# The Black Pigeon

## By Anne Austin

Originally published in 1929

# The Black Pigeon

© 2012 Resurrected Press
www.ResurrectedPress.com

## Published by Intrepid Ink, LLC

Intrepid Ink, LLC provides full publishing services to authors of fiction and non-fiction books, eBooks and websites. From editing to formatting, to publishing, to marketing, Intrepid Ink gets your creative works into the hands of the people who want to read them.
Find out more at www.IntrepidInk.com.

ISBN 13: 978-1-937022-54-9

Printed in the United States of America

# RESURRECTED PRESS CLASSIC MYSTERY CATALOGUE

## J. S. Fletcher

*The Herapath Property*
*The Rayner-Slade Amalgamation*
*The Chestermarke Instinct*
*The Paradise Mystery*
*Dead Men's Money*
*The Middle of Things*
*Ravensdene Court*
*Scarhaven Keep*
*The Orange-Yellow Diamond*
*The Middle Temple Murder*
*The Tallyrand Maxim*
*The Borough Treasurer*
*In the Mayor's Parlour*
*The Saftey Pin*

## R. Austin Freeman

*The Mystery of 31 New Inn from the Dr. Thorndyke Series*
*John Thorndyke's Cases from the Dr. Thorndyke Series*
*The Red Thumb Mark from The Dr. Thorndyke Series*
*The Eye of Osiris from The Dr. Thorndyke Series*
*A Silent Witness from the Dr. John Thorndyke Series*
*The Cat's Eye from the Dr. John Thorndyke Series*
*Helen Vardon's Confession: A Dr. John Thorndyke Story*
*As a Thief in the Night: A Dr. John Thorndyke Story*
*Mr. Pottermack's Oversight: A Dr. John Thorndyke Story*
*Dr. Thorndyke Intervenes: A Dr. John Thorndyke Story*
*The Singing Bone: The Adventures of Dr. Thorndyke*
*The Stoneware Monkey: A Dr. John Thorndyke Story*
*The Great Portrait Mystery, and Other Stories: A Collection of Dr. John Thorndyke and Other Stories*
*The Penrose Mystery: A Dr. John Thorndyke Story*
*The Uttermost Farthing: A Savant's Vendetta*

**Arthur Griffiths**
*The Passenger From Calais*
*The Rome Express*

**Fergus Hume**
*The Mystery of a Hansom Cab*
*The Green Mummy*
*The Silent House*
*The Secret Passage*

**Edgar Jepson**
*The Loudwater Mystery*

**A. E. W. Mason**
*At the Villa Rose*

**A. A. Milne**
*The Red House Mystery*
**Baroness Emma Orczy**
*The Old Man in the Corner*

**Edgar Allan Poe**
*The Detective Stories of Edgar Allan Poe*

**Arthur J. Rees**
*The Hampstead Mystery*
*The Shrieking Pit*
*The Hand In The Dark*
*The Moon Rock*
*The Mystery of the Downs*

**Mary Roberts Rinehart**
*Sight Unseen and The Confession*

**Dorothy L. Sayers**
*Whose Body?*

*The Bride of a Moment*
*Faulkner's Folly*
*The Diamond Pin*
*The Gold Bag*
*The Mystery of the Sycamore*
*The Come Back*

**Raoul Whitfield**
*Death in a Bowl*

*And much more!*
*Visit ResurrectedPress.com*
*for our complete catalogue*

# FOREWORD

Anne Austin early novels were in the romance genre but with The Black Pigeon in 1929 she turned her hand to mysteries, which she would continue to write through the 1930's, most of which featured the young detective, James "Bonnie" Dundee, who is employed first by the police department and later by the district attorney's office in the small Midwestern city of Hamilton. The Black Pigeon, however is a stand alone mystery which takes place in a large city which is not named, but is presumably New York.

When I first read The Black Pigeon it immediately struck me that Austin had written the novel in a form that could readily be turned into a radio or movie serial. Each chapter seemed to end with a new revelation which would then be resolved in the next chapter. As I was researching Austin for the notes for this book and her other mysteries it soon became clear that I had this backwards. The Black Pigeon and several of her other mysteries such as Murder Backstairs and Murder at Bridge had first appeared in syndicated serial form in a number of newspapers around the country before coming out in book format. There is in fact a sly accusation that the heroine of the novel is writing a "serial story" in chapter 25.

In the late twenties and especially the 1930's serials in a variety of media were an extremely popular format. At a time of extreme economic depression, they provided a cheap form of entertainment for audiences who would be reluctant to spend limit cash on books. In newspapers, they were seen as a way to boost circulation in the competitive market of the time, while weekly fifteen or twenty minute episodes could serve as the anchor for an evening of radio programs or to draw audiences back to the theater week after week as part of a movie matinee. A variety of genres appeared in serials including westerns, adventure, science fiction, and particularly mysteries.

Mysteries were well suited to the format. At the end of each episode or chapter a new clue or suspect could be revealed only to be discounted in the next installment only to be replaced by another. As this rhythm matched that of traditional mysteries, very little modification was necessary to fit the serial. Detectives such as Sherlock Holmes had long appeared in magazines such as the Strand, and some of the longer novels such as The Hound of the Baskervilles had first appeared in serial form.

The format seems to have suited Austin's style perfectly, or perhaps her style evolved to meet the form. In either case, her mysteries depended not on some intricate plot revealed step by step, but rather on providing a plethora of suspects, each of whom would seem to have motive, access to the means, and opportunity. Actions are open to misinterpretation, coincidences abound and red herrings appear at every turn. While she might lack the flair of such masters as Agatha Christie or the depth of Dorothy L. Sayers, Austin's mysteries are entertaining and well paced, the latter a necessity of the serial format.

While little known today and with her mysteries mostly unavailable, Anne Austin was obviously popular enough at the time for her works to appear throughout the 1930's. It is with great pleasure that Resurrected Press brings out this new edition of The Black Pigeon.

## About the Author

Born in 1895, Anne Austin began by writing romance novels about young women in the mid 1920's but soon turned her talents to producing a string of mysteries through the 1930's, some of which appeared as serials in newspapers.. Many of these mysteries feature as the detective "Bonnie" Dundee, Special Investigator for the District Attorney, including *Murder Backstairs*, *The Avenging Parrot*, *Murder at Bridge*, and *One Drop of Blood*. Several of her mysteries were translated into French, including *Le Pigeon Noir* and *Le Crime Parfume*. Despite her success as a novelist, Anne Austin disappears from the public record after the 1930's.

Greg Fowlkes
Editor-In-Chief
Resurrected Press
www.ResurrectedPress.com

# Part of Floor Plan of the Seventh Floor of the
## STARBRIDGE BUILDING
### Facing Thirty-Fourth Street near Seventh Avenue

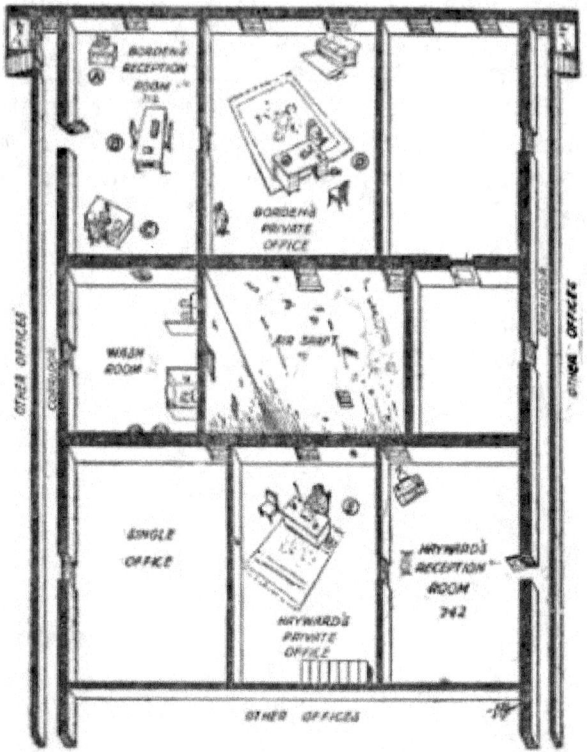

The above diagram shows the relative positions of the office suites occupied by Henry P. Borden, murdered promoter, and John C. Hayward, insurance broker. Note that the windows opening upon the narrow airshaft from both Hayward's private office and the private office of Henry Borden are directly opposite each other.

    **A**—Benny Smith's desk in Borden's reception room, Suite 712
    **B**—Large table for callers in Borden's reception room, Suite 712
    **C**—Ruth Lester's desk
    **D**—Borden's desk in his private office
    **E**—Hayward's desk in his private office, Suite 742
    **1**—Elevator nearest Borden's offices, run by Micky Moran
    **2**—Elevator nearest Hayward's offices, run by Otto Pfluger

# CHAPTER ONE

A BLACK pigeon, its iridescent breast gleaming in the sunshine of the January morning, circled warily above the open window, then fluttered to the white stone ledge. The tiny head jerked back and forth, a brilliant black diamond eye cocked suspiciously, as the little three toed feet pattered just out of reach of the hand extended invitingly, palm upward.

"Satan, you old humbug!" the girl laughed softly. "Don't Ritz me! I'm sure I don't look so different this morning that you don't know me. Is it because I have no crumbs to give you, greedy?"

The black pigeon stood still and studied the girl, his graceful head cocked consideringly. Then, as if reassured, the gleaming black wings spread to the cold sunshine and a second later the tiny red claws were gripping Ruth Lester's forefinger.

As if they had been waiting for a signal from their leader, whom Ruth had named Satan, a flock of pigeons whose home was the roof of the seven story Starbridge Building, came swooping down upon the broad ledge of the window outside the private office of Henry P. Borden, to pay court to the suddenly revealed beauty of Borden's private secretary.

Ruth, with an exultant laugh, which was rich with new tenderness, spread her arms wide, leaning far out of the window. In a moment she was a living pigeon perch. On her little white hands, along her pink sweatered arms, on her shoulders, even on her golden head, pigeons settled trustingly. Brown pigeons; blue gray pigeons with enchanting breasts of bronze and gold and purple; black and white pigeons; white pigeons—no, only one that was pure white and only one, Satan, that was inky black.

An exclamation made the girl raise her blue eyes, but did not startle her, for she had been expecting it. Directly across the narrow airshaft that separated the two wings of the Starbridge Building, a broad window, exactly like the one from which Ruth leaned, framed a young man's head and torso.

Ruth leaned further out of the window, impetuously, her arms reaching toward the man to whom she had be come engaged only the night before. Jealously, the pigeons took wing and fluttered indignantly away—all but the black pigeon, which clung stubbornly to her finger, his beady black eyes flashing from the girl to the man.

"Oh, beautiful!" Jack Hayward called softly. "Little snow princess with the sun on her golden hair! You're too beautiful! Go put on your big yellow spectacles and slick back your hair. I'm jealous even of Satan and he's jealous of me. Look! I believe he'd like to peck my eyes out!"

Ruth laughed, then very gently, so as not to frighten Satan away, she reached into the pocket of her shell pink sweater. In a moment she was holding the struggling pigeon against her breast, as her quick, deft fingers wrapped a slip of paper with a typed message—"I love you"—about one of the tiny red legs, securing it with a bit of black silk thread.

"If you have any bread crumbs, Mr. Hayward," she laughed, "you may be able to learn something to your advantage." And she let the black pigeon flutter away.

Then, because she heard the opening of the door to the outer office, where she was supposed to be sorting the morning mail, she drew in her golden head, and crossed the soberly but richly furnished room where "Handsome Harry" Borden conducted a business which had need of every artificial aid to make it appear respectable. For Henry P. Borden was one of those financial vultures that prey upon the cupidity of men and the credulity of women who have hard earned savings or small legacies to invest. His favorite boast to the sleek haired, collegiate young stock salesman who worked for him was that he was "always within the law," but Ruth Lester, in growing disgust, had come to hope that the law would not always be so obligingly elastic.

But now there was no need for her to worry about Harry Borden's crookedness or about his offensive private life, or about anything in the world. For since exactly twelve o'clock last night she had been engaged to be married to John Carrington Hayward, who was listed on the bulletin board of the Starbridge Building as "Insurance Broker." Broker! Ruth smiled tenderly at the boyish bravado of that title, for Jack hardly made enough selling insurance to pay the rent of his suite of two small offices, and the fifteen dollar a week salary to the incompetent stenographer whom he grandly referred to as "my private secretary." She loved his boyish cocksureness of success, but then—she loved everything; about him, every inch of his tall, lean body, every hair on his coppery brown head. . . .

"Hullo, Ruth! Any mail for the future President of the United States?" a cocky, nasal young voice called from the outer office.

Ruth smiled, a dimple which she did not have to repress any longer tugging at the corner of her adorable little mouth. Then she stepped through the door that divided Borden's private office from the big outer office which served as a reception room for clients and as an office for Borden's secretary and office boy.

Benny Smith, seventeen, and just beginning to be very girl conscious, was sprawled in Ruth's narrow backed swivel chair, pawing the pile of mail on her desk. His sandy hair was still wet from its morning brush, his big ears very red from the scrubbing to which they were not yet accustomed. Benny had told Ruth recently that he was using freckle cream on his speckled cheeks and neck.

"Nothing from your girl this morning, Benny," Ruth answered, in the meek, repressed little voice which had been so necessary a part of the disguise she had temporarily discarded.

"Girl? Who said I had a girl?" Benny sputtered, whirling about in the little swivel chair. Then he saw Ruth and his prominent, pale gray eyes glared until the girl, coloring and laughing, was afraid they would pop from his head.

The boy's gaze traveled in slow, stupefied amazement from the tip of Ruth's smart watersnake pumps—size 4 AA, up to the slender, rounded little legs, shining softly in beige silk stockings, to the knife pleated edge of the short, cream colored serge skirt which barely covered the dimples in her knees; took in the shell pink sweater which molded her almost childishly slim torso; on to the ivory and rose face, with its wide, curling lashed blue eyes— pausing there while the office boy took a deep breath; then arrived at last at the riotously curling mop of golden hair.

"Gee, gosh!" he exploded at last. "All right! I bite! Who *are* you?"

"Don't be silly, Benny! It's just Ruth Lester, of course—"

"Jul yus Caesar!" Benny breathed. "'It's just Ruth Lester, of course,' " he mimicked her precise, repressed voice. "Gosh, what have you went and done to yourself, Ruth? Gee! Be yourself! I ain't feelin' so strong this mornin'—"

Ruth laughed, all the richness and exultation of her new happiness ringing out in her voice. "That's what I'm doing at last, Benny! I'm being myself! Do you like Ruth Lester *herself?*"

Benny rose slowly from Ruth's chair, then lifted a crooked elbow as if to ward her off. "Gosh, woman! Turn them lamps off me! You'll blind me! Where're your specs? Better put 'em on, or I'm liable to get primitive! And say, what have you done to your hair?"

"Nothing—but turn it loose!" Ruth laughed. "It's really too long to be worn as a bob, but—"

"But gosh! You didn't have to slick it back till your head looked like a yellow onion," the office boy protested, curiously angry with her. "I used to think your hair'd pull your eyebrows out by the roots. Say! Maybe that was what give you that scared rabbit look—your hair skinned back like that, pullin' at your eyebrows, and them big yellow, horn rimmed specs of yours, coverin' half of your face. But say, your skin looks diff'runt too—not pale and sickly—"

Ruth opened the top drawer of her desk and took out a box of powder, which she showed him triumphantly. "See! Rachel tinted powder, very heavy. See how yellow it is? Plenty of that slapped on, and my milkmaid complexion was successfully hidden. But—I've got to get to work, Benny! Be a good infant and get me some water for my sponge, and sharpen a bunch of pencils, won't you?"

"Say!" Benny sputtered. "You ain't gonna shut up and not slip me the low down on why you done it, are you? ... To think that all this time—Gosh! I didn't even know you had a figger!" he accused her, his eyes traveling over her beautifully dressed little body again. "You always wore them long skirted, dark old things–"

"Scatter, Benny!" Ruth commanded, her cheeks very pink, her blue eyes brimming with tender mirth. "Remember, this is Saturday—a half holiday. I've something else to do than listen to you sputter 'Gee!' and 'Gosh!' down my neck. No, I'm not going to tell you why I did it! Take these pencils and put a long point on each of them, please."

Her competent little hands began to open the big stack of mail. Only one letter marked "Personal" this morning— another of those big, square, orchid tinted envelopes with the distinctive, angular handwriting in violet ink. The handwriting of a woman of culture and strong character, Ruth had decided long since. She wondered anew why the sight of one of them made her employer so furious. The pencil sharpener had been grinding recklessly, but now the sound dragged, stopped altogether.

"Say, Ruth! I guess I ain't so dumb! I know why you made up to look like a Lillian Gish slavey in specs and long dresses."

"Clever boy!" Ruth laughed, laying aside the orchid tinted letter, unopened of course. She was too happy to scold Benny this morning.

"You done it so's you could keep your job!" Benny deduced triumphantly. "You knowed—all *right! knew*— that the minute 'Handsome Harry' lamped you he'd fall for you like a ton of bricks. Bet that's the reason too that you've worked so many places since you got out of business college, ain't it?"

"Benny, you've been meddling in my desk again!"

"Aw, I ain't either! I just happened to see a bunch of letters of recommendation clipped together and I glanced over 'em," Benny protested. "Say, they had me goin' sure! I couldn't figger out why a whiz of a steno like you worked two or three weeks in a job and then had to blow, and why the guys you worked for give you such swell recommendations if they didn't wanta keep you. I guess they all tried to 'make' you, didn't they?"

"Shut up, Benny, and get to work!" Ruth scolded, her cheeks scarlet.

"Yes, sir, 'at's the ticket, sure's you're born!" Benny applauded his own powers of deduction. "Gosh! I can just imagine! Married man hires you—and who wouldn't? I'm askin' you! Wifey blows in, lamps new secretary—wham! 'Either she goes or I go!' wifey lays the law down. 'Nen— 'I'm awful sorry, Miss Lester, but—er—necessary to re trench—do without a secretary for a while. Best of recommendations, of course—' All 'at stuff! Am I right, fair frail?" Benny concluded, with an impudence he had never been interested enough to show her before.

Ruth's golden head nodded slowly. Yes, Benny was right. No boy of seventeen could know how terribly accurate his slangy version of her past as a business girl was.

"Sure, I'm right! Think I'll be a detective when I get grown. I mean—" and Benny blushed violently, "now that I am grown! Guess it was just as bad when you got a job with a single man, wasn't it, Ruth? Guess it didn't take any guy more'n five seconds to fall in love with you, and more'n two weeks to work you out of a job if you wasn't havin' any, thanks. 'At right?"

"Right!" Ruth agreed. "But do shut up, Benny. If you don't let me do my work I'll spank you."

"Hunh!" Benny snorted. "I'd make two of you. Bet you don't weigh mor'n ninety pounds. . . . Well, I gotta hand it to you, kid! You sure slipped something over on 'Handsome Harry.' No wonder you've stuck here for four months. Sheiks like him don't go round fallin' in love with girls that look Orphant Annies, dying of gallopin' consumption."

At that, joy flooded Ruth's heart, and spilled out in in discreet words. "One man did, Benny!"

The pencil sharpener, which had begun to grind again, stopped with a jerk. "Hey! Spell that out, will you? You ain't gone and got engaged, have you, Ruth? Or—or is it 'Handsome Harry'?" And the boy's freckled face turned a sudden dull crimson. "Guess I mighta knowed that 'Handsome Harry' wasn't missin' nothin"—Gosh!" The last word was a wail of adolescent misery.

"Don't be absurd, Benny!" Ruth cried. Then she rose, drawn to her feet by the boyish agony in Benny's face, and went to him. She tilted his quivering chin with a forefinger and smiled shyly into his eyes. "It isn't Mr. Borden, Benny. It's—can you keep a secret, Benny? I'm engaged to Mr. Hayward. It just happener1 last night, and oh, Benny, I'm so happy I don't think I can bear it!"

The boy did a surprising thing then. He seized the finger which was tilting his chin and pressed it hard against his lips, while a blush ran in crimson waves from his throat to his brow. For an instant his prominent pale gray eyes were not the eyes of an adolescent boy, but those of a man.

"Won't you say you're glad, Benny?" Ruth coaxed tenderly.

"Oh, sure!" the boy mumbled. "Sure 'm glad. Why not? He's a great guy—best lookin' sheik in the Starbridge Building. Gee! What a swell pair you two'll make!" He gulped back his tears manfully. "But say, Ruth, you'd better douse the glim before 'Handsome Harry' surges in. I'm tellin' you—"

"Talk English for a change, Benny!" Ruth laughed. " 'Douse the glim?' "

"Put on them yellow specs of yours and slick back your hair like you been wearin' it," the boy urged, with a curious sort of desperation. "Honest, Ruth—"

"Mr. Borden's affections are so thoroughly engaged at present that I don't think we need worry," Ruth laughed. "But to please you, Benny, I'll revert to the 'Lillian Gish-in spectacles' role."

She was reaching into the top drawer of her desk for the big, yellow lensed, horn rimmed spectacles which made her blue eyes look a sickly, pale green, when the telephone rang.

"Pennsylvania 3500," she announced. Then, after a pause during which she raised her eyebrows significantly as she glanced over her shoulder toward Benny: "No, Mr. Borden has not come in yet. ... I don't know. I'm sorry . . . What name shall I say? Oh ... Thank you!" she hung up the receiver and shrugged. "The woman with the lovely contralto voice. I wonder who she is. I put Mr. Borden on the line once when she called, and he told me to remember her voice and never do it again. Some old flame, I suppose. I can't help feeling sorry for her, though why she should want him back—"

She pushed back the telephone and was reaching for the disguising spectacles when the outer door opened and

Henry P. Borden stepped into the room. Ruth swerved her chair so that her back was turned toward her employer. If only he would go right on into his private office, so that she should have time to—

"Morning, Miss Lester. Anything important?"

Borden was striding toward the door that led into his private office, not vouchsafing a look at that pallid little nonentity whose only appeal to him was that she was an incomparable secretary.

Henry P. Borden, known along Broadway as "Handsome Harry" Borden, deserved both the adjective and the slight sneer with which it was accompanied. For handsome he undoubtedly was, in a bold, striking, black and white way. If he had chosen the movies instead of dubious finance as a career he would inevitably have been cast as the "heavy"—the drawing room, silk hat type of villain. He was tall and large, but not at all fat. Sleek, thick black hair, into which forty years of self indulgence and at least twenty years of fast living had not introduced a single strand of white. Bold, wide, black eyes, which had a trick of staring at a woman until her heart fluttered and her cheeks went either pale or crimson— according to the purity of her heart and the type of response which "Handsome Harry's" eyes called up in her. A stubby black mustache. Extraordinarily fair skin, for a man, despite the thick growth of beard which he shaved close twice a day. Rather thick but well shaped red lips, always slightly moist, as if he had just run an anticipatory tongue over them. If rumor could be trusted, anticipation had nearly always become realization for "Handsome Harry" Borden.

"Nothing very important, Mr. Borden," Ruth answered, without turning her head. Oh, if he would only go on into his office and close the door!

But Borden paused, his hand on the knob of his door. "Any calls?"

Ruth's hands shook a little as she adjusted her spectacles with fumbling haste. "Only one," she answered, in her meek, timid little voice. "The woman with the beautiful contralto voice. I asked her if she would leave her name, and she said no." She rose, gathered up the mail, the orchid tinted letter topping the stack, and faced her employer, inwardly quaking.

"That voice may sound beautiful to you, but believe me, I'd rather listen to a riveting machine. . . . Hullo! What have you done to yourself?"

As Benny Smith had done, Harry Borden took her in, from the top of her curl crowned head to the toes of her new snakeskin pumps. No—not quite as Benny had done, for the boy's eyes had been clean and young and frank, while the man's eyes were bold and suddenly calculating, after the first blankness of astonishment.

Ruth pursed her mouth, banishing the dimple and look ing as much as possible like the mouselike little creature he had become accustomed to and had ignored. "I—it's just these clothes, Mr. Borden. I—I saved some of my salary, and—but, please, Mr. Borden, there's a letter from Hendrickson in Chicago. He's sold ten thousand shares of that Nu Gas stock, in spite of what the chemist reported—"

The potential lover vanished and the shady financier took his place. "Hendrickson's a fool, but a damned good stock salesman. Wire him to—"

They passed on into Borden's private office, and as her employer gave her instructions regarding Hendrickson Ruth laid the stack of opened letters, topped with the orchid tinted "Personal" envelope, upon the immaculate green blotter of the flat topped brown walnut desk. Before she reached her chair on the opposite side of the desk Borden flipped the orchid letter aside, with a muttered oath, then picked it up and thrust it, with an angry gesture, into the breast pocket of his vest.

"I wonder if he ever answers one of those letters, and why she keeps on writing him if he doesn't," Ruth reflected, then looked up from her notebook to find her employer's eyes regarding her quizzically, calculatingly.

"Little Miss Cinderella in person!" he chuckled. "Funny what a permament wave and a box of rouge will do for a girl."

"Yes, Mr. Borden," Ruth answered meekly. "There's an urgent letter from Nathan in Los Angeles. He's demanding a larger commission on Bakersfield Oil, since the new field is failing. What shall I write him?"

Borden consented to be lured into dictation. His manner instantly became sharp, incisive, his words rapid, but Ruth wrote happily. Thank God, he wasn't going to annoy her. . . .

"Write me out a check for five hundred cash," the promoter said at last, flinging his personal check book across the desk to her. "And go to the bank yourself, won't you? Then stop at Penn Station and get me a drawing room and two round trip tickets for Winter Heaven—train leaving at 2:15 this afternoon. Wire the Hotel Winter Heaven for a suite—best in the house. Reserve the rooms in the name of Mr. and Mrs. H. P.—let's see—what other surname begins with a B, so the initials on my luggage will match?"

"Benton?" Ruth suggested, in a small, innocent voice.

"All right. But make a note of it on the ticket envelope for me, please. I was in Atlantic City one time with a temporary missus, and forgot our name. It was damned awkward. 'Mr. and Mrs. H. P. Benton,' eh? Good enough," he chuckled. "Guess who Mrs. Benton will be, Cinderella."

"I—I think I'd better not know, don't you, Mr. Borden?" Ruth answered timidly. "Here's the check. Will you sign it, please, and I'll go to the bank right away, before it's jammed."

"Little prunes and prisms!" Borden laughed, grasping the small hand which extended the check. "You know something?—I believe you've been stringing me! I don't think you're half the timid little rabbit you've been pretending to be." He drew hard on her hand, so that Ruth's small body was strained against the desk. "Come on! Let's see how you really look. Take off those hideous spectacles and let me see your eyes—"

"Please, Mr. Borden!" Ruth gasped. "I—I can't see without them. My eyes are so weak. And—and they blink without my glasses," she lied desperately.

It was Benny who ended the scene, a stormy faced, sullen Benny who jerked open the door as if he had been listening at the keyhole.

"What the devil—?" Borden began furiously. "Have you forgotten how to knock?"

Benny swung the door shut and slouched against it, sullenly defiant. "There's a guy out there wantin' to see you. Says him and his wife's been gypped outa their life savin's—"

Borden stared at the boy as if he thought Benny had suddenly gone crazy. Then the dark blood of anger stained his peculiarly white skin. "Get the hell out of here, or I'll shake your teeth down your throat! And get rid of that man, whoever he is. You know damned well I never see a person of that sort. . . . Wait! You'd better handle him yourself, Miss Lester. Here! Don't forget the check. Five hundred in tens and twenties, please. Here's a fifty to get the drawing room and railroad tickets. I want to have at least five hundred in ready cash, and this fifty is too big a bill anyway."

The promoter had drawn a handsome brown leather wallet from his pocket, and as he extracted the fifty dollar banknote, Ruth caught a glimpse of another yellow backed bill, but did not see its denomination. It might be a hundred or even a five hundred dollar note, Ruth knew, for "Handsome Harry," playboy of Broadway, loved to flash golden tinted bills before the dazzled eyes of headwaiters.

Later, a harsh voiced, flinty eyed detective would be demanding of Ruth Lester a minutely detailed recital of every event of that Saturday morning, expecting prodigious feats of memory of her. Then, everything would be of importance, for murder would have made them so. But now nothing seemed important to Ruth Lester but that she was free to leave Harry Borden's private office, free to close the door upon his staring, bold, greedy, black eyes.

Not even the old man who was tremulously reiterating his story of terrible and crushing financial loss through one of Borden's fake stock schemes seemed important to her then. She eased him out of the office as gently as possible, her ears almost deaf to his muttered threats of vengeance against Henry P. Borden. She had listened to many such stories, heard many versions of the old man's bitter prayer that God should make Harry Borden pay with his life for his sins. But as she hurried into her fur coat and jaunty little felt hat, her heart was singing again, her joy not touched by the slightest hint of premonition that those prayers would be answered so soon and so horribly.

It was half past ten o'clock. In less than three hours she would join Jack Hayward at the elevator, go to lunch with him to celebrate the engagement which had taken place last night. The miracle of it! He had loved her before he knew she looked like—this! And Ruth smiled at her own reflected beauty, thoroughly appreciated by herself for the first time.

"Didn't I tell you?" Benny demanded in a furious whisper. His freckled face was very pale, his hands clenched. "Didn't take him ten minutes to begin pawin' you, the dirty—"

"Hush, Benny!" Ruth interrupted, with an apprehensive glance toward the private office. "I can take care of myself."

As she left the office to fulfill her employer's commissions she was smiling a little at the office boy's sudden infatuation, so like, and yet so different from the greedy interest that had sprung into the bold black eyes of "Handsome Harry" Borden.

# CHAPTER TWO

## I

MICKY MORAN, the jolly, impudent, red headed Irish boy who was lord of the elevator directly across the hall from the Borden offices, did not recognize in the pink and white and gold little beauty the timid secretary who had been a daily, mouse quiet passenger of his for the last four months. His bold eyes took her in at a glance, then he began to whistle significantly: "Yes, sir, that's my baby!"

Just before the elevator reached the ground floor Ruth Lester asked, in the hesitant, meek voice which had been part of her "disguise": "Is your father recovering from that awful automobile accident, Micky?"

Before the astonished boy could reply, Ruth, laughing at him over her furred shoulder, stepped into the lobby of the Starbridge Building.

"Vain little imp!" she characterized herself, as a gust of January wind tugged at her coat. "But oh, I'm so glad I can be me at last. Four months of being some one else! But worth it, worth it, worth it!" she chanted under her breath, as she joined the Saturday morning shoppers who milled about the busy corner—Thirty Fourth Street and Seventh Avenue.

It was uncanny how accurately Benny Smith diagnosed the absurd situation which had made a disguise necessary. Perfect blond beauty had been a pleasant possession, so long as her father had been alive to shield her. Ruth had been as proud of him as he of her, for Colby Lester had been one of the greatest criminal lawyers in New York—a criminal lawyer whose greatness lay in his keenness as a detective rather than in jury swaying oratory. During the last five years of his life

Colby Lester had talked over all his cases with his daughter. Many a night they had sat up until dawn, Ruth curled kitten wise in his arms, her childish brows knit, amusingly, in the same fashion as his, her logical mind keeping pace with his and sometimes leaping ahead of it.

"Good work, Infant! You've got the makings of a Grade A detective under those yellow: curls. But, please God, you'll never, have to earn your living in any such sordid fashion as this," he had told her once, when she had pounced upon the missing link in a chain of evidence which was to acquit a man of murder.

A dignified home, exquisite clothes, private school, association with keen and cultured minds—all these things Ruth had enjoyed until Colby Lester's sudden, tragic death. He had been defending a woman on the charge of poisoning her lover, a married man, and had been shot down by the grief and jealousy crazed widow of the victim, because she had believed that Colby Lester would win the defendant's freedom for her. And he had, although his funeral took place while the jury was bringing in its just verdict of "Not guilty."

Even now Ruth could scarcely understand why there had been so little for her when her father's estate was settled. But his books showed that he had defended more penniless victims of tragic circumstance than wealthy ones, because their cases presented problems which intrigued his detective instincts. And he had been a connoisseur of comfortable living, had thought he could always make enough money to gratify the exquisite tastes he had cultivated in himself and his daughter. And then he had died. . . .

Ruth Lester shivered, but not because a high January wind was whipping about her slender legs. She mustn't think about her father's death now. She was happy again, and he would be happy, too, at last. For Ruth had had the feeling all through. the two years since her father's death that Colby Lester was wandering about, an earth bound spirit, stricken with remorse that he was not able to protect her from the wolves who wanted to gobble her up.

She had used what little money there was to take an eight months' secretarial course, and had come out of the Miller Business College primed with all sorts of useful knowledge, her fingers capable of astonishing speed in shorthand and typing. Her only desire had been to become an expert secretary and to earn a decent living by her Work. But men had not let her do it. Apparently no man could look at her without wanting to touch her. She had had to flee, from this job to that, from one humiliating experience to another. As Benny Smith, the office boy, had guessed, the wives of the married men she had tried to work for had been the worst. . . . But those scenes would not bear thinking of now, when she was so happy...

It was a motion picture, finally, which pointed a way out of her difficulty. Out of work, having had ten jobs in eight months, she had gone forlornly into a movie theater in an effort to forget her rather absurd troubles. And she had seen, on a screen, a timid, mousy little secretary with skinned back hair, ill fitting clothes and horn rimmed spectacles, suddenly transform herself into a beauty, so that she might win the love of her employer.

The next day, Ruth Lester, transformed from a beauty into an exact copy of the motion picture's heroine as she had appeared in the earlier reels, presented herself at the offices of Henry P. Borden, who had advertised for a secretary.

And for four months, although "Handsome Harry" Borden was notoriously fond of beautiful women, Ruth had been permitted to work in peace. Sometimes it had been cruelly hard to keep her pose and her deliberately achieved homeliness, for three of those months had been the loneliest she had ever spent. In all that time no man had asked her for a "date." But, oh, this last month!

Ruth drew a deep breath of joy. The pain of recalling the past had been wiped out by the ecstasy of arriving, inevitably, at Jack Hayward's name. Her little high heeled pumps clicked a staccato accompaniment to her joy as she turned in at the bank. Reaching into the inside pocket of her fur coat she retrieved her spectacles, straddled her short nose with them, so that the teller could recognize her and make no difficulty about cashing Burden's check for five hundred dollars.

In the street again, on her way to the Pennsylvania station, to buy two tickets and a drawing room for Harry Borden and the woman he was to take to Winter Heaven with him, Ruth had a few more precious minutes in which to review her strange romance. . . .

She laughed softly as she remembered how she must have looked, in her "disguise," leaning out of the window opening upon the airshaft, coaxing the black pigeon to her with crumbs held invitingly in the hollow of her palm. But the young insurance broker, watching her across the airshaft, had not laughed. He had smiled, a frank, jolly smile. And she had smiled, forgetting for the moment that the dimple must be sternly repressed. Two days later, when she was feeding the whole greedy flock with crumbs sprinkled upon the window ledge, Jack Hayward—she had learned his name, of course, from the bulletin board— had tried to lure them away from her, with crumbs of his own. It had become a game between them—or rather, between the handsomest man in the Starbridge Building and the dowdiest, most timid looking little secretary.

Then one day he had appeared at the elevator—not the elevator in his wing of the building, but at the one across the hall from Borden's offices.

She could hear him now:

"I wonder if you'll let me lunch with you, Miss Lester. so I can find where you get such potent bread crumbs. My greatest ambition in life is to have that black rascal of a pigeon eating out of my hand!"

She had wanted to turn back then, into her own office, for five swift minutes at the mirror—just long enough to remove her spectacles, scrub off that sickly yellowish powder, release the golden glory of her curls, but the elevator had come, and her opportunity to show him how Ruth Lester really looked had been lost.

It was during that first luncheon of theirs that Ruth's resolve was made. For Jack Hayward had talked to her as no man since her father's death had talked—as if she had a mind worthy of his; as if she were something more than a beautiful little scrap of femininity made to be gobbled up by a man.

"I won't show him the outside me until he has a chance to learn and love the inside me," Ruth resolved, and trembled lest the great experiment should fail, for she already loved him—the outside and the inside of him. "What if he should only like and feel congenial with her mind, and fail, because of her disguise, to love her as a man must love the woman he marries?

But that would have to be her risk, she resolved.

"Oh!" Ruth came to herself with a start, and smiled at the ticket agent. She had not even realized that she had arrived at the station. "Two round trip tickets and a drawing room for Winter Heaven, please. The 2:15 train for this afternoon."

When the ticket envelope was handed to her, she jotted upon it, as her employer had requested, the name under which he would register at the Winter Heaven Hotel— H. P. Benton. As she hurried back to the Starbridge Building, she wondered who "Mrs. Benton" would be—this time. And she shivered a little, at the thought that but for the grace of God, it might have been she. Soon such sordid things would not touch her, for she would be Jack Hayward's wife. Mrs. John Carrington Hayward! . . But oddly enough, she shivered again, and wondered if she were taking cold.

## II

. ."Hul-lo, Miss Lester! Is God's gift to women in his office? I phoned and he's expecting me. Oh, pardon me! I thought it was Miss Lester! But I guess Handsome Harry canned her, the poor little scared bunny! Can't say I blame him—why!—what—?"

Ruth turned in the little swivel chair and faced the girl who had announced herself so nonchalantly. So it was Rita Dubois who was going to be "Mrs. Benton" for a week end! Ruth was hardly surprised, but a little sorry, for she liked the vivacious, dark eyed, black haired little French American, singer and dancer in the noisiest, most garish night club in the city.

"I've just turned my hair loose," Ruth smiled, putting on her timid manner and peering upward at Rita through her enormous horn rimmed spectacles.

"Attagirl!" Rita applauded, as she touched up her already vividly rouged lips. "So you've fallen for Handsome Harry, too, you poor little simp! Been to the movies and got a few hot tips on how to vamp your boss? . . . "Well, Bunny, don't be jealous of little Rita, no matter what you hear! You can have him—next week! But listen, don't you toddle in and tell him I said so, after I'm gone, or I'll snatch those golden curls of yours out by the roots. . . . Pretty stuff!" And Rita, finished with her lips, lifted one of Ruth's curls and fingered its yellow silk almost tenderly.

Ruth laughed, then glanced apprehensively toward Harry Borden's closed door. "The curls are out in someone else's honor. Miss Dubois. And don't yon tell Mr. Borden, but—I'm engaged to be married. It just happened last night, you're the second person I've told—"

"Good child! Wise little baby!" Rita approved, her voice curiously gentle and low. Then she stooped and laid her heavily rouged and scented lips against Ruth's cheek.

"That's the only way, Infant! Lasso 'em with a wedding ring when you're young and you won't have to—oh, hul-lo, Harry! The top of the morning to you, darling!"

Harry Borden held his door wide, and, regardless of Ruth's presence, his arms, too. "Glad to see you, sweet heart! Miss Lester's just bought the tickets. Drawing room, too, if you're a good girl!"

"You mean," Rita corrected him coolly, "If I'm *not* a good girl! But remember, Harry, I haven't said I'd go yet."

As Harry Borden, laughing indulgently, was about to close the door, Rita Dubois turned her head and gave Ruth a confidential, mocking grin, along with a significant wink.

Ruth's fingers were flying over the typewriter keys again when Benny Smith's voice, sullen and indignant, interrupted her.

"Hunh! Thought it was a secret—you getting engaged!" he flung at her from his own desk in the corner. " 'Nen you go and tell everybody!"

"I haven't told anyone but Miss Dubois and you, Benny," Ruth protested.

"Well, if you gotta whisper your little secret, looks like you'd pick out somebody besides one of Handsome Harry's dames," the boy persisted sullenly. "I thought you just told me 'cause you—you sorta liked me—"

"I do like you, Benny—lots," she said gently. "Now be a darling and don't interrupt me any more. I want to be through by one."

"Then I guess you don't want to be told that Handsome Harry's frau is coming for her alimony this morning," the boy retorted, grinning again.

"Oh, I'd forgotten that today's the fifteenth!" Ruth cried. "Does Mr. Borden know she's coming?"

Benny chuckled. "I didn't tell him. He was talking to this Dubois dame on the other line when his missus called up, and then you come back and I forgot to mention it. I'm going to be forgettin' a lot o' things if you don't slick back them curls again."

"Benny, remember that I'm an engaged woman!" Ruth laughed. "But what am I going to do if Mrs. Borden comes while—?"

There was a faint rat-tat upon the outer door and Benny sprang to answer, knowing who it was, for no one but Harry Borden's wife bothered to knock when she came to his offices.

"Morning, Mrs. Borden," Benny mumbled, as he opened the door wide. "Say, Ruth, I gotta beat it to the post office for them stamps. Anything else you need?"

"No, thanks, Benny. Fifty twos, a hundred ones, and ten specials. . . . Good morning, Mrs. Borden. I'm sorry I wasn't here when you telephoned. I'd gone to the bank for Mr. Borden."

Ruth had risen as she spoke, and now faced Mrs. Borden nervously, but smiling the little timid smile which Mrs. Borden would expect of her, for it had greeted her once a month for four months.

Elizabeth Borden was the kind of woman whom Ruth had met when her father was alive—well born, cultured, gentle. Colby Lester would have called her a thorough bred, and that was the label which his daughter instinctively gave her. A rather faded, tired thirty-eight, as against Harry Borden's triumphant forty. Soft, fine skin, going a little lax beneath high, aristocratic cheek bones, and wrinkling faintly around tragic eyes and a patient but bitter mouth. Leaf brown eyes, no longer glowing with the fire of spring. Leaf brown, smooth hair, touched with the rime of premature winter at temples and brow. A thin, high bridged nose, whose nostrils quivered with pain when Harry Borden flung some veiled insult at her. The ghost of a pretty woman, perhaps of a beautiful one, for Handsome Harry Borden would never have married a homely girl. But a ghost who had not done with suffering. . . .

Of all the varied duties which she was called upon to perform as Harry Borden's confidential secretary, none was so painful to Ruth as this monthly encounter with Mrs. Borden. For Borden forced his wife to come to his offices that he might humilate her. There had been a legal separation, but no divorce, and Borden had arrogantly stipulated that he would pay the court allotment of $500 a month for the support of his wife and two children, a boy of twelve and a girl of seven, only if Elizabeth Borden came to him each month and asked for it. And Ruth knew that if Elizabeth Borden had had only herself to consider, she would have died rather than so humiliate her self before him.

"Benny told me Mr. Borden was in," Mrs. Borden answered Ruth's greeting.

Ruth glanced miserably toward the closed door, behind which Harry Borden and Rita Dubois were arranging details of their week end trip to Winter Heaven. "Yes, he's in, Mrs. Borden, but he—he's in conference."

A burst of high pitched laughter penetrated that closed door, and Mrs. Borden flinched, her nostrils quivering, her gloved hands clenching upon the handbag she held. Ruth did not consciously notice the discarded wife's reaction then, but later, when every tiny thing was of so much importance, she remembered—and wished she could forget.

"I—then I—" Mrs. Borden stammered. "Shall I come back a little later, Miss Lester? I brought the children downtown with me, and they're waiting in the rest room of a department store. I—you know it is—necessary that I—that I ask—that I see Mr. Borden today."

"Yes," Ruth nodded. Harry Borden's ultimatum was that the monthly five hundred would be paid on the fifteenth day of the month and on no other. If his wife did not call for it then, and ask in so many words for what was hers and the children's by right, she would have to wait until the same date the next month. "I suggest, Mrs. Borden, that you come back in about an hour. I am sure he will be out of—conference—by then."

Mrs. Borden flushed. "The children have a dentist's appointment at twelve, and then I'm to take them to lunch. I wonder if Mr. Borden will be here about half past one?"

Ruth agreed eagerly. She was glad she would not have to see poor Mrs. Borden again on that, her own happy day. "Yes. He will be here until nearly two. He told me so just a few minutes ago. I'm sure half past one will be fine."

"Thank you." Mrs. Borden was turning toward the door, when another burst of laughter—treble wedded to bass—shook the ground glass panel in the door between the outer and inner offices.

Ruth saw the slight, frail body sway, sprang to put her arm about the older woman. "Please sit down just a minute, Mrs. Borden. Here! In my chair. And lay your head on the desk. It's the heat—they keep these offices stifling. I'll get you a drink of water. There! Feeling better?" she asked, as she helped Harry Borden's wife to the little swivel chair and forced her gently down into it.

Ruth darted to the water cooler in the corner near Benny's desk, then discovered that the paper cup container was empty. But there was a carton of them in the bottom drawer of her desk. She ran, frightened a little, for Mrs. Borden looked terribly white and ill. The drawer stuck a bit, and the older woman was leaning downward to help, with trembling hands.

"Don't bother, dear Mrs. Borden," Ruth begged. "There! It often sticks. . . . The cups are here somewhere . . . Oh!" She snatched her hand from the pulled out drawer as if she had touched a snake. Then she laughed, shakily. "What a goose I am! Please don't be frightened, Mrs. Borden. I keep forgetting that the gun is in there—"

"Gun?" Mrs. Borden quavered, shrinking away from the drawer, her hand going to her throat.

Ruth laughed nervously. "Yes—an automatic pistol. Isn't it ridiculous—my having a pistol? But there were so many hold ups in the building last month that a— friend of mine—" she could not yet toss off Jack Hayward's name nonchalantly—"bought one for me, and for himself, too. He has offices in this building, and he was terribly in earnest about my keeping the thing here in case of another hold up. As if I'd touch it! I'm more afraid of it than I am of a bandit! Here are the cups. Sorry to be so long."

Five minutes later—just four minutes after Mrs. Borden had left, looking so strange and ill that Ruth was genuinely frightened—the door of Harry Borden's private office opened and he emerged, or rather was pulled along, for Rita Dubois, in high good humor, was tugging at his hand.

"Don't worry! I'll be at the station on time," the dancer was reassuring him gaily. "I can do more shopping in a couple of hours than most girls could do in a day. And mind you don't call up the stores and limit these charge accounts, old dear!"

"Mind you don't fail to keep your part of the bargain!" Harry Borden reminded her, as they reached the door. "I'll keep mine—all of it! But—no double crossing, Rita!"

Ruth glanced up, her spectacled eyes taking in the laugh ing but mutually suspicious couple. She saw Harry Borden wave good bye to Rita, and many hours later she was to try to recall every detail of that picture, though now she only noted, idly, that the man seemed to be waving a torn banknote, and that Rita's finger tip kiss was for the torn bill rather than for Harry Borden.

# CHAPTER THREE

HARRY BORDEN was chuckling as he closed the outer door upon Rita Dubois. "They all fall sooner or later, eh, Miss Lester? Some little jazz queen—Rita. You ought to see her and her dancing partner, Ramon Romero, do their turn at the Golden Slipper. Maybe I'll take you some night—hmm? Make Rita jealous. A little jealousy's good for 'em. That would be a neat way of paying her back for keeping me on the anxious seat for a week. . . . Hard to 'make'—Rita. But I don't like 'em if they're too easy."

Ruth said nothing, but her back was rigid and her fingers, flying over the keys, were spoiling a letter by interpolating, "Now is the time for all good men to come to the aid of their party."

"How're the letters coming on?" Borden suddenly be came brisk and businesslike again. "Nearly through? Where's Benny?"

"Gone to the postoffice for stamps," Ruth answered. "He should be back any minute now. I have five more letters to write, including that long one to Hendrickson. . . . And oh, Mr. Borden," she detained him meekly, "Mrs. Borden was here while Miss Dubois was with you. I told her you were in conference and she said she would return at half past one. You'd said you would be here until about two."

Harry Borden dropped an angry oath. Then, "I don't know whether I'll be here or not. Why the devil didn't she come earlier in the morning? She knows damned well that if she doesn't ask for her money—my money!—on the fifteenth, she'll have to do without. It would serve her right if I cleared out at one."

A vision of Elizabeth Borden's white, suffering face turned Ruth ill. "Then won't you please leave a check with me for her?" she pleaded, raising her spectacled eyes to the man who stood scowling in the door of his private office. "I'll be glad to wait here until she comes, although I have an engagement for one myself—"

"No!" Borden was curiously violent. "I'll be here, and I'll make her ask me for it, make her beg for it. It's an outrage that I have to fork over five hundred a month for her and the children. The judge that made the award was a sentimental fool. Three hundred would be more than ample."

Ruth's eyes, looking very meek behind their spectacles, did not falter, however. "Hadn't I better leave the door on the latch? You might not hear her knock—"

"Let her pound on it, then!" Borden retorted grimly. "You know I never stay in these offices alone without the door being locked. What with hold up men and bellyaching investors dropping in with their pretty little threats because they haven't the guts to take their losses like men, my life wouldn't be worth a nickel, if I hung around here alone with the outside door unlocked. Don't you worry your pretty head—and who'd have guessed it 'was pretty?—over Mrs. Borden, child. She looks soft, but believe me—"

Benny Smith's noisy arrival cut short whatever confidence Harry Borden may have been about to make. The employer spoke curtly to the office boy: "Well, Benny, about time you were drifting back! Been shooting craps in the alley again?"

"No, sir," the boy mumbled, flushing darkly. "They was a long line at the stamp window."

"There's always a long line at the stamp window when you go to the postoffice," Borden agreed sarcastically. "Listen—and get this through your thick head: I want you to go to my apartment and pick up a couple of bags that my man has packed for me. Take them to the station and check them, bringing me the checks. And make it snappy—hear ?"

Borden passed into his private office, but almost immediately reappeared. "Bring in the letters you have finished, Ruth. I'll sign them now, and Benny, you'd better hold down this office until Miss Lester comes back. I don't want it to be left unattended. No telling who'll stroll in. I'm expecting Adams this morning, and if he comes in, tell him to wait."

At Borden's first use of her Christian name Ruth flushed with resentment, but she obediently gathered up the finished correspondence and followed Borden into the private office, but not before she had caught the look of sullen hatred with which Benny was glaring at his employer's back. So Benny had noticed that casually dropped "Ruth," too, and was resenting it passionately. . .

"Guess I'm sort of nervous today," Borden confessed, with a wry grin. "A week end at Winter Heaven will do me good. . . . Who was that chap that came in this morning, all het up over losing money on some of my stock?" he asked suddenly.

"He wouldn't give me his name," Ruth answered. "He insisted on seeing you personally—said he would be back. I dealt with him as tactfully as I could—"

"Tact and efficiency are your long suits, aren't they, child?" Borden smiled. "Draw your chair around to this side of the desk. We'd better go over the figures in this letter to Nathan. I'm not sure I'm going to let him hold me up for a bigger commission. Looks confoundedly like blackmail to me."

There was nothing for Ruth to do but to obey. She dragged her chair from its usual place at the big flat-topped desk opposite to Borden, and placed it where Borden indicated, with a pointing finger—so close to his own chair that the legs almost touched. Borden drew out the stenographer's leaf of the desk and shifted the letters to it. Ruth sat very still, her little hands tightly clasped in her lap, as Borden dipped his pen in the onyx ink well

and leaned toward her—closer and closer, so that her
nostrils were assailed by the odor of pomade with which
he kept every lock of his black hair in gleaming order.

"Look!" he pointed to the letter under his large, well
manicured hands. "Wouldn't you think that was a big
enough commission for any fly by night like Nathan to
make?"

Ruth leaned forward and peered through her
spectacles. Borden laughed suddenly. "Bet you could see
better with out those goggles, Ruth! Come! I'm going to
take 'em off for you. I'll bet a hundred dollars your eyes
are just the right shade of blue to go with these yellow
curls of yours," and his hands reached out, were about to
lay hold upon the last item of the girl's disguise, which
men of Harry Borden's type had made necessary, if she
was to be allowed to work in peace.

Ruth's head jerked back, her hands going up to
restrain his. "Please, Mr. Borden! The light really hurts
my eyes," she lied frantically.

Then somehow she was out of her chair, and Borden's
left arm was about her shoulders, as his right hand
reached determinedly for the spectacles. A hundred
times, afterwards, she reproached herself bitterly for the
scream that tore out of her throat. After all, he was only
trying, half jokingly, to take her glasses off. . . . But as his
flushed face almost touched hers, and his eyes glittered
with some thing more than laughter, she lost control of
nerves which had been curiously taut all morning—and
screamed.

"What are you trying to do, you little devil?—arouse
the building?—make them think I'm murdering you?"
Borden demanded furiously. "Look! That chap's getting
an eyeful across the airshaft and—get out of here and
stay out, or I'll knock those pop eyes out of your head!"

Ruth, who had obeyed his command to look, and who
was taking a staggering, uncertain step toward Jack
Hayward, framed in the opposite window and being
forcibly restrained by another man from leaping through

it, thought at first that Borden's last furious sentence was directed at her. But Benny's voice from the doorway told her the truth.

"If you're hurting Miss Lester, I'll—I'll—" Benny was sputtering, his fists clenched.

"Get out, and mind your own business! You, too!" Borden added viciously, nodding furiously and gesticulating toward Jack Hayward, who was calling out something in a rage strangled voice. "Sit down again, Miss Lester," he added, more normally. "And keep your confounded glasses on, if you're so crazy about them. Where's that letter to my lawyer?"

Before she obeyed, Ruth turned toward the window again, shaking her head slightly and laying her finger against her lips. Then, trembling, she sat down and was not again molested while Borden signed the letters.

"Tell that fool office boy to go on to my apartment for my bags," Borden reminded her gruffly. Then, "I'm sorry, Miss Lester, but damned if I can see why you kicked up such a fuss. Didn't mean any harm."

"It's—all right, Mr. Borden," Ruth said meekly. "And —I'm sorry I screamed. I'm—easily frightened." And indeed she was sorry she had screamed, for now the blight on her perfect happiness had been communicated to Jack Hayward. But her remorse then over having "kicked up a fuss" was nothing to compare with the agony of self reproach which was to come to her later. . . .

She found Benny Smith at her desk, bending over the pulled out bottom drawer. "What are you doing, Benny?" she demanded sharply. "You must keep out of my desk!"

"Looking for a towel," the boy muttered. Then, tensely: "Listen, Ruth, if that guy gets fresh with you again—"

"Hush, Benny!" Ruth cut short his threat. "Run along to his apartment now for his bags. I can take care of my self, Benny. It's sweet of you to mind, but I don't want you to lose your job on my account," she added gently.

The boy closed the bottom drawer of her desk and snatching up his overcoat and cap, strode out of the office, fancying himself, Ruth reflected tenderly, every inch a man, and—what's more—a man in love! "Oh, I wish I hadn't screamed!" she told herself disgustedly.

The door had scarcely closed upon Benny when it opened to admit Carl Adams, one of Borden's dapper, collegiate young stock salesmen. Few of the men worked on Saturdays, since it was a half holiday.

"Hullo, Miss Lester. Saw Benny at the elevator. What's this about you and Borden? Benny seemed to think you might need protection. And I don't wonder. . . . What have you done to yourself? Why, the scared little bunny turned into a beauty! . . . Greetings, chief!" the sales man broke off his confidential compliments and hailed his employer jovially.

"Come on in, Adams," Borden answered grimly. "Bring me Adams' sales record, Miss Lester, please."

Except for an unimportant telephone call or two, Ruth was allowed to finish her letters in peace, for the conference between Borden and his dilatory stock salesman proved to be a long one. It was ten minutes after one when the flushed, angry eyed young man jerked out of the office, and twenty minutes past when Ruth, the last letters signed and stamped, hurried to the elevator to keep her overdue appointment with Jack Hayward. She had telephoned him, in a guardedly low voice, that she would be a little late, and she knew that he would be waiting. . . . If only she hadn't screamed, so that nothing but joy could have entered into the rest of this day. . . .

"Lord, darling! I thought you were never coming. Just one more minute and I'd have gone in after you," Jack Hayward greeted her. "Did that beast—?"

"Sh!" Ruth warned. "Look! Here come Minnie and Letty, lugging their brooms and scrub pails, poor things! I wonder if they'll recognize me? . . . Hello, Minnie! Letty! Aren't you going to speak to me?"

The two calico clad, gray haired, stoop shouldered old women who had been gossiping together as they plodded down the hall, stopped and stared, then grinned humbly, apologetically.

"They really don't know me!" Ruth laughed, hugging Jack's arm delightedly.

The older of the two women nudged her companion with her broom handle. "It's Miss Lester, Letty! Now, don't that beat all? Ye've took your specs off, ain't you, dearie? My, what a change! Letty, maybe if us girls 'ud take off our specs we'd catch us a beau, too, eh?" and Minnie cackled shrill mirth at the idea.

Letty Miller shook her gray head slowly. "Reckon our day is over, Minnie. But it's nice to see a young couple sweetheartin', one as handsome as the other—"

"Just for that, Letty!" Jack laughed, drew a dollar bill out of his pocket, and tucked it into the torn, sagging pocket of the calico dress.

The arrival of the elevator cut short his cleaning woman's eager thanks. As they stepped into the car Ruth squeezed her sweetheart's arm and whispered with mock severity: "Prodigal! Don't you know you've got to save money now? But it was dear of you!"

As the car shot down to the main floor Micky Moran, the elevator operator, commented with impudent frankness on Ruth's changed appearance, and it amused the girl to see how jealously Jack resented the boy's familiarity. Imagine being jealous of Micky! They were passing through the lobby of the office building when Ruth suddenly remembered that she had left her savings bank book in the office.

"Wait here for me, darling," she told Jack. "I forgot something. Be right back. No, don't come up with me," and she darted back into the elevator.

A few precious seconds were lost while she fished in her handbag for her key. Darn Harry Borden anyway! Afraid to stay alone in his own offices if the outer door was unlocked! Praying that he would not hear her, she ran to the filing cabinet and pulled out a folder marked "Ruth Lester—Personal." The bank book was not there. She went through the contents of the folder twice, then darted to her desk and searched through the two top drawers unsuccessfully. From Borden's office came the rumble of his voice. Probably he was talking over the phone. Whirling back to the filing cabinet she dug into half a dozen folders with panicky aimlessness. At last, after at least five or six precious minutes had been wasted, she found the thin brown booklet in the folder devoted to her employer's returned checks and bank statements. As she thrust the passbook into her handbag she heard the sound of a receiver being slammed upon its hook. In her haste to be gone before Harry Borden could come out to investigate, she jerked open the outer door so violently that it struck her across the mouth.

She was panting a little, her handkerchief pressed to her bruised lip, when the elevator, which she had just signalled, stopped at her floor and Jack Hayward emerged, his face very white, his eyes stormy with anger and fear.

"What kept you so long? Why, Ruth! What's wrong? You're crying!" And almost roughly, as Micky Moran looked on, Jack pulled Ruth's hand from her mouth and saw the swelling lip. "God! That beast! I'll kill him for this! I was afraid—let me go, Ruth!"

"Jack, please, darling, please!" Ruth begged, pulling at his arms frantically. "Come on into the elevator. It wasn't Mr. Borden! I swear it wasn't! I struck my face against the door! You've got to believe me! Jack!" Her voice changed suddenly, became ominously quiet and steady, as the young man flung off her clinging hands. "If you don't come with me now, if you won't believe me when I say it wasn't Mr. Borden who hurt me, in spite of—what you saw this morning, I'll take back the promise I gave you last night. I mean it!"

Jack Hayward came to his senses. He shook his head, as if to clear from his eyes the red mists of anger. "You—

mean that, Ruth?" She nodded, her blue eyes imploring him through tears. "All right! But on one condition—that you give Borden notice on Monday morning. I'm not going to have you in that devil's office another day!"

Ruth would have promised anything to get him to go quietly with her. The elevator boy regarded the silent, flushed pair with humorously upraised brows, as he shot the car down to the main floor.

"Where shall we eat?" Jack asked in a strained, unnatural voice when they had reached the sidewalk.

Ruth swallowed hard at the lump in her throat. "Anywhere, dear. The—the McAlpin Hotel? It's closest—"

"What did it matter now? Jack thought she had lied to him, believed Borden had kissed her so violently that her lip had been bruised . . . Her "perfect day" was spoiled. . . . She shivered, could not stop shivering, even as she followed her fiance into the big, warm dining room of the McAlpin.

She stood miserably beside the table while Jack and the waiter stooped to pick up the widely scattered contents of her handbag. Suddenly she knew she could not get through the meal which was to have been so gay, without the relief of tears. "Will you excuse me a minute, dear? I want to telephone," she choked, and fled.

"No, thanks," she quavered, as he reached for her coat. "I'll keep it on. I'm—cold. Oh—I'm so sorry!"

She found the ladies' rest room deserted. Flinging herself upon a settee, Ruth Lester shed hot tears for lost ecstasy. Joy would come again, she knew, but today, which was to have been so perfect, was hopelessly blighted. . . . Maybe Jack was feeling as cheated and unhappy as she was. . . . The thought pulled her out of despair. She bathed her eyes, powdered her face, and was smiling tremulously when Jack looked up from the menu card he was studying grimly.

"I suppose you telephoned Borden to warn him of my murderous intentions," the jealousy crazed young man challenged her, as he stumbled to his feet.

"Ruth, you've got to resign Monday. I mean it!" Jack interrupted, leaning across the table to cover her icy little hands with his. "I'm jealous as—as the devil, honey. I couldn't bear it—having you near that beast. Bill Cowan had to hold me back today, when I saw Borden pawing at you precious little face, his arm about your shoulders. I believe I could have leaped across that eight foot airshaft, I was so wild, and if I had—"

"No," Ruth quivered, slipping into the chair he pulled out for her. "I—I had to powder my face. I hope you ordered something good. I'm—"

Ruth's fingers curled over his tightly. "Let's not think of Harry Borden any more, darling. He doesn't really matter, you know. He shan't ever touch me again. I promise! Of course I'll resign Monday. . . . But who is Bill Cowan, darling? I'm sorry he had to see—"

"Cowan?" Jack laughed, reassured, happy again. "Oh, Cowan's a real estate man. Sells lots out in Scarsdale. Know why I wanted to see him, sweet?"

Color swept over Ruth's cheeks. "Oh!—Really, Jack? But—how can you? Oh, it would be heavenly to build a home!"

Jack leaned as far across the table as he could, his brown eyes holding her blue ones adoringly. "Oh, I'll manage the money, darling! I signed up old T. Q. Garnett yesterday for fifty thousand dollars worth of additional insurance. My commission will more than pay for a lot in Scarsdale—"

"Has his application been accepted?" Ruth interrupted, practical even in her joy.

"Not yet, but he was to see the medical examiner this morning. I'm sure he'll pass. . . . Here comes food! Now look here, young lady, if you dare cry again, I'll go back and finish that beast, and I don't mean maybe. . . . The broiled mushrooms are for the young lady, waiter, the sweetbreads for me. I ordered for you, honey."

The waiter left them in peace for several minutes, for his services were in demand elsewhere. They scarcely touched their food, for neither had an appetite just then for anything but long, sweet, significant glances.

"You'd better have some very hot coffee," Jack decided suddenly, as Ruth, wrapped though she was in her thick fur coat, shivered again, uncontrollably. He signalled the waiter. "Wonder what time that matinee begins—2:30 or 2:45? Maybe the tickets say—" and he took out his wallet to consult them. "That's funny! They're not here, and yet I distinctly remember Miss Barnes' handing them to me this morning. ... By George, I left them on my desk! I remember now. Cowan came in just as she gave them to me and I laid them down to shake hands with him. . . . Waiter! Bring a pot of very hot coffee for the young lady, and some almond ice cream, with a lot of those little buttery cakes. Right, darling? . . . I'll dash back to the office and get the tickets. Won't take me more than ten minutes. We'll have ample time to make the theater. It's only ten of two now," he added, looking at his watch.

He kissed her with his adoring eyes, and she watched him swing down the room, her heart almost bursting with pride and joy in him. He was so tall and lean and handsome, so vital, with his dark, red brown hair, his tanned skin, his bronze brown eyes. . . . Oh, she loved him! Even his jealous rage against Borden was precious, because it sprang out of his love for her. . . .

"No," she roused herself from her reverie several minutes later, to answer the waiter. "There's nothing wrong with the ice cream, thank you. I'm just not hungry. Oh, yes, I would like another cup of coffee. Bring a pot for two. The gentleman will be back soon."

But, strangely, he was not. When her second cup of coffee had been drunk, Ruth consulted her tiny wristwatch, and was startled to see that it was five minutes past two. Jack had been gone fifteen minutes! Her whole body was shivering with a chill as she poured her third cup of coffee, and sipped it slowly. Fear mounted in her heart until she felt nauseated. . . . Ten minutes after two—

A couple leaving the next table obscured her view of the door for a minute and Jack was almost at her side before she saw him. "Oh, darling!" she cried out with relief. "I was getting so worried—why, Jack! Jack! What's the matter? What has happened?" Her lips went white and cold. "Borden?"

# CHAPTER FOUR

## I

JACK made an impatient gesture toward the waiter who had hurried to the table, order pad in hand. "No dessert. But you can bring the check. . . . What do you mean—Borden?" he demanded of Ruth, in an odd, constrained voice, as the waiter was removing Ruth's dish of melted ice cream.

"You—you look so queer that I thought you might have had a quarrel with Borden," Ruth quivered, oblivious of the waiter's presence. "Oh, Jack, what is the matter? Did you see him?"

Jack frowned, then poured himself a cup of coffee with a hand that trembled slightly. "Why should I see him? Watching Borden isn't my favorite indoor sport!" He must have realized then how violent his voice was, for he softened it suddenly. "There's nothing the matter, honey. I—just thought I'd gather up some work to do over the week end," and he pointed to the big, well filled brief case he had propped against the wall.

"You're—going to work tomorrow?" Ruth asked slowly.

Jack smiled at her, with oddly pale, taut lips. "Just during the day. We'll have our evening together. Sorry to have kept you waiting, sweetheart. A little matter of business came up while I was in my office—something I—hadn't expected. I've been very unchivalrous today; I've kept two ladies waiting!" he added, with a sorry attempt at lightness.

"Yes?" Ruth could not trust herself to say more. What *had* happened? Jack was keeping something back, some thing important. . . .

"The first lady of the land—" he jerked a courtly little bow in her direction— "and my friend, Letty. She was just about to clean my office when I got there. She wouldn't stay, though I urged her to. I always feel like a dog when I keep one of those poor old women from their work." He was talking rapidly, not looking at her, and Ruth knew he was deliberately trying to divert her attention, so that she would not question him.

She tried gallantly to play up, though her heart felt like a stone in her breast. "Poor Letty! She's like a ghost, isn't she, dear? A drab, gray old ghost, haunting a scrub pail and a mop. But I'll never forget Letty. You know, darling, it was your sweetness to old Letty that made me first realize that I loved you."

His smile became more natural, eager. "Yes? I thought you said last night you'd loved me since the first time you saw me, when you were feeding the pigeons."

"Of course!" she nodded, almost happy again. "But I didn't *realize* until the other day—Tuesday, wasn't it? How long ago it seems now!—when you were showing me your offices so proudly. Remember? You'd sent Miss Barnes out for a quart of hot chocolate, and you made poor old Letty have some, too."

"Oh, Letty and I are pals," Jack laughed. "Ever since her first day in the building, when I noticed that she was new, and told her I was glad to meet her, she's thought your precious Jack is a 'really remarkable fellow.' "

"And he is!" Ruth cried, completely happy again. Then she laughed softly, her blue eyes limpid with love. "Darling, I'll never forget how comical you looked last night when I came back into the room without my spectacles, with my curls turned loose and that awful yellowish powder scrubbed off my face—"

"That was a mean trick to play on a man!" Jack chided her tenderly. "Let him get himself engaged to one girl and then find himself saddled with an entirely different one!"

"Are you sorry, darling?" she teased, the dimple tugging at the corner of her beautiful little mouth.

"I suppose I'll have to make the best of you," Jack retorted. Then, to the waiter. "The check? Oh, yes."

Ruth, watching his face because she loved it so, saw a frown pass quickly over it as his eyes scanned the check. And again joy fled from her heart. . . . She tried to grasp its flying wings: "Oh, no! Jack isn't stingy! Why, he's the soul of generosity. I've seen him tip Letty and the elevator boys—"

She turned away her eyes, lest she see that the tip was small. . . . She could not have borne that—not today!

"Your briefcase, sir!" the waiter called to Jack, as he and Ruth were leaving.

Jack accepted the heavy bag with muttered thanks and Ruth thought he looked at it with distaste—disgust even. "The poor dear doesn't want to work, but feels that he has to, now that he's an engaged man, planning to get married!" she deduced, trying to recapture joy. "Of course! That's why the bill dismayed him. He wants to save for our home—now."

At the theater Jack refused the singsong offer, "Check your hat and coat and bag, sir. Check your hat and—" with a curt "No!" And he nursed the heavy bag on his knees during the entire performance of the play.

The show they had chosen so happily the night before, when making their plans, proved a disappointment. It was a murder mystery, with the action taking place in a courtroom. Ruth had wanted to see it because of her familiarity with the law and with trial procedure, but unfortunately the district attorney looked something like her father, who had lost his life in a courtroom, and during the second act she burst into tears and cried so hard that people around them looked at her with impatient disapproval.

"I think we'd better duck the rest of this," Jack urged, his mouth tight and grim. "I never realized—I'm not enjoying it any better than you are, darling. I've already guessed who the murderer is anyway—pretty obvious, and it's rather a sordid way to spend our big afternoon."

"No, let's stay," Ruth choked. "I—I want you to get your money's worth." When she had said it she could have bitten out her tongue. Her only excuse was that by this time she was so nervous and ill—she must be taking a dreadful cold!—that she hardly knew what she was saying. They sat through the third act, their hands touching only once. And she had dreamed all morning of that glorious opportunity for holding hands!

"Let's go to the savings bank first, then on to my apartment for dinner," Ruth suggested, almost timidly, when they left the theater. "I want to cook for you—to get into practice."

"That's the spirit!" Jack applauded, but the smile on his lips scarcely touched his eyes. What—oh, what had happened? Ruth wondered desperately.

But in the bank, open Saturday afternoons for savings bank depositors, he seemed more himself again, teasing her about her thriftiness, and gallantly relieving her of her handbag while she made out her deposit slip and endorsed her salary check.

"Peeking to see what kind of lipstick I use?" she laughed at him, when she left the teller's window.

Jack closed her little brown leather handbag, and flushed as if he had been caught in the act of stealing. "Just curious to see what a girl stuffs into a handbag," he grinned at her. "I never saw one that didn't look ready to burst. I see that the little inside mirror broke when you dropped your bag in the hotel dining room. Are you superstitious?"

Ruth shivered. "Seven years bad luck, you mean? Pooh! You can't scare me! I've just entered on seven years divine luck—and seven more and seven more—and seven more—" she chanted.

Jack's mobile, sensitive face went grave again, almost shadowed. "Please God, you're right, dear."

And do what she would that evening and the next evening, Ruth Lester could not long keep the shadow of trouble, even fear, out of her lover's eyes. True, he ate the dinner that she cooked for him, and praised her culinary art extravagantly. But after the dishes were washed and restored to the tiny cupboard in the miniature kitchenette, he slumped into gloom again, forgetting to kiss her for as long as half an hour at a time. Ruth spent most of Sunday in bed, but contrary to her fears, an actual cold did not develop. There was just that odd shiver that ran along her nerves at the most unexpected moment. . . .

Sunday evening they ate dinner in the little restaurant to which Ruth had taken Jack the first time they had ever eaten together, in obedience to his whimsical request that she show him where she got such potent crumbs that the black pigeon would eat out of her hand.

"Oh, Jack, the poor pigeons!" Ruth remembered the birds contritely. "I was so happy yesterday that I forgot to buy peanuts to feed them before I left for the week end. I meant to do it when I was getting Mr. Borden's money and tickets. Poor Satan! Do you think he'll starve to death before Monday? I'll take a lot of crumbs with me in the morning—"

"I don't like that black pigeon!" Jack surprised Ruth by saying the absurd words grimly. "He looks too much like his namesake—'Handsome Harry.' "

"Darling!" Ruth laughed. "I do believe you're jealous of the black pigeon! He's a greedy scamp. But have you noticed how the little white pigeon adores him? She's never far from his side, although she's too timid to eat out of my hand yet. I wonder if most of the pigeons aren't ladies who are in love with Black Satan. He struts about as if he were the lord of creation. ... I wonder, too," she mused, "how Rita Dubois is enjoying this week end. I know she doesn't really care for Harry Borden—"

"Let's not talk about that man again!" Jack interrupted vehemently. Then, as Ruth's delicate little face flushed and quivered: "Sorry, darling! I'm all on edge. . . . Keyed up, I suppose, to my new responsibilities. Shall we go out to Scarsdale with Cowan next Sunday and look at the lots? Oh, Ruth! I do love you so! Forgive me for being so difficult last night and tonight. I—lots on my mind. Got to plan a future for Mr. and Mrs. John Carrington Hayward. Love me? Say it, Ruth!"

It was not until she was dressing to go to the office Monday morning that Ruth realized that Jack had not reminded her of her promise to resign her position as Harry Borden's secretary. "But—why should he remind me?" she reasoned. "He knows I'll keep my promise, and I can understand his not wanting to talk about it under the circumstances."

She arrived at the office at nine fifteen, though Borden never required her presence until half past. And his train was not due from Winter Heaven until twelve ten. There was a great pile of letters on the floor, beneath the slot in the door, but there was something Ruth had to do before she opened, read and sorted the mail. She had not forgotten the pigeons this time. Benny Smith had not arrived, although he was supposed to open the offices at nine o'clock sharp. Of course he was taking advantage of Borden's absence. . . .

Ruth took the dried sponge out of the little glass dish on her desk, then emptied into it an envelope of peanuts and a larger package of crumbs. Satan and his harem should have a feast and not have to wait until noon for it, either!

Smiling, she opened the door between the reception room and Borden's private office, and, with the glass dish in her hand, stepped across the threshold. The ghastly spectacle that met her eyes robbed her of all power of motion for the moment, and the pigeons of their meal. The glass dish fell to the floor, the peanuts and crumbs scattering upon the thick velvet rug. . . . But Ruth did not see them, for her eyes were fixed in a trance of horror upon the thing that lay near the window on the floor. . . .

## II

Slowly, her feet feeling as stiff and cold as the thing that lay on the floor, Ruth Lester backed toward the door which led into the reception room, her hand groping for the knob, in a desperate need for something to cling to, for her whole world was whirling madly about her. But her staring, unwinking blue eyes could not tear them selves away from the sight which filled them—the prostrate body of her employer, "Handsome Harry" Borden.

Even in death he looked handsome. His still face, very white against the polished dark brown wood of the floor and in contrast with the sleek blackness of his unruffled hair, was pillowed upon his up flung left arm, so that he looked as if he slept. But the rigid stillness of that sprawled body was not the peace of sleep. From beneath the slightly raised right shoulder—he had fallen upon his side—something which had once been warm and red had spurted, forming a dark, irregularly shaped pool, dry now at the edges.

Ruth Lester had a queer, half mad desire to apologize to the man she had served for intruding upon the awesome peace which had come somehow, terribly, swiftly, to put a period upon his forty years of turbulent living. Oddly enough, knowing the man as she did, her first conscious, coherent thought was that he had killed himself. And instinctively her eyes, breaking away after long seconds or minutes—she never knew which—from their horrified contemplation of that strangely ennobled face, searched the room, or as much of it as she could see without advancing again into that chamber of horror. It was only when she saw no pistol or other weapon that the word "murder" went zigzagging through her mind like a streak of lightning. She whispered the word, her lips feeling icy as they touched each other. But—who? Why?

Her groping hand found the door knob, and she clung to it, swaying dizzily for a moment. Then, frenzy taking the place of stunned horror, she banged the door upon that ghastly sight and staggered across her own office, both hands reaching for the outer door. When she had come in, she had left it on the latch, so that visitors to the office might gain access, and as she let it swing shut behind her fleeing, horror driven figure, she had the impulse, born of long habit, to click on the latch, so that no one could enter during her absence.

"Nobody can hurt him now. He needn't be afraid of unlocked doors any more," Ruth's mind babbled crazily, as she ran down the hall, past the suites of offices that lay beyond Borden's, turned the corner, raced on.

From the very first moment of discovery there had been only one thing she could do. She must see Jack. The journey along the two corridors had never seemed long to her before, but now she felt as if she would never reach the man she was engaged to, the man who . . . But as if something too frightful for contemplation were pushing upward from her subconscious mind, she veered her thoughts. Why hadn't she stepped to Borden's window and called across the airshaft to Jack, screamed at him until he answered? But to do so, she would have had to step over the stiff, still legs of that thing that lay so near the window. . . .

Two men who had offices in Jack's wing of the Starbridge Building looked at the white faced, running girl, but she did not see them, did not hear one of them call out to her. If she had, she would not have answered. No one but Jack could do now, and he ... Oh, no, no!

She found his outer office door closed but not locked, tore it open, gasped out Jack's name to the girl who was calmly opening mail.

"Mr. Hayward? Yes, he's here, or rather, he's in the building. Just stepped out of the office a minute. Won't you wait for him?" Miss Barnes asked, her light brown eyes taking Ruth in curiously, then with a little cynical half smile, which betrayed her thought that the engaged couple had quarreled already. "Go right into his private office, Miss Lester. I'll see if I can find him for you. I think he went into the typewriter agency next door—"

Ruth had no power to listen, did not know that she shut the door of Jack's private office upon the uncompleted sentence of his secretary. Gasping, her hand pressing hard upon her heart, she sank down into Jack's desk chair, her whole body trembling so that the chair quivered and squeaked.

If only Jack would come! Come quickly and take her in his arms, and tell her what to do, tell her that he hadn't— Oh, no! not that! She mustn't go mad, with so much to do. . . . Afterwards, Ruth had no memory of reaching a shaking hand down, down, to the bottom drawer of Jack Hayward's desk, no memory at all of jerking it open. But there memory began, recording a moment of such transcendent horror as was never to be entirely erased from her mind.

Every finger of her groping hand seemed to have an eye, as if her wide, terrified blue ones were not enough. But all the eyes in the world could not have found Jack's automatic pistol in the drawer, for it was not there. . . . For a frantic minute, kneeling now beside that pulled out drawer, she pawed among towels and rubber banded bundles of ancient life insurance "literature," but she knew that the thing she had never had the courage to touch but which now, if she had found it, she would have hugged to her breast in a transport of relief and joy, was not there—not there . . .

She heard Jack's voice in the outer office. Rose, trembling and nauseated, from her kneeling position. Held tightly to his desk for support as she faced him.

"Hello, darling! Sweet of you to pay me a good morning visit," his cheerful, eager voice began. Then he saw her white, stricken face, the horror in her widened blue eyes. "Why—what's up, Ruth? Wait! Hold everything! Jack's here, sweet!"

And his arms were about her, steadying her, holding her close against his heart. Her fingers dug into his shoulders. "Mr. Borden! He's—dead! Murdered! Blood, Jack—oh! What am I to do? The police—oh, Jack!"

The young man's arms went lax for a moment, then tightened about her so that she gasped for breath. "God! That you had to see it!" His exclamation, uttered on jerky gusts of breath, might mean anything—anything!

Ruth struggled in his arms, hid her eyes against her elbow. "My fault! I—I screamed! If only I hadn't screamed, Jack! I won't have to tell the police, will I, Jack? I'll lie! I'll lie, Jack! Nobody will have to know! I'll lie!"

The man seized her roughly, shook her a bit to stop that hysterical babbling. "Shut up, Ruth! Do you hear me?—stop it, I say! You've got to get hold of your nerves, darling! Oh, my God!" he groaned, pressing his cheek hard against the golden curls. "Listen, Ruth. The man deserved to be shot. Hold fast to that, darling! He deserved it, I tell you! There's only one thing for you to remember—that we love each other. Now, we'll go—over there—" and he nodded, his face grim, to the window across the airshaft, "and face this thing together. Take my arm, darling. Hold tight!"

Dimly Ruth heard the man she was engaged to, the man who loved her so much that he—but she mustn't think, yet!—give instructions to his secretary, but she did not take in the words, had no idea whether Miss Barnes had heard any or all of their conversation. The two corridors seemed infinitely long, stretching away like interminable paths in a nightmare, but at last they were in her own office again. Jack gently unlocked her rigid fingers from his arm and lifted her bodily into her little swivel chair. She laid her head on her desk, pillowing it on her crossed arms, while Jack, in a brisk, businesslike voice, called police headquarters. Fragments of his conversation pierced the swirling chaos of her mind— "Yes, Borden! B o r d e n. Henry P. Borden. Murdered in his office, suite 712, the Starbridge Building. . . . This is John C. Hayward speaking. . . . Of course I shall stay until police arrive."

As from a great distance, Ruth heard him turn the knob of the door which she had closed upon the thing which had been "Handsome Harry" Borden. He must be looking. ... Oh, how could he? His automatic gone from the drawer of his desk. . . . That heavy briefcase which he had not let out of his possession after he had returned to her at luncheon, during the whole of the matinee. . . . "Check your hat and coat and bag, sir. . . ." Jack's scowl at the boy, his curt refusal. . . . All the time, even when they were holding hands across the briefcase, that horrible thing of blue steel had been there. . . . Oh, no, no! Ruth wrenched her mind back, forced it to reconstruct the events of Saturday afternoon. But that, too, was more than her mind could bear, without shuddering away and being dragged back. . . . Her bruised lip. Jack's white hot anger against Borden, his refusal to believe that it had not been Borden who had hurt her. . . . His threats, in sanely uttered in the presence of Micky Moran, the elevator operator. . . . She had had to hold him back with all her strength to keep him from forcing his way into Borden's offices. . . . His declaration that he had forgotten the theater tickets, his return to his office to get them. . . . Had he really forgotten them, or had he *intended* to do what—oh, she mustn't say it, even to herself! Again that agonized wrenching of her mind, to bring it back to the subject, no matter how horrible it was. . . . Had Jack seen Borden across the airshaft? Oh, God, why had the architect set two windows exactly opposite each other, so terribly close? . . . Had Jack furiously delivered an ultimatum to Borden about her? Had they quarreled then, so that Jack's fury became insanity? "What easier than to snatch his automatic from the drawer of his desk and fire at Borden, drawn to his own window by the quarrel?

Suddenly Ruth's small body was galvanized with purpose. If Jack had done this thing, he had done it for her— for her! And now, before the police came, she could do something for him. . . .

"Where are you going, Ruth?" Jack demanded, harshly. "Stay out of there! It's no sight for your eyes. Stop, I tell you!"

"Oh, let me go!" Ruth sobbed, tearing at his hands. "I've got to go! I've got to do it before the police come! Don't you—understand?"

"Do what? Are you crazy? Please, darling, get control of yourself! It wasn't your fault, really! The man deserved to die—"

"Don't say that again! I can't bear it!" Ruth screamed. "Don't you realize?—I've got to close the window, before the police come!"

He let her go, or her strength for the moment was greater than his, for she flung herself upon the connecting door, tore at the knob until it yielded, stepped in—then stumbled backward into Jack's arms.

"The window's closed, Jack! Closed! Do you hear? Closed! Oh, God, I thank thee! Forgive me, Jack—"

There was a loud knock upon the outer door, followed immediately by the turning of the knob. The police had arrived to inquire into the death of "Handsome Harry" Borden.

# CHAPTER FIVE

IN the brief instant between the turning of the knob of the outer door and the entrance of the police, Ruth had time to get control of her nerves. For fear so horrible that she now wondered how she had been able to bear it had been lifted from her mind and heart. The window of Borden's private office, opening upon the airshaft, and directly opposite to Jack Hayward's window, was closed. How could she, even for a moment have believed her man was guilty of murder? Her reasoning was exquisitely clear and simple: The only way Jack Hayward could have shot Borden was through the window. She herself had left Borden's door locked, because of his deadly fear of hold up men or the assaults of loss crazed investors in his stocks. Borden would never in the world have unlocked it for Jack Hayward, for it was his custom, she knew, to demand to know who wanted to see him, if he was alone and unprotected in his office. The only person, probably, whom he had admitted was his wife, whom he was expecting, and she undoubtedly had already called before Jack's return to his office to get the forgotten theater tickets.

"Henry P. Borden's offices?" an aggressive voice demanded unnecessarily, for the name was painted on the door. "What's happened here?"

Ruth Lester was still standing in the protective circle of Jack Hayward's arm. She looked curiously, no longer afraid, at the detective in plain clothes who was addressing her. Behind him stood two policemen in uniform, but Ruth scarcely saw them. The detective towered over her—a gigantic man, at least six feet three inches tall and broad in proportion. He looked as if he had grown grizzled in the service of justice, but was still not satiated, getting a savage joy out of running criminals to earth. There was a gleam of almost lustful anticipation in his small, pale gray eyes, overhung with portentously scowling brows.

"I am John C. Hayward—offices in this building, and this is Miss Lester—Ruth Lester, secretary to Mr. Borden, who is—in there. Murdered," Jack answered the detective quietly.

"I'm Detective Sergeant McMann," the huge man completed the strange introductions curtly. "Move aside, please. Let's see him. Who discovered the body?"

"I did," Ruth whispered, horror of that thing inside swooping down upon her again. "I—I got to the office this morning at nine fifteen, and—and found him there."

"You've been in there, too?" McMann jerked his head at Jack.

"Just looked in. I didn't touch anything," Jack answered.

"Except the door knob. No good having it photographed for fingerprints since both of you've touched it," McMann answered, as he grasped the knob in his own hands. Another jerk of his head indicated that the two uniformed policemen were to enter the room behind him.

Ruth and Jack stood aside to let the three of them pass, then watched from the doorway. The detective stopped just inside the door and gave a keen, searching glance about, apparently less interested in the body on the floor near the window than in what he hoped to find in the room.

"What are these crumbs and peanuts doing on the rug?" he demanded, whirling upon Ruth.

"Oh!" she gasped, guiltily. "I—I must have dropped them when I saw—Mr. Borden. I—I was going to feed the pigeons the first thing this morning because I forgot to Saturday and I thought—"

"Pigeons!" McMann ejaculated. "What pigeons?"

Ruth's soft, tremulous voice explained: "This is the top floor of the building. A flock of pigeons nests on the roof and I've been feeding them at noon for several weeks. I—I was so startled at seeing—Mr. Borden—when I opened the door that I dropped the little glass bowl full of crumbs and peanuts."

"Hmm!" McMann beetled his eyebrows at her, then strode about the room, his eyes searching the floor, the walls, the desk. Then, at last, after so long a time that Ruth felt like screaming to him to get it over with, he went and knelt beside the dead man's body and lifted the outflung right hand, whose fist, Ruth noticed for the first time, was clenched convulsively.

"Stiff!" McMann pronounced. "Dead a good many hours, I'd say. Shot through the heart. Must have died quickly, but Dr. Nielson will tell us that. Rand—" he adressed one of the policemen—"put in a call for headquarters. Tell the chief it's murder all right, and to send Dr. Nielson over right away. And Biggers, you stand outside the door in the hall and keep the crowds away. The news will go through the building like wildfire, once it gets started. Did you spill it?" he demanded of Ruth.

She shook her head. "I told no one but Mr. Hayward. I went to him immediately after—after I saw Mr. Borden. Mr. Hayward has offices on this floor, around in the next wing. We are—engaged to be married. That's why I went to him."

"That so?" McMann's little, squinted gray eyes studied the pair in die doorway. He seemed about to ask some questions concerning their relationship to each other or to the dead man, and then, to Ruth's great relief, to decide upon a query of more immediate importance. "Did Borden keep any money or valuables in the office? Do you know what he had on him Saturday? Looks like he must have been murdered as long ago as Saturday."

"I know that he had five hundred dollars in tens and twenties," Ruth answered steadily. "He had me go to the bank to get it for him, as he was going to Winter Heaven for the week end. His train was to leave at 2:15. I don't know how much more he had. I caught a glimpse of a yellow backed note in his wallet when he put the five hundred in, but I didn't see the denomination. He also had a pair of railroad tickets with a Pullman drawing room ticket, which he had had me buy for him."

As she spoke, the detective was searching the pockets of the dead man's coat, trousers and vest. "Here are the tickets O.K., a couple of baggage checks and some loose change in a pocket. But there are no banknotes at all. . . . Hmm! Looks like robbery."

"There have been a number of hold ups in the building in the last few weeks," Jack volunteered. "Someone who knew Miss Lester to be Mr. Borden's secretary may have seen her cashing the check for five hundred and—"

"I'll do the maybes on this job, thanks!" McMann interrupted harshly. "Now, Miss Lester—by the way, any relation to Colby Lester, the lawyer?"

Tears sprang into Ruth's eyes. "He was my father."

McMann's glinting gray eyes were gentle for a moment, as they took in the small figure, with its crown of golden curls and wide, limpid blue eyes. "Sorry, Miss Lester! I had no idea. Do remember the boys saying he had a kid— I mean a daughter—that he was crazy about. . . . Now, child, in your own words, tell me all you know about this business. When you last saw Borden, everything of importance that happened Saturday, anything you can think of to help me."

"Please, may I sit down—in my own office?" Ruth faltered.

The detective took a chair beside Ruth's desk, making notes on sheets of yellow paper, as the girl told her story.

"Saturday is always a quiet day, since it is a half holiday," Ruth began, her hands tight locked on the desk before her, her brows knit in an effort at concentration. "I arrived first, at half past nine, then Benny Smith, the office boy, came in—"

"Where is he now?" McMann rapped out, as he made a note of the name.

"He hasn't come in yet," Ruth admitted. "He some times soldiers on the job when he knows Mr. Borden is out of town. He was to go away for—"

"The boy's address?" McMann demanded, pencil poised.

"Why, I don't know," Ruth acknowledged reluctantly. "I have an old address on file, but his family moved the first of January. I told him to give me his new address, but someone interrupted, and I'm sure he didn't."

"Guess he'll stroll in later," McMann dismissed the office boy. "Now go on, please. When did Borden come in Saturday?"

"About ten, as usual. Some woman, who would not give her name, had just called for him on the phone, and I told him, describing her voice. He knew who she was, but he didn't mention her name."

"Ever hear her voice before?" McMann was instantly alert.

"She had called several times during the four months I worked here," Ruth answered. "Once I put her through to Mr. Borden, and he told me to remember her voice and never do so again. She has a beautiful, throaty contralto. . . . Yes, I'd know it if I heard it again, over the phone anyway."

"All right. Go on," McMann, obviously disappointed, urged her impatiently.

"Mr. Borden dictated for about half an hour." The girl's clear voice faltered as she remembered that foolish first scene between her and Borden, when he had seized her hand and tried to pull her toward him across the desk, urging her to take off her spectacles. Perhaps Benny would tell of it later when he was questioned, but now she could only pray that he would not. . . .

"Any trouble between you and Borden, Miss Lester?" McMann pounced.

"Trouble? Oh, no!" Ruth protested, flushing. "He was always very considerate of me, till the very day of his death—" Which was literally true—until the very day of his death! "He dictated, as I said, until Benny interrupted to say that an old man was in this office, demanding to see Mr. Borden. I went out to talk with him, because Mr. Borden wouldn't see him, of course—"

"Why 'of course'?" McMann demanded.

Ruth gazed at the detective blankly for a moment, then her blue eyes filled with a sudden, glad light. How could she have forgotten that the old man had muttered threats against Borden's life? . . . But, oh, he had looked so ill and beaten! Her eyes clouded again, but she answered honestly: "Mr. Borden would never see any one who had a grievance. The old man—he wouldn't give me his name, insisted on seeing Mr. Borden—said he had lost a fortune —all his savings—in one of Mr. Borden's stock promoting schemes."

"Did the old man make any threats against Borden?"

"Yes," Ruth admitted slowly. "But—I thought he was just talking, as people do who are furious and helpless. They frequently say things they don't mean—" She checked herself abruptly. She mustn't babble like this and give Jack away. Of course he hadn't killed Borden, but McMann would seize upon the least thing.

"Suppose you describe the old man and let his lawyers worry about his defense, if it comes to that." McMann brought the girl back sharply to the business in hand. "Remember, Miss Lester, your employer has been murdered, and I'm counting on you to help me find out who the murderer is."

Ruth pressed her fingers into her temples, in a mighty effort to remember clearly. "He was old—about sixty, I think," she told the detective slowly, and did not see McMann, who was past fifty himself, wince at her unintentionally cruel words. "He was wearing a shabby black overcoat with a velvet collar, which had flakes of dandruff on it, I remember, for I felt sorry for him, he looked so helpless. I can't tell what color his eyes were, but he had on old fashioned steel rimmed spectacles. His hair, sort of long, I think, was gray, and his face thin and hollow, with deep lines. He seemed tall, but I'm so short that nearly everyone seems tall to me," she confessed. "I can't really remember what he said, for he was muttering most of the time, but he did make threats of 'getting even.' Said he'd teach 'that crook' a lesson, bring him to his knees—things like that. I don't really remember, for I was trying to soothe him and get rid of him. I had a lot of work to do, and I knew it was all so hopeless, that Mr. Borden wouldn't see him or make any restitution."

McMann, who had been jotting down her description of the defrauded old man, scowled and then told her to go on with her story.

"Before writing the letters I went to the bank and to Penn station to get Mr. Borden's tickets for Winter Heaven. After I returned and gave the money and tickets to Mr. Borden, Benny told me that Mrs. Borden had called on the phone to say she was coming in. She and Mr. Borden were not living together."

"I know. Legal separation, with court allowance for her and the children. About five years ago," McMann interpolated. "What did she come to see him for?"

"To get her separation allowance," Ruth answered reluctantly. "Mr. Borden had been ordered by the court to pay her each month on the fifteenth, and he made her come for it in person. To—to get news of the children, I suppose," she added, in a futile attempt to gloss over the dead man's malicious cruelty to his wife.

"Well? Did she come?" McMann asked, busily taking notes.

"Later," Ruth answered, flushing. "But before Mrs. Borden arrived Mr. Borden had another caller—Miss Dubois, Rita Dubois."

"Oh!" McMann whistled, raising his thick eyebrows. "The dancer from the Golden Slipper, eh?"

"Yes. Mr. Borden saw her there two or three weeks ago, and—and—liked her."

"So the other ticket and the drawing room were for Rita Dubois!" McMann deduced triumphantly. "Rand, get headquarters on the line again—or say, have the central telephone office tie up one of these lines for headquarters calls. Tell the chief to have Rita Dubois brought here as soon as she can be found. What's her telephone number, Miss Lester? I suppose you know it, if she and Borden were friendly."

Ruth reached for her desk calendar and turned to the leaf devoted to the previous Tuesday. "It's Trafalgar 0400. Miss Dubois has a private phone and I don't know her address."

"Got that, Rand? . . . All right, Miss Lester. Did Rita and Borden quarrel? Will you please tell me exactly what happened?"

Jack Hayward sat down upon the edge of Ruth's desk and laid one of his hands upon her two clenched, icy little fists. She looked at him gratefully, her eyes brimming with love, before she went on: "No, they didn't quarrel. They—seemed very happy. I could hear them laughing, although the door was closed, while they were in—there," and Ruth jerked her head toward the private office which was a temporary morgue for the man who had laughed and loved on Saturday. "Mrs. Borden came while Miss Dubois was with Mr. Borden and I told her he was—in conference, and she made an appointment to come back between half past one and two. Mr. Borden had told me he would be in his office until about two, since his train would not leave until two fifteen and he planned to lunch on the diner."

"With Rita Dubois?" McMann shot at her.

"He did not tell me who was to go with him," Ruth answered truthfully. "And Miss Dubois did not take me into her confidence either. I do know, however, that he planned to take—a woman, for he had me wire for reservations at the Winter Heaven Hotel, in the name of

Mr. and Mrs. H. P. Benton. The drawing room reservation was made in that name also."

"All right!" McMann made a note. "What next? When did Rita leave?"

"Shortly after Mrs. Borden—about five minutes," Ruth answered. McMann's constant interruptions and questions had shunted her off the subject of Mrs. Borden, but she was not sorry that there was no opportunity now to tell him of the poor, discarded wife's jealousy and humiliation —a humiliation so keen that she had become ill. Why tell McMann now about Mrs. Borden's having seen the automatic pistol in the bottom drawer of the desk? Time enough to tell if it should become necessary...

McMann turned again to the policeman who sat at the telephone, an extension of which was on the absent office boy's desk. "Get me Captain Foster, Rand." As he waited for the connection, the detective turned to Ruth with an other question: "Hear or see anything between Borden and Rita when she was leaving?"

Ruth knit her brows. "Mr. Borden and Miss Dubois came out of the private office together, laughing and talking. Miss Dubois said something about shopping. Said she could do more shopping in two hours than most women could do in a day. And jokingly told him not to call up the stores and limit the charge accounts he was opening for her."

"And what did Borden say?" McMann demanded, his pencil busy. "Gold digging him, eh?"

"He answered something which I didn't understand about her keeping her bargain and he'd keep his. He said, 'Mind you don't double cross me, Rita'—or words to that effect. But he was in great good humor, and waved good bye to her—"

"Just a minute," McMann interrupted, and reached for the phone extension on Ruth's desk. "Hello, Captain. McMann. . . . Yeah. Oh, sure! Robbery or a passion crime, I don't know which yet. Might even be revenge. Too many leads, if you ask me. . . . Say, chief, send Clay out to get Mrs. Borden—Wait! I'll get the address."

Ruth supplied it, from memory: "Mrs. Elizabeth Borden, No. — East Sixty first Street." Her lips felt dry and stiff as she uttered the words. After all, Mrs. Borden was Borden's wife—or rather, his widow! And she loved him. ... It had been so painfully obvious to Ruth on Saturday, when the wife had been forced to listen to the ribald laughter of her husband and his new love, that the wife did love him, was jealous. . . .

". . . That's right, chief. Tell Clay not to spill the beans, see? Just tell her she's wanted at her husband's office, see? . . . Yeah! Plenty! . . . Dr. Nielsen's just leaving? Good? Say, Chief, guess who Borden's private secretary was? Colby Lester's little daughter! Fact! . . . Sure I'll show her every consideration. No man could help it—"

Jack Hayward leaned close to whisper to Ruth, the first smile of that dreadful morning twinkling in his bronze brown eyes. "Better get out your spectacles, darling!"

McMann continued his telephone conversation with the chief of police. "And say, Chief, have Ferber, the fingerprint expert, come right over with his camera. . . . Yeah, I've got this wire plugged up with headquarters until further notice, but there's another line. Rand will take all calls coming in on it; may get some tips that way. . . . And send me over two or three plainclothes men, won't you? All right!" He hung up the receiver and turned to Ruth again, dismissing, to her vast relief, both Mrs. Borden and Rita Dubois, with his first question: "Now, Miss Lester, what other visitors did Borden have Saturday morning and when did you leave the office?"

Ruth considered. "No one else—oh, I'm forgetting Mr. Adams. He's one of the stock salesmen. Mr. Borden had asked him to come in on Saturday to go over his sales record. Mr. Adams had been in a slump--"

"Quarrel?" McMann tapped impatiently with his pencil.

"I didn't hear any quarrel, but Mr. Adams looked rather exasperated when he came out of Mr. Borden's office—"

Ruth was interrupted by Patrolman Biggers, who had been stationed outside the door in the hall. "Lady here wants to see Mr. Borden," he announced to McMann, winking broadly. "Says she's his—"

"I *am* his wife!" a quivering voice cut short the police man's explanation. "I want to see my husband! . . . Oh! Has anything happened to Harry? I knew it! . . . Oh, Harry, Harry!"

# CHAPTER SIX

DETECTIVE SERGEANT McMANN and Ruth Lester sprang to their feet as Mrs. Borden's voice rose in a wail of terror and grief. But it was Ruth who reached the pale faced, red eyed woman first, her arm which went around the swaying body. Jack Hayward strode to the magazine cluttered table in the center of the office, which also served as a reception room for clients, picked up a chair, and helped Ruth to lower the almost hysterical woman into it. McMann, immense, tall, watched the scene with narrowed gray eyes, then, when Mrs. Borden was seated, stepped forward.

"Mrs. Borden," he began slowly, portentously, "just what makes you think something has happened to—your husband?"

Mrs. Borden's tear reddened, leaf brown eyes fluttered uncertainly before they met the hard eyes of the detective. Then, like a thoroughbred, she drew the hysteria rent cloak of her dignity about her slight figure. "Are you from the—the police, too, sir?"

"I am Detective Sergeant McMann," the big man answered curtly. "I repeat: how did you know that some thing had happened to Mr. Borden?"

The pale face of the new made widow went even whiter. "Why—why," she stammered, "the policeman stationed outside the door, of course. Tell me the truth, Mr. McMann: has my husband been arrested? Oh, I was afraid it would come to this sometime! Where did they take him? I must see him, I must! I have a right—"

McMann stepped toward the closed door leading into the private office as he answered. "No, Mrs. Borden, your husband has not been arrested. And you may see him. He is— here. "Won't you step in, please?" and McMann held the door wide.

Ruth cried out sharply at that cruel invitation, but the detective silenced her with a scowl and a peremptory gesture. After returning his scowl with a long, level, contemptuous look of her blue eyes, Ruth bent over the widow and assisted her to rise. The detective made no objection to the girl's entering the room, nor to Jack's following, his tanned face drained of color.

For many nights to come Ruth Lester was to be haunted by that long drawn wail of agony and grief that rose from Mrs. Borden's throat when she caught sight of that which lay sprawled and still on the floor. For a dreadful second that seemed eternal Ruth thought the widow was going to kneel in that horrible, brownish, drying pool of blood, but she must have seen it just in time, for she shuddered away from it, then flung her body beside that of the man who had been her husband and the father of her children. Ruth tried to tear her eyes away, so that she might not see that lifting of the stiffened face, the cradling of it upon a bosom Harry Borden had scorned in life and come back to in death.

McMann stood by, grimly, watching that heartbreaking tableau, listening for the widow to betray herself. But the only words that came were choked endearments, spaced by shuddering sobs and moans of grief. At last the detective bent over the kneeling woman and gently forced her convulsively clinging hands from the dead face. With considerable care, McMann restored the body to its exact former position, while Ruth on one side of her and Jack on the other half carried the widow into the outer office.

McMann joined the group, and spoke quietly to the collapsed figure in the chair. "Mrs. Borden, why did you come to see your husband this morning?"

Mrs. Borden raised a shaking hand and passed it over her dazed eyes. "Please! I—feel—faint. I'll be better in a moment."

"I'll get you a drink!" Ruth offered pityingly, eagerly. As she ran to the water cooler in the corner she had a vivid mental picture of performing that same service for Mrs. Borden on Saturday, saw herself pulling open the stuck bottom drawer of the desk, with Mrs. Borden's assistance, saw again the blue black Colt's automatic lying on a stack of clean towels, heard again her own hurried explanation to Mrs. Borden of the gun's presence there. . . .

"Thank you, Miss—oh, yes, Miss Lester. You're very kind. Will you tell me why—he—killed himself, sir?" Mrs. Borden addressed the detective with an effort, after she had moistened her lips with the water Ruth had brought.

"My question first, please, Mrs. Borden," McMann answered. "Why did you come to see your husband this morning? You have had ample time to think of a good reason."

"Oh!" Ruth cried, but Jack, taking her hand and pressing it hard, warned her to silence.

Mrs. Borden stiffened. "I came this morning to tell my— my husband that our daughter, Betty, is ill. Harry—Mr. Borden—is—was very fond of Betty, and Betty of him." Waveringly, she raised her handkerchief to hide the trem bling of her lips.

"You were here Saturday, Mrs. Borden. Was Betty ill then?"

"Oh, no, she was quite well then, but Betty is delicate, easily upset. She awoke this morning with a fever, and cried for her—her father."

"I see," McMann said, with apparent sympathy. "You came Saturday morning and were told Mr. Borden was busy and that you had better come back later?"

"Yes." A brief spasm distorted the pale face. Ruth, watching her with her heart in her blue eyes, knew that the widow was hearing again those bursts of treble and bass laughter. . . .

"You said you would return about half past one?" McMann pressed. "And did?"

Fresh tears swam in the widow's leaf brown eyes. "I did. Harry—Mr. Borden—"

"Just a minute, Mrs. Borden! How did you get in? With your own latchkey?"

Humiliation flooded the woman's face with scarlet. "I— had no latchkey, Mr. McMann. Mr. Borden and I— were— living apart. I came to give Mr. Borden news of our children and to—to—"

"To get your monthly allowance check for five hundred dollars, which he stipulated that you must ask for in person on the fifteenth day of the month, without fail— unless the fifteenth fell on a Sunday?" McMann supplied with slow significance.

The color became mottled on Mrs. Borden's thin cheeks. "Yes, sir. I knocked on the door, then when no one answered, I realized that Miss Lester had gone for the day and that Harry—Mr. Borden—was in his private office. I tried the door and found it locked, then I knocked quite loudly. He came and—and let me in."

"Was your husband glad to see you?" McMann shot at her.

Ruth quivered, but Mrs. Borden's reclaimed dignity was equal to the answer. "He was—courteous, as— always. We did not—quarrel—ever."

"Hmm!" McMann commented, nodding his head and narrowing his hard gray eyes. "Just exactly what happened, Mrs. Borden? Everything that you can remember, please."

"Harry—Mr. Borden—asked me into his private office, and I sat down across the desk from him. I—I told him little bits of news about the children, and he asked particularly about—about Betty. Then—then he wrote the check and gave it to me—"

"Did you have to remind him to do so?"

Ruth felt like screaming at the man not to persecute the poor woman so. But Mrs. Borden, quite pale again, answered simply: "It was part of the—the separation agreement that I should specifically ask for the allowance. I did so. And Harry wrote the check immediately. I have it here with me. I was going to deposit it to my account this morning. The bank was closed Saturday afternoon." And she drew the unpaid check from her handbag and passed it to the detective, who scanned it briefly and put it in his pocket.

"By the way, Mrs. Borden, at exactly what time did you arrive Saturday?" McMann remembered to ask, as he jotted down notes on her story.

"It was just two or three minutes after half past one when I left the children in the lobby of the McAlpin Hotel, where the three of us had lunched. It must have been twenty minutes of two when Mr. Borden admitted me. I had rather a long wait for the elevator, I remember walking was slow through the Saturday crowds. Yes, it must have been as late as twenty minutes to two."

McMann considered, then: "Now, Mrs. Borden, was there anything at all unusual in Mr. Borden's manner?"

Again that wave of scarlet. "He—was obviously in a hurry," she faltered. "He said something about having to catch a train. He was much the same as—usual, except perhaps a little more—more exuberant, as if—as if—" her voice choked on a sob—"as if he were delighted about something. I'm—glad he was happy. Something terrible must have happened later to make him want to—to commit suicide. Did he learn that he was to be arrested for— for promoting a—an unsound company, Mr. McMann."

The detective regarded her narrowly for a long time, as if trying to make up his mind whether she was acting or not, before he answered:

"Your husband did not commit suicide, Mrs. Borden. He was murdered."

The slight figure which had been holding itself rigid under McMann's bombardment of questions slumped suddenly, and again Ruth ran to her side, offering water, with little soothing murmurs of consolation which the widow obviously did not hear.

"Murdered! My husband—murdered? Who? Why?"

McMann's tall, big body teetered slowly back and forth on its heels as his hard gray eyes met and held those horror-filled brown ones. "I believe you can answer both those questions, Mrs. Borden—who—and why."

The widow thrust out a wavering hand, as if groping for support. Ruth gave it, her eyes blazing upon the detective. "I?—I don't know—what you mean, sir!"

McMann spoke slowly through hard, straight lips: "Let me remind you of several things, Mrs. Borden: You were separated from your husband and you still loved him: You suffered agonies of humiliation each month, through having to beg him for support for yourself and children. You came here Saturday to see him, and found that he was closeted with a girl he loved, a girl with whom he meant to spend the week end at Winter Heaven. You were crazed with love, jealousy and humiliation. You came back here, demanded that he give up his trip with this other woman, quarreled violently with him after he had given you the check, and, when he laughed at you for your interference —you shot him! Doesn't that answer both your questions, Mrs. Borden—who, and why?"

As McMann's ruthlessly logical sentences peppered like bullets upon poor Mrs. Borden's shrinking figure, Ruth Lester thanked God that she had not told the detective about the automatic pistol in the bottom drawer of her desk—that fearsome blue black thing which Mrs. Borden had seen and shuddered away from on Saturday. Even if the pistol was still there and unfired—as it undoubtedly was, Ruth told herself, McMann would believe that the sight of it had planted the idea of murder in the jealousy tormented mind of the discarded wife.

Ruth's own small body stiffened with indignation and sympathy as Mrs. Borden pulled herself together to answer McMann's brutal charge. Tears in the leaf brown eyes were suddenly dried in the fire of anger. A brilliant flush took the place of the pallor which had spread over the sensitive, aristocratic face. Words, when they came, were uttered quietly but firmly:

"I did not kill my husband, sir. He was alive, well and —happy when I left him Saturday afternoon. I never saw him again until—a few minutes ago."

Whatever answer the scowling, obviously skeptical detective might have made was checked by the opening of the outer door and the entrance of three plainclothes men, whom McMann greeted curtly, assigning them rapidly to their tasks:

"Carlson, I want you to take charge of all visitors whom Biggers stops at the door. They'll be stock salesmen and other business callers who don't know that Borden is dead. Herd them into Suite 715 down the hall. It's vacant. Question all comers and send for me if anything develops. Get the alibi of every salesman who reports. Biggers is holding a couple of them now. . . . Yeah, that's all, but don't let anything slip through your fingers. . . . Covey, get hold of the superintendent of the building, and tell him to round up every employe that was on the premises Saturday afternoon. Ask him also to make an office to office canvass for every tenant that was in the building after one o'clock —not many of them, I guess. Question them one by one as to whether they heard a shot, and when. Keep a complete record, of course. Better get the 'super' to give you another vacant suite for your job, and have the gang brought to you, one by one. I don't want them to have a chance to compare notes. And don't put out anything, see? Just ask for information, don't give it."

Covey, a little bright eyed, gleeful looking detective, nodded happily. "And shall I send the elevator boys to you straight off, Chief?"

McMann nodded, but his attention was not so engrossed with his subordinates that he did not see Ruth Lester start, grow very pale, and reach instinctively for Jack Hayward's hand. And he missed not a flicker of the changing expressions that succeeded each other rapidly on the young insurance broker's handsome face—sudden realization of what that order to Covey meant to him and to Ruth, fear—then grim determination.

Ruth did not hear a word of McMann's instructions to Birdwell, the third of the plainclothes men, for she was reliving that damning scene with Jack Hayward at the elevator, when he had come up to rescue her, as he thought, from Borden's amorous importunities. The room spun dizzily about the girl, as she realized that Micky Moran, the elevator operator, would tell—would be forced to tell —how, with her bruised lip trembling with fright and her eyes swimming with tears, she had struggled with Jack to keep him from forcing his way into Borden's office. ...

The crushing pressure of her sweetheart's hand steadied her finally, so that she became conscious of what was going on about her. McMann was bending over Mrs. Borden again, demanding sternly:

"Now, Mrs. Borden, just one more question for the present: did you encounter any one as you left your hus band's offices Saturday afternoon?"

What sounded like a sigh of relief quivered the white lips of the widow. "No one, sir. . . . No, wait! There was a scrubwoman coming out of the office next to the elevator, across the hall. I remember thinking how old and bent she was, how—how harshly life must have used her. . . . That is the only person I saw, Mr. McMann, before the elevator came."

Ruth wondered how many people poor old Minnie Cassidy, the cleaning woman who "did" Borden's offices, had served in this ironic way. She, too, had never been so downhearted but that a sight of rheumatic, bent, but humbly cheerful old Minnie had made her think to her self, gratefully: "Thank God, I'm better off than that. I have a lot to be thankful for." Now, for the first time, with unspeakable ordeals stretching ahead of her and her sweetheart, she fleetingly wished that she could change places with old Minnie, who could not, by the most absurd stretch of the imagination, become involved in this implacable, hard eyed man's investigation into the murder of Henry P. Borden. . . . The convulsive pressure of Jack's hand told her that he was following her thoughts, and she looked up fearfully into his eyes. He was smiling, but his face was very pale, with two little knots of muscle to indicate that his jaws were clenched. She wanted to reach up and touch those clenched jaws, to reassure him: "*I* know you didn't do it, darling! Remember, the window was closed, *closed!* Don't you see? They can't really think you did it, no matter what Micky Moran tells!" But she did not dare, with McMann's narrowed gray eyes flashing keenly from her face to Jack's. . . .

"Oh, hello, Dr. Nielson! Glad you've got here!" McMann strode to the half closed door and extended his hand to a slender, oldish man, whose bared head was thinly covered with graying fair hair, through which the scalp showed pinkly. Pale blue eyes, enlarged by thick lensed spectacles, surveyed the room diffidently. "The body is in the next room, Doctor, exactly as Miss Lester here found it when she came to work this morning. It's pretty obvious that death took place as long ago as Saturday afternoon."

"Nothing is obvious, my dear McMann," the doctor protested mildly. "The building is open on Sundays, I take it?" Without waiting for an answer, the medical examiner stepped over the threshold, removing his gloves as he did so. "Ah! Near the window, I see."

"Yes," McMann admitted, following the doctor and not bothering to close the door behind him. "He was killed in his private office, and not near the door. Looks pretty certain that whoever bumped him off was known to Borden; otherwise he—or more likely *she*—wouldn't have been admitted to the private office."

"These Sherlock Holmes deductions are your field, not mine, my dear McMann," Dr. Nielson said placidly, as he dropped to his knees beside the corpse. "Hmm! Shot through the heart, I think, but of course only an autopsy can tell us the exact facts. No powder burns on the coat or vest, so the weapon must have been fired at a distance of some feet. I'll take a sample of this blood, naturally," he added, opening the small black bag he carried. "The extent of coagulation will help us to arrive at the approximate time of the murder. I presume it is murder? Have you found a weapon?"

McMann indicated the floor of the room with a wave of his hand. "No gun anywhere near the body, doctor. He could have committed suicide and flung the weapon out of the window as he fell, but the window was closed. It was closed when you arrived, Miss Lester?" and he whirled toward Ruth, who was standing beside Jack Hayward in the doorway.

"Oh, yes!" Ruth cried eagerly, too eagerly, so that the detective's eyes narrowed suspiciously. "I did not go near the—the body or the window and Mr. Hayward just touched his hand to be sure Mr. Borden was—dead. He never touched the window, either."

With a piece of chalk the medical examiner outlined the sprawled body on the polished, rug free strip of floor. Around the upflung arm, the head half pillowed upon it, the out thrust right arm, down the torso, around the big, long legs rigidly crooked in death, the chalk speeded, lifting only to avoid that dark, drying pool of blood. While the doctor worked a thick, pugnacious young man, shouldering a camera, pushed his way into the room, saluted McMann, grinned appreciatively at Ruth, then went about his first gruesome task—that of photographing the dead man where he lay. At the explosion of the flashlight Mrs. Borden, still sitting in a forlorn huddle in the outer office, screamed, and Ruth turned back to her, to comfort her with an explanation and little murmurs which were scarcely words.

But she could hear McMann's big voice: "I've left everything just as it was till you got here, Ferber. Finger prints may play a big part in this case. Go over the whole room, especially the desk, doors and windows. Oh, Miss

Lester!" Then, as Ruth reappeared in the doorway, "Were these windows looking out on the street closed, too?"

"They were kept closed in the winter," Ruth answered. "Ventilation came from the window on the airshaft between the wings. Minnie Cassidy, the cleaning woman, must have closed it when she cleaned Saturday afternoon, although Mr. Borden was still here. It's a rule of the building that no windows are to be left open overnight."

"Think the woman cleaned, do you?" McMann shot at her.

"Why, yes," Ruth answered, surprised at his lack of astuteness. "The wastebaskets have been emptied, as you see, both in my office and in Mr. Borden's. Minnie came down the hall toward this office just as I was getting on the elevator Saturday afternoon. I suppose she cleaned then." Her lips went dry with fear that her ordeal was upon her —that McMann would question her then and there about her departure, would learn that she had come back for her forgotten bank book. But the detective merely nodded as he said:

"I'll get Minnie's story when Covey rounds her up."

"The cleaning women don't come on duty week days until four," Ruth volunteered. "Saturdays they work from twelve to four."

McMann thanked her with another curt nod, then, since the finger print expert had finished with Borden's desk, he began to pull out drawers. "I don't see any gun here," he remarked, to no one in particular. "In view of all these hold ups in the building, I'm surprised he didn't keep one."

Because she knew his search would soon extend to her own desk, Ruth volunteered, a little breathlessly: "I have an automatic in my desk, Mr. McMann. A Colt's .38, I believe it is."

"What!" the detective exploded. Then, "Bring it to me! No, wait! I'll get it," he corrected himself grimly, with a significant glance at the finger print expert, who followed close at his heels as McMann strode into the outer office. "Show me where you keep it."

Obediently, without glancing at Mrs. Borden, who was straining forward to see, Ruth pulled open the bottom drawer of her desk, and pointed, shrinking a little, as she always shrank from sight or touch of that blue black thing.

"Where?" McMann was burrowing among the dean towels, cartons of paper cups, and bundles of old station ery with which the bottom drawer was filled. "There's no automatic here, or any other kind of gun!"

"Not—there?" Ruth repeated stupidly. "Not there! Why—" and involuntarily she turned on icy feet and stared at Mrs. Borden.

# CHAPTER SEVEN

DETECTIVE McMANN'S eyes were like glinting bits of steel as he surveyed Ruth's small body from the topmost golden curl to the toes of her beige kid pumps. Those hard gray eyes did not miss the fact that her little hands were locked tightly together, her blue eyes fixed in a wide, unwinking stare of horror—upon Elizabeth Borden.

"When did you last see your automatic, Miss Lester? Come now—the truth, the whole truth and nothing but the truth! Colby Lester's daughter should be familiar with that phrase, and know that the truth is always the best policy."

Ruth nodded weakly, and moistened her lips. "I—saw it Saturday morning, when I opened the bottom drawer to get a new carton of paper cups. It was there then, lying on top of those clean towels. I—I never saw it again, Mr. McMann. I never touched it. It frightened me even to look at it."

McMann's narrowed eyes searched her face. "Who else knew you kept a gun in that drawer?"

Ruth silently prayed that Mrs. Borden would forgive her, as she answered: "A number of people. I can't remember all of them at the moment, but Benny, the office boy, of course, and Mr. Borden, and—and Mrs. Borden—"

"Ah! So Mrs. Borden knew!" McMann interrupted triumphantly. "And how did Mrs. Borden know you kept a gun there? Did she ask you?"

"She—saw it there," Ruth said faintly, reaching out dizzily for the desk. A low exclamation, that might have been either of fear or of startled realization had broken from Mrs. Borden's ashen lips.

"When?" McMann barked.

"Saturday morning," Ruth admitted in a low, trembling voice. "I pulled out the drawer to get the paper cups and Mrs. Borden, who was sitting at my desk, helped me with the drawer because it stuck, and—and I explained how I happened to have a gun—about the hold ups in the building, you know."

"And why was Mrs. Borden sitting at your desk?" Mcmann caught her up sharply, relentlessly. "You'd made her sit down because she was feeling faint, hadn't you? And you were after a cup to give her a drink, weren't you?"

Ruth stared her amazement at his accurate deduction. "Mrs. Borden did not look—well, so I thought—"

"Look here, Miss Lester," McMann interrupted her stumbling speech. "This is murder, you know, and I'm here to find out who did it. If you're trying to shield Mrs. Borden—"

"I'm grateful." Mrs. Borden, who had risen and was holding to her chair, finished his sentence for him. "And I don't want you to bully this child. It is true: I did see the weapon. I was feeling sick and faint because I heard a woman and my husband laughing loudly together."

"You admit that?" McMann demanded. "I guess we're about through here, doctor," he called to the medical examiner who was still in the private office with the corpse. "Mrs. Borden, I ar—"

"Wait, Mr. McMann!" Mrs. Borden commanded, and Ruth admired the calm courage which had come to Harry Borden's widow. "I have made no confession, and will make none, for I did not kill my husband. I have merely relieved Miss Lester of a painful duty—that of telling what happened between her and myself Saturday morning. I admit that I was hurt—jealous, if you will— because my husband was so evidently finding happiness with another woman. But for many years he has given me cause to be jealous, and I have borne it uncomplainingly for the sake of my children."

McMann nodded, his lips twisting in a brief, cruel smile. "But on Saturday you reached the end of your rope, didn't you, Mrs. Borden? You quarreled with him about this other woman, after he had given you your check—"

"I did not!" Mrs. Borden interrupted firmly. "We parted as amicably as usual, and my husband was alive. I did not even remember that Miss Lester had a pistol in her desk. My husband gave me no cause to remember, and I was thinking only of getting back to the McAlpin, where I had left my children."

Again McMann grinned, but he suddenly switched his glinting, hard gaze to Ruth again. "Did Borden buy the automatic and instruct you to use it on bandits, Miss Lester?"

"No." Ruth breathed the word, rather than spoke it.

"I bought the gun for Miss Lester, Mr. McMann," Jack Hayward spoke up. "As I told you, we are engaged to be married. I bought the automatic several weeks ago, after there had been two hold ups in the building, but she was afraid to learn to shoot it."

McMann scowled at the young man, thought deeply for a moment, then pounced upon Ruth again. "If you were so afraid of the gun, Miss Lester, how did it happen that so many people knew you had it?"

The memory of past humiliations painted Ruth's cheeks scarlet. "Mr. Borden made me get it out sometimes and show people that we—we were armed," she faltered. "It— amused him to see how frightened of the gun I was. Several of the stock salesmen were in his office one afternoon, and he made me bring it in—and— and pretend I was a bandit."

"Swell sense of humor!" McMann commented. "You weren't so crazy about your boss, were you, Miss Lester?" he challenged suddenly.

Ruth stared at the detective with frightened blue eyes. "I—he was always a considerate employer. I had no cause at all for complaint, until the day of his death." She could have bitten her tongue after she had again uttered that phrase of double meaning, but apparently it had made no impression upon McMann, or he had accepted it at its face value.

"You seem pretty sure that Borden died on Saturday, Miss Lester," the detective commented. "Let's see what the medical examiner has to say. He must be able to give some sort of report by now . . . Oh, Doctor!"

Dr. Nielson appeared in the doorway between the two offices, his pale eyes blinking mildly behind his thick lensed spectacles.

"When was Borden killed, Doctor? Of course I know you can't say to the minute or even the hour, before you perform the autopsy but it would help me in my work if you could tell me approximately when death took place."

The doctor cocked his thin haired head and smiled quizzically. "You have so little regard for the niceties of science, McMann. It is truly deplorable. But, offhand, and on the condition that you shall not hold me to this opinion or make a hasty arrest based upon it, I shall say to you now that the deceased has been dead between forty one and forty five hours. I draw my conclusions from—"

McMann waved away the medical explanation. "So he was killed after one o'clock Saturday, eh? Let me know later, Doc, if you can fix the time more accurately. Of course we may have a dozen witnesses among the employes and tenants of the buildings as to when the shot was fired. And say, Doc, phone me as soon as you extract the bullet, won't you? I'll bet you a hundred it's a .38 calibre, if you're in a betting frame of mind."

"Not this morning," the doctor repudiated the offer drily. "Now, if I may, I'll phone the morgue to send for the body." And he stepped to the telephone.

"Where the devil is Covey?" McMann began to fume, but before the words were well out of his mouth, the outer door opened and the plainclothesman appeared, followed by two very young men in the uniform of the Starbridge Building.

"Elevator operators on duty Saturday until six," Covey introduced them to his chief.

"All right, boys. Come on in," McMann invited. "I'm not going to arrest you—yet," he added with grim humor, as the boys continued to hug the wall. "Guess this room's getting a little crowded. I'll take you boys into the private office and treat you to a sight you'll never forget."

Micky Moran and Otto Pfluger, whom Ruth recognized as the silent, tow headed boy who ran the car nearest Jack Hayward's offices, stumbled nervously across the outer office in the wake of the detective. Covey, chuckling, indicated by pantomime that the boys had no idea what had happened.

Ruth had no answering smile for his chuckles. The moment, which had been hurtling toward her like a flaming meteor out of hell, was upon her. Micky Moran was behind Otto Pfluger, and before she realized the folly of her action, Ruth caught his eye with her imploring, terrified gaze, then raised a finger to her lips, shaking her head ever so slightly.

"Don't, darling!" Jack whispered, his breath stirring the curls over her ear. "Just keep a stiff upper lip. You've been marvelous. And I love you, no matter what—"

"Will he let us listen, do you think?" she whispered, clinging to his hands, afraid to have him finish that ominous sentence.

Micky did not close the communicating door behind him and the young lovers dared take their place within it. McMann, seated at Borden's desk, glanced up, but did not object. Possibly Ruth thought, he wanted to observe their faces as the elevator operators told their stories.

"Which of you runs the elevator just across the hall?" McMann demanded "You? All right," as Micky Moran stepped jerkily toward the desk, his eyes turned to that awful, huddled thing on the floor. "Henry P. Borden was murdered Saturday afternoon, and undoubtedly, or rather, in all probability, his murderer—or murderess rode up and down in your elevator, my lad. What's your name?"

"Michael Dennis Moran," Micky answered automatically, then: "Gees! Murdered! Do I *have* to stay in here, boss? Honest—ow!"

"What the devil—?" McMann sprang to his feet, as the boy's howl of fear followed upon an eerie sound.

Ruth enlightened him, her eyes upon the black pigeon which was flying about the airshaft window, as if seeking admission: "It's just a pigeon, Mr. McMann. Sometimes they fly into the glass, thinking the window is open."

As she spoke, McMann strode to the window and peered out interestedly, just as the black pigeon settled upon the white stone ledge and began to strut up and down, pecking at something—

"Lord! And I nearly missed it!" McMann shouted. "Here, Ferber! Look! Have you photographed this window for finger prints? Fine! I can open it then. . . . Has Nielson gone? Hey, Doctor!"

A minute later Ruth, in a bitterly lucid flash through the darkness of horror and fear, rechristened the black pigeon. She would never again call him Satan. His true name was Nemesis. . . .

# CHAPTER EIGHT

## I

DR. NIELSON, with his little black bag of instruments, and Ferber, the finger print expert, with his camera, were crowding the detective at the window as McMann pushed up the sash. Ruth, still not knowing what had caused the detective's jubilant excitement, stepped forward slowly on icy feet, a cold little hand dragging at Jack Hayward.

"Look, Doctor! "What would you say that is—and that— and that?" McMann pointed from spot to spot on the white stone ledge of the window which opened upon the airshaft.

Nielson smiled his diffident, wintry smile. "I'd say, unofficially, that it is blood, my dear Sherlock, but only a laboratory test—"

McMann barked out a laugh. "And what would you say made those peculiarly shaped blood spots, Ferber? You don't have to be so confoundedly cautious in your opinions. Look!"

The heads of the two men bumped together as they studied their find.

"I'd say they are the footprints of a pigeon, made in blood," Ferber answered, awe in his voice. "Now—how the deuce, if the window was *closed?*"

McMann drew in his head and dropped to his knees, going over every inch of the strip of bare floor which bordered the rug, from the farthest corner of the room to where the stiff, crumpled body of Harry Borden still lay. A sharply triumphant exclamation announced discovery.

"Look, Ferber—Nielson! The same identical tracks— two of 'em, between the body and the window! Three pronged tracks, as clear as the nose on Doc's face! Funny I didn't notice them before, but naturally I was working on the theory that the window was closed when Borden was shot. Let's see the finger prints you got off this window, Ferber, as soon as you can. If I'm half the Sherlock that Nielson is so fond of calling me, those finger prints will be as good as a picture of the man or woman who put a bullet through Borden's heart. Right, Ferber?"

"You might be if there were any finger prints," Ferber grinned. "It happens that the window had been wiped clean. I'm afraid Borden's murderer was a little too clever to leave a calling card, McMann."

McMann scowled, his brows beetling so that they almost hid his glinting gray eyes. "He—or she—may not have left a calling card, but the pigeon did. Nice, obliging bird, that black pigeon!"

It was then that Ruth Lester renamed Satan. In horror and fear she rechristened him Nemesis. For long before McMann reached the inevitable conclusion to which the footprints of the pigeon were to lead him, Ruth had realized fully what ungrateful payment the black pigeon, or one of his flock, had made to her and Jack Hayward for the crumbs they had fed him every day.

"I'm afraid my stodgy, scientific mind fails to follow your brilliant deductions, McMann," Dr. Nielson gibed mildly. "I'll play Watson to your Sherlock. Just what do these alleged footprints of a pigeon in blood tell you, my dear Holmes?"

McMann flushed with resentment at the doctor's mild raillery, but decided to answer. "I should think it is obvious, Doc, even to a stodgy, scientific mind. This window was open before and after the murder, and possibly while it was being committed. Certainly it was open afterwards, or the pigeon could not have flown into the room and walked about in Borden's blood. Also Borden's body was alone in the room when the pigeon entered, unless—by George!"

"Please don't go mysterious on me, Sherlock," Dr. Nielson begged. "I assure you I'm all agog. Unless—what?"

"Unless," McMann explained impressively, "the room was occupied by someone the pigeon was not afraid of—to whom it was accustomed!" On the last portentous word, the detective swung about so that he was facing Ruth Lester, who involuntarily cried out, as if he had accused her then and there of the murder.

Jack Hayward flung a protecting arm about the shoulders of the trembling girl. "McMann, I resent the insinuation you have made against Miss Lester! I—"

"Please, Jack!" Ruth begged, in a panic of fear as to what his next words might be. She turned to McMann then, her exquisite, pale little face lifted bravely to meet any verbal blows he might give her. "The pigeons are accustomed to no one but me, Mr. McMann, and I was not in this room when Mr. Borden was shot, or afterwards, until I found him this morning."

"In the next office, perhaps, with the door open?" McMann shot at her.

"No!" She was trembling no longer, was almost glad that his suspicions were directed against her, rather than against Jack Hayward. She knew *she* was innocent. ...

"Gees!" an awed voice broke the tension.

McMann swerved instantly to the red headed elevator operator, who was regarding Ruth with a curious mixture of awe, admiration and fear.

"All right, Moran! Snap out of it! You've got to do a lot of plain and fancy remembering, my lad, if you don't want to spend a night in jail to refresh your memory," McMann snapped at the instantly terrified boy. "First, I want you to give me the name of every person who used your elevator after one o'clock Saturday."

Micky Moran rumpled his red hair in despair. "Gees! 'At's gonna be a big order, boss. Nearly every tenant and steno on this side of the building beat it at one o'clock. Car was jammed, boss, for two or three trips."

"Give me as many names as you can," McMann ordered, seating himself at Borden's desk, to make notes. ""Wait a minute! . . . You're getting samples of blood from those pigeon footprints outside and inside, aren't you, Doc? And Ferber, you'd better photograph 'em before the Doc scrapes 'em up. . . . Now, Moran—"

The boy drew a deep breath and then rattled off a dozen names, which McMann listed, with the number of the office to which each belonged. "Now, Moran, when did Miss Lester leave? With the others at one o'clock?"

The boy shot an apologetic glance at the girl who was 'waiting, breath drawn in, hands tightly locked over Jack Hazard's rigid arm. "No, she didn't get off till the rush was over. Musta been about a quarter past one. Mr. Hayward was waitin' for her at the elevator. He usually goes down in Otto's car, on the other side, but when he's got a date with Miss Lester—"

"All right, Moran," McMann interrupted. "Mr. Hayward was waiting for her and they got into your elevator about one fifteen—"

"One twenty," Ruth corrected. "I had looked at my watch several times, as I knew I was keeping Mr. Hayward waiting. Mr. Borden had to sign some letters before I could leave, and Mr. Adams stayed until after one."

"All right—one twenty," McMann accepted the correction and made a note of the time. "Anything unusual happen as the couple went down in your elevator, Moran? Did Miss Lester or Mr. Hayward seem upset or worried, or anything out of the ordinary?"

Micky considered. Then his face lighted up. "Gees! Guess I did most of the talkin', boss. I just couldn't get over how different Miss Lester looked, and I kept tellin' her so—"

"Different?" McMann pounced. "Was she crying, or pale?"

"Gees, no! She was lookin' swell! If I hadn't seen her when she went out on an errand in the middle of the mornin', and spoke to me so's I'd recognize her, I'd never a knowed her, honest! Like I told her, she looked like a movie star, only sweller. And I said to Mr. Hayward I had to hand it to him—he could pick a winner that anybody else woulda passed up."

McMann knit his brows in a puzzled frown. "I'm afraid I can't see why anyone would have 'passed up' Miss Lester, Moran. What do you mean?"

The elevator operator chuckled. "If you'd a seen her Friday or any day before that, boss! Hair all slicked back tight so's her ears showed, and great big yellow spectacles over them swell blue lamps of hers, and old fashioned clothes that looked like they come from the Salvation Army. Guess she was disguised so's 'Handsome Harry' wouldn't make no passes at her."

"I see!" McMann commented drily, his narrowed gray eyes flicking from Ruth's exquisite, flushed face to the angry, tight lipped face of the man to whom she was engaged. "And this amazing transformation had taken place for the first time on Saturday, Moran?"

"It wasn't no transformation. It's her own hair. Any guy with half an eye could see that! She'd just had it slicked back tight till Saturday," Micky corrected indignantly.

McMann had been answered. In the utter stillness of the room the tap tapping of the detective's pencil upon the edge of the dead man's desk sounded as loud as hammer blows. Then suddenly McMann spoke, and his words were directed to Ruth Lester:

"Twice this morning you've used the phrase, 'until the day of his death.' Borden, you said, had been a considerate employer—'until the day of his death.' You had never quarreled with Borden—'until the day of his death.' But —what about the *day* of his death, Miss Lester?"

Every vestige of color left Ruth's cheeks and lips, but her blue eyes were steady as she answered: "I meant, of course, until and including the day of his death."

McMann rose slowly from the desk and strolled toward the girl, towering over her as he summed up: "You feared the effect of your beauty on a man like 'Handsome Harry' Borden. You wore a sort of disguise to keep him from wanting you. Saturday, happy in your engagement to Mr. Hayward, you left off your disguise of homeliness and let Borden see what he'd been missing. He made love to you, just as Mr. Hayward had feared he would—"

"Mr. Hayward!" Ruth repeated indignantly. "He himself didn't know I was any prettier than I seemed until Friday night after we became engaged! It never occurred to him that Mr. Borden—"

"But he gave you an automatic pistol to protect yourself against a man who was notorious where women were concerned," McMann interrupted sharply. "And Saturday, when Borden saw you as you really are, you were glad you had that means of protecting yourself, weren't you, Miss Lester?"

"Gees!" Again Micky Moran's awed exclamation shattered a moment of intolerable suspense. "You didn't shoot him when you come back, did you, Miss Lester? . . . Gees! A little frail like that, and a big guy like him!" And Micky's wholly admiring gray green eyes popped from Ruth to Borden's body and back again.

"When she *came back?*" McMann repeated triumphantly. "Suppose you tell me all about Miss Lester's return to the office, Moran."

Ruth's blue eyes were so piteous with fear and frantic appeal that the elevator operator flushed and stammered as he began his story. But Ruth's terror was not for her self. . . .

## II

"She came right back up. I heard her tell Mr. Hayward she'd forgot her bank book, and aw, gees, boss, I didn't mean nothing by what I said," Micky Moran protested unhappily. "Honest, she couldn't a killed him! Why, boss, you only gotta take one look at Miss Ruth to see she wouldn't hurt a fly—"

"Stick to your story, Moran!" McMann jerked him up. "Miss Lester came right back up to her office, you say. Mr. Hayward with her?"

"Naw, she told him to wait for her in the lobby, and he did. I took her up and was gonna hold the car for her, but I got a signal from the fifth floor and had to shoot down again. Mr. Hayward was walking up and down in the lobby nervous like, and looked awful worried when he seen I hadn't brought Miss Lester down with me. Pretty soon—"

"How long?"

"Oh, four or five minutes, I guess, maybe six or seven. I dunno," Micky protested miserably. "Honest, I dunno! Mr. Hayward kept draggin' out his watch and lookin' at it, then finally he rushed into my car and told me to shoot up to the seventh floor. We was nearly there when the seventh floor signal flashed on, and there Miss Lester was, breathin' hard, like she'd been runnin' and tears in her eyes—"

"Tears!" McMann interrupted. "You're sure of that, Moran?"

"Sure!" the boy affirmed eagerly. "She'd banged her head against the door and hurt her lip. She was holdin' her handkerchief up to it, and when Mr. Hayward pulled her hand down I could see her lip was swellin' up and gettin' red. Mr. Hayward thought 'Handsome Harry' done it and was raisin' an awful roughhouse, down in the hall, but Miss Ruth—"

"Just what did Mr. Hayward say, Moran?" McMann interrupted.

"Gees, I dunno! Somepin about killin' Borden for hurtin' her—just like any guy'd say if he thought—"

"Stick to your story, Moran!" McMann commanded curtly. "Tell me exactly what happened. What Hayward said, what Miss Lester said, what they did."

Micky stuck out his lower lip sullenly. "Gees, I'm tryin' to, ain't I? Mr. Hayward started toward Borden's office and Miss Ruth swung onto him and held him back. She told him it wasn't 'Handsome Harry' that had hurt her lip, said she'd banged it on the door, like I told you. And she said if Mr. Hayward wouldn't believe her, she'd take back the promise she'd made him. That cooled him off and he piped down, but he told her she'd have to resign Monday. She said she would, and she got him in the car and I took 'em back down, and honest to God, that's all I know about it, boss!"

McMann's pencil tapped an ominous accompaniment to the slow, painful beating of Ruth's heart. Finally she could stand that slow tapping no longer. She stepped to ward the desk. "Please, Mr. McMann! I ask you to believe me when I say that I didn't see Mr. Borden when I returned to my office to look for my savings bank book. The door between the offices was closed, and Mr. Borden was talking over the telephone."

McMann looked up at her from under beetling brows. "And I'm to believe, too, that you spent from four to six minutes looking for your bank book?"

"I did! I had filed it in Mr. Borden's bank folder by mistake, instead of in the folder I use for my personal papers. I looked everywhere before it occurred to me that I had done so. I tell you, I didn't see Mr. Borden, that my lip *was* bruised against the door when I swung it open. I was in a hurry to rejoin Mr. Hayward—"

"Moran, your car was down at the main floor all the time you were waiting for Miss Lester, wasn't it? You couldn't have heard a shot if one had been fired on the seventh floor? Or did you hear one?"

"I didn't hear no shot!" Micky Moran denied emphatically. "I swear to—"

"Aren't you forgetting, McMann, that Mrs. Borden has already told of seeing Mr. Borden *alive* at twenty minutes of two?" Jack Hayward interrupted, his voice quivering with anger.

"I'm not forgetting anything, Hayward—thanks!" McMann grinned crookedly. "If you want to know, here are three things I'm not forgetting: first, that you had given Miss Lester a gun to protect herself against Borden's advances, if he ever took a fancy to your girl. Second, that everything points to the conclusion that Miss Lester's changed appearance had just the effect on 'Handsome Harry' Borden that you had feared it would. Third, that five hundred dollars in cash—the exact amount of Mrs. Borden's separation allowance—is missing from Borden's body. Get my point?"

"I'm afraid I don't!" Jack retorted furiously.

"All right, if I have to spell it out in words of one syllable! Miss Lester comes back for her bank book. Borden is alone, hears her return, comes out, tries to kiss her, does kiss her so hard that her lip is bruised. She struggles with him, manages to reach her desk, gets out her gun, holds him off with it, until he backs into his private office—"

Jack Hayward laughed abruptly, sarcastically. "I was wondering how you were going to get him back in here!"

"Is that so?" McMann almost snarled. "Any man'll back up if a gun's leveled at his heart! She gets him in here and thinks she's safe, but he starts for her again, knowing she's afraid of the gun, doesn't think she'll have the nerve to shoot it. He starts after her again and she lets him have it. She sticks the gun in the pocket of her fur coat and tears out of the office, crying and panting for breath. You meet her at the elevator. She forcibly restrains you from pounding on Borden's door, to make him let you in to beat him up—because she knows he's already dead!"

Jack laughed again, harshly. "I didn't know a detective could have such a sense of humor, McMann! Again I remind you that Mrs. Borden came here about twelve minutes after Miss Lester had left the building for the day and found her husband—"

"Dead!" McMann interrupted. "Why not? She didn't report the murder because she was afraid to, afraid she'd be accused of it. The body was still warm, you know. And she needed that five hundred she found on him when she was feeling his heart to see if he was really dead. She knew well enough that the check he'd written for her and left on his desk was nothing but a scrap of paper, since he was dead. Isn't that right, Mrs. Borden?" And the detective's glinting eyes shifted suddenly from Jack Hayward's livid face to the cowering, trembling figure of Borden's widow, who was holding to the jamb of the communicating door to support herself.

"No! No, no!" Mrs. Borden sobbed out the denial. "Harry was alive when I came—alive when I left! And while you're wasting time accusing first me, then this poor child, the real murderer is escaping! Oh, you're being cruel and stupid—stupid!"

"Stupid, am I?" McMann flushed darkly. "Stupid because I've hit on the truth, and you don't want to admit that you robbed the dead body of your husband? Stupid, because I've found the explanation of that closed window? I'm stupid and I'm cruel and I forget," he reiterated the charges against himself, with heavy sarcasm. "But I haven't forgotten that someone closed that window after Harry Borden was killed, after he'd been dead long enough for a pigeon to take a stroll in his blood!"

"And why did Mrs. Borden close the window, McMann?" Jack asked more quietly, taking Ruth's shuddering little figure into his arms and holding her close.

"For the same reason that made her come here this morning," McMann retorted. "Because she loved her husband. No wife who loved her husband would want a January wind blowing in upon him, even if he was dead and unable to feel it. And knowing he was dead, she came here this morning to claim his body. . . . Going, Dr. Nielson?" the detective broke off to inquire, as the medical examiner stepped softly toward the door. "You can tell the chief just how stupid McMann is, and ask him to prepare a warrant for the arrest of Ruth Lester. My only hope is that she gets as able a lawyer as Colby Lester to defend her, but I don't suppose she'll have much trouble getting out of it, under the circumstances."

Jack Hayward lunged toward McMann, trying to free himself of Ruth's convulsive embrace, but a mild, diffident voice halted him.

"Before you arrest anyone, especially Miss Lester, my dear Sherlock," Dr. Nielson spoke from the doorway, "I advise you to interview the woman who cleaned these offices Saturday afternoon. She, at least, would have no reason to conceal the murder. The chaps from the morgue will be here any minute now, and I'll phone you a report of my findings after I complete the autopsy. Good day— and step softly, McMann."

Ferber, the finger print expert, shouldered his camera and picked up his kit. "I'll amble on, too, McMann. I'll develop these negatives and send you copies in an hour or so."

As the two men were leaving, Coghlan, superintendent of the building, pushed his way in. "About through with my boys, chief? My elevator service is crippled."

McMann had risen and was pacing the office, from the airshaft window to the desk and back to the window again, his face darkly flushed, his eyes almost hidden under his bushed eyebrows. "Get substitutes!" he shouted irritably. "I'm not through with them and won't be any time soon. ... By the way, Coghlan," he demanded suddenly, stop ping at the raised window and peering out of it, "who has the office directly opposite?"

The superintendent made a wide detour to avoid the thing that lay on the floor. "Let's see," he considered, scratching his head. "This murder's got me so upset I can't think right clear—"

Ruth had feared that question and its inevitable answer so long that she had no power now to feel more fear as Jack Hayward interrupted, his voice quiet and matter of fact:

"That is my office, McMann."

McMann looked from the corpse upon the floor to the window near which it lay, then, squarely facing the window, he stood for a moment, before staggering backward. A choked scream checked his too realistic pantomime of the falling of a mortally wounded body.

"Stupid, eh?" he gasped, as he righted himself, without a glance at the dead man whose last movements he be lieved he had imitated. "Moran! At what time did Hayward return to his office?"

"He didn't—so far as I know!" Micky Moran retorted.

McMann was nonplused only for a moment. His pointing finger aimed itself at Otto Pfluger, who had been lean ing, silent and sullen, against the wall during the entire time he had been in the room. "You, there, towhead! You run the car nearest Hayward's office, don't you? What time Saturday afternoon did you bring him up?"

Ruth did not scream again. Now that the inevitable had happened strength and courage came to her from somewhere, possibly from the thought that whatever Jack had done, he had done for love of her. . . .

# CHAPTER NINE

## I

OTTO PFLUGER hunched his shoulders and rammed his hands deeper into the pockets of his uniform. "I dunno—about two o'clock, I guess. I ain't keepin' tabs on them that's got a right to come and go."

"Isn't there a register record for Saturday afternoons, Coghlan?" McMann demanded. "You require every one to sign in and out, don't you?"

Coghlan shook his head. "Not until four o'clock Saturdays. Too many tenants coming and going before then."

"I can tell you almost to the minute when I returned and when I left the building," Jack settled the question matter of factly. "Miss Lester and I went to lunch at the McAlpin Hotel, and just before dessert was served I discovered that I had left the theater tickets on my desk. We were going to a matinee. I looked at my watch, found that it was ten minutes to two, and walked rapidly from the McAlpin to the Starbridge Building—a distance of less than two blocks. I didn't have to wait for the elevator, so it must have been not later than five or six minutes of two when I got off at the seventh floor. I went to my office and—"

"Just a minute!" McMann interrupted, sharply. "I'd just a little bit rather have Otto's story before you have a chance to tell him what he remembers. And you might unclench that fist of yours, Hayward. I'm afraid you'll sprain your fingers, and that would be too, too bad! . . . Now, Otto, how long was Mr. Hayward in his office before he went back down again in your car?"

"I ain't saying he was in his office a tall," Otto denied sullenly.

"Oh!" McMann pounced. "So you saw him head toward this wing of the building when he left the elevator, did you?"

Otto Pfluger shrugged, and slouched lower against the wall. "Naw! I ain't sayin' he was in his office or he wasn't in his office, because I didn't follow him—see? I 'tended to my business and that was runnin' my elevator."

"And right now, young man, your business is to answer my questions civilly!" McMann retorted angrily. "I may not give you a tip to keep your mouth shut, as Mr. Hayward evidently did, but I can give you a free pass to the jail if you don't open up and spill what you know."

"Mr. Hayward didn't give me no tip Saturday—naw, nor this mornin' neither!" Otto anticipated the next question of the angry detective. "He tips us boys reg'lar the first of the month, like most of the other tenants do. . . . Aw, all right! I'm tellin' you, if you'll let me! It was about ten minutes after I took him up before I took him down again, I guess, because I sent my kid brother, what was hangin' around in the lobby, over to the drug store across the street to get me a cup of coffee, right after I'd took Mr. Hayward up, and I'd drunk it before he rung for me to take him down."

McMann grinned crookedly as he made rapid notes of the boy's story. "You didn't have any other passenger during those ten minutes, Otto?"

"Naw."

"And when Mr. Hayward left, did you notice anything peculiar about his behavior?" McMann suggested.

Otto glowered. "Naw!"

Ruth could have kissed the sullen young towhead for his failure to mention a fact which might yet assume vast importance—that Jack Hayward had returned to his office empty handed and left it with a heavy briefcase.

"Who else rode in your car between two and four o'clock Saturday?" McMann prodded the unwilling witness.

"I ain't been taking no memory course," Otto Pfluger shrugged. "But far as I remember, I didn't take down no passengers from the seventh floor after Mr. Hayward left."

McMann scowled, then turned upon Micky Moran, who grinned cheerfully. "How about you, Moran? Who were your passengers for the seventh floor after Miss Lester's and Mr. Hayward's second trip?"

Micky scratched his thatch of red hair, to aid his memory. "First I brought up Benny Smith, the kid that works here."

"Benny!" Ruth exclaimed. "Why, he left for the day at exactly one o'clock!"

"Well, he come back," Micky grinned. "Said he'd forgot something. I took him back down three or four minutes later . . . And say, I guess 'at lets Miss Lester out, all O. K.! If the kid had found his boss dead he wouldn't a rode back down without tellin' nobody, would he?"

Ruth smiled gratefully at the boy who was so obviously anxious to lift suspicion from her.

"If the boy came back for something he'd forgotten, it was undoubtedly in the outer office," McMann pointed out. "And the door was closed between the two offices after Borden was killed, according to Miss Lester's own story of her discovery of the body. But you stick to your own story, Moran, and let the office boy tell his when he comes in—if he ever gets here," McMann added curtly. "Who else came to the seventh floor Saturday afternoon?"

"That lady I heard you call Mrs. Borden," Micky answered sullenly. "Gees! I didn't know the sheik was married!" he added, brightening. "He sure didn't let it cramp his style none."

McMann frowned. "Keep your opinions to yourself until they're called for, Moran! When did you bring Mrs. Borden up?"

Micky stuck out his lower jaw pugnaciously and seemed about to go into a stubborn silence. Then, "I dunno! Pretty soon after I took Benny down, I guess. After half past one, anyway."

"Did you notice her manner? Anything unusual?" McMann rapped out.

"I didn't pay no attention to her. She didn't mean nothing in my young life," Micky retorted. "She just got in the elevator and I took her up—that's all."

"And when she came down?" McMann was having hard work to restrain his anger and impatience. "Was she up set? Crying? Pale?"

"Gees! I didn't give her a second look, after I seen it was the same lady I'd took up," Micky protested disgustedly. "I ain't got no time for dames her age."

McMann looked as if he could cheerfully have clouted the impudent youngster over the head, but he limited the expression of his anger to a black scowl. "Any one else?"

"Sure. A frail that was here Saturday morning, and two or three times before then," Micky answered sulkily. "Looked like a chorus girl."

"Rita Dubois!" Ruth cried. "I thought she was to meet Mr. Borden at the station—"

"Just a minute," McMann silenced her peremptorily. "Describe the girl, Moran—hair, eyes, clothes, anything you can remember."

"Black hair, black eyes. Kinda tall and slinky, like a movie vamp," Micky obliged. "I didn't notice her clothes, 'cept she had on a swell fur coat with a real live white orchid pinned on the collar."

McMann looked at Ruth, who nodded an eager confirmation of the girl's identity. "All right, Moran. When did you bring her up and what happened, that you know of? Did you talk with her?"

"Not when I brought her up," Micky answered the last question first. "She was looking so sore, tapping her foot and acting so impatient, that I kept my mouth shut."

"When was this?" McMann pounced.

"Gees, I dunno! 'Bout half an hour after Mrs. Borden left, I reckon. I ain't got no way of tellin' the time each party come up. I let her off at the seventh floor and then I went back down. While my car was down, the telephone in the booth started ringin' and I answered it. The starter goes off at half past one, and they wasn't anybody else but me down there."

"Yes? What of it?" McMann demanded impatiently. "How long before Miss Dubois rang for the elevator?"

" 'At's what I don't know—not exactly," Micky admitted, flushing. "It—'at was my girl on the phone, and I made a date with her for Sunday, and—and kidded her along for awhile, 'nen when I got back in my car the seventh floor red light was on."

"Five minutes? Seven minutes? Ten minutes?" McMann suggested impatiently.

"Maybe ten minutes, maybe more," Micky admitted, his flush deepening. "This Rita dame looked sore because I've kept her waitin', and I jolly her up a bit. I says to her, 'Sorry if I kept you waitin', Miss. I was makin' a date with my sweetie,' I says. 'Nen she says, 'Well, be sure you don't stand her up, old dear. Nothing makes a girl more sore than to be stood up,' she says, tappin' her foot again, like she was sore as all get out. An' I says, 'Gees! Did Borden stand up a swell frail like you?' An' she grins a little at that an' cracks right back, I'll say he did! And how!'"

"What else?" McMann demanded.

"Gees, ain't 'at enough for one trip?" Micky grinned. "'She got off and beat it out of the elevator, like she was in a hurry. She run into the telephone booth and that's the last I seen of her, 'cause I had a call from the fourth floor then—or maybe it was the fifth. Naw, it was the fourth. Old man Cohen—wholesale shoes."

"Any other passengers for the seventh floor Saturday afternoon?" McMann demanded impatiently.

"Naw, not a soul," Micky answered promptly. "I thought Borden had gone down by the other elevator, for some reason or other. Gees! He musta been dead already,

and his sweetie thought he'd stood her up! Gees! She
musta stood there poundin' on the door—"

"That'll do, Moran!" the detective cut him short. "You
and Otto can get back on your jobs, but don't leave the
building till I give you permission. Understand?"

When the door had closed upon the elevator boys,
McMann faced Jack Hayward, his eyes narrowed to
glinting gray slits. "Well, how about it, Hayward? I
suppose you're going to tell me it took you ten minutes to
find those conveniently forgotten theater tickets."

Before Jack could answer Patrolman Biggers
appeared, with the information that the men from the
morgue had arrived to remove the body of the murdered
man.

"Just a minute, Biggers. Hold 'em back until I get
Mrs. Borden out of the way. I'll put her in Covey's charge
down the hall till I need her."

Some of Ruth's hatred of the detective evaporated as
she witnessed his gentleness with the widow whom he
had, a few minutes before, tried to bully into confessing
that she had killed her husband. But when the body had
been removed on a stretcher, and McMann was free to
devote his entire attention to Jack Hayward, fear for the
man she loved fanned her hatred of McMann into a high,
hot blaze.

## II

"Well, Hayward," McMann opened the attack with his
short bark of a laugh, "you've had plenty of time to figure
out why it took you at least ten minutes to find those
theater tickets."

Jack flushed darkly but his voice was steady: "I had
no trouble finding the tickets. They were in plain sight on
my desk. But when I entered my office the phone was
ringing and I answered it, of course."

"And talked ten minutes? Who was the girl?" McMann
was heavily sarcastic.

"The call was from an insurance company with which I do business," Jack answered, his flush deepening and his eyes involuntarily glancing toward Ruth.

"A business call at two o'clock on Saturday afternoon? Pretty thin," McMann commented drily. "I suppose you can give me the name of your caller?"

"I can," Jack answered reluctantly. "And also the substance of the conversation, though I had hoped to spare Miss Lester the bad news for a while longer. The call came from the branch manager of the Pinnacle Life Insurance Company. He was still in his office, and took a chance on finding me in mine. He called to tell me that Mr. T. Q. Garnett, whom I had signed up for a fifty thousand dollar policy, had been turned down after a medical examination, because of high blood pressure." His handsome young face was very grim and pale as he acknowledged the collapse of his plans for an immediate wedding.

"Oh, Jack, darling!" Ruth reached for one of his tightly clenched fists and laid it tenderly against her cheek. "You should have told me! If you had—" But she checked the sentence that was tumbling out on the receding tide of doubt and fear which had made the last two hours a nightmare. So much was clear now—his worried, harassed manner on Saturday, his moodiness Saturday evening and Sunday evening, that work stuffed briefcase—

"Birdwell!" McMann shouted, and the detective who had been stationed at the telephone in the outer office, in place of Patrolman Rand, appeared in the doorway. "Check up on this by phone. Pinnacle Life Insurance Company. Ask for the manager. Find out if and when he called John C. Hayward Saturday afternoon. . . . Any news, Birdwell? That phone's been ringing enough."

Birdwell, middle aged, laconic, and permanently bored with life, answered tiredly: "Much ringing, little news! Clay's out to round up the Dubois woman."

McMann consulted his notes, checked an item or two, then demanded irritably: "Hasn't that office boy blown in yet? . . . No? What's the last address you have, Miss Lester? We've got to pull him in."

Ruth got the information from her files and gave the memorandum to Birdwell, without comment.

"I'll put Callahan on the job, sir," Birdwell volunteered wearily. "Anything else?"

"No. Yes, wait! Hayward, you say you and Miss Lester lunched at the McAlpin? . . . Which table?"

Jack answered concisely, coolly, but Ruth, who had returned to his side, tightened her hands convulsively about his rigid arm.

"Tell the manager of the hotel to send me the waiter who served this couple on Saturday, Birdwell, and tell him to make it snappy," McMann directed.

"Biggers is holding off a swarm of reporters out there in the hall," Birdwell volunteered uninterestedly. "Ready for 'em yet, sir?"

"No!" McMann barked. "Just tell the boys that Detective Sergeant Thomas H. McMann expects to make an arrest within a few hours. And that's no lie! Be sure they get my name spelled right. . . . And Birdwell, bring Rita Dubois to me as soon as Clay drags her in."

McMann waved his subordinate away, then concentrated upon Jack Hayward again. "So it took you ten minutes to answer the phone and pick up a couple of theater tickets. That right?"

"Not exactly," Jack answered evenly. "I was pretty well knocked out by the bad news from the insurance company, since I'd counted on the commission to get married on, so I sat at my desk for two or three minutes, trying to get hold of myself before seeing Miss Lester again. I didn't want to spoil her day—the first after our engagement—" He drew a quick, sharp breath, then smiled down at the girl who was clinging to his arm.

"Needed money pretty badly, didn't you, Hayward?" McMann interrupted significantly.

"I was sorry to lose the commission, because it might mean a postponement of our marriage," Jack admitted curtly. "Then it occurred to me that since I'd lost that commission I'd better be lining up other business, so I packed my briefcase with work to do over the week end. It took me several minutes to find a list of prospects I wanted to work on, for I'm not familiar with my secretary's filing system. "When I had found it I left the office and rejoined Miss Lester at the hotel."

"At what time?"

"At ten minutes past two. I glanced at the big clock in the hotel lobby as I passed through it on my way to the dining room, and congratulated myself that we wouldn't be late for the matinee, although I had been gone longer than I had intended."

"You've got the time down pretty pat, haven't you?" McMann insinuated, grinning crookedly as he made a note. Then, more directly, "You were already thinking in terms of alibis, weren't you, Hayward?"

"You're certainly open minded, McMann!" Jack laughed contemptuously. "First you sum up a magnificent case against Mrs. Borden, until the poor woman herself must have half believed she did it. Then you make an equally strong case against Miss Lester, and now both of them must give way to your new favorite—John Carrington Hayward!" And the foolhardy, angry young man bowed ironically.

"Oh, Jack, don't!" Ruth cried. "Please, darling—"

"Give him enough rope—" McMann shrugged, but his face was livid with anger. "I admit your charge, Mr. Hayward: I *am* open minded, and you can oblige me with a little more information. You saw Borden across the airshaft, didn't you?"

Ruth held her breath, then released it with a sigh of relief as Jack retorted emphatically: "I did not! I never even went near the window. I had other things to think about, besides Borden."

"And yet you knew he'd been making violent love to Miss Lester," McMann reminded him. "You'd threatened, in the presence of Moran, the elevator boy, to kill Border., remember!"

"I did—before she had assured me that Borden had not touched her," Jack answered evenly. "I believed Miss Lester when she assured me that she had hurt her lip against the door."

"Yes, you did! You believed her so firmly that you came back later to kill Borden!" McMann shouted, banging his fist upon the desk. "Come clean, Hayward! You own a gun yourself, don't you? You didn't spend good money—hard up as you are—to protect Borden's offices from hold up men and neglect your own safety—did you?"

Again, when she most needed it, courage from some unseen, beneficent source sustained Ruth Lester, just as sickening waves of nausea began to pour over her brain.

"I own a .38 calibre Colt's automatic, exactly like the pistol I gave Miss Lester," Jack answered steadily. "You will find it in the bottom drawer of my desk, unfired. I have never used it."

As he spoke, Ruth stared at him in terror she was powerless to conceal, wanted to clap her hand over his mouth to hold back that damning admission. Then light broke through the blackness of her despair. "Why, he doesn't know the gun is gone!" she realized, with almost hysterical joy. "He doesn't know! How stupid I've been! Of course he'd have cleaned it and put it back if he had killed Borden! He had plenty of time—"

McMann rose. "As you say, Hayward, I'm open-minded! I'll have a look at that gun, and then, still open minded, I'll wait for Pederson's report on whether it's been fired or not. Pederson's our firearms expert, and if he says it's never been fired, I'll take his word for it— but not yours. Pretty clever of you to admit possession of a gun, but you knew damned well that the record would show when and where you purchased it." He strode to the communicating door, opened it, flung it wide, and addressed the detective who was talking over the telephone: "Back in a minute, Birdwell. Keep an eye on this couple for me, won't you? Come on out—both of you!" and he motioned to Ruth and Jack, who still stood beside Borden's desk.

Flushed, but with heads held high, they obeyed, silently taking seats at the large table in the center of the reception room, where every word they uttered could be heard by Birdwell, who had taken possession of the desk of the unaccountably missing office boy.

"I haven't scattered the reporters yet, sir," Birdwell volunteered. "Been busy on the phone. The waiter's coming right over."

"Well, guess I'll have to give 'em a minute," McMann conceded, with feigned reluctance, smoothing his hair and adjusting his tie, as he opened the outer door.

A barrage of questions halted him on the threshold.

"No, nothing for you yet, boys," the massive detective shook his head, raising his hand impressively for silence. "Just say the murder of Henry P. Borden, known as 'Handsome Harry' Borden, promises to be one of the biggest crime sensations of the year, and that Detective Sergeant Thomas H. McMann, in charge of the investigation, expects to make an arrest before the day is over. . . ."

News photographers pressed forward, cameras were aimed, flashlight powder, already prepared, exploded, while the flattered detective posed in the doorway.

"Is it true, McMann, that the widow is under suspicion?" a reporter asked, when the photographers had finished.

"Mrs. Borden's testimony is of the highest importance. She is being detained for further questioning," McMann answered. "But really, boys—"

"Just a minute, Chief," another reporter insisted, using a title that could not fail to flatter the detective sergeant.

"What about Borden's secretary—Ruth Lester? Headquarters tells us that she is a daughter of the late Colby Lester, the big criminal lawyer. That right? Is she being grilled, too?"

Ruth uttered a low, strangled cry and her sweetheart's arms went out, embraced her trembling little body with fierce pity, as McMann closed the door upon whatever answer he made to the importunate reporters.

"Don't mind so terribly, sweet!" Jack pleaded. "He's just a blundering fool—"

"Oh, don't!" Ruth shuddered. "Try not to antagonize him, darling! Listen—" and her voice dropped to a whisper, as she glanced over her shoulder fearfully.

Birdwell's weary but watchful eye was upon her. She knew then that it was useless to try to warn Jack. Totally unprepared, he would have to face McMann when the detective returned—empty handed, gloating over the disappearance of his latest suspect's gun. . . .

After what seemed an interminable time to Ruth, but was probably not more than ten minutes, McMann reappeared, calling over his shoulder to some one in the hall: "Wait outside here till I call for you—and don't talk."

As the detective strode on across the reception room of the suite toward the private office, he commanded the couple to follow him, with a jerk of his leonine head.

"Well, Hayward," the detective opened his attack with one of the short, ugly barks that served him as a laugh, "spin your yarn! You've had ten minutes to think up a good one. Where's the gun? We'll find it, you know, sooner or later, and you might as well come clean!"

Anger gave way to startled surprise on Jack Hyward's face. Ruth drew a shuddering sigh of relief; his surprise was as genuine as the anger which had preceded it.

"What do you mean, McMann? The gun is where I told you it was—in the bottom drawer of my desk."

"I don't doubt it was there Saturday, Hayward, but I guess you weren't taking any chances on cleaning it and putting it back," McMann retorted. "All right! I'm waiting—what did you do with the gun, my lad?"

"I tell you, McMann," Jack answered furiously, his face very pale now, "I have no more idea where that gun is than you have! All I know is that I had a Colt's automatic, that I kept it in the bottom drawer of my desk, and that I haven't seen it for at least a week."

McMann's short laugh barked again. "I told you I'm open minded, Hayward! I bite: when did you see it last?"

The young man flushed at the sneer in the detective's voice, returned the pressure of Ruth's cold little fingers, then answered readily: "When Miss Barnes, my secretary, gave me a stack of fresh towels last Monday morning. The delivery man for the towel service makes his rounds every Monday. Miss Barnes usually puts my towels in that drawer herself, but last Monday I happened to be sitting at the desk when she brought them in and I pulled open the drawer, shifted the automatic slightly to the front, where it would be easily accessible in case of a hold up, and placed the clean towels behind it. That is absolutely the last time I saw the thing."

"Used one towel all week, eh?" McMann sneered.

"No." Jack was obviously fighting for self control. "Miss Barnes puts out a fresh one for me each morning before I get to the office. We have a cabinet with towel rack above the stationary washbasin in the outer office, just as this suite has. Miss Barnes can tell you whether the gun was there Saturday or not. I don't know myself, for I didn't open the drawer."

"She says it was there, all right," McMann assured him. "Real handy for you when you had your quarrel with Harry Borden."

"I had no quarrel with Harry Borden," Jack denied, wearily. "I have never spoken a word to the man in my life."

"Is *that* so?" McMann exclaimed triumphantly. "Birdwell! Birdwell!" he shouted till the room reverberated with the sound. When his subordinate opened the door, the detective sergeant barked out an order: "There's a chap named Cowan waiting outside in the hall. Bring him in!" He turned to the couple who were gazing at each other, the girl's eyes frankly terrified, the young man's face very pale, but under better control. "Your good friend, Bill Cowan, Hayward! Won't you be glad to see him? I found him waiting for you in your office—said he made an appointment with you for this morning. Made it Saturday morning when he was in your office— remember?"

"Yes," Jack answered quietly.

"I thought you'd remember," McMann agreed significantly. "Funny, but your friend Cowan didn't know *his* old pal, Borden, had been murdered. I had to break the news to him, and I wonder if you can imagine why Cowan wasn't as surprised as he might have been?"

The badgered young man was saved the necessity of a reply by the entrance of Bill Cowan, the real estate man, ushered in by Birdwell, who immediately retired to his duties in the outer office.

Ruth, clinging to her sweetheart's arm for much needed support, turned to face the man who undoubtedly had it in his power to send Jack Hayward before a grand jury. She saw a medium sized, foppishly dressed man of thirty eight or forty, running an embarrassed hand over sleek brown hair.

"Lord, Jack. I'm sorry I stumbled into this! Tough break, old boy! If I'd seen a paper—" Cowan began nervously, apologetically.

"You wouldn't have kept your appointment," McMann finished his sentence for him. "That right? You'd have been pretty sure that your friend, Jack Hayward, was in trouble, wouldn't you?"

"I—I wouldn't say that," Cowan hedged miserably. "But no man wants to get mixed up in a murder case—"

"I'm afraid you are mixed up in one, Cowan," McMann interrupted. "And I don't need to remind you that it's the duty of a citizen to aid justice in any way possible, when circumstances force him into the unpleasant role of witness. Just repeat the story you told me, Cowan. I may as well tell you, Hayward, that your friend gave you away by accident, when I told him you were being questioned concerning Borden's death."

"That's right, Jack, old man," Cowan assured the grim-faced young man anxiously. "God knows I wouldn't for the world—"

"That's all right, Cowan," Jack interrupted, his pale lips twitching into a faint smile. "Naturally it's your duty to tell anything you know which may seem to have any bearing on this case. But I want you to know, Cowan, that I had no more to do with Borden's murder than you did."

"That's fine, old man!" Cowan thrust out a hand with eager friendliness, and seemed much relieved when Jack shook it. "As Mr. McMann here has just said, Jack, I spilled the beans accidentally. Said something foolish and hasty about being afraid Saturday that there'd be a row. He wouldn't let up on me till I'd shot the works, of course." The embarrassed real estate man mopped his brow. "Lord! If I'd only learned to keep my mouth shut! ... I had to tell him, Jack, about that nasty little business Saturday morning, when you saw Borden struggling with the young lady here—"

"Pardon me, Cowan. This is Miss Lester, my fiancee," Jack interrupted. "I believe I told you Saturday that Miss Lester and I were to be married soon."

"Glad to meet you, Miss Lester," the embarrassed man acknowledged the introduction. "I told Jack Saturday that I didn't blame him for going off his nut when he saw Borden getting fresh."

"Both you and Mr. Hayward were mistaken as to Mr. Borden's intentions," Ruth said, in a clear, calm voice. "Mr. Borden was merely trying to take off my spectacles, and I was determined to prevent his doing so."

"Get on with your story, Cowan. We're wasting time," McMann ordered curtly. "You told me that both you and

Hayward, standing in that window across the airshaft, saw Harry Borden struggling with Miss Lester, his arms about her, and that she screamed. Is that right?"

"We—ell—that's what it looked like," Cowan stammered and flushed. "But I guess it doesn't take much to make a girl scream."

"In this case, there was enough to make Jack Hayward want to jump across an eight foot airshaft and kill the man who was forcing his attentions upon Miss Lester," McMann pointed out. "It took all your strength to hold Hayward, didn't it, Cowan? And he swore he'd kill 'that beast' if he laid hands on Miss Lester again, didn't he?"

Cowan mopped his glistening forehead again. "Something like that. I can't remember his exact words. I asked him why he was so 'het up' about Borden's making love to his secretary, and he told me then, after I'd got him away from the window, that he and Miss Lester were going to be married and that that was why he was interested in buying a lot in Scarsdale, the suburban property I represent. I advised him to have Miss Lester resign her position with Borden, and to get married immediately. He said that's just what he'd do, and agreed to talk with Miss Lester that evening about building a home in Scarsdale."

"All right, Cowan," McMann prodded the unwilling witness. "Get along to the telephone call."

Jack and Ruth both started, and stared at each for a moment in obvious bewilderment. Then Jack spoke directly to Cowan: "I had no call from you, Cowan."

McMann let out his harsh, short laugh. "For a very good reason, Hayward! But tell him exactly what you told me, Cowan. I'm anxious to wind this business up."

"You see, old man," Cowan began reluctantly, turning to Jack and the girl who clung to his arm, "I was at Penn Station, just a block away, to see my wife off for a week's visit to Winter Heaven, when I remembered that I'd left my blueprint of the Scarsdale property on your desk. I knew I'd need it to show my Sunday prospects, so I took a chance on finding you still in your office and called you on the phone. The line—"

"Just a minute, Cowan," McMann interrupted. "Exactly when did you make the call?"

"At ten minutes after two," Cowan answered unhesitatingly. "I'd put my wife on the train, and when I was crossing the waiting room on my way toward the telephone booths I noticed the clock—nine minutes after two, and glanced at my own watch to see if I was with the railroad time. Then I stepped into the booth and called Hayward's number. The line was busy—"

"If it was, it was someone else trying to get me on the phone," Jack interrupted, his voice steady but emphatic. "For I rejoined Miss Lester at the McAlpin Hotel at ten minutes after two."

"That would be a perfectly swell explanation and I'd be the first to congratulate you upon it, Hayward—except for one little thing," McMann chuckled.

"And that is?" Jack demanded, with angry contempt.

"The accident that happens to nearly every 'perfect alibi,'" McMann retorted. "Cowan didn't get the busy signal. *He was plugged in on a busy line!*"

# CHAPTER TEN

JACK HAYWARD shrugged angrily. "Then maybe Cowan can tell me who uses my phone in my absence. The bills are outrageous. I've told you before, McMann, and Miss Lester has corroborated me, that I rejoined her in the dining room of the McAlpin Hotel at ten minutes after two. It is obvious that I could not have been talking over the telephone in my office at the same moment. Central probably gave you a wrong number as well as a busy number, Cowan. If you think you recognized my voice, you're mistaken—that's all."

"I didn't say I recognized your voice, Jack, old man," Cowan protested unhappily. "I merely told Mr. McMann that I heard Borden giving you the devil—"

"Borden!" Ruth and Jack exclaimed simultaneously, incredulously.

"Yes—Borden!" McMann repeated triumphantly. "From what Cowan says, there not a doubt in the world but that you called Harry Borden on the phone, and had your quarrel with him in that way, rather than across the airshaft."

"And shot him over the telephone, too, I suppose?" Jack retorted contemptuously. "Very ingenious of me, I'm sure."

"Please, Jack!" Ruth begged, her voice piteous with terror. "Mr. Cowan," she turned tremulously to the embarrassed, unwilling witness, "Isn't it very possible that you're mistaken in thinking you recognized Mr. Borden's voice over the phone?"

"Oh, sure! Of course!" Cowan succumbed instantly to the appeal in those blue eyes.

But McMann was of sterner stuff. "Look here, Cowan! You told me that you heard a man's voice, which you recognized as that of your friend, Harry Borden, shouting, in great anger: 'I'm not going to have you interfering in my affairs! Who are you, to tell Harry Borden what he can do and can't do?' Is that the truth, Cowan? Are those substantially the words you heard before you hung up the receiver?"

The harassed real estate man mopped his brow again. "As near as I can remember—yes."

"You distinctly heard the speaker call himself Harry Borden?" McMann insisted.

"Yes, I did, for a fact," Cowan admitted unhappily. "I said to myself that there'd be trouble yet between those two, but I never dreamed—"

"Well, I guess my case is pretty clear," McMann broke in, smiling with grim satisfaction. "Saturday morning, Hayward, you see the girl you're engaged to struggling in Borden's arms. You threaten to kill Borden if he lays hands on her again. Cowan has to hold you by main strength to keep you from trying to jump across the airshaft to get at your man. You meet Miss Lester at one twenty; she comes back to her office for her forgotten bank book, has another struggle with Borden who bruises her lip in kissing her—"

"I've told you that is not true!" Ruth cried.

McMann went on as if she had not spoken: "You find her at the elevator with tears in her eyes and her lip swelling, and it takes all her strength and threats of breaking the engagement to keep you from killing Borden then. You two go to lunch together, she confesses that Borden had manhandled her—"

"That also is not true!" Ruth interrupted furiously.

McMann ploughed on imperturbably, inexorably. "You're so angry with Borden, Hayward, that you leave the hotel dining room in the midst of your luncheon and hurry back to the Starbridge Building, determined to have it out with him, possibly with your mind already made up to kill him. You call him on the phone—"

Jack laughed contemptuously. "That's likely, isn't it? If I had wanted to telephone Harry Borden, I could have done so from the hotel, without making a trip to the Starbridge Building."

"But you couldn't have shot him from the hotel!" McMann retorted angrily. "Maybe you did forget your theater tickets, as you say you did, and had to come back for them. Maybe you didn't intend to kill Borden until after you quarreled with him over the phone. It's not up to me to figure out just why you telephoned Harry Borden before you shot him. All I'm concerned with is that Harry Borden was shot as he stood in front of that window, that he had been heard defying your threats over the telephone, that you had a gun, which is missing now, and that the window of your private office is directly opposite the open window at which Borden was standing when he was killed. That's enough for me!"

"But not for me, Mr. McMann!" Ruth cried, her blue eyes flashing as she shook off Jack's restraining hand and stepped toward the detective. "And I know enough about criminal law and criminal court procedure to know that it will not be enough to warrant Mr. Hayward's arrest. Remember I'm Colby Lester's daughter!"

"You had a good teacher—the best in the world, Miss Lester," McMann answered with surprising gentleness. "But I am also remembering that you're engaged to be married to Jack Hayward, and I believe he killed the man who insulted and mistreated you. I'm mighty sorry—"

"Please listen to me for a minute, Mr. McMann," Ruth pleaded. "I know you're only trying to do your duty— that you want to be fair. But there are so many things you aren't taking into consideration. First, you are making a mistake in believing that Jack had a motive for killing Mr. Borden. I admit that he saw, from his window, the struggle that Mr. Cowan has told you about, but Mr. Cowan will gladly assure you that Mr. Borden was not making love to me—kissing me, or anything like that. He was simply trying to take off my spectacles, and it was foolish of me to scream. I admit that I was afraid Mr. Borden would like my appearance too well, if he saw me without my glasses. I knew he liked pretty girls, and other men had made my business life rather hard for me, before I made myself as plain as possible. But that is absolutely all that happened between Mr. Borden and myself, I did not see him when I returned for my bank book, and I was able to convince Mr. Hayward that Mr. Borden was not responsible for my bruised lip."

The detective shifted in his chair. "I'm afraid all this isn't getting us anywhere, Miss Lester—"

"Please!" the girl begged. "The second important fact that you're ignoring is that my automatic is missing, too!"

"I'm not exactly ignoring that fact, Miss Lester," McMann answered, not unkindly, "but I didn't like to drag Colby Lester's daughter into this case as an accessory either before or after the fact."

"I—I don't know what you mean!" Ruth gasped. "No, please, Jack!" she pleaded, as the young man sprang to ward McMann's desk.

"Better try to control that temper of yours, Hayward," McMann advised grimly. "I'm afraid it's already got you into enough trouble. . . . What I meant, Miss Lester, was that a frantic girl may hit upon strange ways to confuse evidence, when she fears for the life of the man she loves. I'm not saying that you hid that pistol of yours this morning after you discovered that your employer had been killed and that your sweetheart's gun was missing-"

Ruth went very pale, but her voice was steady as she challenged the detective: "What makes you think I knew his gun was missing?"

McMann smiled. "You betrayed yourself when Hayward mentioned his automatic. He has better control of his expression than you have, child; he should have warned you that he was going to admit ownership of the gun. But I didn't rely entirely on reading your expression. Miss Barnes told me that you were alone in Mr. Hayward's office for two or three minutes this morning, when you went there to tell him what you had found in here. It was easy to deduce how you had spent those minutes— and why. You were afraid your sweetheart had killed your employer, and you looked for his pistol, to make sure. You didn't find it—and came to the same conclusion that I did."

"You're wrong there, at least!" Ruth blazed. "I did find that his gun was gone, but I know Jack Hayward did not kill Harry Borden!"

"And how do you know that, Miss Lester?" McMann asked quietly.

"Because the person who killed Borden was in this office, not in one across the airshaft. Oh, I know a shot *could* have been fired from one window through the other, but there are two excellent, irrefutable proofs that the person who killed him was in this office either during or after the murder. First—the body was robbed of five hundred dollars—"

"Just a minute!" McMann interrupted. "We have no proof that Borden was robbed, beyond the fact that the money is missing. How do you know that he did not give the money to some one before his death?"

"He gave Mrs. Borden a check!" Ruth flashed. "And he had no other visitor except Mrs. Borden until Rita Dubois came, according to the evidence of the elevator operator, Micky Moran. . . . Oh, yes! Benny Smith was here, too, about half past one, but surely you can't imagine Borden's making his office boy a present of five hundred dollars! Can't you see that it isn't fair to Jack to convict him in your own mind until you've talked with Rita Dubois? We know she was here—"

"And that she didn't see Borden, in all probability, if we're to put the natural interpretation on what she said to Moran, the elevator operator, about Borden's having 'stood her up,'" McMann pointed out patiently.

"That's ridiculous!" Ruth cried, forgetting tact in her anger. "The natural supposition is that she was referring to Borden's having failed to meet her at the station, to take her away on the week end trip to Winter Heaven, as they had planned. Why give *her* the benefit of the doubt, when you've been so ruthless with Mrs. Borden, Jack and myself? Oh, please be fair! Don't you see how likely it is that it was Rita Dubois who—who last saw Mr. Borden alive? Since for some reason he failed to keep his appointment with her, he would be expecting her here. Probably she telephoned him and he asked her to come, or she simply came to see why he had 'stood her up' at the station. He would admit Rita, would unlock the door for her, but not for Jack Hayward. And don't forget— *someone closed that window after Harry Borden was murdered.* Jack could not have done so. He couldn't have got in. He has no key to this office, of course—"

The girl's passionate outburst was interrupted by Birdwell. "Phillips, the waiter from the McAlpin Hotel has arrived, sir."

"Just a minute, Birdwell," McMann answered, then turned to the real estate man, Bill Cowan, who was obviously eager to escape. "Cowan, I'm inclined to let you go on about your business and not hold you as a material witness, if you give me your promise not to talk with any one—reporters, your wife, any one else—about this case, and will promise further not to leave town, but hold yourself available for further questioning."

Cowan gave both promises with almost ludicrous alacrity and bolted, after another apologetic grip of Jack Hayward's hand. The waiter, Phillips, was ushered in— a small, neat, middle aged man in a well brushed black overcoat, snugly buttoned over his waiter's uniform.

After preliminary questions as to his name, place of residence and occupation, McMann asked: "Ever see this couple before, Phillips?"

Meek brown eyes studied Ruth Lester and Jack Hayward conscientiously. "Yes, sir. They lunched at one of my tables in the McAlpin dining room Saturday."

"At what time?"

The waiter shrugged slightly and smiled apologetically. "That I could not say, sir. After the twelve thirty to one thirty rush, sir, I should say."

"Did you notice them particularly, Phillips? Anything at all to fix this couple in your mind?" McMann pursued.

"Well, sir, there were several things," the waiter began deprecatingly. "I thought it odd that the young lady wouldn't take her fur coat off, sir, as the dining room was quite warm."

"Ah!" McMann commented with satisfaction, as he made a note of what he undoubtedly considered an important point.

"I didn't take my coat off because I was chilled—felt as if I were taking cold," Ruth explained, taking care to keep defiance out of her voice.

"You seem to have recovered from the cold," McMann reminded her. "Perhaps there was something—heavy in the lining pocket which you didn't want the waiter to feel or see?"

Ruth knew that he was referring to her missing automatic. "There was nothing in the pocket, Mr. McMann!"

McMann smiled, shrugged, then turned to the waiter again. "You said there were *several* things that impressed this couple on your memory. What else, Phillips?"

"Well, sir, the young lady dropped her pocketbook and while I was stooping to pick up the scattered contents of the bag, the little lady excused herself, saying she had to telephone—"

"To warn Borden not to let Jack Hayward into his office?" McMann pounced, his glinting, narrowed gray eyes fixed upon Ruth.

The girl's face flamed. "No! I simply made the conventional excuse, and went to the ladies' rest room to— powder my face. I telephoned no one."

"Hmm!" McMann obviously did not believe her. "What else, Phillips?"

"While I was picking up the scattered objects, the young gentleman was studying the menu card," the waiter went on, in his deprecating, hesitant manner. "He put the things back in the young lady's bag and gave me the order, without waiting for the young lady—"

"What was the order?" McMann demanded.

"I wouldn't like to swear to that, sir—"

"I ordered broiled mushrooms on toast for Miss Lester, and sweetbread patties for myself," Jack interrupted. "They were on the ready to serve list, and both of us are in the habit of eating light luncheons."

"That's right, sir! I remember now!" the waiter corroborated eagerly. "I brought the orders right out, but first, before the young lady came back, I brought the rolls and butter and gave the young gentleman the key—"

"The key! What key?" McMann demanded, his eyes taking quick note of Ruth's startled surprise.

"Why, sir, the key that had fell out of the young lady's handbag. I kicked against it when I was putting the rolls and butter on the table, or I would never have noticed it. I handed it to the young gentleman, sir."

"And what did he do with it?" McMann prodded, a twisted grin of supreme satisfaction upon his thin lips.

"I didn't notice, sir."

"Did you see him reach for Miss Lester's handbag to put it there?"

"No, sir. I'm quite sure he didn't, sir, at the time, at least. Probably he handed it to her when she returned to the table, sir."

"Do you think so?" McMann grinned. "Just what kind of key was this, Phillips?"

"An ordinary Yale lock key, sir."

"Miss Lester, show Phillips your key to this suite, please!" McMann rapped out.

Ruth obeyed, going to the outer office to get her hand bag. When she returned she silently handed a Yale lock key to the waiter, who fingered it briefly, then laid it upon the extended palm of the detective.

"Is that the key, Phillips?"

"It looks like it, sir, but of course I couldn't say—"

"Or *is* this the key you found on the floor?" Ruth asked, with quiet triumph, offering a second key, differing only slightly in size and shape from the first, which she took from a small coin purse.

The waiter shook his head helplessly. "It looks like it, miss, but since most Yale keys look alike—"

"Exactly!" Ruth cried. "Mr. McMann, *this*—" and she handed him the second key—"is the key to the office. You can try it and see for yourself. Yale lock keys are so much alike that I was always mistaking my apartment key for my office key, and the other way round. So I solved the difficulty by keeping my office key in my coin purse, and the apartment key loose in my handbag. And the coin purse, which has a firm fastening, and fits snugly into its pocket in my handbag, did not fall out when I dropped the bag. That is correct, isn't it, Phillips?"

"Yes, miss. I didn't pick up a coin purse," the waiter agreed eagerly. "And it must not have come open, for there was only the one key and no small change on the floor."

McMann chuckled again, as if the by play amused him immensely. "All right, Phillips. Anything else to impress this couple on your memory?"

"Well, sir, the gentleman excused himself to the young lady pretty soon after I'd served the entrees, and left the dining room," the waiter resumed his story.

"How soon after? And how long had they been there when the entrees were served?" McMann prodded.

"As I said, sir, the entrees were ready in the kitchen and I brought them right out. I judge they hadn't been in the dining room more than five or six minutes when I served the food, since the gentleman ordered immediately, without waiting for the young lady. I couldn't say exactly how long it was before the gentleman left, but the food was scarcely touched, sir."

"Not hungry, eh?" McMann commented, sweeping Ruth and Jack with his narrowed eyes. "Well, Phillips, how long was the young man gone?"

"I couldn't say that, sir, to the minute, but it was quite a while—fifteen to twenty five minutes, I should think, for the young lady was becoming very restless."

"Very restless!" McMann repeated slowly, as he wrote the words down. "Then when the young man returned, how did he behave, Phillips? How did he look?"

"Flustered, sir, and worried, sort of. "Wouldn't have any dessert, sir, and seemed to be in a hurry to get away," the waiter answered.

"Remember what they talked about when you came for the dessert order?" McMann demanded sharply.

"I didn't listen, sir, of course," the waiter deprecated, "but I heard the gentleman answer some question the young lady had asked—something about Mr. Borden, sir."

"About Borden!" McMann triumphed. "You're sure of that, Phillips? Just what was said and how did you happen to remember the name?"

"Why, sir, Mr. Borden is—or rather, was, sir—a frequent guest for luncheon in our dining room, so naturally when his name was mentioned I noticed it."

"Yes?" McMann smiled at the pale girl with the blazing eyes and at the pale young man whose hands were clenched.

"Yes, sir. He was saying something like, 'What makes you think I saw Borden?' and the young lady answered, or in words to this effect, sir: 'You were gone so long and look so awful I thought you were having a quarrel with Borden.' That's all I heard, sir, for I left the table then to get the check from the cashier, with the amount stamped on it."

"I'm afraid, Miss Lester," McMann turned to Ruth, "that, like most people, you're inclined to forget that waiters have eyes and ears, as well as hands." Before the flushed, indignant girl could answer, the detective turned to the waiter again. "When did the couple leave, Phillips? Give me the time, as nearly as you can place it."

The waiter shook his head. "I really couldn't say, sir. I go off duty at three, and all I can say is that I worked for some time after the young couple had gone."

"In quite a hurry to get away, weren't they, Phillips?" McMann suggested.

"I couldn't say as to that, sir, except that the young gentleman left his briefcase and I hurried after him with it."

"His briefcase, eh? Pretty heavy, was it, Phillips? Sides stuffed out?"

"Do you think, Mr. McMann, that it's fair to lead the witness like that?" Ruth demanded furiously. "In a court of law—"

"This isn't a trial—yet," McMann reminded her grimly. "Answer the question, Phillips."

"It was a large bag and quite heavy, but I don't remember whether it was bulging or not," the waiter answered conscientiously.

"Did the gentleman leave you a big tip, Phillips?" McMann asked, grinning.

The waiter shrugged and spread his hands. "He left the change from two one dollar bills and a half dollar. The bill came to two forty five, sir."

McMann roared with sudden laugher. "A nickel tip! No wonder you've got such a good memory where this gentleman is concerned, Phillips!"

Jack Hayward's face flamed with humiliation. With furious haste he thrust his hand into his pocket and drew out a dollar bill. "Here, waiter! I apologize. I don't think I even looked at the amount of the bill. God knows no one has ever before been able to accuse me of being a niggardly tipper. Here!"

But McMann halted the advance of the waiter's eager hand. "Put up your money, Hayward! What would have been a big tip on Saturday might look to the jury like a small bribe to make this man forget some of the things he has—unfortunately for you—so well remembered!"

Birdwell opened the communicating door. "A report on Benny Smith, the office boy, sir."

# CHAPTER ELEVEN

## I

"'WELL, what about the office boy, Birdwell? Why the devil hasn't he shown up?" McMann demanded of his subordinate, after the waiter had been dismissed, with the usual instructions.

"Callahan traced the Smith family to their new address, and has just phoned from the neighborhood, sir," Birdwell answered wearily. "The boy, Benny Smith, is sick in bed. Callahan says the doctor has been there, and won't let the boy out of the house until the middle of the afternoon, if then."

"What's the matter with the boy?" McMann barked impatiently.

Birdwell coughed. "Upset stomach, it seems. The boy was sick this morning, but insisted on coming down to the office, Callahan says, leaving the house about half past ten. At eleven he was back, and seemed so sick that his mother had a doctor in."

"Benny *sick!*" Ruth marvelled to herself. "Why, he has the constitution of an ox! I wonder—"

Whatever it was she was about to ask herself was cut short by McMann's next question, aimed at Birdwell: "What about Rita Dubois? Any word from Clay?"

"Yes, sir. Clay has traced her to the home of a friend of hers—a Miss Wilbur—Willette Wilbur. Another dancer, living with her mother at—" and he consulted a memorandum for the address.

"Then why doesn't he bring her in?" McMann demanded impatiently.

Birdwell refused to be hurried. "The girls are out, sir, according to Mrs. Wilbur. She says Miss Dubois spent the night with her daughter, and that after breakfast this morning the two girls went downtown together to do some shopping. They expected to have lunch with Mrs. Wilbur, and mentioned that they would be back by one o'clock."

"Well, I guess there's nothing to do but to wait," McMann admitted grudgingly. "By the way, Birdwell, Clay didn't tip off Mrs. Wilbur that Rita was wanted by the police, did he?"

Birdwell smiled slightly. "Not Clay! He's watching the house and has instructed the central telephone office to plug in any calls from or to the Wilbur number on the phone I'm holding down out here. Just in case Mrs. Wilbur might try to warn the girl, you know."

"Good!" McMann applauded. "That's all—no, send Covey in to me. He's in 715 down the hall, you know. . . . And now, Hayward, another question, if you can spare the time," he called out sarcastically to the young man who stood at one of the two front windows, his arm about Ruth Lester's shoulders, as they both stared with miserable, unseeing eyes downward at the mid day throngs in the street below.

"Yes?" Jack wheeled, swinging Ruth's slight little body with his, not dropping his arm.

"You've said you and Miss Lester attended a matinee. Which theater? When did the curtain go up?"

Ruth saw the drift of the question before it was apparent to Jack, but there was nothing to do but to stand quietly in the circle of his arm as he answered:

"The Princess Theater. The play was 'Murder.' The curtain rose at two forty five."

" 'Murder!' Rather a neat coincidence, eh? I hope you both enjoyed the show?"

Ruth, remembering how she had wept uncontrollably during the second act because the district attorney reminded her of her dead father, did not answer except with a nervous flicker of her eyelashes, and Jack's only response was a tightening of his arm about the girl's shoulders.

"Two forty five curtain, eh?" McMann nodded, his eyes narrowing to points of steely light. "You say you were not in your office at 2:10 when Cowan was plugged in on a busy line after he'd called your number, that you were rejoining Miss Lester at the McAlpin Hotel at that moment. Right?"

"That's correct," Jack retorted curtly.

McMann shuffled his notes, pretending to consult them to refresh his memory. "And yet, Hayward, you were in such a hurry to leave the hotel that you didn't take time to read the figures on your check, and started off in a rush without your briefcase. According to the waiter's story, you didn't have dessert after you got back to the hotel. If, as you say, it was only ten after two when you returned, what was your hurry?"

"I was not in a hurry," Jack contradicted. "I had a cup of coffee, sat talking with Miss Lester for a few minutes, and left the dining room at two twenty five. We were both under the impression that it was a two thirty curtain and walked directly to the theater, which is five blocks from the McAlpin Hotel."

"Hmm!" McMann considered. Then, "So you were among the first arrivals, eh? The doorman and the usher would be likely to remember you, I suppose, and could corroborate your story?"

Jack's hand closed so tightly over Ruth's shoulder that she winced, but his voice was steady as he answered: "No, we were not among the first arrivals—in the theater, itself, that is. There was a notice in the lobby, giving curtain time, and we turned away, walking about in the neighborhood of the theater for ten minutes or so."

"Really?" McMann was politely surprised. "With Miss Lester suffering from a cold, you walked her about in Saturday's high wind? I'm surprised at you, Hayward!"

"I was not cold any longer. I'd had two or three cups of hot coffee while waiting for Mr. Hayward!" Ruth cut in determinedly. "I preferred walking to sitting in a drafty theater."

"I suppose you checked your briefcase, Hayward?" McMann demanded, after a brief, measuring glance at Ruth.

Again that convulsive pressure on Ruth's shoulder. "No. I kept it with me—my overcoat also."

"Not taking any chances on the check room girl's curiosity, were you?" McMann insinuated.

"I don't think she would have been interested in the contents—life insurance literature and lists of prospects," Jack answered evenly. "There was no gun in that brief case, McMann."

"That's your story and you're going to stick to it, eh?" McMann growled. "Listen, Hayward, you must realize that I've got the goods on you! Three people—the elevator operator, Moran; Cowan, a friend of yours, who would have lied to protect you if he had dared; and Phillips the waiter—have told substantially the same story: you were in a white hot rage against Harry Borden and threatened to kill him. By your own admission you returned to your office, where you kept a gun. Your secretary says it was still there Saturday morning and it's not there now. Cowan hears Borden defying your interference and threats over the telephone at ten minutes after two. I submit that Borden came to the window on the airshaft, directly opposite your own window, not knowing that you had been telephoning from your own office, that you saw him, reached for your gun and shot him down before he suspected his danger; that you then came to his office, opened the outer door with the key so providentially placed in your hands by the waiter, closed the window without taking time to notice that one of the pigeons had already betrayed you, by leaving tracks of *blood* outside the window as well as on the floor inside the room; that you then robbed the dead man's body of the five hundred dollars so that it would look like the work of a hold up man, or because you badly needed the money. That's my case, Hayward, and if I were a prosecuting attorney, I'd be willing to take it to court as is!"

"Just a minute, Jack!" Ruth cried peremptorily, as the furious young man started forward. "Listen, Mr. McMann, before you make a false arrest! I know you don't want that blot against your record. I admit that, as you sum it up, it looks like a strong case against Mr. Hayward, but remember that you've got to find someone who saw him in this wing of the building after he returned to his office. There were cleaning women and undoubtedly other tenants on the floor, and Rita Dubois was certainly here about the time you insist that Jack was in Borden's office. I know he wasn't, for he couldn't have got in, and my evidence about the key would not be ignored in court as you have chosen to ignore it."

There was a flicker of admiration in McMann's hard gray eyes as they studied the girl. "When did Hayward return your key, Miss Lester?" he asked at last, very quietly. "The key to Borden's office?"

"He did not return it, because he had never seen it or touched it," Ruth denied passionately. "As I explained a while ago, the key the waiter found on the floor could not have been the office key. It was my apartment key, the only one that could have fallen out of my bag when I dropped it. He returned it immediately to my bag, for it was there when I reached the apartment Saturday evening, and the bag had not been out of my possession after I returned to the table—before Mr. Hayward left for the theater tickets." But as Ruth was concluding her argument in a triumphant rush of words her too clear memory betrayed her. Like a scrap of motion picture film, a scene passed before her mind's eye: Jack and herself in the bank Saturday evening; Jack, waiting for her to make her deposit, and holding her handbag for her; Jack's guilty flush when she rallied him on having opened it: "Peeking to see what kind of lipstick I use, darling?"

"Haven't you remembered something you'd like to forget, Miss Lester?" McMann asked, almost kindly.

"No!" Ruth denied. No, no! She had told him the truth. It must have been her apartment key which had fallen out of her purse and which Jack had been returning. But—why hadn't he explained then?

"Detective Covey, sir," Birdwell announced, and the jaunty, jolly little detective swaggered into the dead man's private office.

"What about the cleaning women, Covey?" McMann demanded impatiently.

"Haven't been able to find either one of them—Minnie Cassidy and Letty Miller are the names, sir," Covey answered cheerfully. "The Cassidy woman left home at ten this morning, according to her daughter, to visit some friend of hers in another part of town, but the daughter don't know the name or address, and the Miller woman hasn't been living at the address Coghlan, the superintendent, gave us, since about the first. It's a rooming house and the landlady says old Mrs. Miller didn't leave a forwarding address."

"I suppose there's nothing to do but to wait until they show up for work at four this afternoon," McMann growled. "All right, Birdwell—what is it?" as his other subordinate again appeared in the communicating door way.

"Dr. Nielson on the phone, sir," Birdwell answered. "Ready with his report, sir."

As McMann reached for the extension on Borden's desk, Ruth's cold right hand went involuntarily to her throat. If the calibre of the bullet which had killed Borden matched the calibre of the pistol missing from Jack's desk . . .

"Hello, Dr. Nielson! McMann speaking. What's the dope? . . . Fine! And can you tell me any more definitely when death occurred? . . . Hm! Close enough, I guess! Let's see—that places the murder between two and four o'clock Saturday, eh? ... Thanks, Doc!" McMann hung up the receiver and faced the couple who waited, scarcely breathing. "Well, Hayward, I don't think you'll be surprised to learn that the bullet which killed Harry Borden was the regulation bullet for a Colt's .38 calibre automatic. Anything to say now, my lad?"

"Nothing—except that I did not kill Borden and have no idea who did," Jack Hayward answered steadily.

"Mr. McMann, please don't forget that my gun was exactly like Mr. Hayward's—a Colt's .38, and that it too is missing," Ruth begged earnestly, her blue eyes enormous in the pallor of her exquisite little face. "Can't you see that if Jack had—had killed Mr. Borden he would not have disposed of my gun as well as his own, *because he would know that the absence of my pistol would make suspicion fall on me?*"

Again that gleam of admiration in the detective's grim gray eyes. "Covey, this is Colby Lester's daughter," he remarked, with a grin, to his subordinate. "A chip off the old block, eh? . . . Now, Miss Lester, there's just one more question for the present: did you yourself dispose of your pistol, either before the crime on Saturday, so that it would not be available if Hayward forced his way into these offices and quarreled with Borden, or this morning after your discovery of the body, to confuse the investigation with two missing pistols? Just a minute, please! I'm asking that question of the daughter of Colby Lester, the finest and most honorable criminal lawyer it has ever been my privilege to know."

Color swept from Ruth's throat to the fringe of golden curls on her forehead, as she drew her small body very erect and faced Detective Sergeant McMann with wide, unflinching blue eyes. "Mr. McMann, I swear on the name of my dead father, who taught me truth and honor—I did not touch the gun, I did not remove it, for any reason whatsoever, from my desk, and I do not know where it is!"

McMann gazed keenly into her eyes as she swore her solemn oath, then beckoned Covey to his side. The two men conversed in whispers for a minute or two, while

Ruth and Jack retreated, hand in hand, toward the front windows.

## II

"Well—twelve o'clock! Time for lunch!" McMann surprised them both by booming out cheerfully. "I'd like you to be back by one, if convenient, Miss Lester. I may need you to help me go over Borden's private papers. You may go about your business as usual, Hayward, but I'll have to ask you to hold yourself available for further questioning."

"Then I am not under arrest?" Jack asked quietly, as Ruth drew a sobbing breath of relief.

"Not yet," McMann answered curtly.

"And—and may we go to lunch together?" Ruth begged tremulously.

"Sure! Why not?" the detective grinned. "But if I were you, Hayward, I wouldn't forget to tip the waiter this time. Now clear out, both of you, and don't waste time gossiping with the reporters."

"Thank you, Mr. McMann!" Ruth cried, tears of relief quivering on her thick lashes. "I'll wait in my office for you, Jack, till you get your hat and coat."

As she was washing her hands at the stationary basin in the corner of the outer office, Detective Covey came out of the private office, waved at the girl with airy cheerfulness, and disappeared into the hall. Only twelve o'clock! Ruth kept glancing incredulously at her tiny wrist watch. Less than three hours since she had found the body of Harry Borden on the floor of his private office!

As she was powdering her face with hurrying, trembling hands, McMann appeared in the communicating doorway, and spoke to the detective stationed at Benny Smith's desk. "Phone down to the Childs Restaurant on the corner to send me up a couple of sandwiches, some apple pie, and a cup of coffee, Birdwell. Better have them send up your own lunch, too. I'm too busy to leave here now. . . . By the way, Miss Lester, I'm afraid I'll have to ask you to stay all afternoon. You undoubtedly know more about Borden's business and personal affairs than anyone else."

"I'll be glad to stay, Mr. McMann," Ruth assured him. "I'm more anxious than you can possibly be to have this mystery cleared up."

"Have a good lunch," McMann called, almost gently, as he closed the door upon himself again.

Biggers, the patrolman stationed outside Borden's offices, proved extremely useful in holding off reporters as the girl and her sweetheart waited for the elevator, but not even he could prevent the explosion of a flashlight or two as cameras were aimed at the couple who, reporters knew, were involved somehow in the investigation into the death of "Handsome Harry" Borden.

Ruth was grateful for the presence of other passengers in the car, since Micky Moran was prevented from asking embarrassing questions. As a matter of fact, the red headed elevator operator was a much subdued youngster, with the fear of the law heavy upon him.

"Where shall we eat, darling?" Jack asked, when they were upon the street, drinking in deep draughts of cold air and freedom.

"Anywhere but the McAlpin," Ruth shuddered. "How about our own little tearoom? But no! We've been too happy there. Let's not go back there until we've waked up from this awful nightmare." .

"Then the Colonnade is as good a place as any," Jack decided. "I want to talk, and there's no chance in this mob. Since it's a cafeteria, there won't be any waiter hanging over us," he added grimly, as he guided her through the storm doors.

A few minutes later they deposited their lightly burdened trays upon a small table in a far corner of the big, noisy room. Ruth automatically raised a spoon of luke-warm vegetable soup to her lips, then repudiated it with a violent gesture.

"Oh, Jack, I can't eat! Talk to me—say something! Oh—I'm sorry! But—it's been so—so horrible!"

Jack Hayward quietly laid down his fork and reached for the girl's twisting, cold hands. "You want me to say I didn't do it, don't you, darling? Do I have to say it in so many words? Well, then, darling—I didn't kill Borden."

"Thank you, Jack!" Tears welled up in her eyes, splashed upon her pale cheeks. "If you had, I would have stood by you. You know that, don't you? But Jack, who did? And where is your gun? You didn't take it home, did you— to have it out of reach, in case—?"

"No!" Jack denied, his hands tight upon hers. "When you first told me this morning I thought you had done it—

"I?" Ruth cried.

Jack nodded, his bronze brown eyes pleading with her to forgive him. "From some hysterical things you said about it's being your fault—"

"I meant it was my fault that *you* had killed him," she interrupted. "I had discovered that your gun was missing. I didn't know mine was, too. I thought you had quarreled with him when you came back Saturday afternoon, and had shot him before you realized what you were doing. And I knew that if you had, it was my fault, for having screamed and hurt my lip against the door. But tell me again that you didn't!"

Jack frowned and withdrew his hands, and Ruth knew that he was hurt and angry at her insistence. "I did not kill Borden, Ruth. I don't know who did. I wish to God I did know."

"Thank you, dear," she repeated, smiling at him eagerly and not casting a glance toward the man who had followed them along the food counters and taken his seat at the next table. There was no need to look; she knew that his apparently uninterested gaze was upon her and Jack Hayward, that, although he was not close enough to have heard their low voiced conversation, he had "listened" nevertheless. For Ruth had recognized in their "shadow" a man who had testified in one of Colby Lester's cases, for the prosecution—a detective who was a trained lip reader. So that was why McMann had permitted her and Jack to lunch together! He had hoped to get a confession in this way, since all other means had failed. If Jack had been guilty—Ruth shuddered to think of the desperate chance she had taken when, knowing that the "shadow" was reading every word that fell from their lips, she had dared lead Jack into declaring his guilt or innocence. But it was innocence, thank God! McMann might not be convinced, would not be, of course, but she was. . . . No chance now to explain to Jack, or everything would be spoiled. . . .

"Aren't you going to eat?" Jack asked, a little stiffly.

She smiled at him, brilliantly, through tears. "I'm not very hungry, but I'll eat one bite for every bite you take. And when we've finished, we'll talk about the house we're going to build in Scarsdale. No more murder talk now, darling! We're too wrought up. All that matters is that you didn't do it and I didn't, and we love each other. . . . Oh, Jack, I do love you so, even if you are a hot headed, detective baiting, young idiot! Come, now! Bite for bite!"

When they had finished their lunch, Ruth, smiling to herself at the lip reading shadow's undoubted annoyance, insisted on taking Jack to see Macy's window display of modernistic furniture, refusing all the while, with almost hysterical gayety, to discuss the murder or any scrap of evidence that had developed in the morning's investigation.

In the elevator she had a chance to whisper an explanation to her bewildered fiance, for the lip reading shadow had not boarded the car with them: "We were followed, darling. I had to make you repeat your assurances to me for the benefit of the detective. We mustn't forget that McMann is clever."

Loving admiration routed the shadow of resentment from Jack's eyes. "You're worth two of him—Colby Lester's daughter!"

They parted at the door of Borden's offices, Jack to go to his own suite, where his comings and goings would undoubtedly be under closest supervision.

As Ruth entered her office, Birdwell hung up the telephone receiver and announced to McMann, who stood in the communicating door: "Clay's got the Dubois woman. Says he'll have her here in fifteen minutes."

# CHAPTER TWELVE

"MISS LESTER," McMann called to Ruth, who was hanging up her hat and coat, "you're familiar with Borden's letter files, of course. I wish you'd go through them and bring me every letter you can find that contains a threat of any kind. A promoter of his ilk is bound to have made bitter enemies, and I don't want to overlook any bets. Also, bring me his cancelled checks for the last year. If he has been paying blackmail to anyone, I'd like to know it."

"Yes, Mr. McMann," Ruth agreed eagerly. She was grateful for any task that would keep her mind off Jack Hayward's almost inevitable arrest. And her respect for the detective rose. He was not letting the blackness of his case against Jack Hayward make him indolent or careless in opening up new avenues of investigation. A detective —McMann; not just a third degree bully as she had feared.

A few minutes later she entered Borden's private office, which the detective had made his own, and laid two bulky folders before him. "When I first came to work for him, Mr. Borden told me he received many blackmail and death threat letters from ruined investors, and instructed me to file all that I found in his mail in this folder. He pretended to laugh at them, but I'm sure he was afraid. I think he had a private detective or some sort of bodyguard."

McMann, obviously impressed, opened the folder and began to riffle through the odd collection of letters it contained. "That so? What gave you that impression, Miss Lester?"

"A big, uncouth looking man, whom Mr. Borden called Jake—I never heard his last name—was in and out of the offices frequently, and Mr. Borden always saw him," Ruth answered eagerly. "And if a new threat had been received in the mail, Mr. Borden always called for the folder when Jake made his next visit. Frequently, also, when Mr. Borden was still in his offices when I left, I saw Jake hanging around in the hall, as if waiting to protect Mr. Borden. At least, that is the only explanation I could think of."

McMann frowned in intense concentration. Then: "Did this Jake have a key to the offices, Miss Lester?"

Ruth shook her head. "I don't know. I don't know any thing else about him at all. Of course I never asked Mr. Borden any questions, and he never volunteered any in formation."

McMann left the room, apparently to give instructions to Detective Birdwell in the outer office, then returned and began to study the letters again, frowningly. "Nothing recent here," he said at last, closing the folder, "but of course I'll put a man on this job. Something may turn up, but I doubt it. Now let's see these cancelled checks. You checked his bank statements for him, I suppose?"

"Yes. It was difficult, for he seldom made an entry on a check stub, and when I questioned him about a blank stub, in an effort to keep the record straight so that he would not overdraw, he would say, 'Oh, I don't know! Two or three hundred, I guess. Just charge it to 'cash,'" Ruth answered. "Sometimes he drew as much as two or three thousand dollars out of the bank in a single week."

"Any checks to women?" McMann demanded.

"Only to Mrs. Borden," Ruth told him.

"So 'Handsome Harry' was no woman's fool," McMann approved, smiling crookedly. "Any charge accounts for his lady friends?"

Again Ruth shook her head. "No, not in his name at least. But from what he said to Rita Dubois on Saturday, I gathered that he had given her letters to the credit managers of several shops. I imagine the accounts were to be opened in her name, with his name as guarantee of payment, but of course I can't be sure."

"Just one of the little points that Rita can clear up for us," McMann commented drily. "By the way, how long had Borden's affair with the dancer been going on?"

"I don't think it had really begun," Ruth answered honestly. "From what I overheard between them on Saturday and from what Mr. Borden said after Rita had left—"

"What did he say?" McMann interrupted sharply.

"Something about 'they all fall sooner or later,' and that he liked them when they weren't too easy," Ruth answered, flushing. "He met Rita Dubois at the Golden Slipper about three weeks ago, and was infatuated with her from the first. He talked about her to me, and when she came to the office it was easy to see that he was in love with her."

"And she with him?" McMann pounced.

Ruth's flush deepened. "N—no. She hated for him even to touch her hand. I was surprised that she had agreed to go to Winter Heaven with him Saturday."

McMann studied the girl keenly. "There's something else, Miss Lester. Out with it!"

"Well," Ruth admitted reluctantly, "she practically admitted to me that she was gold digging Mr. Borden. That was Saturday morning. She noticed the change in my appearance, too, and charged me, good naturedly, with having 'dolled up' to 'vamp' Mr. Borden. She laughed then, and said I could have him 'next week,' implying that she would get all she wanted out of him over the week end. Then she warned me not to tell Borden what she had said. I replied by telling her of my engagement to Mr. Hayward. Mr. Borden came out of his private office then and ended the conversation between Miss Dubois and myself."

"Hmm!" McMann frowned, as he scrawled notes on a sheet of yellow paper. "No wonder she was sore when he 'stood her up.' Now, Miss Lester, I'd like you to tell me, if you can, who preceded Rita Dubois in Borden's affections. There *was* someone, of course?"

Ruth hesitated, loath to involve another woman, probably as innocent as herself of Borden's murder, but she realized that now, when the shadow of arrest hung over the man she loved, was no time to be scrupulously ethical. And if she did not tell, McMann would learn from other sources. . . . "From the time I came to work for Mr. Borden until he met Miss Dubois," she began slowly, "Mr. Borden was very attentive to a Miss Gilman—Cleo Gilman."

"Were they lovers?" McMann asked bluntly.

"I don't know, but—I presume so," Ruth answered reluctantly. "I heard her remind him, on the fifth of December, I believe it was, that her rent was due, and I saw him give her cash to pay it. She did not come to the office very frequently, but until he met Miss Dubois he made an engagement with her by telephone nearly every day."

"Her telephone number and address?" McMann demanded.

"I don't know her address but the telephone number was Circle 3412," Ruth told him.

"And did they quarrel over Miss Dubois?"

"I don't know. He simply stopped calling her on the phone and gave me instructions to tell her he was not in, if she called him. She only called twice after that, I believe."

"And what did she say to you when you told her Borden wasn't in?"

The ghost of a smile tugged at the dimple in the corner of Ruth's enchanting little mouth. "The first time she left word for him to call her, and he didn't, of course. The second time she laughed and said, 'Well, well! So that's that! Listen, darling, tell him Cleo says 'Good bye, good luck and God bless you.' She never called again when I was here."

"You sure of that? Sure she wasn't the woman who called him Saturday morning and wouldn't leave her name?" McMann prodded.

"No. The voice was not the same at all," Ruth replied unhesitatingly. "The woman who called Saturday morning had a beautiful, throaty contralto voice. Miss Gilman's is a little nasal and quite high pitched."

McMann reached for the extension of the telephone which he had had hooked up with police headquarters. "Hello! That you, Captain? McMann speaking. Another little job for one of the boys. Have a good man sent out to bring in Cleo Gilman. Yes—that's right. One of Borden's lady friends, that he broke with about three weeks ago. Telephone number, Circle 3412. . . . Yes . . . Too damned much rather than too little. I got enough suspects to crowd the Tombs. . . . No, I'm not making any arrests yet. . . . What's that? The boys didn't find a gun in either place? . . . Well, I didn't think they would. ... By the way, Captain, any report on Borden's manservant, Ashe, yet? I told Birdwell an hour ago to have him brought here. . . . Not at Borden's apartment, eh? Well, I want him brought here as soon as he shows up. . . . Yes, here! I'm making these offices my headquarters for today, at least. . . . Yes, she's a lot of help to me, and I don't want to drag her down to headquarters, if I can help it," and McMann nodded and smiled at Ruth, to indicate that he was referring to her. "Mrs Borden? I sent her home at noon. She has a sick child. No, no danger of her blowing. . . . Oh, sure, she's still in the picture. O'Brien's keeping an eye on her. . . . All right, Captain. See you soon," and McMann hung up the receiver, just as Birdwell opened the door between the two offices.

"Detective Clay and Rita Dubois, sir."

"Good! Show Rita in. I'll speak to Clay out there," McMann directed as he rose from Borden's desk.

"Shall I leave the room, Mr. McMann?" Ruth asked, but so wistfully that the stern faced detective smiled again, with something like paternal fondness.

"I should say not! I'm counting on your help," he boomed and bolted from the room before she could thank him.

A minute later the door opened to admit Rita Dubois. The dancer's black eyes looked enormous in the thin, exotically beautiful face, but there was a nonchalant smile on the vividly rouged lips.

"Well, well! We meet again, darling," she drawled, as she swayed, gloved hand on a slim hip, toward Ruth Lester. "I see you've shed the horn rimmed spectacles, along with the rest of your scared bunny disguise, and believe me, you're a riot." She had come quite close, and suddenly her voice dropped to a whisper: "Listen, Infant! Slip me a tip, won't you? Does that big stiff of a detective know I was here Saturday afternoon? Is that why he sent a dick out to drag me in?"

Ruth smiled, felt again that warm rush of friendliness toward the breezy, slangy dancer. "The elevator operator told him he brought you up about two o'clock Saturday afternoon," she answered in a whisper.

"Thanks, kid!" The dancer drew a sharp breath, the nonchalant smile was wiped from the rouged lips. Suddenly she looked old and tired and very much afraid.

Detective Sergeant McMann made quick work of his preliminary questioning of Rita Dubois. Her replies as to name, age, profession and place of employment were given coolly, even nonchalantly, but Ruth, seated near the dancer, so that both of the girls faced the detective across the dead man's desk, saw that Rita's hands were locked so tightly that her white kid gloves were bursting at the seams.

"And so you and Borden, after your first meeting about three weeks ago, became lovers?" McMann pounced suddenly.

"That's a lie!" Rita denied vehemently, her black eyes blazing.

"Then—" McMann grinned crookedly—"I take it that your week end at Winter Heaven with 'Handsome Harry' was to have been in the nature of a honeymoon? Let's not waste time, Miss Dubois! I know that you and Borden had planned to go to Winter Heaven on the 2:15 Saturday afternoon, that Borden had bought a drawing room for the trip and that he had reserved a suite for you and him self at the Winter Heaven Hotel. Now what I want you to tell me is—why didn't Borden meet you at the station as he had planned?"

The dancer laughed, but it was not a gay sound. "That was what I wanted to know, too—and I found out when I saw the headlines about the murder at noon today."

For two hours Ruth Lester had been praying that Rita Dubois would furnish Jack Hayward an alibi, by admitting that Borden was alive when she had visited him after 2:15. The collapse of that hope now was so unnerving that the girl feared she would faint.

"So it was news to you that Borden was dead, was it, Rita?" McMann grinned.

"I'll say it was!" Rita assured him, nonchalant again. "I was knocked out. Fainted right on the street. My girl friend, Willette Wilbur, was downtown with me, had to call a cab and take me to her home. She can tell you. And then I find a dick waiting to grab me—"

"Were you in love with Harry Borden, Rita?" McMann interrupted suddenly.

Color swept over the thin, exotic face. "That's my business! . . . Well, all right then—I wasn't! But God knows I didn't wish him any harm."

McMann studied the girl for a long minute through narrowed, glinting gray eyes. Then: "Well, Rita, let's have your story. Did you go to the station?"

Rita flung up her head defiantly. "Sure I did! I'd promised to go away with him for the week end, and I was ready to keep my bargain. I got to Penn Station at two, and went to the information desk, where he'd said he would meet me. At five minutes after two, I began to get nervous for fear we'd miss the train and decided to phone him. There's a telephone booth near the information desk, and I called from there, where I could see Harry if he came while I was phoning. His line was busy, so I knew he'd not left the office. I waited for about five minutes more and called again, and his line was still busy—"

"Just a minute!" McMann interrupted. "Can you fix the time of that second call exactly?"

"Sure! Ten minutes after two," Rita asserted confidently. "I had my eye on the big clock."

Ruth did not need the flick of McMann's narrowed gray eyes in her direction to remind her that the dancer had partially corroborated Bill Cowan's damaging testimony against Jack Hayward—that, when he had called Jack's number at 2:10, he had been plugged in on a busy line and had heard Harry Borden's voice raised in violent anger. With a tremendous effort of will she controlled the waves of dizziness that were pouring over her brain and braced herself to listen to McMann's next question:

"Did you call his number again?"

"Of course!" Rita answered promptly. "I knew he was in his office or his line wouldn't be busy. I waited about a minute, and then I got him, and he told me to come over to the office—"

"Wait!" McMann interrupted sharply. "Exactly what did you say to Borden and what did he say to you?"

The dancer hesitated for a moment, while Ruth held her breath. "Well, he didn't give me a chance to say much. I said, 'My God, Harry, do you know what time it is, or have you forgot you were to catch a train at 2:15?' And he said, 'No, I hadn't forgot, Rita, but I've been unavoidably detained. What time is it?' I told him it was twelve minutes after two and he swore a blue streak, and then he said we'd have to take a later train and for me to come on up to the office, that we'd make new plans when I got there."

McMann frowned and tapped his pencil against the dead man's desk. Ruth held her breath.

"Well, Rita, go on," McMann directed at last. "You came, and you were hopping mad, too, weren't you?"

"Well, I wasn't what you might call delirious with delight," Rita admitted flippantly. Then her eyes widened with fear. "Say, what are you trying to do? Pin something on me? Well, you've got a fat chance, old dear, because I didn't even see Harry, much less bump him off, if that's what you're insinuating."

McMann's thin lips twisted in that slow, crooked grin of his. "Stick to your story, Rita. When did you get here? What happened?"

The dancer's hands gripped each other so tightly that a knuckle cracked. Her big black eyes flashed from McMann's heavy, grinning face to Ruth's pale one, as if seeking help. Then, on a quickly drawn breath, Rita answered: "I came right over from the station, just a block away. Just took time to check my bags. I suppose I was here within five minutes after I hung up the receiver."

"You got here about eighteen or twenty minutes after two, then?" McMann asked, with pencil poised.

Rita shrugged. "I guess so. Maybe a minute or two sooner—I don't know. I knocked on the door and there wasn't any answer. I knocked several times and then tried the knob and found the door was locked, so—I went away again. There wasn't anything else to do," she added defiantly.

"Of course not!" McMann agreed blandly. "Nothing to do but to turn right around and go right back home, and wait for Borden to call you there, so that's what you did, eh?"

"Yes," the dancer agreed eagerly—and fell headlong into McMann's trap.

"Then, Rita," McMann asked, as Ruth leaned forward tensely, "how do you account for the fact that you spent at least ten minutes on the seventh floor?"

"I didn't!" Rita denied recklessly.

Ruth could hardly suppress a gasp of relief. Now, at least, Rita Dubois was lying. Micky Moran, the elevator operator, had said that after taking the dancer to the seventh floor he had spent at least ten minutes in the telephone booth in the lobby of the Starbridge Building, in conversation with his girl. But of course Rita could not know this—

Suddenly an incident which she had completely forgotten until that moment recurred to Ruth Lester like a flash of lightning across a dark sky. "Please, Mr. McMann," she cried, her voice quivering with excited hope, "may I speak with you privately for a minute?"

The detective led the trembling girl to a far corner of Borden's office, while Rita stared after them with enormous, frightened black eyes.

"I've just remembered something, Mr. McMann," Ruth whispered, as the big man bent low to listen. "Saturday morning, when Mr. Borden was in the outer office with Rita, he waved good bye to her with the torn half of a yellow backed banknote. I didn't see the denomination, and I didn't think much of it at the time, but now I believe I know what had happened, and what Mr. Borden meant when he said that about keeping his part of the bargain if she kept hers."

"Yes, yes," McMann urged impatiently, as Ruth paused for breath.

"I'm sure now that they had been scuffling playfully, Rita trying to take the bill away from him, and tearing it in two. I'm *sure—sure!*—that he let her keep half of the torn bill, and had promised to give her the other half after she'd kept her promise about—about going away with him."

"Well?" McMann grunted, frowning in deep concentration.

"Oh, don't you see?" Ruth implored. "If she's telling the truth—if she really didn't see Mr. Borden again, she still has her half of the bill! But I believe she's lying! I believe Mr. Borden was alive when she came, and that he either gave her the other half of the bill, as he had undoubtedly promised he would, or that—that they quarreled because he wouldn't, and she—she—" Her whispering voice faltered. She could not bring herself to utter an accusation of murder. "Oh, Mr. McMann, please believe I'm not just talking wildly, to—to help someone else! I *know* Rita must have been desperate for money, and yet I don't think she's just a gold digger either—"

McMann frowned prodigiously, in deep thought. Then, "Was Borden in the habit of carrying bills of large denomination?"

"He was, he was!" Ruth replied in an eager, breathless whisper. "He was terribly vain about money—loved to flash hundred dollar bills. Just last week he showed me a five hundred dollar banknote—told me to take a good look at it, as I might never see one again. I told him he was foolish to carry such big sums on his person, but he just laughed at me and looked pleased with himself. Maybe—maybe he showed it to Rita Saturday morning—" She faltered again, her blue eyes raised imploringly to McMann's stern face.

McMann nodded slowly, the frown clearing. "And Borden's half of the bill was not on his body this morning. Of course whoever took the five hundred in smaller bills might have taken the useless torn half—"

"It wouldn't have been useless to one person—Rita Dubois!" Ruth reminded him. "And she could have passed it, *no matter how she got it,* for she would have thought no one knew of Borden's having had the other half! Please ask her for her half of the bill, Mr. McMann! If she still has it, I'll believe she did not see Mr. Borden when she came back Saturday afternoon."

Detective Birdwell interrupted the whispered conference. "Headquarters on the line, sir. The Golden Slipper safe was robbed sometime between closing time early Sunday morning and noon today. The manager of the club has some sort of tip about a five hundred dollar bill—"

As McMann reached for the extension on Borden's desk, Rita Dubois rose, looked wildly about as if for a way of escape, then braced herself against the desk, her enormous black eyes fixed in an agony of suspense upon the detective.

# CHAPTER THIRTEEN

"HELLO, Captain! McMann speaking," the detective in charge of the investigation into the murder of Henry P. Borden greeted his superior on the other end of the wire. "The Golden Slipper's safe has been cracked, eh? . . . Lose much? . . . Hmm! Guess I know what graft to get into when I retire from this game! . . . What's that? A five hundred dollar bill, eh? ... When did she get it changed?" and McMann raised his brows and smiled his sinister, crooked smile at Rita Dubois, who was leaning toward him, her lovely face white and drawn with suspense. "Listen, Captain, is the club's manager there now? . . . All right, ask him if he remembers *whether the bill had been torn half in two and pasted or pinned together*." The words were uttered with slow, dreadful significance, the detective's narrowed, little gray eyes never leaving Rita's stricken face. The answer, when it came, brought a grunt of satisfaction from the detective, who quickly concluded the conversation.

"Well, Rita?" McMann grinned, as he hung up the receiver. Suddenly he leaned forward and addressed the pitiably frightened dancer, his pencil tapping staccato periods to his brief sentences: "No use wasting time! Saturday morning Borden gave you half of a five hundred dollar bill. He kept the other half. He had bargained to give it to you when you had kept your promise to go to Winter Heaven with him. In addition to the torn half of a five hundred dollar bill, Borden had more than five hundred dollars in smaller bills to pay for the week end jaunt. *No money was found on his body this morning!* You say you did not see Harry Borden Saturday afternoon, yet Saturday night, when the Golden Slipper opened at eleven o'clock, you were there with a five hundred dollar bill which had been torn in two and pasted together, and which you had the club manager change into smaller bills for you. Now—that's all true, and there's no use your denying any of it. What I want to know is—how did you get the other half of the five hundred dollar banknote? Come clean, Rita—and no hysterics!"

As McMann hammered out his damning sentences, Rita Dubois slowly straightened until she stood, tall and slim and rigid, her chin elevated, her blue tinted lids curtaining the agony of her great black eyes. When he had finished and shot his question at her, she shrugged slightly, and slowly opened her eyes, staring at the detective steadily, blindly, as she answered:

"Yes—it's all true. I lied. I did see Harry Borden Saturday afternoon."

"Dead or alive—or both?" McMann pounced.

Rita's voice was the monotone of a woman who is restraining hysterics. "Alive. I didn't kill him, if that is what you mean. He was alive and well when I left, after having been with him only about ten minutes."

"Thank God, oh, thank God!" Ruth cried, in a voice shaking with laughter and tears. "At half past two, when Rita left Mr. Borden—alive, alive!—Jack and I were in the lobby of the Princess Theater, Mr. McMann!"

"And the curtain did not rise until two forty five," McMann reminded her, but almost absent mindedly. "Of course someone may remember seeing you and Hayward there at half past two. Did you ask the box office man when the matinee was to start?"

"No, of course not," Ruth admitted reluctantly. "There was a sign in the lobby giving curtain time, so we just walked about for ten minutes, as Jack told you."

"I remember," McMann granted, that twisted smile on his lips again. "But Rita has the floor now. Well, Rita, how did you get in Saturday afternoon at about seventeen minutes after two? Did you use the key Borden had given you?"

Ruth gasped her surprise, and the dancer, apparently, was no less startled. "I—I didn't have a key," she retorted defiantly, her agitated hands instinctively gripping her handbag.

"Oh, yes, you did!" McMann laughed harshly, as he rose, strode to the girl and forced the expensive alligator bag out of her desperately clinging hands. Ruthlessly, without apology, he dumped its contents upon the desk top, until a Yale lock key clattered upon the polished surface. "And here it is! You amateurs are always so sloppy," he reproved the dancer jocularly. "An old hand at the game would have remembered to throw this thing away."

"How did you know I had a key to Harry's office?" Rita demanded.

"Because of a little memo that Borden jotted down on the envelope that held his railroad tickets," McMann enlightened her. " 'Get key from Rita.' Now, why didn't Borden 'get key from Rita,' *If he was alive when you entered these offices Saturday afternoon?*"

Ruth saw only too clearly the drift of McMann's questions. He undoubtedly believed that the promoter was dead when Rita arrived, that he had been shot immediately after his telephone conversation with her, in which he had told her to come to the office, that she had arrived, knocked, received no answer, entered with the key Borden had lent her, had found her would be lover dead, and had, in her desperate need for money, robbed the body. If only Rita had not had a key, could not have entered unless Borden had been alive to admit her, then Jack Hayward would automatically have been eliminated as a suspect. But Rita was answering, and Ruth forced herself to listen.

"He forgot to ask me for the key, I suppose," Rita retorted defiantly. "Anyway, he made a date to meet me at the station for the 5:32, the next train for Winter Heaven. He wouldn't have needed the key before then, since he told me he was going to stay in his office all afternoon. He'd given me the key Friday when I was having lunch with him—breakfast for me, lunch for him. I was to meet him at the office about six Friday evening and go out to dinner with him, and he said as he might not be in when I got there, I'd better take the key and let myself in with it, so I would not have to wait in the hall. Later he phoned me to meet him at the Crillon, instead, and I did, and forgot to give him the key. But I didn't use it Saturday— didn't even remember I had it. I knocked and he let me in. He was expecting me, of course, but before he opened the door he asked who it was and when I shouted, 'Rita,' he let me in."

"And then?" McMann grinned skeptically, as Rita paused. "What explanation did he give you for missing the train?"

Rita hesitated, flushed, then seemed to choose her words carefully. "He didn't give any explanation—just apologized, and promised to make it up to me. He—he seemed to be in a hurry to get me out of the office, as if he were expecting someone. I thought he'd been having a row with Cleo Gilman over the phone and that he was afraid she'd come while I was there. Harry and Cleo had been— 'friends' for about a year before I met him. He had told me about her, said he was through with her—"

"Did he mention Miss Gilman Saturday afternoon?" McMann interrupted.

"No, he didn't mention any one's name, except Jake Bailey, who was always hanging around, like a body guard or something. I jokingly asked him if Jake was going to Winter Heaven with us, and he said no, that Jake had left Friday night for a week end visit with his people somewhere upstate—he didn't say just where," Rita answered, still in that careful, hesitating manner which was branding her as a liar in McMann's eyes, as Ruth could clearly see.

Her fear was confirmed when McMann asked, smiling twistedly: "You're sure he told you that Saturday *afternoon,* Rita? Wasn't it Saturday morning or Friday evening?"

"It was Saturday afternoon," Rita replied stubbornly.

"Borden was in a hurry to get rid of you but you took time to joke with him about Jake Bailey, eh?" McMann grinned. "All right, Rita, all right! Go on with your story. How did he happen to give you the other half of the five hundred dollar bill? Why didn't he wait until you were in Winter Heaven? He wouldn't give it to you Saturday morning, remember!"

An ugly splotch of red suddenly glowed on the slim throat of the dancer. "I asked him for it. I was pretty sore because he'd missed the train, and he wanted to make up with me, so he gave me the other half of the bill. I told him *I* might miss the 5:32 if he didn't—so he gave it to me."

McMann chuckled. "Just like that, eh? You make an awfully poor liar, Rita. . . . Here! Keep your shirt on!" he commanded uglily, as the dancer sprang toward him, her teeth bared, her slim, long fingers curved into talons. "So you went to the station to make the 5:32, did you, and he stood you up again?"

Rita hesitated, then answered desperately, angrily, "Yes, I did!"

McMann leaned back in his chair, grinning and nodding with what seemed, to Ruth, like ghoulish satisfaction. "What do you think the police department has been doing all day, Rita? I'll tell you one little job they've cleaned up: you beat it from here, after stopping in the lobby to telephone someone, straight to the station, got the bags you'd checked there, and took them to your hotel. *And yon didn't take them out again Saturday afternoon!* You did take out a small overnight bag about midnight Saturday, on your way to spend the night with your girl friend, Willette Wilbur. *Now* how about it, Rita?"

The red splotch on the dancer's throat extended to her face, suffused it. She swayed dizzily for a moment, closing her terror stricken black eyes. "I—I didn't go to the station," she gasped. Then the words came in a passionate torrent: "I was only going away with him to get the five hundred. I—I needed it, and I won't tell you why, if you kill me! After he'd given it to me, I didn't care what happened between him and me later. I was just happy that I didn't have to—to pay for it, by—by—" She choked, and suddenly began to cry, horribly, without hiding her convulsed face.

"Listen, Rita," McMann urged, almost gently. "You've admitted you needed five hundred dollars in a whale of a hurry, that you were willing to do almost anything to get it. Now admit just a little bit more and tell me the whole truth. I'll put it up to you straight: either Borden was alive when you came and you killed him—wait till I'm through!—killed him to get the money that would come too late if he waited until night to give it to you, or he was dead when you got here. No, wait! Isn't this what happened?—you came, got no answer to your knock, used Borden's passkey, found him dead on the floor—yes! just where you're looking," he interrupted himself, as the dancer's eyes involuntarily shot a glance of horror toward the spot where Borden had lain in death— "You remembered that he had the other half of the five hundred dollar bill he had given you; you looked for it, found it and more than five hundred more in smaller bills, took it all— over a thousand dollars counting your half of the bill—"

"No, no!" Rita screamed, beating the air with frantic, clenched fists. "I didn't rob a dead man! I'd die first! He was alive, I tell you—alive! He gave me his half of the bill, and not a cent more! Not a cent!"

Birdwell's weary, bored voice from the doorway interrupted Rita's passionate avowal. "Ferber's here with the pictures of the finger prints, sir. And Borden's manservant, Ashe. Mrs. Borden's come back, too, sir."

"All right, Birdwell," McMann nodded to his subordinate. "I told Mrs. Borden to come back at two o'clock. How's her sick child? . . . Better? That's good!" and oddly, Ruth Lester thought, the stern detective seemed to be genuinely pleased. "We won't keep her from the kid longer than necessary. Sick all right. I talked to the doctor myself. Tell Ferber to come in. Hold Ashe out there till I'm ready for him. And send around for Mr. Hayward. He's in his own office."

Ruth's eyes dilated with fear. Was McMann going to arrest Jack now, convinced, as she was sure the detective was, that Hayward had shot Harry Borden through the open windows facing each other across the airshaft, and that Rita, arriving very soon afterwards, had robbed his body?

Ferber, the finger print expert, was entering the private office, a large portfolio under his arm, when McMann shot another question at Rita Dubois:

"Was that window open or closed when you were in this office Saturday afternoon?" And he pointed to the window looking out upon the airshaft.

Rita's terror stricken black eyes went blank. "Window? ... I don't know. . . . Yes, I do! It was open, because I noticed some pigeons—or at least one black pigeon—walking up and down the window ledge."

"Then why did you close it?" McMann snapped at her.

"I? I didn't close it! Why on earth should I?" Rita cried, and Ruth's heart echoed the question. If, as McMann seemed to believe, Borden was dead when Rita Dubois arrived, and she had robbed his body, why should she have stopped in her dreadful, ghoulish work, to close the window? Rita did not love Harry Borden. It would have meant nothing to *her* that the cold wind would have blown upon his dead body. . . .

"Hello, Ferber! Let's see what you've got there? Good, clear prints?"

"Lots of 'em, McMann," the finger print expert answered cheerfully, smiling and nodding at Ruth Lester. He spread the sheaf of enlarged photographed finger prints upon Borden's desk. "Here's one peculiar set—

found it half a dozen places," and he pointed to a picture. "Look! The middle finger of the right hand is a stub— about half an inch of it missing, I'd say."

Ruth started eagerly toward the desk. "Those are Minnie Cassidy's finger prints. Half of the first joint of her middle right finger was cut off in an accident when she was a child. She told me about it when she was dusting my desk one afternoon."

"Thanks, Miss Lester," McMann grunted, as he bent over the photographs, studying them frowningly. He looked up as Jack Hayward entered the room, jerked a nod at him, which Jack answered with smiling courtesy, before he crossed the room to take his place beside Ruth Lester.

"Send Mrs. Borden in, Birdwell," McMann called through the door which Jack had left ajar.

When Mrs. Borden, very pale but dignifiedly composed, was shown into the private office by Birdwell, McMann stuck his hands deep into his pockets and regarded his collection of "guests" with upraised brows and that now familiar twisted smile on his wide, thin mouth.

"Now, folks," McMann said at last, after his glance had lingered for unbearable seconds upon Jack Hayward, "I'm going to ask all of you to permit Mr. Ferber here to take your finger prints. It is my duty to tell you that none of you is compelled to do so—unless you are placed under arrest as a suspect," he added, with slow, terrible significance. "How about it? Anybody got any objections?"

"I have no objection," Mrs. Borden answered promptly, in her low, cultured voice, and immediately began to strip her gray gloves from her hands.

"It's all right with me!" Rita Dubois answered defiantly.

Ruth and Jack agreed almost simultaneously, and five minutes later the ugly, shameful business was accomplished. Seated at the desk again, McMann compared the fresh prints with the enlarged photographs of the finger prints which Ferber had found in the "death chamber."

"Mrs. Borden, you were wearing gloves Saturday, I presume? Did you remove them during either visit?" the detective sergeant asked.

"I was wearing gloves on both my visits, of course, and I did not remove them," Mrs. Borden answered.

"That accounts for it!" McMann muttered to Ferber, who was bending over him. "You, too, Rita?" he asked casually, without looking up.

"Yes! I was wearing gloves and I didn't take them off while I was here."

"Then how do you account for the fact that the print of your right thumb was found on each drawer of Miss Lester's desk?" McMann demanded.

Jack's hand closed so hard over Ruth's that the girl winced, but she was not conscious that she was hurt; she only knew that here was evidence that Rita Dubois had been searching her—Ruth's—desk for *something!* Had Rita found the thing she was looking for—the gun with which to kill Harry Borden, perhaps?

"Oh! ... I forgot!" Rita was answering, defiantly. "I wanted to paste together the two halves of the five hundred dollar bill Harry had given me. I was looking for paste, and had taken off my glove to do the job."

"With Borden in a hurry to get rid of you?" McMann reminded her.

"It was Harry who suggested it," Rita answered. "We were in the outer office, saying good bye—" She glanced, ashamed, at Mrs. Borden, who was looking steadily at her own clasped hands. "I'd just stuffed the two halves of the bill in my handbag and Harry said I might lose one of them, and suggested I paste them together. I looked for the paste and couldn't find it, and he was in such a fidget that I went on without bothering about the paste, and later bought a little tube at the drug store."

"There's a paste pot in plain sight on Benny's desk," Ruth could not refrain from telling the detective.

McMann glanced at her and smiled slightly, as if to assure her that he was very much on the job. Then, with the suddenness of a cat pouncing upon a mouse: "What did you do with the gun, Rita? Of course we'll find it sooner or later, but you might as well save us the trouble!"

Ruth gasped, tried to realize all that McMann's question meant, as Jack's hand again closed with fiercely exultant pressure upon hers.

"Gun? What the hell are you talking about?" Rita almost screamed, in a fear roughened voice. "I've never had a gun in my hands in my life—"

"The .38 calibre Colt's automatic that you found in the bottom drawer of Miss Lester's desk," McMann interrupted coolly. "You were looking for it, and you found it. Borden had told you, as he had told several other people, that Miss Lester owned a gun, kept it in her desk in case of a hold up. Borden wouldn't give you the other half of that all important five hundred dollar bill, and you were desperate for need of it. You couldn't wait till Saturday night. You quarreled with him, pretended to be leaving, went into the outer office, got the gun out of the drawer, and—shot him."

Rita had gone dead white as the detective summed up against her, but when he had finished she laughed, her vividly rouged lips twisting in an ugly loop of disdain. "Sounds simply swell, don't it? But listen here, and get this straight: I didn't know Baby face had a gun in her desk; there wasn't one in the bottom drawer when I looked for the paste, and I didn't kill Harry Borden! That's the truth, and you can third degree me till hell freezes over if you want to!"

"Then—someone else had already killed him with that gun when you looked for the paste to stick together that bill you'd taken off his body?" McMann shot at the superbly defiant dancer.

"Wrong again, big boy!" Rita answered insolently, though her cheeks were still chalky white. "He was alive when I came and alive when I left, as I seem to remember having told you before!"

Ferber said something to McMann in a low voice, and the detective frowningly studied two photographs of finger prints. Then: "I suppose Borden helped you look for the paste tube, Rita?"

The girl flushed. "No, he didn't. He went over to the cooler and got a drink while I was going through Miss Lester's desk."

"He didn't touch the desk?" McMann persisted strangely.

"No!"

"And yet," McMann said slowly, to no one in particular, "Borden's finger prints—or rather his right thumb print—is on top of the wooden handle of the bottom drawer of Miss Lester's desk. The other four fingers would be inserted beneath the long wooden handle, of course. That right, Ferber?"

"Yes. I didn't photograph the underside of the handles, but I can, by removing them," Ferber answered.

"Not necessary," McMann assured him. "Miss Lester, did Borden, to your knowledge, open the bottom drawer of your desk on Saturday?"

"No," Ruth answered. "To my knowledge, he never opened a drawer of my desk during the entire time I worked for him, but he may have when I was not there, of course. Benny Smith, the office boy, opened that drawer Saturday morning. He was looking for a towel, he said, when I asked him what he was doing at my desk. I'd just come out of Mr. Borden's office, after having taken dictation."

"That accounts for these thumb prints," Ferber said to McMann, pointing to a picture. "Found a number of them on the kid's desk."

"Any one else touch your desk Saturday that you know of?" McMann asked Ruth.

"No. I did, of course. I opened the bottom drawer, as I have told you, to get a paper cup to give Mrs. Borden a drink. She started to help me, but didn't touch the drawer—and she had on gloves, I remember," Ruth answered.

"One of Borden's thumb prints half obliterated by Rita's thumb print," McMann mused, in a low voice, that was just loud enough for Ruth's straining ears to catch. "That means he opened the drawer first—"

"Well, if he did, he did it before I came!" Rita cut in. "He certainly didn't touch that desk while I was with him."

Ruth's head spun with conjectures. If Borden had opened that bottom drawer on Saturday afternoon, after her departure, and before Rita's arrival, was it not possible that he had done so to get the gun, to protect him self against some threatened trouble—trouble arising from that mysterious telephone call which had kept him so long that he had missed his train? But Bill Cowan had testified that Borden had been connected with Jack Hayward's number! Had McMann, whose ability she was be ginning to respect as much as she feared it, arrived at the same conclusion? If so, he had again arrived at Jack Hayward as the most likely suspect. . . . Ruth forced her mind away from that too terrible possibility. Supposing Borden, fearful of an attack at the hands of some one who had not yet come into the investigation—for she herself was convinced that Jack had not talked to Borden over the phone or across the airshaft—had taken the gun from her desk. When Rita came—Ruth went on building up her suppositious case—the gun was on top of Borden's desk, handy for his defense against the person from whom he undoubtedly feared a visit. Else why should he have planned to remain all afternoon in his office, instead of spending the hours between trains with Rita? But that, she told herself despairingly, was built on the theory that Rita was telling the truth about the agreement between her and Borden to make the later train.

"Why suppose Rita had told the truth? She had lied so much! No, it was better to hold tight to facts. Borden had undoubtedly opened the bottom drawer of the desk. In all probability he had done so to get the gun kept there. Rita had come. She had quarreled with Borden. She had seen the gun on his desk. She had shot him to get the money he would not give her. Then Rita had robbed the body. Perhaps she was telling the truth about the paste— or part truth! Who could say how Rita's mind would function after she had killed Borden? The bill was all important. It was torn in two. In an office there would be paste. She had hunted for the paste in the outer office, and in the meantime the black pigeon—or one of his flock —had flown in through the open window, had dipped his tiny feet in the fresh flowing blood of the dead man, leaving telltale tracks behind.

But why had Rita come back into that death room to close the window? Ruth knit her brows in a terrific effort to think straight. Then light burst upon her. Rita had heard the flutter of the pigeon's wings or the sound of its body caroming against the glass of the upper sash and had run back into the private office, frightened half to death. She had seen the pigeon—or maybe several of them—on the window ledge, and had had a sudden horror of the feathered creatures pecking at Harry Borden's dead face. Instinctively cautious, even in her panic, she had closed the window with her gloved left hand, so that there were no finger prints. Ruth started to draw a deep breath of relief, when suddenly the whole structure top pled and fell, stricken by one question which her relentlessly logical mind insisted upon asking: if Rita had done all this, where did Jack's missing automatic fit into the picture?

Then hope thrust up its head again. Why try to fit Jack's gun into any theory of the murder? It was missing—true. But wasn't it entirely possible that Jack's gun had been stolen by a petty thief, prowling through the almost deserted office building, glad to lay his hands on any thing of value? The long arm of coincidence, of course, but wasn't real life full of just such amazing coincidences? But Ruth knew, even as she consoled herself with this philosophic reflection, that Detective Sergeant McMann would emit a loud roar of derisive laughter if she told him her theory. He might be trying, with true police conscientiousness, to bully Rita Dubois into confessing to both murder and robbery, but Ruth was sure that in his heart McMann believed the dancer had done nothing worse than rob a dead man's body, after Harry Borden had been killed by Jack Hayward, in a jealous rage.

The newly discovered evidence that Borden had had Ruth's gun in his possession that Saturday afternoon would do much, Ruth realized sickly, to confirm McMann's suspicions against Jack. He would argue, undoubtedly, that Borden and Jack had quarreled over the telephone—that inexplicable one sided conversation of Borden's which Bill Cowan had overheard when he had called Jack Hayward's number at ten minutes after two— and that consequently, fearing an attack upon his life, Borden had possessed himself of Ruth's gun, had gone to the open window with it in his hand, and had been shot down by Hayward before he could aim Ruth's weapon.

But—Ruth argued with herself desperately—if McMann believed this to be the truth about Borden's murder, how could he account for the disappearance of *her* gun? Would he be so stupid as to try to convince himself that Rita Dubois had stolen it, too, along with the money on Borden's body? Ruth herself was sure that if Rita had come into Borden's office and found him dead, with a gun lying on the floor, she would have concluded that he had committed suicide, would not have dreamed of touching the weapon with which he had done it, for fear of its being found in her possession and incriminating her. . . .

"Miss Lester!" McMann's harsh voice broke into the girl's troubled maze of theory and conjecture. "Do you know when the glass panels of these office doors were washed last?"

Ruth considered for a moment, then answered confidently: "On Friday. The window washer always comes on Friday, and does the door panels at the same time. It was late Friday afternoon."

"Was any other woman, besides yourself, Rita and Mrs. Borden in these offices after the window washer's visit?"

Ruth shook her head, her puzzled blue eyes taking in the fact that McMann's narrowed eyes were fixed upon a set of photographed finger prints. "No. Not while I was here, Mr. McMann."

"Well," McMann grunted, frowning, "some woman was here all right. She left her calling card on the glass panel of the door between this office and the outer one. Three fine finger prints." He reached for the phone, which was plugged up with police headquarters. "Hello! Captain Foster, please! McMann speaking . . . Oh, Captain, any report yet on Cleo Gilman? . . . *Is that so?*"

# CHAPTER FOURTEEN

RUTH LESTER'S hand tightened convulsively over Jack Hayward's as she listened, with incredulous hope, to McMann's half of the telephone conversation which the detective sergeant was carrying on with his superior officer at police headquarters.

"So Cleo skipped out Saturday noon, bag and baggage, eh?" McMann spoke into the mouthpiece of the telephone, his voice registering the frown which was beetling his thick brows and snarling the corners of his mouth. "Who's on the job? . . . Clay, eh? Put him on the phone if he's there now, please . . . Hello, Clay! What's the dope on this Gilman dame? Did she say where she was going? . . . No? . . . Oh, back Monday or Tuesday morning, hunh? Well, be on hand to welcome her home and tell her that McMann wants a chat with her. . . . Sure, go through her apartment! What do you think this is—a tea party?"

The detective slammed the receiver upon the hook, strode to the door between the private office and the outer office of the Borden suite. "Birdwell! Take Mrs. Borden and Miss Dubois down the hall and put them in Covey's charge until I need them again. He's still in that vacant suite, isn't he?"

"Yes, sir—interviewing tenants who could have heard the shot fired, sir," Birdwell answered in his weary voice. "Frank Ashe, Borden's manservant, waiting to see you, sir."

"All right—show him in," McMann directed, as he held the door wide for Mrs. Borden and Rita to pass through, the widow thanking him with a faint, sad smile, the dancer wrapping her fur coat about her slim body with assumed nonchalance, utterly belied by the chalky pallor of her face.

As a gray haired, anemic looking man was about to enter the private office, McMann held him back with an arm stretched across the doorway, and turned his head to address Jack Hayward:

"That's all for the present, Hayward. Thanks for the finger prints," and he grinned crookedly. "Guess you knew they wouldn't help us much, since you'd been here this morning after Miss Lester discovered the body. By the way, while you were out to lunch, I performed an interesting experiment." He reached out for the door and closed it in the manservant's face.

Jack Hayward's steady bronze brown eyes did not flicker, nor did his color change. "Yes?"

"Yes! . . . When I was in your office this morning, looking for the gun you seemed to be so sure I'd find in the bottom drawer of your desk and which wasn't there — oddly enough!—I found something else. A missing link, you might say," and the detective paused, his terrible, twisted grin widening until Ruth felt she must scream.

"That's interesting," Jack said evenly, despite the frantic warning of Ruth's tightened fingers upon his arm. "May I ask what it was?"

"Oh—nothing much," the detective grinned. "Just a nice long ten foot pole with a hook on the end of it— the kind of pole that's ordinarily used to pull windows down from the top, but which—as I took pains to prove— can be used very nicely for closing windows across an eight foot airshaft, if a chap gets just the right leverage. A nice useful sort of pole, if a fellow very badly wants a window closed and doesn't want to be seen walking along a hall and unlocking another fellow's door in order to close it. You found it very handy, didn't you, Hayward?"

Jack's handsome, tanned face darkened with anger, but his voice was steady as he answered: "I did not close Borden's window with a pole or in any other manner, McMann. There was no reason why I should. But it must have been a very interesting experiment. Did you also demonstrate to your own satisfaction how I robbed the body and secured Miss Lester's automatic, all with this very useful window pole?"

McMann's grin widened. "I admit that at noon I was a little bit worried about those details, but a charming visitor has pretty well cleared them up for me."

Ruth could remain silent no longer. Her voice quivered with anger as she lashed out at the self satisfied detective: "That's not fair, Mr. McMann! Rita Dubois has cleared Jack by insisting that Mr. Borden was alive when she came here Saturday afternoon at seventeen minutes after two, at which time Jack was with me in the McAlpin dining room."

The grin left McMann's broad, thin mouth. He looked at the angry, trembling girl gravely, almost compassionately. "I'm sorry, Miss Lester, but what Rita Dubois says doesn't mean *that* to me!" and the detective snapped his fingers. "You saw me catch her in lie after lie. The facts are all I'm interested in: Rita had a key to this office. She could have entered, whether Borden was alive or dead. She got from him—alive or dead—half of a five hundred dollar bill and five hundred more in smaller bills. At least we *know* she got the torn half of the five hundred dollar banknote, and we can take the other for granted, I think. Alive, Borden wouldn't have given her a cent until she'd come across—kept her part of the bargain, which was to go away with him and become his mistress. You heard him say so yourself. Therefore, she got the money from Borden dead, not Borden alive."

But Ruth was not defeated by the detective's logic. "Then you think she was so greedy that she stole my gun, too—walked out of here with the very weapon which she must have believed had killed Mr. Borden? And which did kill him! I *know* it did—"

McMann shrugged. "And Hayward's gun? What about that?"

Ruth tried to control her anger, to speak reasonably, convincingly: "Mr. McMann, I don't believe the disappearance of Mr. Hayward's gun has any connection at all with this case. He himself told you he owned it, where to look for it. Was that the action of a guilty man? Won't you work—just for the sake of fairness—on the theory that Mr. Hayward's gun was stolen by a petty thief, prowling through the building Saturday? There was a gun in *these* offices—please don't forget that! We know, from the thumb prints on the bottom drawer of my desk, that Mr. Borden opened that drawer, in all probability to get the gun to defend himself against threatened attack. Maybe he always kept it handy when he was alone in the office. I don't know! But he almost certainly had it in his possession or on his desk Saturday before he was killed. An unknown woman was in these offices sometime Saturday afternoon. You have her finger prints. I believe that Rita was telling the truth when she said that Borden was alive, that he gave her his half of the five hundred dollar bill to make his peace with her, for having missing the train to Winter Heaven. After all, she *had* kept her part of the bargain. She had waited for him at the station; he could not know that she would ditch him after getting the money. The five hundred dollars, for some reason, was of vital importance to Rita Dubois. Either Mr. Borden gave it to her of his own accord, or— she killed him in desperation when he refused. That is the only reason why Rita Dubois would have taken my gun away with her—because she had used it upon Harry Borden."

McMann had listened patiently, even respectfully to Ruth's long, passionately sincere speech. When she paused, breathless, he asked quietly: "You don't believe that Rita killed Borden, do you, Miss Lester?"

"No! I know she lied a lot, and that she was desperate for money, but I don't believe she killed him. Neither do I believe she robbed his dead body. What I do believe, Mr. McMann, is that Harry Borden's murderer—or murderess—has not yet been questioned."

McMann smiled, but not derisively. "Cleo Gilman? If she was here Saturday afternoon, she walked up—part of the way, at least. Moran, the elevator operator, seemed pretty sure that he had brought no other passengers to this floor."

"I wouldn't count too heavily on Micky Moran's memory, Mr. McMann," Ruth flashed. "And granting that Micky is infallible, isn't it reasonable to suppose that a person coming here to see Mr. Borden after a telephone quarrel with him, a person he feared and armed himself against, would have walked at least a flight or two, rather than be seen getting off the elevator right in front of Mr. Borden's offices?"

"Just a minute, Miss Lester," McMann brushed her question aside. "You refer to a *telephone quarrel*. Surely you're not forgetting that that telephone quarrel, or part of it, was overheard by Bill Cowan, when he was cut in on Hayward's busy line? How can you explain that? You don't think it was your petty thief, prowling through the Starbridge Building, who called up Borden and quarreled with him, after stealing Hayward's gun?"

Ruth looked staggered for a moment, then triumphant. "Telephone operators have been known to give wrong numbers as well as plugging new calls in on busy lines. Mr. Borden's telephone numbers are Pennsylvania 3500 and 3501. Mr. Hayward's number is Pennsylvania 3051. Mr. Cowan was formerly rather a close friend of Mr. Borden's. He could easily have given the operator the Borden number, which he must have called many times in the past, thinking that he was giving Mr. Hayward's number. Remember, he did not hear Jack's voice—only Borden's!"

McMann chuckled. "You're very clever, Ruth Lester. You can have a job under me any time you like. . . . That's all for the present, Hayward. You can get back to your work."

"Thanks!" Jack bowed ironically. Then, to Ruth, in a low voice: "You're a darling and I love you."

"All right, Ashe!" McMann called through the door by which Jack was leaving.

The gray haired, bloodless looking little man who had been Harry Borden's manservant slipped noiselessly, diffidently through the door, and took the chair which McMann indicated—the one opposite to his own—at Borden's desk.

"Sit down, Miss Lester," McMann invited. "I may need you. . . . Now, Ashe, how long had you been with Mr. Borden?"

"Ten months, sir."

"When did you last see your employer?"

"Saturday morning, sir. He left his apartment at half past nine, as usual. He told me he would be out of town for the week end, and that I was to pack his bags. I was to expect him for dinner Monday evening—him and a young lady," the valet answered.

"Did he say who the young lady was?"

"Yes, sir. He said Miss Dubois would dine with him."

"Where were you Saturday afternoon, Ashe?" McMann pounced suddenly.

The valet looked startled, then faintly indignant. "I, sir? I had lunch with my daughter—my married daughter, Mrs. Bernard Williams, in Washington Heights, and took her to a neighborhood movie—my daughter and her two children. At half past four her husband met us in the lobby of the theater and all of us—"

"All right, Ashe!" McMann interrupted the iron clad alibi impatiently. "Now tell me: have you any knowledge or suspicion as to who killed your 'master?"

The anemic little man straightened in his chair, then leaned forward slightly toward the detective as he said in a curiously impressive voice:

"Yes sir. I think I have, sir!"

# CHAPTER FIFTEEN

DETECTIVE SERGEANT MCMANN betrayed no surprise or pleasure when Frank Ashe, Borden's man servant made his startling assertion, but Ruth Lester leaned forward tensely, one hand trembling against her throat.

"So you think you know who killed Borden, Ashe. . . . Well, who was it?" McMann asked matter of factly.

"I don't know her name, sir, but I do know he was in mortal terror of a woman, sir," the valet answered earnestly.

"Tell me what you know, Ashe, and make it snappy," McMann directed, with pencil poised over a pad of scratch paper.

"Well, sir," the valet began, with diffident eagerness, "it happened on Christmas Eve. Mr. Borden was going to a big party at the Dancing Bear, with Miss Gilman, but to dinner and the theater first—"

"With Miss Cleo Gilman?" McMann interrupted sharply. "How do you know?"

"I heard him talking with Miss Gilman over the telephone about the party, sir," the valet answered readily. "He had had me call her number, as he frequently did. Miss Gilman was—" the man coughed apologetically— "Mr. Borden's lady friend until recently, sir, until he took a fancy to Miss Dubois, the dancer at the Golden Slipper, sir."

"You didn't let much slip past you, did you, Ashe?" McMann grinned. "Well, I'm glad you didn't. Now what happened on Christmas Eve?"

"Mr. Borden came home about six o'clock to dress for dinner, and Mr. Bailey was with him."

"Jake Bailey?" McMann cut in.

"Yes, sir, Mr. Jake Bailey. Mr. Borden never said so, but I got the idea that Mr. Bailey was a sort of bodyguard to Mr. Borden. I know that Mr. Bailey carried a gun, for I have seen it in his hip pocket when he'd take his coat off to play poker with Mr. Borden late at night sometimes, when Mr. Borden couldn't sleep and wanted company. A nervous sort of man, Mr. Borden was. On Christmas Eve the two of them came in together, and Mr. Borden told me to mix some cocktails. He wanted creme de menthe in them, and it happened that the bootlegger, who's on the third floor of our apartment hotel, though I hope, sir, you won't use this against him—"

"I'm not in the prohibition enforcement department," McMann grinned. "Go on. You went down for the stuff, eh, because the bootlegger was behind on his Christmas deliveries?"

"Why, yes, sir," the valet assented, surprised. "And knowing I'd be right back, and that Mr. Bailey was with Mr. Borden, I left the foyer door on the latch—clicked it, you know, to save the bother of unlocking it when I came back with my hands full. Mr. Borden wanted a few other things besides the creme de menthe, since I was going to the bootlegger's anyway. She must have been watching and waiting for her opportunity—"

"She? Who?" McMann broke in sharply.

"I don't know her name, sir, but the woman who was quarreling with Mr. Borden when I came back with the liquor, sir. The three of them—Mr. Borden, Mr. Bailey and the woman were in Mr. Borden's bedroom with the door closed when I got back. I could hear Mr. Borden's voice and the lady's voice and I knew they were quarreling, but I couldn't hear what they said. I didn't want to be mixed up in any trouble, sir, so I went about my business—mixing the cocktails that Mr. Borden had ordered. That was in the pantry, right off the dining room—"

"But you did hear the woman's voice?" McMann interrupted. "What sort of voice? High, low, harsh, soft?"

The valet hesitated, groping for words, and a faint flush crept up his anemic cheeks. "It's odd, sir, but I did notice her voice particularly, because I recognized it as one I'd heard over the telephone several times. A beautiful voice, sir, sort of—sort of like the deep notes of an organ, if you know what I mean."

Ruth leaned forward, too excited to keep out of it any longer. "A contralto voice, Mr. Ashe—musical, but low pitched?"

"That's it, miss, exactly!" the valet nodded gratefully. "Maybe she's telephoned here at his office, too. I take it you were his secretary, miss? He mentioned that he had a little bit of a blond girl for his secretary, but he didn't—didn't say—"

"What a little beauty she is?" McMann helped him out, chuckling. "Yes, Miss Lester was Mr. Borden's secretary, Ashe. You say this mysterious female with the contralto voice telephoned Borden frequently before Christmas Eve?"

"Not frequently, but several times, sir. The first time, although she wouldn't give her name, I put Mr. Borden on the phone, and he told me when he'd hung up as quick as if the receiver burned his ear, that he'd fire me if I ever did it again. After that, the three or four times she called, I mean, I always said my master was out, for I couldn't mistake that voice. But once she changed her voice completely, so that I was fooled. Said she was Miss Gilman, and made her voice sound almost like Miss Gilman's, too. So of course I called Mr. Borden to the phone, but he didn't fire me, under the circumstances, though he bawled me out proper for having let him in for it."

"All right, Ashe. Get along with your story," McMann directed impatiently. "You're sure this was the same woman—I mean, that the woman who slipped in after you'd left the door unlocked was the woman Borden wouldn't talk to on the telephone?"

"Yes, sir. Sure of that, sir," the valet nodded emphatically. "As I was saying, I mixed the cocktails, and just as I was shaking them I saw, through the archway between the dining room and the living room, a sight that fair turned me sick, sir." The valet paused dramatically.

"Well, what was it?" McMann demanded.

"A woman being half dragged, half carried, from the bedroom through the living room to the foyer," the valet said impressively. "Mr. Borden holding her up by one arm, Mr. Bailey by the other. She looked like she was drunk or asleep, but it wasn't that, for there was blood on her mouth, which Mr. Bailey wiped off twice as they crossed the living room. Knocked out, she was, sir."

"What did she look like—hair, eyes, complexion, clothes?" McMann rapped out, thoroughly interested at last.

"I couldn't see so plain at that distance, sir, but I had the idea she was not old and not young, and her eyes were closed, so I couldn't say as to the color of them. She was wearing one of those little tightfitting hats, but there was some dark hair—black, maybe—against her cheeks. Very white, they were, sir, in spite of her rouge. As to clothes I couldn't say, except that she looked like a lady, sir—dressed fine, but quiet, in a dark cloth coat, I believe, with a fur collar, but I couldn't be sure. They stopped at the door and I heard Mr. Borden say something to Mr. Bailey, then Mr. Borden held her up while Mr. Bailey came running for some of the brandy I'd just bought from the bootlegger. He spoke pretty rough to me, sir, told me to get into the kitchen and stay there till I was called for. When I came out, Mr. Borden having called me from the dining room, he was alone. He took two or three drinks, one right after the other, and then Mr. Bailey came back. I gathered he'd taken the poor lady down and put her in a taxi, after she'd been brought to a little with the brandy."

"Any conversation between Bailey and Borden about the woman, that you overheard?" McMann demanded, when the valet paused.

"Yes, sir. While I was pouring out drinks for both of them, Mr. Borden said to Mr. Bailey: 'Jake,' he said—he always called him Jake—'that was a rotten thing to do, but honest to God, I thought she was pulling a gun on me when she opened her handbag. And next time it'll be a gun—if there is any next time.' And Mr. Bailey laughed, like he was trying to make Mr. Borden feel better, and said, 'You let Jake take care of her, Harry, and there won't be any next time. Either that, or give her what she wants.' Mr. Borden slammed his fist down on the side board and said, 'I'll be damned if I do!' And then he noticed me and told me to run his bath. And that's all, sir, except that after that, until last Friday night, Mr. Bailey slept in the apartment, and hardly let Mr. Borden out of his sight."

"Did the woman telephone again?" McMann asked, frowning mightily.

"No sir. Nor come back either, so far as I know."

"Do you know Mrs. Borden by sight, Ashe?" McMann asked suddenly.

"Yes, sir. Mr. Borden sent me to his wife's home on Christmas day with presents for the children, and I talked with her then. She sent Mr. Borden a gift, sir, though he hadn't sent anything with her name on it."

"You're sure Mr. Borden's visitor was not Mrs. Borden?"

"Absolutely sure, sir. There's no resemblance at all, sir, except that both the ladies may be about the same age," the valet answered positively.

For half an hour longer the detective quizzed the valet on every possible phase of Borden's life, but beyond the fact that Borden had entertained rather frequently, giving "wild parties" in his apartment, Ashe could tell nothing of importance. From him, however, McMann got the names of three of the dead man's male friends, though Ashe seemed dubious when asked to choose "friends" from among the murdered promoter's host of convivial companions.

"And where is Jake Bailey, Ashe?" McMann concluded his rapid fire grilling of the valet.

"That I couldn't say, sir. He left Friday night for a bit of vacation, since Mr. Borden was to be away for the week end. He had given up his room at the Mills Hotel, where he was staying until Christmas Eve, and was staying with Mr. Borden nights, as I've told you. I expect he'll be back tonight, sir, unless he stays away to keep from being questioned. A man don't relish being a witness in a case like this, sir."

"You're right, Ashe, and thanks for coming in," McMann said, extending his hand with sudden heartiness. "Stay on at Borden's apartment for the present and let me know anything at all that develops. The police department will take charge of his mail, of course. Give my men any assistance you can when they go through Borden's apartment tonight. I may be along myself. Of course you know you're not to leave town until this thing is cleared up?"

"Yes, sir," the valet admitted gravely, as he sidled diffidently toward the door.

"Well!" McMann drew a deep breath and flashed a humorous glance at Ruth Lester. "There are enough women in this case to make up a Ziegfeld chorus. It shouldn't be hard to get a line on a woman with a voice like you and Ashe describe. I believe the poor old duffer fell in love with her voice. I thought he was going to bust into poetry. You say she called Borden at ten o'clock Saturday morning?"

"Yes. Just before he came in. When he asked if there were any calls, I said that the woman with the beautiful contralto voice had called and he said something that I've just remembered: 'That voice may sound beautiful to you, but I'd rather listen to a riveting machine,' and he shuddered, as if the thought of her frightened or disgusted him—"

She was interrupted by the sound of a scuffle in the outer office, and of a body hurling itself against the communicating door. A moment later the door was torn open and Benny Smith, fighting off the restraining hands of Detective Birdwell, plunged into the private office.

"I wanta see Miss Lester, I tell you! Turn me loose, you big stiff! I gotta see Miss Lester—oh, gosh, Ruth! Gee!" the boy cried weakly, as Ruth ran toward him. He put out his hands blindly as if he were going to faint. . . .

"Here's Ruth, Benny!" Ruth cried, flinging her arms about the swaying figure of the seventeen year old office boy. "Oh, Benny dear, what *is* the matter?"

The boy clung to the girl weakly, his pale gray eyes, suffused with tears, searching her face in an agony of suspense. "Aw, Ruth, they ain't pinched you, have they?"

"No, Benny, no!" Ruth was laughing and sobbing at the same time. "Who said I'd been arrested?"

"Micky Moran. I'm gonna knock his block off, the big liar," Benny gasped, swiping a sleeve across his unmanly tears. "I knowed *you* didn't do it—"

"And how did you know, Benny?" McMann demanded, in a deceptively casual and friendly voice, from his chair at Borden's desk. "Come on over here and tell me all about it, if you're able to walk. . . . Been sick all day, Benny? Just what seems to be the trouble?"

"Who wants to know?" the office boy countered in a quavering, belligerent voice.

"This is Detective Sergeant McMann, in charge of the investigation of Mr. Borden's murder, Benny," Ruth told the boy gently.

"Pleased to meetcha!" Benny slumped into the chair the detective was indicating and jerked his head in a funny, frightened nod.

"Now that we've been properly introduced, Benny," McMann grinned, "suppose we start all over again. Why didn't you come to work this morning?"

"Cause I was sick, mister," Benny quavered. "Honest to God I was! Sick to my stummick. Guess I et too many hot dogs yesterday. Or maybe it was ptomaine poisoning."

"Or maybe—" and McMann leaned toward the boy across the desk—"the thought of killing a man sort of uspet your stomach!"

Benny shrank from McMann's narrowed menacing eyes as far as the back of his chair would permit. "Me?" Benny's adolescent voice quavered and broke. "I ain't killed nobody! Gosh! You don't acshully think I killed Mr. Borden, do you, mister?"

"Please, Mr. McMann!" Ruth begged. "Don't frighten him to death. Of course Benny didn't do it! Why in the world should he?" And she laid a hand protectingly, fondly upon the boy's shaking shoulder and challenged the detective with flashing blue eyes.

"When did you last see Henry Borden, Benny?" the detective demanded sternly.

"Saturday, 'bout half past one," the boy answered sullenly. "I had to come back to the office for something I'd forgot—"

"What was it?" the detective interrupted harshly.

To Ruth's amazement, color flooded the boy's pale, freckled face. "I—I—just something—I don't remember," he stammered.

"Listen here, my boy, I'll clap the handcuffs on you too quick to talk about if you don't answer my questions and answer them truthfully!" McMann threatened, emphasizing his words with a thump of his fist upon the dead man's desk. "What did you come back for?"

Benny cowered lower in his chair and shivered, his prominent, pale gray eyes looking wildly toward Ruth for help. "Tell the truth, Benny," the girl urged, pity and fear in her wide blue eyes.

"I—I come back to get Miss Lester's—gun," the boy gasped. "I took it Saturday before last for target practice out in the country and brought it back Monday morning, without Ruth knowing nothing about it. I didn't mean no harm—"

"Oh!" The exclamation seemed to burst from Ruth's despairing heart, rather than from her throat. If Benny had taken her automatic, McMann would of course consider the mystery entirely solved. With that troublesome second weapon thus eliminated, how could she expect the detective to have any doubt that it was Jack Hayward's gun which had fired the fatal shot? And it was she who had urged Benny to tell the truth!

"All right, Benny!" McMann interrupted harshly. "Where's the gun now? Did you bring it in with you?"

At Ruth's cry of anguish the office boy had raised his terror stricken eyes to search her face. But at the detective's question he faced his tormentor, his chin thrust out belligerently. "I don't know where it is! I didn't take it Saturday, 'cause it wasn't there! And that's the truth, so help me God!"

Ruth, in her joy, could have kissed every freckle on the homely young face, but the detective's savage effort to make the boy confess that he had lied killed that joy in the moment of its birth.

Finally, since the boy, miserably ill and frightened though he was, stuck stubbornly to his story, McMann tried a new tack: "And you saw Borden, did you, when you came back to swipe Miss Lester's gun?"

"Wasn't gonna swipe it; was just gonna borrow it," Benny quavered. "Yes, I seen him all right. He was settin' at his desk. I seen him through the door. Old Minnie left it open when she was emptyin' his wastebasket. I was closin' the drawer of Miss Lester's desk, and he thought I was her, 'cause he called out, 'That you, Miss Lester?' and I stepped into the middle of the office, so's he could see me, and I said, 'No, sir, it's me, Mr. Borden.' And he yelled out, 'Then what the devil are you hangin' around here for? What are you lookin' for in Miss Lester's desk?' And I said I was lookin' for a stamp, and he said to get t'ell out of here, and—and I beat it. An' 'at's all—honest to God!"

"Benny," Ruth asked quickly, before McMann could spring his next question, "did you see my pistol on Mr. Borden's desk when you were talking to him?"

"You keep out of this, Miss Lester!" McMann said sharply. "This lovesick young puppy would swear black was white if he thought you wanted him to."

"I didn't see the gun, but I wasn't looking at his desk," Benny answered the question, in defiance of the detective, but his freckled young face was beet red at the charge McMann had cruelly made against him.

"Did any one see you leave Borden's office?" McMann shot at the boy.

"Sure! Old Minnie, the cleaning woman. She come back with the wastebaskets just as Mr. Borden was yellin' at me to get out."

"And just what time did you come back?" McMann sprung his trap casually.

"Back?" Benny echoed, blankly. "I didn't come back, and if anybody says I did, he's a double dog liar!"

"Then I suppose you've got an alibi for the rest of Saturday afternoon?" McMann suggested, his narrowed eyes holding the boy's grimly.

"You mean—what did I do Saturday afternoon?" Benny was obviously stalling for time. "I—I went to a movie— down on Fourteenth Street, 'nen I went home to supper—"

"Went to a movie alone?"

"Naw—with a frail—I mean, with a girl—"

"Her name?"

"I—I don't know her name. A dizzy little kid I picked up," Benny confessed, in an agony of embarrassment. "She said I could call her Fritzie, 'cause 'at wasn't her name, but what she liked to be called. A tough baby. I didn't try to date her up," he added, with a comical attempt to confide, as man to man, in the scowling detective.

"Miss Lester," McMann addressed the girl suddenly, "I wish you'd go down the hall to that vacant suite where Detective Covey is stationed and ask him to send Minnie Cassidy, the cleaning woman, to me if she's come in."

"Certainly, Mr. McMann," Ruth agreed, trying to smile cheerfully, though she was convinced that the detective was merely resorting to a ruse to get rid of her while he grilled Benny Smith on the subject of Borden's unwelcome advances to her.

She found the cocky little detective with his feet on a rickety desk, abandoned by the recent occupants of the office suite. Several men, whom she recognized as tenants of the Starbridge Building, stood about the desk, smoking, exchanging theories.

"Hello, Beautiful!" Detective Covey greeted her, his bright eyes roving her small body appreciatively. "You and the Big Cheese having a good time down there? Believe me, child, he musta taken a shine to you, to let you in on this investigation like he has."

"Mr. McMann has been very kind to me," Ruth said, forcing herself to smile. "Has Minnie Cassidy, the clean ing woman, come in yet, Mr. Covey? Mr. McMann wants to see her."

"And what a treat that'll be!" Covey chortled. "Yeah, she's in the building. I saw her a minute or two ago. She's changing her clothes to get on the job. I told her to come back here and I'd take her to the sergeant. "Wanta wait? Mrs. Borden and Rita are in there—" and he jerked his thumb toward the inner office of the suite—"but why not brighten up the day for old Jim Covey?" and he swung out of the chair he had borrowed from the next door office and pushed it toward her invitingly.

Ruth seated herself, glanced around the circle of men diffidently, then turned the full glory of her wide blue eyes upon the little detective. "Did all these men hear the shot fired, Mr. Covey?" she asked innocently.

Covey chuckled. "Five of 'em think maybe they did and maybe they didn't and if you can get any two of 'em to agree on the time, I'll give you my nice silver shield. According to these birds—no offense, fellows!—guns were popping off in the Starbridge Building last Saturday afternoon from half past one to half past three o'clock, but just try to pin one of these guys down, Miss Lester, and he'll crawfish instanter—tell you that at the time he thought it was the backfire of an automobile, and that he really didn't pay no attention. Can't say I blame a chap with a business of his own to look after—nobody's fool enough to want to testify in a murder case that may drag out for weeks and be tried two or three times. Ho, hum! It's a great game, Beautiful!" and he grinned impishly at Ruth. "But it has its compensations. . . . Have you seen this extra?" he added, reaching for a paper which he had tossed to the floor beside his desk, "Got a swell snapshot of you—you didn't duck your head quick enough," he chuckled. "Your sweetie looks sore enough to bite nails in two, but he's a good looking guy at that. How the sob sisters will love *him!* Wanta see, girlie?"

"No," Ruth shuddered, warding off the proffered sheet with a trembling hand. "I—I'll go back to my office now. Will you please send Minnie Cas—"

"Here's the old girl now!" Covey interrupted cheerfully. "All togged out in the what the well dressed scrub woman will wear. Took your time, didn't you, Mother Machree?"

Minnie Cassidy's work roughened hands plucked nervously at the baggy front of her calico dress. "I'm sorry to have kept you waiting, sir, but one of the cleaning ladies was sick—kinda fainty, and I—"

"Sure, sure!" Covey interrupted, chuckling. "Wanted your bit of gossip, didn't you? Well, I can't blame you. It ain't every 'scrub lady' that can brag of being one of the last to see a murdered man alive. Come along now and have a good time telling it all over again to Detective Sergeant McMann. . . . No, reckon I'd better stick right here and keep an eye on Mrs. Borden and Ritzy Rita. Can't tell what might happen."

"I'll take Minnie to Mr. McMann," Ruth volunteered eagerly, so eagerly that the little bantam rooster of a detective gave her a long, measuring glance before he opened the door and permitted her and Minnie Cassidy to pass into the corridor.

# CHAPTER SIXTEEN

POOR dearie!" Minnie Cassidy, the cleaning woman, murmured commiseratingly, as she and Ruth started together down the hall toward the Borden offices. "They do say the fool cops are sayin' your man did it, but as me and Letty was tellin' each other not five minutes ago, Mr. Hayward is not the boy as would hurt a fly—so kind hearted and open handed he is. Just you pray the Blessed Mother, miss, and—oh, Lordy! What's that?"

"Flashlights," Ruth informed her, behind hands she had flung up to cover her face.

"Me picture in the papers?" Minnie cried, as delighted as a child. "And me with this old calico mother hubbard on!"

"Let's run!" Ruth begged, dragging at Minnie's gnarled old hand. Patrolman Biggers, still on guard outside the Borden offices, grinned sympathetically as he swung open the door for them.

"Mr. McMann is in Mr. Borden's private office, Minnie. I'll take you in—oh!" she broke off, with a startled exclamation, then ran to her own desk, where Benny Smith was sitting, his head bowed on his outflung arms, terrible sobs shaking his thin, adolescent body. "What's the matter, Benny? Benny dear, what is the matter?" she implored, stroking his sandy hair.

"The big stiff! The big old bully!" Benny sobbed. "I'll punch his nose through his face, I will—"

The door to the private office opened, and McMann's curt voice interrupted any confidence that Benny might have been about to make.

"Come in, Miss Lester! Is this Minnie Cassidy?"

"Missus Minnie Cassidy!" the cleaning woman corrected the detective with surprising spirit. "And ye're

Tommy McMann. Me husband—God rest his soul!—was a rookie along with ye, Tommy McMann. Many's the poker game he's won your good money off ye and brought it home to Minnie Cassidy."

McMann chuckled and thrust out a big hand which Minnie Cassidy seized and shook warmly. "So you're Tim Cassidy's widow, Minnie! Poor Tim! As grand a 'big foot' as ever walked a beat! Come in, Minnie. Miss Lester will stand by and see that I don't use any third degree methods on you."

"As if ye could!" Minnie wagged her head at him derisively. "I'm on to ye cops, I am! Hot air and bluff, the lot of ye. ... Now what did ye want to know, Tommy McMann? ... So ye're a detective sergeant now? My Tim would a been your Captain if the gangsters hadn't got him."

"I'm sure of it, Minnie!" McMann answered heartily, with a humorous lift of his bushy eyebrows toward Ruth, who had slipped into a chair beside the one he had drawn up for Minnie Cassidy. "You cleaned these offices on Saturday, Minnie?"

"That I did! And not a slipshod job like most of the girls get by with on a Saturday," Minnie answered emphat ically. "Emptied the wastebaskets, wiped off the desks and window sills and chairs with me oiled rag—"

"That's fine, Minnie!" McMann'grinned. "You left us a fine surface for finger prints. But to go back a little— "Was Mr. Borden in this office when you came to clean, and at what time did you come in here?"

"That he was, and looking like he'd live to be a hundred!" Minnie answered. "It was near the death of me, and yes, of Letty, too, when Mr. Coghlan, the superintendent of the building, told us the poor gentleman had been murdered."

"What time was it when you cleaned these offices, if you remember, Minnie?" McMann was plainly trying to be patient with his former colleague's widow.

"Half past one it was when I finished in 713, Mr. Green's offices across the hall. They've got a big fancy clock in the front office, and I noticed the time by it. Then I come straight over here, and let myself in with my passkey—"

"The door was locked?"

"That it was, and I thought Mr. Borden was gone. I knew Miss Ruth had left, for me and Letty seen her and her young man—and a nicer man ain't in the land of the living than Mr. Hayward, Tommy McMann!—seen them at the elevator, we did."

"When?"

"Just before I went into Mr. Green's offices—musta been fifteen or twenty minutes past one," Minnie an swered readily. "So I thought nobody wasn't in here and I come in. There wasn't no light on in Mr. Borden's private office—not that he needs it, what with two windows on the street and one on the airshaft. Anyways, there wasn't no light, so I opened the door without knockin' and then I seen Mr. Borden a settin' at his desk, and I started to back out, saying, 'Excuse me, sir, I didn't know ye was still here,' and he said, 'Come on in. I'm going to be here till two. You won't bother me.' "

"Pleasant, was he?" McMann demanded. "Didn't look worried or angry?"

"He spoke sort of short, but Lordy, I'm used to that," Minnie confessed resignedly. "I went on about me work, and was carryin' out his wastebasket when Benny, his office boy, come in."

"Tell me exactly what passed between Benny and his boss," McMann directed.

"Now, Tommy McMann, ye're not going to make me help ye scare that poor kid to death!" Minnie assured the detective spiritedly. "I didn't pay no attention to what passed between 'em—none of my business. I took out the wastebasket and when I come back Mr. Borden had stepped out. Well the telephone rang so I answered it and says "Mr. Borden will be back in a minute,' and she

said, 'Then I'll hold the wire, thank you,' as sweet and
ladylike as you please—"

"Wait!" Ruth cried, leaning toward Minnie excitedly.

"What kind of voice did she have, Minnie? Oh, please
try to remember! Was it?—"

"Just a minute, Miss Lester!" the detective reproved
her sternly. "No leading the witness, if you please.
Describe the woman's voice, if you can, Minnie. Anything
at all unusual about it?"

Minnie Cassidy reached out and patted Ruth's hand,
as if to console her for McMann's sharpness. "As sweet a
voice as ever I heard, Tommy McMann! Put me in mind of
a singer I heard one time on my daughter's radio—an alto
singer, she was—"

"The woman with the contralto voice!" Ruth cried
triumphantly.

"Alto or contralto, it was a pretty voice, and fair did
me good to hear it," Minnie asserted cheerfully.

"And did Borden talk with her when he returned?"
McMann demanded.

"No, that he didn't! He done the same as you've
done— asked me what kind of voice the lady had, and I
told him same as I've told ye, and he said, sharp and real
mad like, 'Hang up the receiver!' and I was gonna do like
he told me, though it went agin the grain I can tell you,
when he said, 'Wait a minute! Tell her to call me again in
fifteen or twenty minutes. I can't talk to her now. I'm
expecting my wife any minute,' he says, 'but don't tell her
that,' he says real quick."

"And what—" McMann leaned forward, betraying al
most as much suspense as Ruth—"exactly what did the
lady answer?"

"Let me see now," Minnie Cassidy considered
leisurely, immensely enjoying the fact that "Tommy"
McMann, who had once been a "rookie cop" with her
husband and who was now a detective sergeant, was
hanging on her words. "Jist what did the sweet voiced
lady say? Seeing as how she was on the telephone, and

not here to kill the poor man, I reckon it won't do her no harm for me to tell ye what she said, Tommy McMann. She said, 'Tell Mr. Borden that if he is wise, he will talk to me when I call again.' Then she hung up the receiver, and I told Mr. Borden what she'd said and then I took me things—"

"Just a minute, Minnie," McMann interrupted. "What did Borden say when you gave him that threatening message?"

"He didn't say nothing—just grunted and slammed the door behind him when he went back into his private office. And that's the last sight I ever had of the poor man, so help me God!" Minnie answered fervently.

"As you left Borden's offices, did you see anyone getting off the elevator or knocking at Borden's outer door?"

"That I didn't," Minnie answered. "I took my things down the hall and left them just outside the door of Mr. Feldblum's office till I could go to the supply room, where us cleaning women keep our pails and brooms and rags and suchlike. My bottle of furniture polish was empty and Mr. Feldblum is mighty particular about his desk, so—"

"Could you have heard a shot fired in this office while you were in the supply room?" McMann demanded.

"That I couldn't, Tommy McMann—and I didn't!" Minnie Cassidy answered emphatically. "If I had, I wouldn't have paid no attention. I'd have said to meself, I would—'That's another of them dratted automobiles, explodin' like a pistol shot'—"

"All right!" McMann shrugged, frowning at the notes on the case which he was shuffling through his big, thick hands. Suddenly a memo in his own handwriting caught his eye. "When you were coming out of Feldblum's offices you saw Mrs. Borden leaving. That's right, isn't it? She's already told me a scrubwoman saw her."

"I did see a lady come out," Minnie acknowledged, "but I didn't know it was Mrs. Borden till I saw her pictures in the papers. One of the cleaning ladies had all the papers, and I pointed to Mrs. Borden's picture and told her I'd seen her leaving Mr. Borden's office when I was coming out of Mr. Feldblum's reception room, down the hall."

Ruth, whose mind had been a welter of speculation, shot through with vivid rays of hope that at last real progress was being made in the investigation, suddenly leaned toward Minnie Cassidy, forestalling McMann's next question with one of her own:

"Was there some reason why you noticed Mrs. Borden particularly, Minnie?"

McMann leaned back in his chair, tacitly giving his consent to question and answer.

Minnie hedged. "With so few comin' and goin' on Saturday afternoon, why shouldn't I notice her? And I don't believe for a minute that the poor lady would shoot the father of her two little children—"

"Was Mrs. Borden crying, Minnie?" McMann suddenly interrupted. "I must have the truth—"

"Well, cryin' she was then," Minnie admitted belligerently. "And why shouldn't she be? Separated from her husband and still lovin' him, like the papers say. Not takin' on, jist dabbin' at her eyes with her handkerchief, then pressin' it hard against her mouth."

Detective Sergeant McMann strode to the door and directed Birdwell, in the outer office, to send for Mrs. Borden, who was being detained down the hall by Detective Covey. While awaiting the arrival of the newly made widow, the sergeant resumed his questioning of Minnie Cassidy.

"Now think hard, Minnie," he directed, with brusque kindliness. "Did you see anyone else at all enter or leave these offices on Saturday afternoon?"

"Do ye think I had nothin' to do but watch Mr. Borden's offices, Tommy McMann?" Minnie demanded in dignantly. "I had me work to do—"

"Answer the question, please, Minnie," McMann interrupted impatiently.

"Haven't I answered it?" Minnie was curiously truculent.

"Did you see the dancer whose picture is in the papers, too?" McMann tried a new method. "Rita Dubois, her name is. She's admitted she was here, so you needn't be afraid of getting her into trouble," he added, with some what weary sarcasm. The scrubwoman's reluctance to give any information which would incriminate another was undoubtedly wearing his patience thin.

"That I didn't," Minnie retorted emphatically. "When I finished Mr. Feldblum's offices I went around into the other wing of the building, and was busy there until about half past two, then I went to the supply room again, to rest meself a bit, though ye needn't be tellin' Mr. Coghlan I said that. He thinks us girls is all wheel horses—"

"I shan't tell on you, Minnie," McMann chuckled. "Oh, all right, Birdwell. Show Mrs. Borden in. ... Sorry to bother you again, Mrs. Borden," he apologized brusquely, as the pale faced widow slipped into the room, "but this morning I neglected to ask you how you spent the rest of Saturday afternoon—from the time you left your husband, I mean. About ten minutes of two that was, I believe?"

Mrs. Borden answered in a quiet, controlled voice: "As I told you, sir, I had left my children at the McAlpin Hotel, while I came to see my—my husband. I had left them in the ladies' parlor, in charge of the maid on duty there. She had told me she would be on duty until two o'clock, when she would be relieved by another maid. I promised to be back by two, and I was, for she was still there, though she left immediately after I had tipped her for her services. I took charge of the children myself then, and was with them continuously until they went to bed in the evening. The three of us attended a motion picture downtown—a war picture that my little son was eager to see."

"I see," McMann commented noncommitally. Then, in rapid succession, he fired a half dozen questions designed to pick a flaw in the widow's alibi, his flying pencil making notes of the detailed information she gave him as to the name of the theater, the time she and her children had arrived there, even the musical and dancing numbers of the prologue which had introduced the feature picture. Ruth knew, as the detective left the private office for a conference with Birdwell in the outer room, that every detail of that alibi would be carefully checked, that even Harry Borden's children would be pitilessly cross examined, but she had little hope that Mrs. Borden's alibi would be shaken—and, looking at the sad faced, bereaved woman, Ruth could not but be glad. . . .

McMann returned, sat down, again faced the widow, who was standing, with one hand clenched tightly upon the back of the chair in which Minnie Cassidy sat. She had refused a chair for herself. "Mrs. Borden, Minnie Cassidy here has corroborated what you said about your seeing her when you left your husband's office about ten minutes to two on Saturday. But—she also says that she saw you wiping tears from your eyes. Is that true?"

The pale face quivered, but the leaf brown eyes were steady. "It is true. I don't think I ever left my husband's presence—after our separation—without tears in my eyes. I loved him, and grieved that he would not return to me and our children."

The detective looked at her steadily for a long minute, then said abruptly. "That's all, Mrs. Borden. You may go home to your children, but of course you are not to leave town and are to hold yourself available for further questioning at any time."

"Thank you," Mrs. Borden said in a low voice, as she turned toward the door.

"Please, Mr. McMann," Ruth begged urgently, "may I ask Mrs. Borden just one question?" The detective nodded, frowning slightly, and Ruth turned eagerly toward the murdered man's widow. "Mrs. Borden, I know it is painful for you to have to think of such things now, but won't you please tell Mr. McMann whether Mr. Borden—to your knowledge—knew a woman with a peculiarly beautiful contralto voice?"

Color flamed suddenly in the pale, aristocratic face of Harry Borden's widow. She drew in her breath sharply and her eyelids fluttered, before she answered, almost haughtily: "I am afraid I can give you little help along—those lines, Miss Lester. Naturally Mr. Borden's intimate women friends were not known to me—socially." She opened the door, passed into the outer office, closed the door behind her.

Ruth shrank in her chair as if the widow's words had been blows in her face. But beneath the throb of humiliation two things clamored for recognition—the fact that Mrs. Borden had not really answered her question and the suspicion, amounting to a certainty, that the widow had known only too well the answer to that question. But why should she try to shield, by concealing her name, one of the women who had undoubtedly possessed Harry Borden's love—temporarily at least—after his wife had lost it? Ruth suddenly felt too tired and bewildered to bear any more, but she raised her head, listened wearily as McMann concluded his interview with Minnie Cassidy.

"That's all, Minnie," McMann was saying. "And here's something to pay for a special mass for old Tim's soul, God bless him. . . . How's the baby, by the way? I remember Tim was always bragging about his girl child—"

"Baby?" Minnie cackled. "Ye should see her now! Growed up on me, she did, Tommy McMann. Twenty come June, and as pretty a lass as ye'd hope to see. Ain't that right, Miss Ruth?"

"Rose is a little beauty," Ruth admitted, as heartily as weariness and discouragement would permit. "And a good girl, too. She helps Minnie here with her work, when the rheumatism is bad."

"A good girl," Minnie repeated, tears springing into her watery old eyes. "I'll tell Rose ye was askin' for her, Tommy McMann. It's been hard, with Tim gone and all, but I've tried to do everything for the childer that Tim woulda done."

"And I'm sure you have," McMann agreed absently, his eyes on his notes again. "What's the name of the woman who cleans Hayward's offices? . . . Letty Miller—that's right. Send her in to me, won't you, Minnie?"

Suddenly Ruth remembered something—something which might be of vital importance to Jack Hayward. Her weariness routed by hope, she eagerly awaited the arrival of Letty Miller. . . .

# CHAPTER SEVENTEEN

MINNIE CASSIDY must have found Letty Miller already at work in some office that had closed early for the day, for when the cleaning woman who "did" Jack Hayward's offices appeared within three minutes, she was carrying her broom, floor mop and pail, filled with oily dusting rags. Birdwell, the detective, opened the door for her, and was hailed by his chief, McMann.

"Any further report from Clay on Cleo Gilman?"

"No, sir."

"See if headquarters has got any line yet on Jake Bailey, Borden's bodyguard," McMann directed, then, as Birdwell withdrew, the detective sergeant glanced negligently at Letty Miller. "Come on over here. I won't bite you. . . . Now, take that chair, and don't fidget; I'm not going to keep you long. You'll have plenty of time to do your work. You're Letty Miller, the woman who regularly cleans John C. Hayward's offices?"

Letty's thin, calico clad body accepted the support of the very edge of the chair McMann indicated. Her faded, tired face was raised anxiously; faded brown eyes peered at the detective nearsightedly through ugly, steel rimmed spectacles. Gray haired, frail, timid—no wonder, Ruth thought, Letty Miller had appealed to Jack's tender heart, so that he had tipped her more than he could afford. Was it in her power now to repay him for his kindness? It was hard for Ruth not to take the witness out of the detective sergeant's hands. . . .

"Yes, sir," Letty quavered.

"You cleaned Mr. Hayward's offices last Saturday afternoon?"

"Yes, sir."

"At what time, or approximately what time?"

The cleaning woman pursed her colorless lips in thought, then answered slowly: "I couldn't say exactly, sir, but it was after half past two, because I was in another suite at half past two and happened to look at the clock and remember that I still hadn't cleaned Mr. Hayward's offices, though ordinarily they're among the first I get to."

Ruth's cold hands gripped each other fiercely as she waited for McMann to put his next question: "And why didn't you clean Mr. Hayward's offices earlier, in your regular routine?"

"Because Mr. Hayward came in when I was just ready to begin," Letty answered, with a tiny flash of defiance.

"And ordered you out, eh?" McMann suggested significantly. .

"No, sir," Letty retorted, almost spiritedly. "He told me to go right ahead with my work, but just then his phone rang and while he was answering it I took my things and left."

"Very considerate of you, I'm sure," McMann commented drily. "And what time was this—when Mr. Hayward returned, I mean?"

Again Letty Miller pursed her lips in thought. "I couldn't say to the minute, sir, but it must have been about ten minutes to two. We come on at twelve on Saturdays, but we do halls and baseboards and lavatories until the tenants begin to leave at one. And last Saturday I'd done four suites of offices before I went in to do Mr. Hayward's—and seen him, like I told you. So it must have been pretty near two—say from fifteen to five minutes of two."

"You like Mr. Hayward mighty well, don't you, Letty? He's been good to you—about tips and so on?" McMann asked suddenly.

Letty's lined, pale face flushed a dull red. "Of course I like him, sir. He's a good, kind gentleman, and I'm sure—"

"I thought so!" McMann interrupted grimly. "All right, what next? When did Mr. Hayward leave? I suppose you're going to be very helpful and tell exactly when he did leave?"

Both Ruth and the scrubwoman glared at him then, but McMann did not seem to mind. He did seem a little non plussed, however, when Letty answered defiantly: "No, sir, I'm not, because I don't know when he did leave! I wasn't in that corridor then. When Mr. Hayward come back I took my pail and mop and broom and went around the corner to an office I knew was closed for the day, because it's always closed all day Saturday. And from there I went to the office next to it. I didn't come back to Mr. Hayward's office till after half past two, like I said, and I didn't see him again."

The hope that had routed Ruth's overpowering fatigue when she had remembered that Letty Miller had seen Jack on his return to his office died a violent death, leaving the girl utterly crushed, and so tired that she felt she could not even lift her eyes again, no matter what happened. If only Letty had waited, had watched for Jack to leave, had been in his office from two until ten minutes past two, so that she could have refuted Bill Cowan's damning story about the telephone call!

While McMann continued his questioning of the cleaning woman, Ruth sat in a small, inert heap in her chair, staring with despair dulled eyes at her lax hands. Dimly she realized that McMann gained no further information; Letty had not worked in the corridor on which Borden's offices were located, hence had not had opportunity to witness the arrival or departure of the dead promoter's visitors; she had not heard the shot fired, or, if she had, had not noted it consciously; when she had cleaned Jack Hayward's offices she had not glanced across the airshaft, through Jack's window to Borden's, had, therefore, neither seen the promoter nor noticed whether his window was closed or open. As to Jack's gun, Letty had never seen it, she said; on Saturday, when she had wiped off the desk drawers, the bottom drawer had been closed, and she had not opened it, or any other drawer.

Ruth did not even raise her despair heavy eyes when Letty Miller was dismissed, with the usual instructions from McMann, but she had the impression that Letty's near sighted, dull brown eyes peered at her pityingly, asking her to forgive her for not having been able to clinch Jack Hayward's alibi. But she could not look up, and Letty was gone.

"Detective Carlson wants to report, sir," Birdwell announced from the door.

"All right; show him in," McMann replied curtly. "Hello, Carlson. Any news? You've seen all the stock salesmen that showed up, haven't you?"

"Yes, sir," Carlson answered cheerfully, as he lowered his fat body into the chair vacated by Letty Miller. "Four of 'em blew in, with alibis all neatly wrapped up and ready to deliver. That accounts for all of Borden's boys except Adams, and Grant, one of the salesmen, just received this wire from him. I've checked his alibi with his landlady. He's been renting a room in an apartment, of which he gave the address, and I called the woman on the phone. Looks straight, all right. Here's the wire."

McMann accepted the yellow sheet and scanned it frowningly, then, with courtesy which Ruth was not too utterly tired to appreciate, passed it to the girl. It was a long day letter:

Have just read of Borden's murder. Saw him Saturday, left office about one ten. He ordered me to Chicago, because he thought I was spending too much thought and time there on my girl. Went directly to my room, Mrs. London's apartment, 128 West Sixty fifth Street, talked with Mrs. London for half hour and packed my trunk and bag. Had lunch with Mrs. London. Called my girl, made a date with her, and left apartment about three o'clock. Met girl downtown half

past three. Was with her till my train left for Chicago
eleven ten Saturday night. Don't give my girl's name
unless necessary. Miss Lester knows Borden was sore
at me and I don't want police to think I quarreled
with Borden and killed him. I did not. He did bawl me
out for falling down on job but gave me another
chance. Show this wire to police if they haven't found
real mur derer. Am stopping at Drake Hotel. Will
come back immediately if necessary.
CARL ADAMS.

Ruth read it, and let the sheet flutter down upon
Borden's desk.

"Well, Miss Lester, what do you think?" McMann
asked.

"I think he's telling the truth," Ruth answered dully.
"It had not occurred to me to suspect Mr. Adams. I think
it was fine of him to volunteer this information so
promptly."

"Or very clever," McMann said slowly. "Get the name
of the girl from Grant, Carlson, and go see this Mrs.
London personally. I don't quite like the looks of this. Too
pat. Give the girl the works, too. . . . Did any of the
salesmen have keys to this office, Miss Lester?" he added,
when Carlson had left.

"No. No one was supposed to have a key but Mr.
Borden, Benny Smith and myself," Ruth answered. "Rita
Dubois had Mr. Borden's key from Friday until today, but
I never knew Mr. Borden to trust any one else so far."

"Of course Borden would have admitted Adams,
unless they had quarreled so violently that Adams had
threatened Borden's life," McMann reflected aloud. "After
Adams left—assuming that he has told the truth about
Borden's having ordered him to Chicago—he may have
decided to make another appeal to his boss, to be allowed
to stay here—"

"In that case, he would have ridden up in the elevator," Ruth pointed out drearily. "And Micky Moran did not bring him up. Micky knows Adams well. He would not have forgotten if Adams had returned. Of course if Adams came back with the intention of killing Mr. Borden, with the gun he knew was kept in my desk, he would have walked up, but if the quarrel had been so bitter as all that, Mr. Borden would not have admitted him, and Adams had no key."

McMann regarded the girl steadily through narrowed eyes, and slowly a smile twisted at his grim mouth. "You're a new experience to me, Ruth Lester! You'd give your life to save Jack Hayward's, if it comes to that, but you won't throw the weight of a word against any other person that you don't believe is guilty."

"I want the truth to save Jack," Ruth answered quietly. "I know he is innocent, but I can't blame you for suspecting he is guilty—except for one thing. All this long, dreadful day, Mr. McMann, no matter how much I wanted to help Jack, I have told you the truth, and have suppressed nothing—nothing! And I ask you now not to forget that I have corroborated Jack's alibi—that he rejoined me at the McAlpin Hotel at ten minutes after two, and did not leave me again. According to Bill Cowan's story, Borden was alive and talking over the telephone at ten minutes after two—"

"With Jack Hayward!" McMann reminded her, with curious gentleness.

"No!" Ruth cried desperately. "Perhaps with someone in Jack Hayward's office, but not with Jack Hayward! I'd stake my life on that. I've pointed out the similarity of Jack's and Mr. Borden's telephone numbers. Either Cowan or the operator could have got the wrong number. And though I know you don't believe her, believe instead that she robbed a dead man's body, Rita Dubois has told you that Borden was alive until half past two—when Jack and I stood in the lobby of the Princess Theater."

"Then you believe that Rita killed Borden?" McMann asked suddenly.

Ruth struggled with temptation, then raised her miserable but wholly honest blue eyes to meet the narrowed, probing gray eyes of the detective."I—don't—know," she answered despairingly. Then, desperately, her voice like a sob: "No, I don't believe she did. But I know Jack didn't!"

"I don't think Rita did it, either," McMann said quietly, "Because of—this," and the detective thrust a hand into the pocket of his coat, brought out something which he extended toward Ruth on the palm of his hand.

Ruth Lester's hand crept out, but her cringing flesh rebelled. She could not force her fingers to close upon the small, flattened out lead bullet which lay upon the palm of Detective Sergeant McMann's big hand.

"The—bullet which killed—Mr. Borden?" she gasped. "But I don't understand. . . . It's—flat—"

"Yes, it's flat," McMann agreed, with dreadful significance. "And it's not the bullet which killed Borden. It's— the bullet he fired in defense of his life—but just an instant too late."

Ruth shrank into her chair, a trembling, pathetic heap, with enormous, pleading blue eyes. "Please tell me. I don't understand."

McMann's hard gray eyes dropped before the misery in the blue ones. "Detective Carlson found this bullet, while you were out to lunch with Hayward. He found it on that strip of cement seven flights below," and McMann pointed to the window overlooking the airshaft. "And after Carlson found this—" the detective returned the flattened bullet to his pocket and rose from Borden's desk— "I found something else. Come here!"

Ruth followed him jerkily, on ice cold feet, to the window. Two pigeons, strutting about the window ledge, took flight, but she scarcely saw them. Her frightened eyes followed the direction of McMann's pointing finger— a spot in the brick wall beside Jack Hayward's window.

"See?" McMann persisted, but without triumph. "A new scar in one of those old bricks. I've examined it—and it's new all right. That is where this bullet struck—harmlessly. It was aimed at Harry Borden's murderer, who stood in Jack Hayward's window, but the finger which pulled the trigger was that of a man mortally wounded—or the shot would not have gone so wide of its mark. Do you understand now, Miss Lester?"

Ruth raised her trembling hands to her face, pressed her icy finger tips into her throbbing temples. "No! No!" she cried. "I don't understand! All I know is—the person at whom that shot was fired was not Jack Hayward!"

McMann turned from the window, strode to Borden's desk, took his seat again. Ruth followed unsteadily, her knees so weak with fright that they could scarcely support her small body.

"What became of your pistol, which we know from finger print evidence that Borden had secured after you left Saturday, bothered me considerably until this evidence turned up," McMann said slowly. "I believe that Borden was shot as he stood against that open window, that, as he fell, mortally wounded, his pistol—or rather, your pistol—clattered out of his hand to the cement below. His murderer retrieved it, disposed of it along with the weapon with which he had killed Harry Borden."

"Retrieved it?" Ruth cried, suddenly electrified. "How? How? If you mean Jack Hayward when you say 'his murderer,' how could Jack possibly have retrieved my pistol on Saturday? Otto Pfluger, the elevator operator on Jack's corridor, has told you that Jack descended in his car not more than ten minutes after Otto had taken him up. There is no way of entering that court below except through a basement door. I know, because I once dropped my handbag out of that window and had to go clear down to the basement and through a door leading from the basement to get it. If Jack had done that, he would have been seen. Moreover, he did not have time to walk down seven flights of stairs, counting the basement stairs, and all the way up again, in the ten minutes he was in the building. And there has not been one shred of evidence from either of the cleaning women or any tenant, to confirm your earlier suspicion that Jack used my office key to get into this office after Mr. Borden was killed, to retrieve the pistol provided it fell to the floor instead of out of the window."

McMann frowned thoughtfully as the almost hysterically triumphant girl made each of her points. Then, when she had finished, he asked slowly: "What about Saturday night or Sunday? Knowing that the pistol lay there, he could have taken his time about coming back for it."

"And there is no record of his being in the building Saturday night or Sunday," Ruth told him triumphantly. "I haven't seen the register for those days, but I'm sure you have, and since I know Jack wasn't in the Starbridge Building after two o'clock Saturday until nine this morning, I know his name is not on the register. That's true, isn't it?"

"Yes," McMann admitted. "But he could have walked down to the basement without using the elevator, or with out being seen by the one man on duty after four o'clock Saturday."

"But that exit door to the court is kept locked," Ruth cried. "It had to be unlocked for me, by a porter. Furthermore, Jack never had the key to this office, so he could not have come here Saturday night or Sunday and gained access to Mr. Borden's office, even if he could have entered the building and left it unobserved by the elevator man. You must believe me when I tell you that the key which the waiter picked up and handed to Jack was the key to my apartment, not my office key. No, Mr. McMann, you're on the wrong scent. Please believe me, please keep an open mind for some theory which will explain *all* the facts."

"And one of those facts," McMann pointed out, "is that Harry Borden fired a shot which grazed a brick in the wall beside Jack Hayward's window."

"And what does that prove—against Jack?" Ruth challenged. "I'll grant that Mr. Borden was standing near that window when he was killed, but how can you be sure that he was *facing* the window when he took aim? If his murderer—or murderess—fired at him in this office, isn't it easy to picture Mr. Borden's arm flying out, after he was hit, so that the bullet with which he had meant to kill his attacker, was discharged through the window? Why assume that he had aimed at someone in Jack's window? There was simply nowhere else for the bullet to go—"

"Just a minute!" McMann interrupted, as Detective Birdwell opened the door between the private office and the outer office. "What is it, Birdwell?"

"Commissioner Weeks on the wire from headquarters, sir."

McMann reached for the instrument on Borden's desk, but before he removed the receiver he spoke to Ruth: "That's all for the present, Miss Lester. Please remain in the outer office till I need you again. You might open and sort the afternoon mail. I'll take charge of it and go over it later, of course."

As Ruth slipped through the door which Birdwell held for her she heard the detective sergeant greet his superior, the police commissioner, deferentially.

Sadly she realized what that call from the head of the police department meant. Commissioner Weeks was famous for his choleric temper, his impatient demand for quick results, especially in sensational cases, like the murder of "Handsome Harry" Borden. His motto seemed to be "Arrest somebody—anybody—and find out the truth later." In this particular case, Jack Hayward would undoubtedly be the victim of Commissioner Weeks's avid appetite for newspaper praise.

Fifteen minutes later, as she sat at her desk, trying to concentrate upon the thick sheaf of correspondence addressed to a man who would never read it, Police Commissioner Weeks arrived.

Ruth knew the commissioner personally. In the old days, before her father's death, Weeks had occasionally dined with the famous criminal lawyer, Colby Lester. She rose and faced the tall, lean, distinguished looking man who had barked out a curt greeting to Detective Birdwell.

"How do you do, Mr. Weeks?" she faltered, trying to make her trembling lips smile naturally. "I wonder if you remember me?"

Light sprang into Commissioner Weeks's cold, pale blue eyes, a broad smile flashed suddenly beneath the stubby white mustache that adorned his long upper lip. "Remember you, child?" he exclaimed cordially, taking her hand in both his. "Who could forget your pretty face? You're Colby Lester's daughter, of course. And while I'm mighty sorry that you're dragged into this miserable business, I'm glad to see you again. How are you, my dear?"

"Well, and—very happy," Ruth answered steadily. "You see, Mr. Weeks, I'm engaged to be married to a man I love with all my heart—Mr. John C. Hayward. I'm going to invite you to my wedding."

"Hayward?" the commissioner repeated, his eyes going cold again. "Isn't that the young man—? Oh, hello, McMann! I'm renewing an old friendship with little Ruth Lester."

Ruth sank slowly into her chair as the two men—the detective sergeant in charge of the investigation into the murder of Henry P. Borden, and Police Commissioner Weeks—passed into Borden's private office and closed the door behind them. Had she helped or injured Jack's chances by her desperate, indirect appeal to a man who had never been known to permit friendship to interfere with the performance of his duty? Well—and her body sagged tiredly—she had done her best for Jack. . . .

The next hour was a nightmare of suspense for Ruth Lester. From five until six o'clock the rumble of voices, sometimes loud, the words almost intelligible, sometimes low and earnest, came to the girl through the closed door. There were infrequent interruptions, when Birdwell received reports from headquarters or other detectives working on the case, which he had to relay to his superiors closeted in Borden's private office. From these one sided telephone conversations which Birdwell carried on at Benny Smith's desk, Ruth learned that Cleo Gilman had not yet been found, that no information at all had been gleaned as to the present whereabouts of Jake Bailey, the murdered man's bodyguard; that Benny Smith, permitted to return to his home, followed by a detective, was so ill that a doctor's car had been parked before his home for more than an hour.

At six o'clock came the order which Ruth had been expecting and dreading. McMann, looking pale and harassed, opened the door and spoke sharply to Birdwell: "Get Hayward—and Rita Dubois. Rita's in Covey's charge, down the hall. We'll have Hayward in first. Miss Lester will answer the phone if it rings while you're gone."

The phone did not ring during the detective's absence. Ruth, standing tremblingly beside it, wished it would— that something would happen to make those long minutes shorter. At last the door opened and Jack Hayward pushed in ahead of Birdwell. Ruth's anxious, loving eyes devoured him. He had evidently just brushed his thick, copper colored hair, for the deep waves in it gleamed wetly in the electric light. Not the act of a nervous, or a frightened or a guilty man. . . . And his bronze brown eyes, wide open, candid, clear, smiled at her. . . .

They both forgot Detective Birdwell as they moved toward each other, their arms outstretched. They did not even realize that the detective had considerately turned his back.

"Poor little darling!" Jack murmured, his low voice rich with pity and tenderness.

Ruth wanted to warn him that arrest lay before him, to tell him of the flattened bullet found in the court be low his window, but he stopped her first words by laying his lips against hers. That kiss, which Ruth wanted desperately to prolong forever, lest the next time their lips met it should be from between prison bars, lasted until Detective Birdwell slowly crossed the room and opened the door into the private office.

# CHAPTER EIGHTEEN

"NOW, young lady, if you mention the word 'murder' one more time before you've drunk every drop of this hot broth and eaten exactly one half of this gorgeous broiled chicken, your future husband will anticipate his prerogatives and give you a sound spanking!" Jack Hayward addressed the golden haired girl whom he had just forced down into the biggest, softest chair that her small apartment boasted.

Ruth Lester's great, fatigue shadowed blue eyes stared, as if they were looking upon a divine miracle, at the tall young man who was busily, competently setting her little gateleg table with her own gaily patterned dishes and serving the food which he had ordered sent up from the nearest restaurant. Suddenly, as she watched his untrammeled hands—hands which an hour ago she had expected to see shackled with steel bracelets—she began to sob, shudderingly, so that her whole small body was terribly shaken. Instantly Jack Hayward forsook his dinner preparations, dropped to his knees beside her, drew her head to his shoulder.

"Don't, sweet! You've been so splendid, so brave! I'm here with you now because of your faith and courage. Don't you think I know that if it hadn't been for you I'd be in jail tonight, instead of holding my own darling girl in my arms?" Jack pleaded.

"McMann believes you're guilty, and so does Commissioner Weeks!" Ruth sobbed. "They've just let you out, like a dog on a long leash, to see if you'll run to a buried bone, and—and give yourself away."

Jack laughed and kissed her wet eyelashes. "Then the dog is grateful for the leash, darling, since it's long enough to reach to you, and he's going to begin worrying a bone right now—a nice, juicy drumstick." And he sprang to his feet, to pull the big chair, with the tired girl in it, to the gateleg table.

"Do you think Rita has been arrested?" Ruth dared revert to the subject of the murder, when Jack had grudgingly agreed that she had eaten enough for one small person.

Jack dragged her chair to the little fireplace, gave an expert poke at the smouldering logs, and seated himself on a hassock at Ruth's feet, before he answered, gravely:

"I rather imagine she's been let run loose—on a leash, as I've been, and that the cop on the other end of the leash will find her digging for her buried bone—if Rita isn't careful."

Ruth's eyes widened incredulously, but with shamed hope in them. "You think Rita is guilty, Jack?"

The young man's hands closed tightly over hers. "Someone did it, darling. You mustn't be too horrified tomorrow if it develops that Rita Dubois is the one. One big reason why McMann did not arrest me was that he knew he did not have all of Rita's story. I'm sure he'd rather know what Rita did with the five hundred she admits she got from Borden before he takes a chance on clapping me in jail."

Ruth flinched, but nodded in agreement. "She gave it to someone else, of course—someone who was in dire trouble, someone she will shield, even if she has to go to jail to protect him."

Jack laughed. "Him?"

"A man, of course," Ruth retorted. "The man she is in love with, whoever he may be. She loathed the very thought of going away with Mr. Borden—because she was in love with someone else. And, of course, if she'd simply needed the five hundred to pay bills with, she'd have told readily enough what she did with it. Maybe the man saw her with Borden, suspected she was planning to go away with him, followed her to Borden's office, in a jealous rage— "

"Forced his way into the office, in spite of Borden's fear of strangers with possible grievances, found your pistol by instinct, fired one shot at Borden and one through the window, took the rest of Borden's money and your pistol, then strolled over to my office and completed a pleasant afternoon's work by robbing my desk of my automatic," Jack interrupted, smiling broadly. "Pretty thin, sweet heart."

"Well, what if it is?" Ruth cried. "Any theory that could fit all the facts would sound almost as absurd. I'm just groping in the dark, Jack! Someone did it! But who, how and why? It's like an awful puzzle of which you have all the pieces but to which you can't find the key."

"I know, dear," Jack assured her contritely. "It's beastly of me to joke about it. Suppose we try, just you and I— didn't intend to make a rhyme, sweet, so don't frown at me—to fit the pieces of the puzzle together. I know you've been trying all day, but McMann sort of cramped your style. You were trying so desperately to convince him that *I* didn't kill your unpleasant boss, that you had little time to wonder who did. Now—I didn't do it. That's agreed, isn't it?" he added, with sudden gravity, his bronze brown eyes very steady, but so wistful that her heart contracted sharply with pity.

"Of course, darling!" Ruth protested, smiling at him through a mist of tears.

"All right. But let's consider the case against me, as McMann sees it," Jack began briskly. "Three people have testified that I threatened Borden's life, if he laid a hand on you again. Motive. As to opportunity—I was in my office for eight or nine minutes, possibly ten, between a few minutes of two and two or three minutes after two, and that office is directly opposite Borden's private office, with two open windows between us across an eight foot airshaft. A bullet fired from Borden's office toward mine scars a brick beside my window and is found on the cement floor of the court below. My automatic, which my secretary, Miss Barnes, saw in my desk Saturday morning, is discovered to be missing on Monday morning. Accessibility to weapon—the same make and calibre of weapon which killed Harry Borden. At ten minutes after two, according to Bill Cowan's story, Harry Borden was in telephone conversation with someone in my office. Naturally the police don't say 'some one'—they say Jack Hayward. But you and I know that at ten minutes after two, according to your watch and the clock in the lobby of the McAlpin Hotel, I was rejoining you to finish our interrupted lunch. Now—look at that section of the puzzle, little Miss Sherlock: which piece doesn't fit?"

Ruth smiled bravely, trying to meet his mood. "The telephone call, of course, and the shot fired toward your office. Of course Cowan may have called Borden's number, instead of yours, due to the similarity of numbers, or the operator may have made a mistake—"

"Let's not try to explain away the pieces that don't fit," Jack urged. "For the sake of argument, and probably for the sake of truth, let's admit these two fatal pieces into our puzzle, and shift them about until they fit. Let's say that Borden was talking with someone in my office at ten minutes after two—"

"And for several minutes before ten minutes after two," Ruth interrupted. "Rita says she called Mr. Borden from the station at five minutes past two and his line was busy; that she called again at ten minutes after two and it was still busy, and that at eleven or twelve minutes after two she talked with him. If, as McMann thinks, Borden was already dead when Rita arrived about five minutes later, he was killed immediately after she talked with him, by someone in your office, undoubtedly the person with whom he had been quarreling over your telephone. But here is another piece that won't fit into the puzzle: why should Rita, even if she robbed the body, take the gun with which Borden had fired at his murderer?"

"No earthly reason that I can see," Jack agreed.

"Equally, there seems to be no reason why Rita should do the real murderer across the airshaft a good turn by closing the window, and since that real murderer was not I, he would have had no reason himself to close Borden's window by using the window pole in my office. He'd not have cared a whoop about diverting suspicion from me, the lawful tenant of the office—"

"Wait!" Ruth cried, her delicate little face become illuminated with inspiration. "What if the real murderer— supposing that he was in your office, was a friend of yours, and *did* want to protect you from the consequences of his deed?"

"That's a thought!" Jack agreed soberly. "But—that brings us to—Cowan, doesn't it? Cowan is the only friend I have, so far as I know, who also knew Harry Borden."

"And he admits that he had left a blueprint in your office, which was his reason for telephoning you!" Ruth clapped her hands softly together. "Who can corroborate his story that he called you from the station at ten minutes after two? Suppose it was Cowan! Suppose he himself talked with Borden over your telephone, quarreled with him over some woman, then—"

"Hold up!" Jack laughed. "Before you slip the noose about Cowan's neck, tell me first how he got into my office, how he knew I had a gun—"

"Wait!" Ruth interrupted, her brow wrinkled in thought. "I'm about to get something. Let me think! . . . Oh, yes! It was a fleeting thought that occurred to me this afternoon when your cleaning woman, Letty Miller, was telling her story to McMann. She says she was already in your office, had just entered with her cleaning things, when you returned. I think we have there the explanation of how the murderer gained access to your office!"

"I don't quite see," Jack acknowledged, frowning.

"The cleaning women nearly always leave the outer door on latch, so that they won't have to bother with unlocking it each time they make a trip in and out of the

office. Minnie does, I know, for Mr. Borden came back to
his office one evening after we'd all left for the day and
found the door unlocked, with Minnie emptying the
wastebaskets into the sack in the hall. He bawled her out;
told me about it the next morning. Probably Letty had
left your door on latch, for convenience, and in leaving
hurriedly after you returned, she did not click it on again.
Did you try the door when you left, to see if it was
locked?" She waited breathlessly for his answer.

Jack's thoughtful frown deepened. Then, slowly: "I
can't remember giving the door a thought. I was too cut
up over the loss of that big insurance commission, and its
effect on our wedding plans, to think of whether the door
was locked or not. And, of course, I expected Letty to
return immediately to clean."

"I thought so!" Ruth was triumphant. "I'll have
McMann ask her tomorrow if she didn't leave the door on
latch, and if, as I'm sure she will, she says she did, one
big piece in the puzzle slips into place. Someone besides
yourself had access to your office. I suppose no one
besides you and Miss Barnes has a key?"

Jack shook his head, then grinned. "No. And
McMann, being nobody's fool, considered the possibility of
poor little Miss Barnes having murdered the man across
the airshaft, possibly because she didn't like the way he
wore his hair or the color of his necktie. But Miss Barnes
immediately gave an iron clad alibi. She'd gone to lunch,
immediately after one o'clock, with Miss Parkes, a
stenographer across the hall from my office, and the two
girls had shopped after lunch, finishing up a Saturday
afternoon orgy with a movie. He checked her alibi then
and there and found it perfect. But to get back to your
case against Cowan— poor, unsuspecting devil!
Supposing that he did kill Borden, for motives we can
only guess at, there still remains your pistol in Borden's
office. Cowan could not have had time to go after it before
Rita arrived, or if he had had time, how could he have got
in? We can be very sure that Borden's door was locked.

And again, if Cowan did not—and why should he?—retrieve the gun with which Borden had tried to defend himself, firing toward his murderer in my office window, we come smack upon the foolish conclusion that Rita herself, after robbing the body, took the gun away with her, too. No, darling, I'm afraid it won't wash."

"No—o—o," Ruth agreed reluctantly. She had no love for Bill Cowan! "But Jack, there are other bits of the puzzle which we haven't considered at all. The woman with the beautiful contralto voice and—why, Jack! What *is* the matter?"

"Nothing's the matter!" Jack Hayward denied, with peculiar emphasis. "What were you going to say about the woman with the contralto voice?"

"You started and blushed—and you're still blushing," Ruth accused him wonderingly, and a little jealously. "I'm sure my description reminded you of someone you know."

"What about this woman with the voice?" Jack evaded, reaching for the poker, so that Ruth could not see his eyes.

The girl stared at him, bewildered and hurt, then answered steadily, a little coldly: "You were present this morning when I told Mr. McMann about a telephone call for Mr. Borden at ten o'clock Saturday morning. I was familiar with the voice calling then, for the woman had telephoned several times during the four months I worked for Mr. Borden. He always refused to talk with her, though she never gave me her name. Saturday morning Mr. Borden came in a minute or two after I had hung up the receiver, and when I told him that the woman with the beautiful contralto voice had called he said: 'That voice may sound beautiful to you, but believe me, I'd rather listen to a riveting machine,' or words to that effect."

"Not enough to hang her on," Jack commented drily, still poking needlessly at the fire.

"Of course not, dear," Ruth answered reasonably, though her voice trembled slightly. "But the story Minnie

Cassidy told definitely brings the woman with the contralto voice into the puzzle. While Minnie was cleaning in our offices shortly after half past one Mr. Borden left his office for a minute or two, asking Minnie to stay until he returned, since he had no key and didn't want her to go away and leave the door unlocked for him. While he was gone the phone rang, Minnie answered, told the woman to hold the wire. When Mr. Borden returned, he asked her to describe the voice of the woman calling, and Minnie did so, saying the woman had a lovely, sweet voice, like an alto singer, as she puts it. At first Mr. Borden told her curtly to hang up the receiver, then considered a moment, and directed her to tell the woman to call again in fifteen or twenty minutes."

"Well?" Jack said impatiently, as Ruth paused

"The woman, so Minnie says, gave her this message for Mr. Borden: 'Tell Mr. Borden that if he is wise, he will talk to me when I call again.'"

Jack shrugged. "Not nearly so definite a threat as I made against the man." Then, as Ruth stared at him with wide, hurt blue eyes: "If you're thinking that the woman with the voice made her final telephone call over my phone, I'm afraid I can't see it. Fifteen or twenty minutes after Minnie's conversation with the lady of the voice, I was in my office myself."

"I *hadn't* reached that conclusion yet," Ruth said slowly, coldly. "But your reasoning strikes me as a little odd. The woman could not have known that Mr. Borden had a train to make, hence may have delayed a little *until she reached the Starbridge Building.* Jack! Look at me!" she commanded with sudden urgency. "You're probably the world's clumsiest deceiver. It's written all over your face that you know something about this woman. Is this any time to conceal that knowledge from me? It's for your sake, remember!"

Jack shrugged, then laughed ruefully. "I'll never be able to get away with anything, with a wife like you! . . . And may I have a kiss to make up for all I'm going to suffer at your hands in the future? . . . Umm! . . . Now, darling, imitate that voice for me as perfectly as you can. I know you're a good mimic. I've heard you take off Borden, Benny, old Minnie Cassidy, and poor, timid Letty Miller. Go to it, sweet!"

Ruth laughed, happy again, then, her lovely little soprano voice as obliterated as if it had never existed, she enunciated in a throaty, throbbing, exquisite contralto: "Thank you so much, my dear Mr. Hayward! You are too kind!" Then, triumphantly, in her own voice again: "There! You started and blushed again! You can't deny you've heard that voice before—or the one I imitated."

"You're right, of course," Jack admitted reluctantly. "I do know the woman—slightly. She came to my office about two months ago, to inquire about insurance."

"Just picked you out blindly?" Ruth asked skeptically. "Or had someone given her your name?"

"She didn't say, and of course I didn't ask," Jack answered, a little stiffly. "I asked her into my private office and gave her a lot of information about various types of policies—straight life, twenty year endowment, etc. I didn't think, at the time, that she seemed particularly interested, though she had asked for the information—"

"I imagine," Ruth interrupted suddenly, "that she was more interested in the occupant of the office across the airshaft."

"You've hit it again, though I didn't think anything of it at the time," Jack admitted. "Before she left, with her hands full of insurance literature, she stepped to the window and looked out, perhaps towards Borden's office, maybe at Borden himself. I thought she was interested in the pigeons, which were circling about—I made some remark to her about them, I believe."

"What was she like—besides her voice?" Ruth asked eagerly.

"Tall and very slender, big, fine, dark eyes—sad eyes," Jack answered so unhesitatingly that another pang of jealousy shot through the girl's heart. "About thirty five, I imagine. A good deal of make up, but a skilful, artistic job. Good clothes, but just a little shabby, an elegant sort of shabbiness."

"She evidently made a great impression on you," Ruth could not help remarking. "I suppose you remember her name, too?"

"You're delicious when you're angry or jealous," Jack laughed, and kissed the tips of her fingers. "She did make a deep impression on me, because I thought she had the most tragic face I'd ever seen. That's why I hesitated to say a word which might involve her in this nasty business. No man would want to add another bitter line to that tragic face. Her name was Martha Manning."

"Miss or Mrs.?" Ruth persisted.

"She didn't say, but I addressed her as Miss Manning until she made inquiries about a trust fund's being made of the insurance, if she took it out, in favor of her six year old son. Then I called her Mrs. Manning and she did not correct me."

Ruth considered, her eyes growing wider and wider. Then, slowly: "Miss Manning, Jack, and the boy was Harry Borden's illegitimate son. I feel absolutely sure of that. . . . What was her address?" she added suddenly.

"Some little hotel—let me think. . . . Oh, yes, the Acropolis Hotel. I wrote her, asking if she had made up her mind as to the kind of insurance she wanted to take out, and she did not reply. She did come in again, however, and told me that it was quite useless for her to consider any kind of insurance on her life—that she had been to her own physician and he had told her she was in an advanced stage of tuberculosis. And again—she stood at my window, looking out. ... I felt damned sorry for her," Jack added, in a low voice.

"Frank Ashe felt sorry for her, too," Ruth said slowly. And then she related, briefly, the story that Borden's manservant had told Detective Sergeant McMann—how the woman with the beautiful contralto voice had come to

Borden's apartment, gained entrance by watching her chance, and had been knocked half senseless either by Borden himself or by Jake Bailey, his bodyguard.

"Motive!" Jack commented, but without triumph. "Now as to opportunity. Let us suppose she came to the Starbridge Building Saturday afternoon, before calling Borden on the telephone as he had asked her to, through Minnie. But why come to my office to make the call, even if she did remember that it was directly opposite Borden's and that she could see his face, as she talked to him?"

"Maybe she realized that you were interested in her, would go out of your way to do her a good turn. Perhaps she intended to appeal to you to help her plead her case with Borden," Ruth suggested hesitatingly. "She found your door unlocked, thought you were in, and entered. Once inside, she took the liberty of using your phone, although you were not there, quarreled with Borden— and shot him through your window."

"But how did she know I had a pistol?" Jack objected.

"You've just said you gave her a lot of insurance literature," Ruth pointed out eagerly. "You keep stacks of it in the bottom drawer of your desk. Why couldn't she have seen the pistol while you were searching for the printed matter you wanted to give her?"

"Possible, but not highly probable," Jack conceded. "But—if she killed him from my office, how can you account for the disappearance of your gun? Miss Manning could hardly have entered the dead man's locked office, would have had no reason to do so, in the first place—"

"Then maybe she induced Borden, by threats of some sort, to grant her an appointment, told him she was in the building and would be right up, then armed herself with your gun, went to his office, was admitted because he was expecting her, found he was armed too, and shot him just as he was about to shoot her, Borden's bullet going wild— out of the window. How's that?" Ruth concluded triumphantly.

"Fine," Jack smiled mirthlessly, "except for one or two minor details. Why should she take the gun with which he had tried to kill her? Why close the window?"

"But Rita Dubois insists that the window was still open when she was there between twenty after two and half past two," Ruth pointed out.

"And Rita also insists that Borden was alive," Jack reminded her. "If Rita is telling the truth, our whole case against poor Martha Manning topples, unless we conclude that Borden told Miss Manning not to come until half past two or even later—realizing, as he did, that she had already made him miss his train, and that he would have to deal with Rita, between train time— 2:15—and 2:30. But if that's the case, where was Martha Manning after she concluded her telephone quarrel with Borden at two ten, and until half past two? In my office all that time? So far as I know, no one has told of seeing a stranger on the seventh floor all afternoon, and neither Otto Pfluger nor Micky Moran said anything about bringing such a woman to the seventh floor."

"She could have walked up, of course—part of the way, at least," Ruth offered tentatively. "But—Letty went into your offices for the second time to clean them at half past two. I'm sure she would have told Mr. McMann if she had seen anyone coming out of your office or in the corridor. But, Jack, there's no getting around it: *some* woman, Martha Manning, or some other woman, *was* in Borden's offices Saturday—besides Rita, Mrs. Borden, Minnie and myself, I mean, for, as McMann puts it, she left her calling card on the glass panel in the door between the private office and the outer office—three clear finger prints, the only finger prints on the glass panel, which the window washer had cleaned late Friday afternoon. Maybe she had a key to Mr. Borden's office— but no, that's impossible, for Mr. Borden had the lock changed after I started to work for him only four months ago, and all that time he has refused even to talk over the phone with the woman of the contralto voice. . . . Oh!" she sighed suddenly, and slumped in a pathetic little heap. "I'm so ghastly tired I can't think."

"You're going to bed, darling," Jack commanded, contrition and compassion in his voice and eyes. "I could do with a little sleep myself, and it's a shame to keep my poor 'shadow' standing out there in the cold so long. He'll be all the better for taking his 'dog' for a walk on the leash. You're going to the scene of the crime tomorrow morning, I suppose?"

"Me?" Ruth laughed shakily. "Why, I'm going to take charge of the investigation—after I've done one errand—with my own 'shadow' trailing me. . . . No, I won't tell you what I intend to do. Go along. I want to—pray, and then to sleep. Good night, my darling. I love you."

# CHAPTER NINETEEN

PERHAPS it was because she was so tired and suddenly so sleepy that the prayer for help which Ruth Lester addressed, with childlike faith, to her Heavenly Father, ended in an extremely unorthodox manner, designed to confound a less understanding God than the One in Whom she believed. For her last words, before sleep settled upon her, like a smothering eiderdown comfort, were: "Please come back to me, Daddy. I'm not clever enough to save Jack without your help. It's just the kind of case you always loved, darling. You could make all the pieces of the puzzle fit. Come back and laugh at me for being so stupid —so stupid—"

And with miraculous suddenness, part of that drowsy, naive prayer was answered. Subconsciously, Ruth Lester knew that she was dreaming, that her actual body— aching with fatigue—was lying on her couch bed in a tiny bachelor girl apartment, that her adored father, Colby Lester, always referred to as "the famous criminal lawyer," was dead. But her prayer was being answered, and what did it matter that it was only a dream? But she mustn't wake up too soon. . . .

The dream was a kindly one, not fantastic or absurd. She was back again in her father's library, curled kitten wise in his arms, watching with fascinated blue eyes as his long fingers arranged and rearranged bits of a jig saw puzzle spread out on the desk before him.

"What is that big, square shaped piece, Daddy?" she heard her own voice inquiring, as those expert fingers made a quick rearrangement of the pieces of the puzzle.

"That, Infant?" She distinctly heard his beloved, familiar chuckle. "Why, that's the orchid tinted letter, of course—"

Perhaps, Ruth mourned later, if she had not cried out so sharply at that she would not have awakened, would have seen the complete solving of that jig puzzle under the expert manipulation of Colby's Lester's fingers. But she did wake up, with her own exclamation of self disgust and her father's last words ringing in her ears.

With the sharp clarity of mind and memory which comes in the small hours of the night, Ruth recalled every detail of a scene which she had forgotten throughout the dreadful first day of the police investigation into the murder of Henry P. Borden. She saw again the large, square, orchid tinted envelope, with its distinctive, angular hand writing in violet ink, saw herself seated at her desk in the outer office of Borden's suite, sorting Saturday morning's mail, laying aside unopened the exotic missive marked "Personal"; saw, later, the gesture of repulsion and anger with which Henry Borden flicked the unwelcome letter across his desk, then heard again the muttered oath with which he picked it up and thrust it, unopened, into the breast pocket of his vest.

In her excitement, Ruth sat straight up in bed, her hands clasped to her wildly beating heart. *Where was that letter now?* She had seen Detective Sergeant McMann go through the murdered man's pockets, could clearly recall now every item he had taken from them. *And an orchid tinted letter had not been among them!*

Had Borden, sometime between his receipt of the loathed letter and his death, taken it out of his vest pocket, read it, torn it across and tossed it into his wastebasket? Certainly he had not done so before she herself left the office at twenty minutes after one, for her last act of service to the man who had been murdered had been to help him, dear his desk of accumulated memoranda and advertising matter issued by other promoters on stock as dubious as his own. She had tossed the worthless papers into the empty wastebasket which stood beside his desk. Perhaps he had read the letter and thrown it into the wastebasket after she had left, but if so, it was the first of the orchid tinted letters, of which he had received several during the four months she had worked for him, to find its way into his office wastebasket and thence, possibly, into the possession of a curious reader. But if it had not gone into the waste basket and been taken out, with the rest of the papers, by Minnie Cassidy, *where was it now?*

If, as McMann seemed to believe, Rita Dubois had robbed his dead body, why should she also steal a letter written to Borden by another woman? There was no possibility that Rita herself was the writer. The orchid tinted envelopes marked "Personal" had been coming to Borden's office long before he had ever met and fallen in love with the dancer. If Mrs. Borden had killed her husband before Rita's arrival and robbing of the body, she could not have known of the existence of the letter, could have had no motive for taking it if she had known, for the letter had not been written by Elizabeth Borden. Ruth knew the discarded wife's handwriting very well, had seen her delicate, precise signature each month as an endorsement on Borden's check for separation allowance.

Suddenly the obvious course of action occurred to the excited girl. There was no use in puzzling and worrying over the letter now, but tomorrow morning . . . She lay back on her pillows, welcomed the waves of sleep which immediately began to dull her brain, for maybe Colby Lester, her father, would come to her again. . . .

Colby Lester did not come again that night, but the next morning his daughter woke, feeling strangely happy and comforted, quite equal to performing the'two errands she had set herself—without benefit of police sanction— and then, as she had impudently expressed it to Jack Hayward the night before, to taking charge of the investigation into the murder of Henry P. Borden.

While she was dressing, a sudden thought occurred to Ruth, and she ran to the front window of her tiny apartment. As she had expected, she saw a man strolling leisurely up and down the sidewalk across the street from her apartment house, his head turning now and then to glance casually toward the cheaply pretentious entrance.

Ruth blew a finger tip kiss to the unconscious watcher, laughed exultingly, then whirled back to her dressing table. "I'm going to lead you an awful chase, dear, obvious old 'shadow'!" she promised him.

And she kept her promise. Twice, as the detective's taxi drew almost abreast of hers, the girl thought she was going to be stopped and questioned, but undoubtedly the man had his orders not to jerk on the leash.

The first was not a long trip. Ruth's taxi drew up before an old but dignified apartment house in East Sixty first Street.

"Please wait. I shan't be long," Ruth directed her driver.

"Mrs. Borden is not seeing anyone, miss," the uniformed doorman told her, when she had asked to be announced over the house telephone.

"Please get Mrs. Borden on the phone, and tell her that Miss Ruth Lester wants to see her on a matter of vital importance," Ruth directed crisply.

Three minutes later the dead man's widow and his secretary confronted each other in the large foyer of Mrs. Borden's apartment. Deep shadows from a sleepless, grieving night lay like black moth wings beneath the widow's eyes, and accentuated the ghastly pallor of her once pretty face.

Before Mrs. Borden could frame her dignified protest at the intrusion, Ruth put the question she had come to ask. "Mrs. Borden, won't you please tell me what you know about Martha Manning?"

At that name, color flooded the pale face and the leaf brown eyes flashed angry fire. Ruth was almost sorry she had come. . . .

"How dare you mention that woman's name to me?" Mrs. Borden gasped, her hand at her throat, as if the words were choking her. Then, by a visible effort, she regained a measure of control: "I—don't know whom you mean, or why you ask, Miss Lester! If Mr. McMann has any further questions to ask me—"

"Oh, please, dear Mrs. Borden!" Ruth pleaded. "I know you want to protect your husband's—past from the newspapers, but—he is dead, and it is your duty to tell any thing you know which might help—"

"I have nothing to say to you, Miss Lester," Mrs. Borden interrupted coldly.

"I am sorry to have troubled you, Mrs. Borden," Ruth said gently, "and I want you to know that you have my— my deepest sympathy," and without waiting for a reply, she reached for the knob of the door by which she had entered.

Her question had been answered, far more completely than the murdered man's widow could suspect. Ruth knew now why Mrs. Borden had refused on Monday to identify the woman with the contralto voice. The mother of Harry Borden's legitimate children would die before she would admit, and thus publish to the world, her knowledge of the existence of an illegitimate half brother of those children. How dreadful a burden that knowledge must have been all these years. . .

It was a saddened, subdued girl who gave the next address to the taxi driver.

"That gyp cab's following us, with a dick inside," the driver told her, out of the corner of his mouth, as she climbed into her taxi.

"I know," Ruth smiled at him reassuringly. "The 'dick' is only doing his duty. There won't be any trouble."

The driver shook his head, hesitated about starting his motor. "I don't want to get mixed up in nothing, miss—"

"Very well," Ruth agreed cheerfully, preparing to disembark. "If you don't want to drive me, I'll get the 'dick' to take me in his cab. I'll save taxi fare."

"Guess it's all right," her driver concluded, grinning at her self confident impudence.

This time the trip was a long one, over Queensboro Bridge and on into Long Island City, but at last she reached her destination—the little grocery store over which Minnie Cassidy lived in two cheerless rooms. Ruth had made the trip once before—on Christmas Day—to visit the old scrubwoman, temporarily bedridden with rheumatism.

Entrance was through the mean, dirty little store, inefficiently run by Minnie's son in law, with the help of the girl, Rose.

"Hello, Rose!" Ruth greeted the pretty, untidy girl be hind the counter, "I want to see your mother."

"She's upstairs, Miss Lester. Bud isn't here, and I'm alone in the store. Would you mind going up alone?"

Ruth found Minnie Cassidy puttering about a disordered kitchen. "Good land, child! What brings ye here?"

Minnie greeted the girl. "Here take the weight off your pretty feet! . . . Phut! Don't bother! That's only the cat's saucer and it was cracked anyway . . . Now, what's Tommy McMann been up to? Has he arrested your young man, and do ye think old Minnie can help ye out?"

"I do think you can help me out, Minnie," Ruth smiled, "but Mr. McMann has not arrested Mr. Hayward— yet. . . . Listen, Minnie, and try hard to remember: when you were emptying Mr. Borden's wastebasket, did you notice an orchid  or lavender colored letter? It may have been torn up, of course, but I thought you might have noticed the unusual color—"

"There! I knowed I'd forgot something—what with Tommy McMann pestering the life out of me with his fool questions!" Minnie Cassidy interrupted, slapping her fat old thigh with a triumphant hand. "I seen the very letter ye mean, child, but not in the wastebasket. A reading of it the poor man was, his face as black as a thunder cloud, and his fist pounding up and down on the drawer, as if he wished it was the poor lady's face he was poundin', not a drawer without feelin'—"

"Drawer?" Ruth repeated blankly. McMann had gone through every drawer in Borden's desk . . .

# CHAPTER TWENTY

"BUT I tell you, Mr. McMann, there must be another drawer," Ruth Lester insisted. She had arrived at the murdered man's offices at half past ten, and had almost autocratically brushed aside the detective sergeant's brusque inquiries as to the chase she had led the plain clothesman who had been assigned to the task of "shadowing" her. "Minnie Cassidy described the drawer as no deeper than a case knife is broad, and insists that it was pulled out in front of Mr. Borden as he sat at his desk. She had to pass directly behind him to get to his waste basket, and his obvious anger—pounding on the edge of the drawer with his clenched fist—aroused her curiosity, so that she looked over his shoulder as she passed. He was evidently rereading the letter after he had read it once and put it away in the drawer. Minnie is positive that it was a sheet of orchid tinted notepaper, closely written in violet ink."

"Then why the devil didn't she say something about it when I questioned her?" the detective grumbled. But he pulled out the two inch deep middle drawer of the desk, and, stooping, inserted a hand and tapped against the roof of the cavity exposed. A hollow sound rewarded him. "You're right. There's a drawer above this one, a secret drawer. And no apparent means of opening it."

"Let me try!" Ruth suggested, and began to press her fingers against the elaborately carved strip of walnut which was undoubtedly the front end of the secret drawer, though it appeared to be only the edge of the desk top. Her efforts met with failure until her fingers pressed hard upon a carved leaf directly above the right corner of the unconcealed middle drawer. The carved strip swung slowly inward, revealing a shallow drawer less than an inch deep. Triumphantly, the girl pulled it out. There was not one orchid tinted letter, but six of them, with the last received on top, at the front of the little drawer.

"Don't destroy finger prints!" McMann warned Ruth. "Here—let me handle it." And with infinite caution the detective drew the letter from its large, square envelope, touching only one corner of the sheet as he shook it out and laid it on the blotter of the dead man's desk.

"May I read it?" Ruth begged, and as the detective grunted assent their two heads—one grizzled, massive, the other small and golden—bent over the exhibit which Ruth had brought to light. There was a single sheet of notepaper, closely written on both sides.

Harry, my darling—(the letter began, below the two words, Friday afternoon) "After what happened between us on Christmas Eve, I swore that I would never appeal to you again. Oh, Harry, to think that you could strike me and curse me, after all the happiness we have known together! But my pride—which was one of the qualities you admired most in me, you used to say—has been leveled to the dust. I would rather die than ask you for anything for myself, Harry, but where our son is concerned I have no pride—only love, and a ghastly fear for his future. He is your son, Harry—as much your child as Betty and Harry Junior. It was your own suggestion that I place him in boarding school last September, so that he might have his chance at normal little boy happiness and education. You promised then to pay for his board and tuition, but—

"Finished?" McMann grunted at Ruth, and, as she nodded mutely, he turned the sheet over.

Ruth's tear misted eyes resolutely left the signature to the last:

—the money never came. Almost the last cent I had in the world went to pay for his first half year, and now— there is nothing left—less than nothing. I am ill and broken. If you continue to refuse to pay for his second semester—the first ends the last of January— he will have to be put in an orphanage, and that would kill me. You couldn't—couldn't!—let your son— the child of our love —come to that, Harry! Please, Harry! I abase myself before you. I make one last appeal—for him. Create a trust fund for him—your son. You can arrange for a bank— not I—to be his guardian, if you hate me as much as you've said you do. Do this for him! I ask nothing for myself — nothing! But Harry, in all solemnity, I warn you that you will be sorry if you do not do what I ask. I shall telephone you Saturday morning. If your answer is still no— but I won't think of that now!
M.

"'M!'" Ruth breathed. "Martha!—Martha Manning! Oh, the poor thing!"

"Martha Manning!" the detective exploded. "You haven't told me anything about her. If you knew Borden had a discarded mistress and an illegitimate child, why didn't you tell me yesterday?"

"I didn't know until last night," Ruth retorted. Then, rapidly, breathlessly, she related to McMann the series of deductions and suppositions which had led her to an inevitable conclusion.

"Though I didn't, at first, connect the writer of the orchid tinted letters with 'the woman of the contralto voice,'" Ruth acknowledged.

"Some voice!" McMann commented drily. "It seems to have knocked you, Hayward, Minnie Cassidy and Frank Ashe for a goal. I'm getting sort of curious to hear it myself. Did Hayward get her address when she came to him about insurance?"

"Yes. The Acropolis Hotel—one of those small, inexpensive residence hotels," Ruth answered.

"Hard up—and living at a hotel," McMann commented sarcastically. "Trying to pull Borden's leg, I guess. Black mail . . . Well, we'll have a look at this dame, and listen to her carol her story in her 'beautiful contralto voice.'"

The detective was striding toward the door to give an order to Birdwell, who was still on duty in the outer office, when Ruth stopped him with a question:

"And you'll send for Letty Miller, won't you? If she says that she did leave Jack's door on the latch when she first went in to clean his offices, a big part of the mystery can be cleared up, for we shall know then that someone besides Jack could have entered and used his telephone—and his gun."

"Letty Miller would admit anything if she thought it would help Hayward," McMann commented skeptically. "He must have greased her palm with a good bit of silver, first and last. But it won't do any harm to ask her. Just don't bank too much on your pretty little theory, Miss Lester . . . Oh, Birdwell!" he called, as he opened the door into the outer office. "Get hold of Carlson for me. He's on the floor somewhere, talking to tenants. Send him over to the Acropolis Hotel for Martha Manning. That's right—M a n n i n g. If she's not in, or checked out, tell him to get all the facts and let me know immediately. . . . And Birdwell, have headquarters send somebody for Letty Miller, one of those scrubwomen I was interviewing yesterday. They don't come on till four o'clock, and I don't care to wait till then."

"Yes, sir," Birdwell answered. "Did you get the Miller woman's address, sir? You remember we couldn't find her yesterday morning. She'd moved from the rooming house address the superintendent gave us—"

"Oh, damn!" McMann exploded. "I forgot to ask her. See if Coghlan, the superintendent, did. It's his job to keep up with his employes' various changes of address—"

"Yes, sir. Just a minute, sir," Birdwell interrupted his chief, as the telephone rang. He listened for a moment, then turned to McMann: "It's Clay, sir. He's bringing the Gilman woman in. He says she's just returned to her apartment. He's telephoning from her place now."

"Good! Tell Clay to make it snappy," McMann directed. Then, when his subordinate had concluded the telephone conversation: "Any line yet on Jake Bailey, Borden's bodyguard?"

"No, sir. I'll get hold of Carlson now and send him after this Manning woman."

Fifteen minutes later, while Detective Sergeant McMann and Ruth Lester were still engaged in reading the six passionate, despairing, pitiful appeals for a vanished love which Martha Manning had written to Harry Borden, the woman who had taken that love from her was announced:

"Miss Gilman and Detective Clay, sir."

"Show Miss Gilman in here. I'll speak to Clay out there," McMann directed, and a moment later the detective in charge of the investigation and a tall, magnificently proportioned blond woman passed each other in the door way.

"Hul—lo!" Cleo Gilman sang out cheerily, in her slightly nasal, high pitched voice. As the detective pushed on through the door without answering, except with one keen, measuring glance of his gray eyes, the blond woman shrugged, and addressed Ruth Lester, who was seated at Borden's desk: "I always did love these strong, silent men. Hawkshaw, the demon detecatif, I suppose?" she laughed, strolling with exaggerated nonchalance to a chair near Ruth's, and disposing her voluptuous body in it.

"Yes," Ruth smiled. "Or, to be accurate, Detective Sergeant McMann in charge of the investigation into the murder of your late—friend."

"Meow!" Cleo chided, as she took a cigarette from a lovely black and green enameled case which, Ruth knew, had been one of Harry Borden's Christmas gifts to his then adored mistress. "Poor old 'Handsome Harry!' I was always afraid he'd come to some bad end . . . But what have you done to yourself, darling? You are the priceless pearl of a secretary, aren't you? But I seem to remember you as a timid little slavey, with horn rimmed spectacles, Salvation Army clothes, and your hair dragged into a knot on your neck. I wonder! I wonder . . . And yet I'd been led to believe that it was the fascinating Rita who had— Oh! Hawkshaw!" And Cleo rounded her seductive lips to blow a cloud of smoke toward the returning detective.

McMann, pretending not to hear, strode to Borden's desk, took his seat opposite Ruth, poised his pencil over a pad of scratch paper. "Well, when did you see Borden last, Cleo?"

"Miss Gilman—to you, darling—just until we know each other a little better," Cleo Gilman drawled, arching silken brown brows over wide, topaz colored eyes. "Don't scowl so, Hawkshaw. I'm sure you'd be an awfully attractive man, if you'd just cultivate a jolly smile . . . Oh, very well! If you don't want to be sociable— You asked when I last saw Harry, I believe. Well, let me think—" and she regarded the burning tip of her cigarette with a charming frown.

"Last Saturday, wasn't it?" McMann barked.

Cleo Gilman's carefree laugh rang out. "Poor Hawkshaw! You must be terribly hard up for a suspect if you've picked on me! No—I'm awfully sorry to disappoint you, but I haven't seen 'Handsome Harry' since January second. He dropped in to pay the rent on the apartment and to break the sad news to me that all was over between us."

"Just like that, eh?" McMann growled. "I suppose you quarreled?"

"Oh," Cleo shrugged and smiled, "just enough to give the old boy a good time. It would have hurt his feelings if I hadn't pulled the regular 'you done me wrong' line, but to tell you the truth, darling, I wasn't at all sorry— saved me a lot of trouble, for I was really awful busy on a new enterprise—"

"Just where were you last Saturday, after leaving your apartment at noon with your baggage?" McMann cut in impatiently.

"Now, now!" Cleo shook her charming head at the detective reproachfully. "You're spoiling an awfully good story with your crude importunities. There! I've been aching to use that word—importunities. I've just learned it, you know . . . Yes, yes, darling! I realize you want to know where I was Saturday afternoon, but I'm trying to break it to you gently. Large, bad tempered men, who are not so young are so likely to go off like—that!—with apoplexy. All *right,* Hawkshaw, I'll tell you, but you can't say I didn't warn you— At two o'clock," Cleo Gilman announced calmly, after a long draw at a new cigarette, "which, I gather from our unduly excited newspapers, was approximately the hour when poor old Harry was bumped off, I was in Hartford, Connecticut—delightful little town, but rather slow, don't you think?—being married—"

"Married!" McMann exploded.

"I was afraid you'd take it like that," Cleo sympathized. "But bear up, darling. The worst is yet to come. I was being married to—Arthur Dean Pendennis the third—or is it the fourth?"

"Young Pendennis, the multi millionaire clubman," McMann said slowly, gazing with something like awe at the voluptuous blonde who was smiling lazily at him.

"Fie, fie! Hawkshaw, you've been reading the tabloids!" Cleo Gilman Pandennis chided him.

"If you were married Saturday, how does it happen that you returned to your apartment alone today?" McMann demanded skeptically.

"Well, you see," Cleo smiled enchantingly, "our marriage came as quite a surprise—to Arty. I myself thought I could manage it nicely—as I did, but I agreed with Arty that he'd better hurry home and break the news to Mother —a rather terrible person, his mother, I understand. He's with her now, having rather a tough time of it, I'm afraid —since the papers somehow got hold of the fact that his little Cleo was being 'sought' to be 'grilled'—oh, those tabloids! They *are* insidious, aren't they? Arty has been trying to purify my English—"

McMann drew a deep breath and spread his hands in a gesture of defeat. "Sorry to have bothered you, Mrs. Pendennis. And I hope we can hush things up so as not to cause you any serious trouble with your husband—"

"Oh, please don't trouble your darling old head about me!" Cleo interrupted quickly, her smile brilliantly care free. "Really, Hawkshaw— and you can call me Cleo, now that we're so well acquainted—this is an awfully lucky break for me. You see, I'd made a sort of general confession of—uh—naughtiness before Arty proposed to me— one of those blanket confessions that can cover a multitude of sins and sinners, like Harry Borden, and he forgave all. But dear old Mrs. Pendennis won't let her precious boy come near me again, after she realizes that he has married one of the 'women grilled in Borden murder'—which is what I call a perfectly swell break for little Cleo!"

"You mean—you don't want to live with your husband?" McMann stared at her incredulously.

"How quick you are, Hawkshaw! Little Miss Lester here tumbled ten minutes ago, but for a man you're not so dumb! Of course I don't want to live with Arty. He bores me. Would you believe it?—he quotes a couple of poets named Sheats and Kelly, or Shelley and Keats, I can never remember which—quotes them by the yard, and for weeks I've had to listen and say, 'Oh, da—r—ling! How perfectly sweet! And how *beautifully* you recite poetry!' Arty, I may add, so that you will understand all, has never been in a nightclub in his life and intends to leave half his fortune to the Metropolitan Museum of Art."

"If there is anything left of it when you've taken him to the cleaners," McMann grinned. "I suppose you've got your marriage certificate with you?"

"Dated Saturday, and issued at Hartford, a bona fide county seat," Cleo assured him obligingly, as she extracted the precious document from her large, snakeskin handbag. "It took us two hours to drive to Hartford, and we were married at two o'clock. Our honeymoon was spent in the Pendennis shooting lodge, up in some ghastly mountains somewhere—I wanted to go to Atlantic City, but Arty— "

"All right!" McMann interrupted brusquely, as he returned the marriage certificate to its owner. "But just a minute," he detained the nonchalant beauty who had risen and was wrapping her platinum caracul coat about her voluptuously curved figure. "Perhaps you can help me. . . . From your intimacy with Borden, do you know of any one who had threatened his life, or of whom he was actually afraid?"

Cleo laughed. "Harry was afraid of his shadow. I suppose you know he had a bodyguard? I used to think he was dippy on the subject, and I tried to kid him out of it, wouldn't let him talk about it—but sure enough, some one did bump him off, just as—"

"Did he mention names?" McMann interrupted.

"He gave me a long song and dance when I first met him about the sweetie he had before he fell in love with me—used to tell me by the hour about how crazy she was about him, and how scared he was that she'd try to get even. But, Lord, all men talk like that about the women they're through with!"

"Who was the woman you took him away from?" McMann persisted.

"He wasn't hard to take," Cleo laughed. "I gathered he'd been ripe for picking a long time. . . . But—sorry, Hawkshaw! I'm naming no names. Just write it down that I don't know her name." She drew on a beautiful, silvery gray glove, smiling at the scowling detective with wide, topaz eyes, as she added: "I've had a number of labels pinned on me, first and last, and probably the Dowager Queen Pendennis will think up a good, hot new one, but —even Harry Borden, when he gave me my notice on January 2, had the grace to say I was a—good sport. . . . So long, darling! I've had a wonderful time. Good bye, Miss Lester. If I were as pretty as you are, I'd have grabbed off the Prince of Wales, instead of poor old Arty."

When Cleo was gone, McMann refused to meet the eyes of the girl opposite him, making a great ado of shuffling his memoranda on the case.

"A good sport," Ruth said softly.

"Borden must have been crazy to ditch a peach like that for Rita Dubois," McMann agreed, lowering his head so that his blush might not be so apparent.

Ruth laughed. "Maybe Mr. Borden was an exception to the rule *you* follow, Mr. McMann—he was one 'gentleman' who really preferred brunettes. Mrs. Borden is brunette, Martha Manning is—"

"Detective Carlson with Miss Manning, sir," Birdwell interrupted.

As he had done upon the arrival of both Rita Dubois and Cleo Gilman, McMann had the woman shown into the dead man's private office, while he conferred briefly in the outer office with the detective who had brought her in.

In the brief interval before the detective sergeant's return, Ruth Lester had opportunity to study the woman about whom her curiosity had been raised to an extraordinary pitch—the woman who might never have been involved in the investigation of Harry Borden's murder, if it had not been for her—Ruth's—interference.

Ruth saw a no longer young, but still lovely woman— tall, very slender, graceful. Beneath the brim of a long worn but still smart blue felt hat a pair of great dark eyes—their brilliance heightened by the mascara which frankly beaded the lashes—surveyed the room in which her former lover had died, then came to rest inquiringly upon Ruth.

"I'm Ruth Lester. I—worked here," Ruth answered the unspoken inquiry, tactfully avoiding the name of the murdered man.

"Thank you," Martha Manning murmured. Then, releasing the full glory of the voice that Ruth knew so well, and which had been thrice described since Borden had died: "I am Miss Manning. May I take off my coat, please?"

Ruth watched her remove the well cut but slightly shabby garment of dark blue cloth, trimmed with worn black sealskin, revealing a straightline frock of silk crepe, almost exactly the shade of red as the rouge spots on her thin, heavily powdered cheeks, and the brilliant salve on her lips. "Too much make up," Ruth told herself, "But somehow it suits her."

Miss Manning laid her coat on the back of the chair which Ruth offered, then seated herself upon it, crossing her knees, so that one foot swung free, unconsciously revealing to Ruth the fact that the meticulously brushed black suede pumps had been half soled.

She waited calmly, her black gloved hands loosely clasped about a small black leather handbag in her lap, her face in repose, her dark eyes gazing steadily at one of the windows that looked out upon the street. If she was nervous, apprehensive, she concealed it admirably. She made no fluttery movements, did not raise a hand to pat the scallops of soft black hair that outlined her artistically made up face; did not fish in her handbag for lipstick or compact with which to add touches to an already perfect job of personal adornment. Nor did she speak again. She simply waited. And when at last McMann entered the room she greeted him, in that exquisite contralto voice, as courteously and calmly as if they were meeting at a social function.

"You're Miss Manning? Martha Manning?" McMann asked abruptly, when he had seated himself at the dead man's desk and was ready with his inevitable pencil and pad of scratch paper.

"I am."

"Living at the Acropolis Hotel?"

"Yes. I am employed there, as Mr. Carlson has undoubtedly told you," the woman answered courteously, with no hint of resentment.

"Just what do you do there?"

"I operate the switchboard. My salary, exclusive of my room rent, is ten dollars a week."

"And your hours on duty?"

"From six in the morning until half past eleven. I accepted the position because the hours are short. My health is not very good, requiring me to spend a number of hours each day in the open air," Miss Manning replied calmly, but then suddenly she betrayed either nervousness or the call of a long indulged habit, for she asked: "Do you mind if I smoke?"

"Nervous?" McMann grinned, as the woman stripped' the gloves from her hands and opened her bag to extract a package of fifteen cent cigarettes. She had no cigarette case. Perhaps, Ruth thought pityingly, Borden had once given her just such an expensive case as Cleo Gilman had displayed in that office an hour before, but if so, it had undoubtedly gone, along with Borden's other rich gifts, to pay her small son's expenses at boarding school. Ten dollars a week and a tiny hotel room for five and a half hours work a day! Suddenly Ruth felt slightly ill, ashamed . . .

"Draw your chair up to the desk so you can reach this ash tray," McMann suggested, his voice noticeably less harsh.

"Thank you," Martha Manning replied simply, and obeyed. In the new position, her body was turned squarely toward Ruth, but her head, on its long, slender, lined neck —an age revealing neck—inclined courteously toward her inquisitor.

"Miss Manning," McMann began again, in a crisp, businesslike manner, "what was your relationship to Henry F. Borden?"

"Rather less than— nothing," Martha Manning answered slowly. "I was merely a—former—friend."

"A former—mistress, you mean, don't you?" McMann asked bluntly.

Natural color crept from that pathetically thin throat and blended with the brilliant spots of rouge. Martha Manning inclined her head in mute assent.

"When did you and Harry Borden become lovers and how long did the relationship last?" McMann demanded.

The woman stiffened and her nostrils dilated. "I am afraid I must decline to answer that question, Mr. McMann! I have admitted the relationship, which ceased to exist almost a year before Mr. Borden's—death." The lovely voice vibrated with indignation, but it broke just before it uttered that last word.

McMann shrugged, his narrowed gray eyes fixed on her flushed face. "Miss Manning, when did you last see Harry Borden?"

# CHAPTER TWENTY ONE

"I HAVE seen Mr. Borden a number of times during the last few months—at a distance," Martha Manning answered the detective sergeant's question.

"You mean you followed him about?" McMann pounced.

"I ask you again, Miss Manning—when was the last time you saw Harry Borden?" McMann asked with angry impatience.

Martha Manning smiled strangely, but did not answer. But she tamped out her half smoked cigarette in the ash tray which stood on Borden's desk, and dropped her hands into her lap—as if she could not trust one of them under the piercing eye of the detective.

"My last—interview with Mr. Borden was on Christmas Eve. I'm afraid I took rather an unfair advantage of his manservant's carelessness—as he has probably told you— and succeeded in speaking with Mr. Borden."

"Ah!" McMann raised his bushy brows. "And what was the purpose and the result of that impromptu interview, Miss Manning?"

"As to the purpose of that interview, I decline to answer. Its result you undoubtedly know already," the woman answered calmly, but Ruth saw that her hands were gripping each other tightly in her lap.

McMann laughed, an ugly sound. "You're a cool one, all right! . . . Yes, the man Ashe has told us that you and Borden, in the presence of Jake Bailey, Borden's bodyguard, had a row that ended in a fight in which you were almost knocked out. I see the cut on your lip has healed . . . You tried to kill your lover then, didn't you?—and didn't quite make a job of it?"

The woman's great dark eyes blazed with scorn. "May I remind you that it was I, and not Mr. Borden, who was injured in that encounter?"

"But—" McMann leaned forward toward her across the desk, his gray eyes narrowed to slits—"you've hated him and planned revenge ever since that night! That's true, isn't it?"

"No!" The denial rang out sharply, then, in a voice that quivered and broke with emotion: "I loved him. I loved Harry Borden from the day I met him till the day he died. I still love him—wherever he is now, and will love him till I die!"

The detective settled back in his chair, regarding the trembling woman with that twisted smile of his which Ruth Lester longed passionately to strike from his mouth.

"Suppose we get down to brass tacks, Miss Manning. I'll tell you a few things, and then you tell me a few. Tit for tat. Fair exchange. First: you have a son—" he said with awful casualness, then paused to watch the blood slowly drain from Martha Manning's thin face, leaving the rouge spots in ghastly relief. "A son you have tried to force Harry Borden to recognize and support as his illegitimate child—"

"Stop!" Martha Manning half rose from her chair, leaned toward the detective with clenched, trembling hand, as if she were going to strike him. "Harry Borden did not deny that he was the father of my son! He knew—oh, my God, how well he knew!" and she sank back into her chair and pressed her knuckles to her mouth to stifle the sobs that were shaking her whole frail body.

McMann was apparently unmoved. He went on relentlessly: "You loved this man, you bore him a son, you lived with him for years, and yet for months before his death he would not even speak to you on the telephone. He left orders with his secretary and with his manservant that if 'the woman with the contralto voice' called, Mr.

Henry P. Borden was 'not in.' How do you account for this, Miss Manning?"

The woman raised her head, and with tight clasped hands, fought a moment for self control. "I asked some thing of Mr. Borden which he would not—or could not—do. I—demanded that he marry me, so that our son might bear his father's name."

"What do you mean—could not?" McMann caught her up.

"He told me that Mrs. Borden would not give him a divorce. She knew—about my baby, and was determined that her own children should never know of their father's —sin. When I insisted, Harry—Mr. Borden—left me—"

"Because he had fallen in love with Cleo Gilman. Isn't that more like it?" McMann interrupted.

The woman shrank against her chair, but only her great tormented brown eyes answered, with such pitiful appeal that Ruth's own eyes stung with sudden tears.

"And so," McMann went on, "you followed him about, telephoned him here at his office and at his home, wrote him letters which he did not answer, made an excuse to enter another office in this building so that you could observe your intended victim, then, by a lucky chance, discovered how you could use that other office as the scene of your crime—"

"No, no!" Martha Manning screamed, springing to her feet, her eyes blazing, but her face ashen, except for those ghastly spots of rouge. "You're cowardly, despicable! You *know* you have no foundation for a charge like that against me."

"I haven't made any charge—yet," McMann reminded her grimly, as he too rose and pushed back his chair. "Come here, Miss Manning!" and the detective seized one of the woman's wrists and drew her by force to the window looking out upon the airshaft. "Look!" and he pointed to the opposite window. "Whose office is that?"

The woman snatched her imprisoned hand from the detective's hold and rubbed her reddened wrist. "I—don't know! How should I?"

"Then let me remind you," McMann retorted. "That is the private office of Mr. John C. Hayward, insurance broker, the very agreeable and handsome young man whom you consulted, not so long ago, on the subject of a policy in favor of your son. . . . Do you remember now?"

Martha Manning seemed suddenly to get control of her tortured nerves. Almost calmly, though Ruth thought she moved hastily over the spot where Borden's life blood had ebbed away, the woman walked across the room and took her seat again. It was not until the detective was also seated that she answered his question:

"I did consult Mr. Hayward about insurance, but that is not usually considered a criminal offense, Mr. McMann."

"And how did you happen to pick out that particular insurance broker?" McMann asked sarcastically. "Is he famous in his field?"

"I saw his name and business listed on the bulletin board of the Starbridge Building," Miss Manning answered defiantly.

"One of those days when you were trailing Borden? By the way, you were still living with Harry Borden when he took these offices three years ago, weren't you? You were pretty familiar with the layout of this floor, I suppose?"

"When I went to consult Mr. Hayward about insurance, I had no idea that his office was across the airshaft from Harry's," was the positive, almost calmly spoken answer, but Ruth saw a pair of thin, white hands twisting, intertwining—hands that could not lie, no matter how well that beautiful contralto voice could be made to serve its owner's hidden purposes. As Ruth watched those hands she got an odd, subconscious impression that they had a message for her—a message of vital importance—but with that compelling voice to listen to, there was no time for Ruth to heed the mute story that the hands were telling. . . .

"Then may I remind you that when you were in Mr. Hayward's office on two occasions you went to that window, which affords a view of the interior of this office, and stood there—each time—for minutes, looking toward and undoubtedly into this very room?"

"I did not look this way, because I did not realize that by so doing I could see into Mr. Borden's office. My eyes idly followed a number of pigeons circling about the window, but my thoughts were on my son, and how to provide for him in case of my death."

"Your natural death—or by way of the electric chair?" McMann suggested brutally.

The frail body stiffened, but the contralto voice scorned to make a plea for sympathy: "When I first consulted Mr. Hayward about insurance I knew I was not well, but I considered myself a passable insurance risk. But when I saw him the second time, I went with the knowledge that insurance was impossible, for my physician had told me that I have pulmonary tuberculosis. It was with this knowledge that I appealed to Mr. Borden on Christmas Eve for help for my son."

There was a brief silence, almost long enough for Ruth to hear the mute message which Martha Manning's thin, twisting hands seemed to be trying to give her—without their owner's knowledge or consent. But not quite, for McMann interrupted, demanded the girl's whole attention with his next words:

"I submit, Miss Manning," McMann began slowly, "that your need became so desperate that you determined to stop at nothing, not even a threat of murder, to force Harry Borden to provide for your son. Isn't that true?"

"No!"

"You deny then, Miss Manning, that you have ever threatened Harry Borden's life?"

"I do! Of course I deny it!" The beautiful voice throbbed with anger.

McMann smiled. "But you won't deny that you have written to Mr. Borden a number of times in the last few months?"

The woman's eyes dilated, then closed for a moment, before she answered in a voice so low it was almost a 'whisper: "No. I won't deny—that. Of course I wrote him. I could reach him in no other way."

"And when did you write your last letter to your for mer lover?" McMann persisted.

Martha Manning moistened her dry lips. "I—don't remember the exact time."

"Then let me refresh your memory," the detective suggested, slowly drawing a large, orchid tinted envelope from his pocket.

The woman half started from her chair, seemed about to ask a startled question, then subsided, her great, stricken brown eyes fixed in terrible fascination upon the closely written sheet which McMann drew from the envelope and laid before her.

"You recognize this letter? You admit you wrote it?"

There was no need for an answer, and Martha Manning made none.

"You will note," McMann pointed out obligingly, "that it was written Friday afternoon—the day before Henry Borden was—murdered. Now, if you will kindly read aloud the last three sentences of this letter—" and he turned over the single sheet of orchid stationery.

One of those betraying, thin hands reached out, hovered over the sheet, but did not touch it—dropped instead to the green blotter with which the top of the desk was almost entirely covered; lay there, quivering.

"You won't oblige me?" McMann asked cheerfully. "Then let me repeat them from a very good memory: 'But Harry, in all solemnity, *I warn you that you will be sorry if you do not do what I ask. I shall telephone you Saturday morning. If your answer is still no—but I won't think of that now!'"*

That pitiful, quivering hand started to lift itself from the blotter, but with the quickness of a sleight of hand artist's the detective's big hand shot out and covered it, flattening it against the green surface of the blotter. With his other hand he seized a full ink well and tipped it, so that the fluid ran in a dark tide beneath the pressed down fingers of the woman.

"How dare you?" Martha Manning gasped, struggling to release her hand. "What are you doing?"

"Merely saving time by taking your finger prints myself, Miss Manning!" the detective answered, as he lifted her ink stained hand and pressed the fingers upon a sheet of white paper.

# CHAPTER TWENTY TWO

RUTH LESTER felt that she, as well as the frail, tortured woman beside her, could not bear the suspense of the next slow minutes. With nerve racking deliberation, Detective Sergeant McMann drew another sheet of paper from his pocket—the enlarged photograph of the three finger prints discovered by Detective Ferber on the glass panel of the door between the outer and the inner offices of the Borden suite; laid it beside the startlingly clear prints he had just made, in ink, of Martha Manning's fingers; studied both sets of prints through narrowed, gray eyes, then, with maddening lack of haste reached into his coat pocket, secured a small microscope and fitted it into his left eye.

At last he nodded with satisfaction, folded both sheets of paper carefully together and placed them in a breast pocket of his coat. Then he spoke: "Miss Manning, we will save much time if you will tell me frankly at just what time Saturday afternoon you paid your—farewell visit to Harry Borden."

The thin hands were working desperately now with a handkerchief to remove the humiliating ink stains but at the detective's question they gripped each other convulsively.

"I was not here at all on Saturday!"

"Then how do you account for the fact that your finger prints were found yesterday morning on the glass panel of that door?" McMann demanded triumphantly, pointing toward the closed door between the two offices.

Martha Manning drew a sharp, quivering breath, then, to Ruth's amazement she smiled, and the thin shoulders shrugged slightly, as if their owner were admitting defeat. "I am sorry to disappoint you, Mr.

McMann, after your brilliant demonstration of detective story ingenuity, but —my visit to Harry Borden was made on Friday night— not on Saturday afternoon!"

"Is that so?" McMann snorted, after the first impact of the shock. "Well, we'll soon find out if you were here Friday night! Perhaps you're not aware of the fact, Miss Manning, that every tenant or visitor coming into this building after seven o'clock in the evening is required to sign a register kept in the elevator." He rose and was striding toward the communicating door to give an order to Birdwell, when Martha Manning stopped him, with a cool admission:

"I'm quite aware of the custom you mention, Mr. McMann! And you may save yourself the trouble of consulting the register, unless you wish to verify my statement that Mr. Borden was in his office Friday night."

Ruth knew, by the curious expression that distorted the detective's face, that he had failed to check the register for Friday night, and was now disgusted with himself for that omission.

He continued to the door, threw it open, and with harsh impatience gave the necessary instructions to long suffering Detective Birdwell. Then, whirling back toward the woman who was regarding him coolly, with her great, scornful brown eyes, the detective demanded:

"You admit then, that I shall not find your name on that register? I suppose you're going to try to tell me that you signed a fake name, in a disguised handwriting, and that you've forgotten just which name you did sign!"

"Hardly anything so crude and easily exploded as that," Martha Manning smiled. "I am going to do something much more simple—tell you the truth. I walked up and walked down, taking care not to be seen by the elevator operator."

"Why?" McMann demanded. "Because you were planning *then* to kill Borden and didn't have a chance to go through with it?"

"Your conclusion is undoubtedly logical—from your standpoint," Martha Manning agreed, still smiling strangely. "It simply happens to be totally inaccurate. I walked up because I feared Mr. Borden had seen me following him and had given orders to the elevator man not to admit me into the building."

"But if you did see him, why walk down?" McMann caught her up sharply.

"For approximately the same reason," Miss Manning pointed out patiently. "I mean—I did not want Mr. Borden to give orders to the elevator man that the woman he had just taken down was not to be admitted again."

"Then you expected to make another attempt to carry out your plans, which had miscarried?" McMann suggested.

Again the woman shrugged. "My plans never included anything more sinister than an earnest appeal to Mr. Borden's generosity."

"You say that—" McMann pretended honest amazement—"in face of the threat in this last letter of yours—this threat against Borden's life?" He reached for the letter, read again that damning sentence: " 'But, Harry, in all solemnity, I warn you that you will be sorry if you do not do what I ask!' "

"I admit that it is a threat," Martha Manning said coolly, then flashed a brief, almost affectionate smile at Ruth Lester as the girl gasped. "But it happens, Mr. McMann, that it is not a threat against Mr. Borden's life. When I saw him Christmas Eve, by a ruse—just as I saw him Friday night—I warned him that if he did not voluntarily make adequate provision for our son, I should institute legal proceedings to force him to do so. I have an abundance of documentary evidence, including a number of letters from Mr. Borden in which he more than admits paternity—boasts of it, in fact; also letters to my little son from his—father." Her voice faltered over that name for the murdered man, but her head remained high and proud.

"Had you taken steps to institute such legal proceedings?" McMann asked, with obvious skepticism.

"I had—not," the woman admitted reluctantly. "I—had no money, and I wanted Harry—Mr. Borden—to be spared the consequent notoriety; hence my repeated appeals."

McMann drummed on the desk top for a long minute, and was about to speak when Birdwell interrupted with the requested sheets from the loose leaf register kept by the elevator men of the Starbridge Building. The detective snatched at them, then after a moment's study, he smiled that twisted, cynical smile of his and said:

"Suppose you tell me all about Friday night, Miss Manning—your following of Borden, and your cleverly managed interview with him."

"I shall be glad to," Miss Manning assured him composedly, though Ruth saw that the tell tale hands were locking and unlocking nervously in her lap. "I—happened to be walking in this block—on the sidewalk opposite the Starbridge Building, when I saw Mr. Borden and a man whom I recognized as 'Jake'—the man who had been with Mr. Borden on Christmas Eve when I—talked with him. You referred to him as Jake Bailey, a few minutes ago, But I did not know his last name until then."

She paused, and Ruth had an opportunity to note an almost ludicrous expression of chagrin on the detective's face.

"Well! Go on!" McMann ordered brusquely.

"As they turned in toward the entrance of the building, I started across the street, and I was afraid Mr. Borden had seen me, for he glanced over his shoulder just before he entered the storm doors, behind Jake. I waited until I was fairly sure the elevator had risen with them, and then I too entered through the storm doors and, as the lobby was deserted, I opened the door leading to the stairway and walked up."

"Just what time was this?" McMann asked, his frowning eyes on the register sheet which had recorded the time as well as the name of all arrivals and departures on Friday night.

"I can't say exactly, since I—no longer own a watch," Miss Manning admitted, the bitter lines between nostrils and mouth deepening. "But it was about half past eight."

Although Martha Manning was slowly destroying the case which Ruth Lester had, with what she considered quite remarkable ingenuity, built against "the woman with the contralto voice," the girl could hardly keep from smiling at the deepening chagrin on the detective's face.

"Well—why these dramatic pauses?" he demanded irritably.

"I—am rather short of breath," the woman admitted, but with no hint of a bid for sympathy. "I walked up, resting frequently, for I was in no hurry. I had no intention of trying to see Harry while the man Jake was with him. I could only hope that Jake would not stay long, and that I should have an opportunity to speak with Harry—Mr. Borden—alone."

"And did you?" McMann prodded her, as she again paused. He had to wait, however, until a spasm of coughing had spent itself.

"When I reached the seventh floor, I found the corridor deserted, and walked softly to Mr. Borden's office," Miss Manning went on at last, after dabbing at her lips with the ink stained handkerchief. "I listened, and heard faintly the sound of voices. I knew that Jake was still with Mr. Borden, so I withdrew to the head of the stairway again, and waited, listening through a crack in the door. After several minutes I heard footsteps, and peeped out. Jake was at the elevator. When it had taken him in, and was on its way down, I ran to Mr. Borden's door, removed my glove so that I could knock loudly. I counted on Mr. Borden's thinking that Jake had come back for some forgotten last word. Of course I tried the door first, but it was locked, as I had expected. He did open the door—wide, as I had hoped, and before he could prevent me I slipped in."

"Glad to see you?" McMann cut in sarcastically.

"No," the woman answered simply. "But—he did agree to talk with me. We sat here—at his desk—" and the beautiful voice faltered, broke.

"Borden opened the door between the two offices for you, I suppose?" McMann suggested casually.

"Yes—of course! He was willing to talk things over, as I told you."

"Then how do you account for your finger prints on the door between?" McMann sprung his trap.

The woman looked confused, then confident again. "I remember! When I came out of this office—Harry did not accompany me to the outer door—I felt dizzy, ill with relief and joy—and I leaned for a moment against the door, throwing up one hand against the glass panel to steady myself."

Again McMann looked so chagrined that Ruth could have laughed, although Jack Hayward seemed farther than ever from being cleared of the charge of murder which might be officially lodged against him at any moment.

"So you were dizzy with joy, eh?" McMann grunted at last. "What was the good news?"

"Harry—Mr. Borden—had agreed to establish a trust fund for our son, promised me that he would take it up with his lawyer the next day, or Monday at the latest," Martha Manning answered. "He—did not live to do so."

"So—" McMann leaned forward, and leveled a menacing, triumphant forefinger at the woman—"you called him on the telephone on Saturday morning and again about half past one, just to tell him how happy you were, I suppose? . . . Wait! No use thinking up another good lie! I'll not mince words with you, Miss Manning! I don't believe a word of this fine yarn you've spun to account for these finger prints of yours! In some way—I'll find out how, all right!—you knew when Borden and

Bailey entered the building, and when Bailey left it, but when I get hold of Jake Bailey I'll be able to knock your pretty story into a cocked hat—"

As if the detective's words had been endowed with magic, the communicating door opened at that precise moment, and Birdwell's weary, bored voice announced:

"Jake Bailey is here, sir. He wants to know if he can be of any help, he says—"

"He's damned right he can!" McMann exploded. "Show him in!"

A short, broad shouldered man, his face composed of a set of battered, unmatching features, on which a genial smile set oddly, swaggered into the room, his surprisingly falsetto greeting accompanying an enormous hand thrust out toward the detective in charge of the investigation into the murder of Henry P. Borden.

"Hello, Cap! Seen in the papers where my buddy, Harry Borden, got bumped off, and that you was anxious to have a chat with me. Anything I can do—Well, I guess you don't need me after all, Cap!" he broke off, when, on reaching Borden's desk and shaking hands heartily with McMann, he got a full view of the face of the woman whose back had been turned toward him as he entered the room. "So—you got him, did you? Minute my back was turned—"

"Just a minute, Bailey!" McMann interrupted sharply. "You identify this woman?"

"Sure I know her! Harry hisself pointed her out to me not a week after he took me on to look after him. 'Jake,' he says, 'take a good look at that woman and don't let her get any nearer to me than she is now, or you'll lose your job, Jake,' he says—"

"When and where was this?" McMann interrupted impatiently.

"Now—lemme see!" Jake Bailey laid his gray derby on his dead employer's desk and scratched his wet combed brown head. "Must a been 'long about the middle of November, for I had my last bout with Battlin' Demon on

November tent'—a frame up it was, too, Cap, I'll take my Bible oath! All right, Cap! Keep your shirt on!" he admonished the detective genially. "But you ast, didn't you? Well, it must a been about the middle of November, then, and me and Harry was walkin' along Fifth Avenoo when Harry pipes this dame gittin' off a bus. She makes like she's gonna speak to him or bust, and then he says to me, Harry says—"

"Yes, you've already told that!" McMann interrupted impatiently. "Did she speak to him?"

"Say, Cap!" Jake Bailey grinned broadly. "Harry hopped into a taxi so quick I almost got left!"

"Did you ever see her again?"

"Sure! Christmas Eve. That bird that putters around Harry's apartment went to the bootlegger's downstairs and left the door unlatched, and first thing me and Harry knew—in the bedroom we was—there she was, no shame at all—busting in on a man what's changin' his clothes!"

At that expression of Jake's outraged modesty, Martha Manning laughed—a queer, startling blend of scorn and ironic amusement.

"Yeah! You can laugh, can't you?" Jake Bailey's little greenish blue eyes glared at her with hatred. "You got him —jist like he thought you would, and now you laugh!"

Martha Manning's brown eyes swept him scornfully, as if he were an obnoxious insect, and dropped to the now quiescent hands in her lap.

"Jake, this is a serious charge you're making against Miss Manning," the detective began. "What foundation have you for this charge? Have you personal knowledge of Miss Manning's guilt?"

"Personal knowledge—hell!" the ex pugilist retorted. "If you mean—did I see her do it?—no! I left town Friday night and jist got back—"

"Before we go into your own whereabouts on Saturday, when Borden was killed," McMann interrupted, "suppose you tell me exactly what happened on Christmas Eve, between Miss Manning and Harry Borden."

"Well, like I said—me and Harry was in Harry's bedroom, when in she walks, bold as brass. 'Harry,' she says, 'it's Christmas! Aren't you going to give me—and the boy—a Christmas present?' she says, and by that time Harry was at her, tryin' to walk her right back out of his room. But she hung back—like a wildcat she was—and she keeps whinin' something about not wantin' nothin' for Christmas but his promise to git a divorce and marry her, like he promised—oh, no! She didn't want nothin' much!" he laughed sarcastically.

"And then? Borden struck her on the mouth?" McMann prompted impatiently.

Something like a blush ran over the scrambled features of the ex pugilist. "We ell, Cap," he admitted reluctantly, "I reckon that was me. Harry was payin' me a good sal'ry to pertect him, wasn't he? I jist done my duty—'at's all! But I never hit her till she snatched open her handbag— like she was reachin' for a gun—and Harry yelled at me to help him."

"And did she have one?"

"No," the dead man's efficient bodyguard admitted. "Reckon she was after a picture of the kid she had in her bag. Had 'Merry Christmas for my Dad' wrote on it—"

It was not a laugh this time that told that Jake Bailey's words had struck home. It was a long drawn "Oh!" of infinite misery, so heart rending that Ruth Lester involuntarily leaned forward and patted those tight locked hands whose message she had not yet had time to read.

"And after you knocked her out?" McMann prodded his witness.

"Well, me and Harry fixed her up with some brandy, and I took her down and put her in a taxi. Paid for it, too," the ex pugilist added virtuously.

"And did Borden later intimate to you that he feared this woman would kill him?"

Martha Manning raised her head then and stared steadily at the man who leaned nonchalantly against her dead lover's desk.

"Sure!" came the emphatic answer in a cracking falsetto. "He said he'd a swore she was gonna croak him that time, and he bet she'd do it yet—"

"So you offered to put her out of the way for him, didn't you?" McMann asked casually, after a glance at the notes he had made on the story of Frank Ashe, Borden's manservant.

"Well, I didn't, so it won't be me 'at'll sit in the chair," Bailey retorted.

"And did you see Miss Manning again?" McMann pursued his questioning.

"Naw—guess she laid low and waited till I was out of town," Bailey answered.

"You didn't see her on Friday night?"

"No, I left town on Friday night, like I told you."

"But you were with Borden before you left?"

"Sure I was. I went with him to the Crillon, a swell feed joint, and waited outside while he et with his new sweetie, that classy little dancer he picked up at the Golden Slipper. 'Bout half past six it was when he met her there, and around eight when him and her come out. He put the frail in a taxi, and promised to see her at the Golden Slipper about ten, before her act went on at eleven. She wouldn't let him drive over to her hotel with her—always acted pretty ritzy with him—that dame did. So him and me hopped into another cab and come on over to his office. Said he was dopin' out a new scheme and wanted to work awhile before goin' to the Golden Slipper."

"And did you come up with him?"

"Sure! Harry wouldn't go into his own office at night alone, if he could help it. Scared some sucker who was sore at him because he'd lost his money might be layin' for him, or this dame here," and Jake jerked his head toward Martha Manning. "I come up all right, and we set here awhile, chewin' the rag—told me about this dancin' baby he was gonna take to Winter Heaven with him Saturday, if he could get her boss to let her off."

"How long were you with Borden?"

"Oh, 'bout half an hour, I guess," Jake answered readily. "I didn't have nothin' to do but kill time before my train left from the Grand Central—nine twenty four, that was. Must a been 'round nine when I beat it—sure, that's when it was! Eight fifty five! I remember asking the elevator man what time it was, when he shoved his book at me to sign out. They make you write down the time and your name and the office you've been in."

"Please, Mr. McMann, may I ask a question?" Ruth spoke for the first time since Jake Bailey had entered the room. "I've just been wondering how Mr. Borden got into his office, since he'd given his key to Rita Dubois Friday afternoon and never did get it back."

"That's right!" McMann agreed, rather ungraciously. He did not enjoy having been caught napping. "How did Borden get in, Jake?"

"Check, kid!" and Jake touched his forehead in a salute to Ruth. "Harry didn't remember till he got to his door that he didn't have no key, and since I never had none myself, he had to hunt up one of the old janes that cleans the offices to let him in with her passkey. He couldn't find the old lady that took care of his office reg'lar, and had to prove who he was by showin' a letter with his name on it to the woman I scouted around and found for him."

"Hmm! Letty Miller, I suppose. She's the only other cleaning woman on the floor," McMann commented, as he made a note. "Where did you find her?"

"Down the hall," Bailey answered promptly. "Said she wasn't acquainted with the tenants on this corridor, but was jist helpin' out the old lady who belongs on this part of the floor."

For the first time in many minutes, McMann addressed a question to Martha Manning: "Did you see this scrubwoman yourself, Miss Manning?"

The contralto voice was quite steady. "No. As I told you before, I saw no one. I was alone while I waited for — this man—" and she nodded scornfully toward Jake Bailey—"to leave, and no one but myself was in the hall when I left, after seeing Mr. Borden. The scrubwoman who admitted Mr. Borden must have finished her work in this corridor before I had walked up the stairs."

McMann peremptorially commanded the amazed ex pugilist to silence. "You realize, Miss Manning," he said to the now calm, but burning eyed woman, "that if Letty Miller tells me she was working on this corridor while you claim you were in it your story will be blown sky high?"

"I'm not afraid of anything that this Letty Miller may say," Martha Manning retorted scornfully, "for I am tell ing the truth. I *was* here—I *did* wait until—this man had left, I *did* have a talk with Mr. Borden—"

"Say!" Jake Bailey burst out, regardless of McMann's injunction. "Where was you? You wasn't in no hall when *I* come out of here to take the elevator—"

"No, I wasn't. I was behind the stairway door, holding it slightly ajar and watching you," Miss Manning assured him with cool triumph.

"Say!" Jake Bailey turned to McMann. "You got the goods on that dame, ain't you?—and she's tryin' to lie out of it, ain't she? You got proof she was in Harry's office, and she's tryin' to make you believe it was Friday night she was here and not Saturday? That's right, ain't it?"

McMann grinned wryly. "Substantially correct, Jake. We've got her finger prints, left sometime between Friday afternoon and Monday morning on the glass panel of that door between the two offices. Miss Manning insists that those finger prints were made on Friday night, that she followed you and Borden into the building, walked up the stairs, waited at the head of them on the seventh floor until you left Borden, and then immediately knocked on Borden's door, counting on his thinking it was you, returned for a last word."

"Hell!" Bailey spat contemptuously. "Claims Borden let her in—pretty and polite as you please, does she? Ho! Not Harry! Not *this* dame! He'd as soon let a wildcat in—"

"Mr. Borden carelessly opened the door wide, thinking it was you," Martha answered him calmly. "You just told Mr. McMann that you kept a sharp eye out for me, lest I follow Mr. Borden, and that you did not see me again after Christmas Eve. That's correct, isn't it, *Mister* Bailey?"

The man glared at her. ""Well—what of it?"

"I couldn't have passed very close to you on the street without your seeing me?" she persisted.

"Not on your life!"

"Then—" the lovely contralto voice vibrated with triumph, "I think I can convince both you and Mr. McMann that I watched you from the head of the stairs on Friday night!"

# CHAPTER TWENTY THREE

"ALL right, Miss Manning," Detective Sergeant McMann urged impatiently, as the woman's blazing brown eyes swept dramatically from Jake Bailey to him self.

"The stairway door, Mr. Bailey, if you don't happen to have noticed," Martha Manning began quietly, "is next to the elevator. As you waited for the elevator to take you down, I had ample time to note—with some amusement —your taste in shirts and cravats."

"Is that so?" Jake Bailey snarled. "What's wrong with 'em?" and he looked down at the blue and white striped shirt and plain black necktie he was wearing at the moment—the latter obviously a tribute to his dead employer.

"Nothing—with those you have on," Martha Manning smiled. "But Friday night you were wearing a shirt with broad purple stripes, and a bright red cravat. The color combination was—rather noisy."

"Were you wearing such a shirt and tie on Friday night, Bailey?" McMann demanded, and Ruth Lester knew from his frown that he was deeply chagrined.

"Well—what if I was?" Bailey retorted, his scrambled features as red as the tie Martha Manning had accused him of wearing.

"I suppose you yourself have an alibi for Saturday, Bailey?" McMann changed tactics suddenly.

"Alibi? What t'ell do I need with an alibi?" Jake spluttered. "I left town Friday night at 9:24—went to visit my folks up near Brewster. They live on a farm, and I guess at least ten people can tell you that Jake Bailey, the famous prizefighter, was spending Saturday, Sunday and Monday with his family. I'd 'a' beat it home sooner, but I didn't see a city paper till this morning, and then I took the first train."

"Just give me the names of a few of those ten people," McMann suggested, and Jake Bailey promptly obliged.

"You can go now, Jake," McMann said, when that formality was concluded, "but don't leave town. Where are you going to live, now that Borden is dead?"

"Back to the Mills Hotel for Jake, I guess," the expugilist admitted ruefully. "Sure, I'll keep in touch with you, Cap," he added, with his former geniality. Then "And say, Cap, don't let this dame pull the wool over your eyes. Take a tip from Jake Bailey—she got Harry!"

When the man had swaggered out of the office, McMann gave an order to Detective Birdwell: "Bring in Rita Dubois. She's in Covey's charge down the hall." Then, returning to his desk and his inquisition of Martha Manning, he asked the question which Ruth had been expecting him to ask for the last hour: "Miss Manning, where were you on Saturday afternoon? You've said your work at the hotel switchboard keeps you only till half past eleven each morning. Account for your time after that, please."

"I did what I do every afternoon," Miss Manning answered calmly, though Ruth saw that again the thin, age-revealing hands were twisting nervously in the lap of the red crepe dress. "I—walked. My doctor's orders are that I spend at least half the day in the open air. He says it is my only chance to conquer the—lung condition." Again her voice and manner made it clear that she was not asking or wanting sympathy.

McMann tapped on the edge of Borden's desk with his pencil. Then: "If I remember correctly—and I think I do— Saturday was a very cold and windy day."

"But the sun was shining," Miss Manning reminded him quickly.

"Where did you walk? And how long?"

"I had lunch first—milk and fruit and rolls—in my room at the Acropolis, and then I walked the streets until about half past one, when I went into a drug store to telephone to Mr. Borden."

"Which drug store?" McMann caught her up sharply.

Promptly she gave the name of one of the busiest drug stores in the downtown district.

"And talked with Borden?" McMann suggested, with an effect of casualness.

"No," Martha Manning smiled slightly. "A woman with an Irish brogue answered the phone. Said she was the 'cleaning lady,' that Mr. Borden had just stepped out for a minute, but would be right back, and please, wouldn't I hold the line?" Amazingly, the contralto voice was gone, and in its place Minnie Cassidy's pleasant, cracked old voice, rich with the brogue she had brought from Ireland.

Ruth smiled, but McMann did not. "And—then?"

Martha Manning resumed her own voice. "In a minute or two, the 'cleaning lady' told me that Mr. Borden would not talk then, but wanted me to call him again in fifteen or twenty minutes."

"And you said—" McMann leveled a forefinger at her and narrowed his gray eyes to slits—"you said: *'Tell Mr. Borden that if he is wise he will talk to me when I call again.'* Your last warning, wasn't it, Miss Manning?"

"If you wish to call it that," the woman shrugged. "What I meant was that, if he did not keep his promise to establish a trust fund for our son, I would go through with the suit to make him support the child, as I had threatened on Friday night."

"And yet—" McMann pounced—"you were so dizzy with joy and relief when you went out of this office Friday night that you had to lean against the door for support! How do you account for your sudden change of heart?"

The great, dark eyes suddenly looked utterly weary. "I was—afraid he had promised just to get rid of me on Friday night. I wanted to talk with him again, to ask him if he had seen his lawyer, as he had promised he would, or had made the appointment to do so."

Birdwell opened the door. "Here's Miss Dubois, chief."

"Have her wait out there till I call for her," McMann directed impatiently. "Now, Miss Manning, why didn't you call Borden fifteen or twenty minutes later? Why did you wait until after two o'clock?"

Ruth, watching the woman closely, her own heart beating heavily, wondered if it was fear or merely indignation which made those great dark eyes dilate as they did.

"After two?" Miss Manning repeated. "I did *not* wait until after two! I called at five minutes of two, and Mr. Borden answered the phone himself. He again promised to see his lawyer Monday—"

"Just a minute!" McMann cut in sharply. "Suppose *I* tell *you* what happened! You came to the Starbridge Building to see Borden again, after you'd made your first call—"

"That's not true!" the woman cried.

"Shut up and listen to me!" the detective commanded harshly. "You came here, knocked on Borden's door, he asked who it was, you answered, he recognized your voice, refused to admit you, you determined to see him or talk with him somehow; you remembered that John C. Hayward's offices lie directly across the airshaft from Borden's; you went to his door, possibly to ask him to let you use his phone, even to solicit his aid in forcing an interview for you with Borden—"

"No, no! That's not true! None of it is true!" Martha Manning cried passionately, rising from her chair in her excitement.

The detective's mighty voice ploughed through her protestations: "You didn't find Hayward in, but because his cleaning woman was careless, you found his door unlocked, entered, telephoned Borden, quarreled violently with him from a few minutes after two until two ten, learned that he would do nothing for you—Wait!" He commanded roughly, and with ruthless hands forced the agitated woman into her chair. "I even know the exact words with which he refused your demands, Miss Manning! Harry Borden said to you, 'Who are you to tell Harry Borden what he can do and can't do?' A witness overheard Borden say those exact words, Miss Manning!"

"But not to me!" she cried, but she sat still again, except for those twisting hands, watching the detective's face.

"And then," McMann went on inexorably, "you remembered the gun you had seen lying in the bottom drawer of Mr. Hayward's desk, the first time you were in his office. You called Harry Borden from Hayward's window, he stepped to his own window, after first securing the weapon with which he had armed himself against an at tack he evidently feared, and—you shot him, his bullet going wild and hitting the wall beside Hayward's window!"

Oddly, as the detective's charge piled up against her, the woman became more and more calm. When he had finished his terrible harangue, she raised her head and her enormous eyes met his fully, steadily, though her face was ghastly white around the rouge spots. "Mr. McMann, you are merely trying to bully me into confessing a crime I did not commit. You cannot possibly have any proof to back your absurd charges. I will gladly face any one you can bring forward who will say that he or she saw me in this building on Saturday. You know you cannot bring forward such a person, for I was not here."

At the supreme confidence behind those quietly emphatic words, the last of Ruth's hopes of thus clearing the man she loved vanished—or almost vanished. For—if Martha Manning had not so used Jack Hayward's office, *who had?*

McMann, tacitly admitting his lack of proof by not answering her challenge, considered for a long moment, then said, with a shrug of his massive shoulders: "Well, where do you say *you* were? Got a good alibi all framed up, I suppose?

"I called from a booth in a cigar store," Martha Manning replied calmly, and named it. "And I called at five minutes to two, as I told you. After my conversation with Mr. Borden, I was sure he would do as he had promised, and I went directly to Central Park, where I walked or sat on benches reading, until half past four, when I returned to the Acropolis—arriving about fifteen or twenty minutes to five."

"Any proof that you were in the park? See any one you knew?" McMann asked sarcastically.

Martha Manning smiled—that strange, ironic smile that deepened the bitter lines between nostrils and mouth corners. "A lone woman, practically friendless, is not likely to encounter acquaintances in the park."

"I thought so!" McMann commented with grim ambiguity. Then he strode to the door and curtly requested Rita Dubois to enter.

The little dancer showed signs of the strain under which she had lived during at least twenty four hours, but there was a trace of the old jauntiness as she sauntered into the room.

"Old home week for Handsome Harry's sweeties, *n'est ce pas?*" she laughed, as her bright, young, black eyes took in the older woman.

"You recognize Miss Manning?" McMann asked quickly.

"No—just a natural conclusion," the dancer informed him. "Keep your seat, Baby face," she grinned at Ruth Lester, who had risen to offer her chair. "I'm sure Mr. McMann won't keep me long."

She was right. In a series of rapid questions McMann elicited the following story from the dancer, regarding Friday night: She had had dinner at the Crillon with Borden, and had seen Jake Bailey join her "suitor" on the sidewalk before the restaurant. Borden had joined her at ten o'clock at the Golden Slipper, and had arranged with the manager for her to have the night off on Saturday, so that she could go away with Borden on the week end trip to Winter Heaven. Borden had had to pay in advance for Rita's substitute, but had seemed in the best of spirits. No, he had not said a word to her about Martha Manning, or concerning a visit from a woman earlier in the evening.

Throughout the questioning of Rita Dubois, the last woman to whom Borden had given his fickle love, Martha Manning sat with downcast eyes, and when the dancer had been sent back to Detective Covey, a tremulous sigh of relief stirred the bitter mouth of the older woman.

The detective sat for long minutes, making futile marks with his pencil on Borden's desk blotter. Then, at last: "I'm going to let you go now, Miss Manning, but I warn you if you try to leave the city you shall be detained and arrested."

"I shall not leave the city," Martha Manning promised quietly, and left but not before she had smiled mistily, with her great tragic eyes and bitter mouth, at Ruth Lester.

"Nothing to hold her on—now," McMann grumbled in self defense to Ruth. "But—good Lord! What's all the commotion?"

For the second time during the investigation into the murder of Harry Borden, Benny Smith, the office boy, tore open the door, stood swaying in it, but this time he said: "I've come to give myself up. I shot Mr. Borden!"

# CHAPTER TWENTY FOUR

## I

RUTH LESTER was miserably ashamed later to remember that her first emotion upon hearing Benny Smith's quavering, defiant, "I've come to give myself up! I shot Mr. Borden!" was one of almost unbearable relief. Jack Hayward was saved! But that emotion was almost instantly submerged in pity. And she was glad later to remember that she was conscious of no horrified shrinking as she ran to put her arms about the fever flushed, unsteadily swaying body of the boy who had just confessed to murder.

"Here! Let me help!" McMann gruffly commanded the girl, and with as much ease as if he was lifting a baby the giant detective lifted the boy in his arms and carried him to the big, overstuffed leather chair from which the murdered man had manipulated his ruinous schemes and which for two days had served the detective in charge of the investigation into his murder as a vantage point from which to heckle, harass, bully and confound suspects.

When the boy was lying back weakly in the big chair, McMann whirled one of the straight backed chairs to the desk and curtly commandeered Ruth Lester's services as a stenographer, to take down the confession. Her eyes were now so blinded with tears that she could hardly find her notebook and pencils—pencils upon which Benny himself had put such fine, brave points just last Saturday!

"Ready, Miss Lester? ... All right, Benny. Tell us all about it now," the detective commanded, almost gently. A glass of cold water from the tap in the outer office had been fetched by the detective himself and stood beside Benny's trembling, hot, right hand.

"Well, sir," Benny began, after a strange, wistful look out of his fever reddened eyes at Ruth Lester, who waited with pencil poised, as tears dropped upon her notebook, "I lied yesterday when I said I didn't come back. I did come back, but nobody didn't see me, 'cause I walked up."

"Why did you walk up, Benny?" McMann interrupted.

" 'Cause I was sore at Mr. Borden, 'n I—I wanted to have it out with him," Benny answered, his adolescent voice going suddenly soprano on the last word.

"What were you sore about?"

" 'Cause he—he bawled me out!" Benny cried, rolling his head from side to side against the brown leather back of the chair.

"Isn't it true that you were more sore at him because he'd 'got fresh' with Miss Lester Saturday morning?" the detective suggested.

"You keep Ruth's name outa this!" Benny protested shrilly. "I tell you—I was sore at Mr. Borden 'cause he was always pickin' on me, 'n' Saturday he talked to me like a dog, jist 'cause I wanted to borrow Ruth's pistol for target practice."

"Then you were also lying when you said the pistol was not in Miss Lester's desk when you returned the first time —at half past one?" McMann asked.

"Naw—it wasn't there. 'N' say, I didn't come back up the second time to kill him—"

"But you walked up six flights of stairs so you would not be seen entering the building," McMann pointed out grimly. "Listen, Benny, now that you're confessing, make a clean breast of everything. Your actions prove you premeditated murder."

"No, I didn't!" Benny denied, his head rolling wildly against the chair back.

"Well—go on," McMann directed resignedly.

"I come back, like I said, 'n' opened the door with my key," Benny began rapidly, and was again interrupted by McMann,

"At just what time?"

"I—" Benny looked pitifully confused. "I don't know—exactly. 'Bout two o'clock, I reckon—"

"Then—" McMann said parenthetically and triumphantly to Ruth, "my theory that Rita Dubois robbed the body is correct." Then, remembering the mysterious telephone call, a fragment of which Bill Cowan had said he overheard when he had called Jack Hayward's number at 2:10 and was plugged in on a busy line, and Rita's corroborating story of Borden's line being busy from 2:05 to 2:15, the detective asked: "Have you any way of fixing the exact time of your second return, Benny?"

The boy looked at the detective suspiciously, even fearfully, Ruth thought—though what could he fear now, after confessing? "Naw, I don't know, I tell you, but it was about two o'clock. 'At's all I know. I unlocked the door and come in, and Mr. Borden was settin' at his desk, 'n' I—I come right in here, 'n' we—we had a row—"

"What about?" the detective interrupted sharply

"Aw—jist about him pickin' on me, 'n'—everything! 'N' he picked up a—" his fevered eyes roved over the desk and lighted upon the glass ink well, empty now, since McMann had used its contents with which to take Martha Manning's finger prints—"that there ink well and started to throw it at me, 'n' I grabbed Ruth's gun—"

"Wait! Just where was this gun?" McMann cut in.

"Layin' on the desk," Benny answered. "Right—right here!" and he laid his hand in the center of the big green blotter. "The big stiff tried to beat me to it—'n' I thought he was goin' to shoot me—"

"After hitting you with the ink well?" McMann asked mildly.

"He—he put the ink well down," Benny amended desperately. " 'N' I—I pulled the trigger, 'thout knowin' what I was doin', 'n'—'n' the gun went off—'n' 'at's all!" he concluded, seizing the glass for a long draught of the cold water.

"So—you shot Borden while he sat at his desk," McMann said slowly. "That right?"

"Yeah, 'at's right!" Benny retorted defiantly.

"Then how do you account for the fact that his body was found away over there under the airshaft window?" McMann demanded.

"I—I forgot that," Benny confessed. "But—say, don't you go and try to make me say I *didn't* kill him—'cause I did! I—I did it in self defense," he added, obviously a little proud of his use of a legal phrase. "After I shot him, he got up and walked over there and fell down—'at's how I account for it!"

The detective extracted an official looking, typed document from his pocket. As he unfolded it, Ruth caught a glimpse of the wording of the printed letterhead:

OFFICE OF THE CHIEF MEDICAL EXAMINER
Department of Police

McMann studied the detailed report in silence, then folded it slowly and returned it to his pocket.

"Now, Benny, you know it can't make any difference in the long run whether you shot Borden while he was seated at his desk, or while he was standing at that window. Come, now—just where *was* Borden when you shot him?"

"Settin' at his desk!" Benny repeated stubbornly, and began to cry, like a small boy, and not at all like the seventeen year old young man about town that he fancied him self to be.

"And Benny—" McMann's voice was very gentle now— "how many times did you shoot Borden? How many bullets were fired?"

"Just one! I—I sorta come to when I seen what I'd done, 'n' I dropped the gun 'n' beat it—"

Just one bullet! Ruth repeated to herself. And two bullets had been fired on Saturday, one embedding itself in Borden's chest, and the other scarring a brick beside Jack Hayward's office window!

"So you dropped the gun, eh, Benny?" McMann asked gently. "Odd we didn't find it—"

"I—I picked it up again 'n' stuck it in my overcoat pocket, 'n' then I beat it down the stairs," Benny corrected himself feverishly, shrilly. "I—gosh, I was scared! I—I wrapped the gun in a newspaper what I—I found on the stairs—I mean in one of them big sacks in the hall, what the cleaning women use to dump wastebaskets in—'n' I—I chucked the gun in a—a big old D. S. C. can on the sidewalk—"

"Where?" McMann interrupted.

"I—I don't remember. "Aw, gee, Mister, what does all them things matter now? Ain't I told you I done it?" the boy pleaded, wiping his streaming eyes on the sleeve of his coat.

"Benny, after you'd—shot Borden, did you go around to Mr. Hayward's office for any reason whatever?" Ruth interrupted with a question of her own.

The boy stared at her, frankly puzzled. "Naw—why should I?"

"I thought so! Oh, Benny, Benny! Why are you doing all this? For *my* sake, Benny?" the girl cried, her voice shaking with laughter and tears. Jumping up from her chair at the desk, she abandoned her notebook and pencil and ran to the boy. "Ruth *knows* you're just making it all up, Benny, darling! Why, why? Poor Benny!" and she mothered his fever scarlet face against her breast.

"He—he—'at detective—" Benny sobbed—"told me yesterday I'd better come clean, or you—you'd be arrested for murder!"

"Oh!" Ruth cried, her blue eyes blazing scorn at the embarrassed detective. Then, to the boy, soothingly: "Dear Benny, I told you yesterday I was in no danger—"

"But after he'd sent you for Minnie, he said you was 'n' just didn't know it, 'n' all last night 'n' this mornin' I studied how I could get you out of it, 'cause I'm just a kid 'n' they wouldn't 'lectrocute me—" The boy broke off, sobbing heartbrokenly.

The door opened. "Mrs. Smith's here, sir—"

But Benny's mother waited for no permission. A small woman, dressed like a flapper, her sharp featured face framed in frizzy light brown hair, pushed past Detective Birdwell and ran to the sobbing boy.

"Benny Smith, if you wasn't sick, I'd spank you right here in front of these folks!" she scolded the boy sharply, but Ruth knew that the sharpness covered acute maternal anxiety. "I mighta knowed you'd pull some stunt like this, minute my back was turned!" Then she whirled upon Detective Sergeant McMann. "Are you the detective, mister? . . . Well, I hope you're satisfed. You and your third degree have run my boy's fever up till it's something awful! I didn't get a wink of sleep last night, listenin' to this poor child rave about keepin' Miss Lester out of jail! The doctor and my girl friend, Mrs. Thompson, who helped me set up with him and hold him in bed, can tell you how he took on—ravin' in fever he was—about confessin' so this Lester girl wouldn't have to go to jail—"

"Please, please, Mrs. Smith!" McMann at last succeeded in stopping the torrent of words. "I'm very sorry indeed if anything I said to Benny yesterday gave him the impression that I was about to arrest Miss Lester. Now, I think we'd better call an ambulance and have this boy taken to the hospital. I'm afraid he's a pretty sick youngster."

After Benny, who had lapsed into a fever stupor, had been removed on a city hospital ambulance stretcher, the whole proceeding frantically recorded by newspaper cameras outside the Borden suite, a wet eyed girl faced a flushed, penitent detective across the dead man's desk.

"Pretty rotten, I know," McMann admitted defensively, dropping his eyes to the sheaf of notes he was shuffling between his thick fingers, "but if the police didn't use old fashioned third degree methods occasionally, we wouldn't solve half the crimes we do. Don't like 'em myself, but—" He paused and shrugged. "Leaves us pretty much where we were before Benny busted in on us, doesn't it? If you'll pardon my language, Miss Lester, this is a hell of a case! Of course I knew the kid was lying before he'd been 'confessing' five minutes! . . . Well, better go to lunch, child. It's after one—by George! It's half past!"

Ruth rose, her notebook with the stenographic report of Benny's chivalrous lies held against her breast, tenderly. She would transcribe every word, keep the record always. "And—may Mr. Hayward go with me?"

## II

"Well, darling," Ruth said, after she and Jack Hayward had deposited their lightly burdened trays upon a table in a far corner of the Colonnade Cafeteria, "this has been a busy morning! Net result—a confession!"

"What!" Relief and joy flared in the young insurance broker's handsome brown eyes. "Why didn't you tell me as soon as we met?"

Contrition sobered Ruth's vivid little face. "Forgive me, darling! I've raised your hopes, just to dash them. It was just Benny—lying like the darling little idiot that he is, because he thought McMann was going to arrest me! I'll show you his whole 'confession'—I took it down in short hand, at McMann's request—when I've transcribed it. Of course Benny was half delirious with fever, but I'll never have a nobler compliment paid me—"

"You're a siren and a cradle snatcher," Jack told her severely. "It's a good thing I'm going to marry you and withdraw you from circulation. Any other developments this morning?"

Smiling delightedly, the girl told her sweetheart of Cleo Gilman's stimulating visit and its ludicrous effect upon dour old McMann. "I really believe, Jack," she concluded, "that if Cleo hadn't just married one of the most uppity of the Upper Ten, our detective department's shining light would have tried to date her up. He may do it yet. But I wasn't making any idle boast last night when I said I was going to take charge of the murder investigation this morning." And then she told him of her visit to Mrs. Borden and to Minnie Cassidy, resulting in the discovery of the orchid tinted letter in the secret drawer of Borden's desk.

"Good work!" Jack applauded dutifully, but Ruth was quick to see that a shadow settled in the bronze brown eyes she loved. He acknowledged the shadow by adding, hesitantly: "But I can't help feeling sorry, sweet, that poor Martha Manning has to be dragged into this. I'm sure she didn't kill Borden, and—well, there's something about that woman that gets you—"

"Jake Bailey, another of our morning callers, puts it a little differently," Ruth retorted. "He says Miss Manning 'got' Borden, but he doesn't mean exactly what you do. . . . I'm sorry, dear! I understand how you feel, for I've been feeling like a malicious, meddling little beast myself, ever since she told her whole pitiful, tragic story."

"Don't feel too badly," Jack urged tenderly, his hand closing over hers tightly. "McMann would have got on her trail within a few hours anyhow, since there must be any number of people who knew of her and Borden's affair. . . . But what did McMann get out of the poor thing, with his damnable third degree methods?"

Ruth neglected her soup and salad to recount every detail of Martha Manning's story, in the order in which McMann had extracted it.

"I'll like to choke that bully!" Jack interrupted fiercely, when Ruth told him, with astonishing vividness, how the detective had secured the woman's finger prints.

"Haven't you learned your lesson yet, red head?" Ruth chided him gently. "I should think you'd never utter another threat so long as you live."

"I suppose some lip reading detective has already made a note of my slip of the tongue and if McMann is ever bumped off, I'll be accused of the crime. But cut along, sweetheart! I promise to be good!"

Ruth "cut along" rapidly, describing with wry humor the various tilts between Martha Manning and Jake Bailey, Borden's bodyguard.

"But against his will," she concluded, "Jake did do Miss Manning a good turn. His professional pride would not let him admit that Martha could have been close enough to him on the street so that she could see the pattern of his shirt and tie, without his seeing her. So it all boils down to this: Bailey himself, much as he hates Miss Manning, because he believes she killed his boss, corroborated her story of having been in the Starbridge Building Friday night, from about half past eight till a few minutes past nine."

"A few minutes past nine?" Jack repeated thoughtfully. "And she says she walked down the stairs and out of the lobby at that time?"

Sudden comprehension illumined Ruth's lovely face. "I see what you mean! Why didn't I think of that before? That's just when the little army of cleaning women and porters is pouring out of the building. I've seen them a dozen times, at least. They're through work at nine. I'll speak to Mr. McMann as soon as I get back to the office—"

Jack interrupted, grinning: "I thought you were conducting this investigation, young lady! Why not make inquiries yourself? Mrs. Pellow, the grand old dowager in charge of the cleaning women, must be in the building now. She comes on about two o'clock, I think, and acts as a sort of housekeeper for the building, even before the cleaning women come on. Let's have a go at her, darling. Now—eat every leaf of that salad, or Papa spank!"

Ruth obeyed, but now and then a puzzled frown knit her golden brown brows, and her brooding blue eyes darkened almost to sapphire.

"What's the heavy thinking about, honey?" Jack inquired at last.

Ruth shook her golden head, as if to clear it of mists. "I—don't know. That's the funny thing about it. ... In fact, I'm not so much thinking as—listening."

"Listening? Spirit messages?" Jack laughed.

"You needn't laugh!" Ruth protested. "Dad *did* come to me in my dream last night and make me remember the orchid tinted letter. And I believe that letter is more important than it seems now, or Daddy wouldn't have—"

"It was your subconscious, getting in a chance to remind you of something you'd forgotten," Jack explained easily. "But I'm glad, darling, that you had your little visit with your father, even if it was only a dream. He must have been a wonder—Colby Lester."

"He was," Ruth agreed, tears springing into her eyes. "But shut up now, Jack, and let my subconscious work in peace. That's what I'm trying to listen to."

The girl frowned and pressed her fingers into her temples. Those poor, thin, tortured hands of Martha Manning's . . . What mute message had they been trying, without Martha Manning's knowledge or consent, to get across to her? And surely there had been something else —something she'd made a mental note of as Martha Manning talked, something apparently trivial. . . .

"Come along, darling, if you want to see Mrs. Pellow!" Jack interrupted, just as Ruth felt that she was on the verge of receiving a clear, strong message from her subconscious mind.

"Now it's gone!" she reproached her future husband ambiguously, but she rose obediently. "Here's my check. You may as well get used to paying for it, young man!"

It was good to breathe in deep draughts of the sharp, cold air, to feel the winter sunshine on their faces. With mutual, unspoken consent, the two who had lived for two days under a dreadful shadow—a shadow which might materialize into a prison cell for Jack Hayward—stood for two or three minutes on the edge of the sidewalk, content not to talk, merely to breathe deeply.

Micky Moran, the elevator operator of the car Ruth habitually used, told them where to find Mrs. Pellow: "She's in her office on the second floor—238. 'Way at the back of the building. I carried her up at two o'clock myself, and seen her go down toward her office."

The head cleaning woman, or possibly more accurately, the "housekeeper" of the Starbridge Building, was in her little cubbyhole of an office, just as Micky had assured the couple she would be. They found her at her small, cheap desk, talking over the telephone. She nodded, and went on with her conversation:

"Yes, Mr. Feldblum! I understand . . . Yes, I'll ask Minnie if she saw the paper that's missing, but all our cleaning women have strict orders not to move papers that are left out on desks. . . . All right, Mr. Feldblum! Of course, I'm very sorry, but I'm sure—Oh!" she cried angrily, as she replaced the receiver on the hook. "Hung up on me, as if I was dirt under his feet! . . . It's Miss Lester, isn't it? And Mr. Hayward? Any news yet about poor Mr. Borden, though a harder man to get along with —But I shouldn't say a word, seeing as how he's dead—"

"No, nothing yet," Ruth interrupted the voluble flow of conversation, and smiled charmingly at the stately, white haired, white uniformed "house keeper." "But, Mrs. Pellow, there's something I'd like awfully to have you tell me—"

"My land! More questions!" Mrs. Pellow raised her plump hands in resigned despair. "That snooping young upstart, who says his name is Carlson, and that Big Mogul of a detective—what's his name? McMann?—have been deviling the life out of me, so I don't get a minute to do my work!"

Ruth's smile broadened, for she knew that Mrs. Pellow had never enjoyed herself so much in her life. "It *is* awfully annoying, I know, Mrs. Pellow, but I won't keep you a minute. You 'check out' the cleaning women as they leave every evening, don't you—about nine o'clock?"

"I certainly do!" Mrs. Pellow agreed emphatically. "And just let one of those old girls try to slip past me with anything they haven't got a right to! Why, just before Christmas—day before Christmas Eve, it was—I caught one old lady trying to sneak out with a satchel full of Christmas presents she'd swiped from—"

"Oh, how awful!" Ruth interrupted, with apparently deep sympathy for Mrs. Pellow's troubles. "You stand in the lobby and check them out, don't you?"

"Yes, miss, I do! Every single night in the week, from nine o'clock till they're all gone, and Saturdays from four till the building's clear."

"You were on duty Friday night, weren't you, Mrs. Pellow?"

"I certainly was! But none of my cleaning women stole any gun out of your office, Miss Lester! I'll take my oath on that!" Mrs. Pellow bridled.

"Oh, I didn't think that for a minute!" Ruth disclaimed. "But, please, Mrs. Pellow, if you were in the lobby from nine o'clock till—"

"Nine twenty five!" Mrs. Pellow interrupted. "And the time clock will prove my words!"

"Then, please, Mrs. Pellow, did you see a woman— not one of the cleaning women, but a visitor in the building, come out of the stairway door and leave the building Friday evening between nine and nine twenty five?" Ruth finished her question breathlessly, while her heart beat fast.

Mrs. Fellow's answer came promptly: "No, miss, I'd take my Bible oath no woman visitor or any other visitor or tenant come out of the stairway door between nine and nine twenty five Friday night."

But Ruth persisted, describing Martha Manning accurately. Again she received the same positive denial. "There wasn't any such woman in our lobby Friday night at the time you say."

"What about the stairs beside the service elevator?" Jack thought to ask, and for a moment Ruth felt dashed.

But at Mrs. Pellow's answer hope flowed back, full and strong: "No way for a woman to get in or out of them stairs. The door's kept locked after six, when the elevator man goes off duty. No freight accepted after six."

When Ruth and Jack escaped from Mrs. Pellow's own eager questions as to the progress of the investigation, Ruth said thoughtfully: "I think that proves pretty conclusively that Martha Manning was lying about Friday night, that she *must* have been here Saturday afternoon instead—or how could her finger prints have been on the glass panel of the door? But if she was here Saturday, how *could* she have managed both her entrance and exit without being seen by any one? She's not a ghost, even if she is almost as thin as one—oh!" and she broke off her spoken reflections with a sharp gasp.

"Old subconscious working at last?" Jack teased, just as the elevator door opened for them.

# CHAPTER TWENTY FIVE

"Yes– subconscious working at last, darling!" Ruth answered, when the elevator had discharged them at the seventh floor. Her cheeks were rose pink with excitement and her eyes were shining like blue diamonds, but even if she had wanted to confide in her sweetheart, the inevitable group of reporters clustered about Borden's door would have prevented her.

Throwing Jack Hayward a brilliant smile by way of farewell—a smile destined to grace the front page of an extra a few hours later—Ruth slipped into her office, or rather the office which had been hers until her employer had been murdered.

She found Detective Birdwell with his feet on Benny Smith's desk, his black derby tilted low over his perpetually weary eyes. At the girl's entrance, down came the feet and off came the derby, but the expression of bored gloom on the detective's face deepened.

"Has anything happened?" Ruth asked, as she hung up bat and coat, and fluffed her golden curls before the wash stand mirror.

"Oh, nothing much," Birdwell drawled wearily. "Nothing except that Commissioner Weeks has been here handing out nice, hot little samples of hell. You'd think, to hear that guy talk, that nobody hadn't done nothing but twiddle their thumbs or play tiddledy winks since you stumbled over Borden's stiff yesterday morning. As the chief says to him—" and Birdwell jerked his head toward Borden's private office, where McMann was presumably hard at work—" he says: 'Give us time, Commissioner. We ain't been on this job thirty hours yet,' he says, and the Big Noise comes back at him with this kinda proposition: 'If you can't make an arrest by five o'clock

today, McMann,' he says, I'll assign the case to
Lieutenant Pryor.' Hunh! I know Pryor! He'll clap
everybody in sight in jail, and then say 'Eenie meenie
miney mo' to see which one did it."

"And what did Mr. McMann say to that?" Ruth asked,
smiling cheerfully.

"Oh, this and that," Birdwell told her wearily, "but the
gist of it was that he guessed your sweetie, Hayward,
would have to be the goat. Thought I'd tip you off—"

"Thanks, awfully, Mr. Birdwell!" Ruth replied, but to
the detective's obvious amazement her smile was not a
whit less cheerful. "Is Commissioner Weeks still with Mr.
McMann?"

"No, he's toddled on off to brighten up another dark
corner," Birdwell grinned, "but Borden's lawyer—a la de
da chappie, with a cane and spats and everything—
dropped in a few minutes ago to lend a helping hand.
McMann phoned him to bring in 'Handsome Harry's' will.
But if you want to see the chief, I'll call him out for you."

"No. I've got a job to do that's going to keep me very
busy indeed for the next few minutes," Ruth answered, as
she sat down to her desk and took the cover from the type
writer that had stood idle since the abrupt termination of
her career as private secretary to "Handsome Harry"
Borden.

For a few minutes, however, the little hands lay inert
on the keys, and the golden brown brows were knit in a
mighty frown of concentration above brooding blue eyes.
Then, with an exclamation of excited triumph, she
quickly rolled a sheet of paper into the machine and
began to type with furious haste.

As page after page was filled with her flawless typing,
Birdwell looked on with growing interest, when he was
not engaged in answering telephone calls from police
head quarters.

"What are you writing—a serial story?" he asked at
last, unable to restrain his curiosity.

"I'm afraid it does sound a lot like fiction—of the old fashioned, penny dreadful kind," Ruth laughed, without halting her flying fingers.

She had just drawn the last sheet from her typewriter with an excited, triumphant "There!" when the door between the two offices opened and the detective sergeant emerged, followed closely by a dapper little man, who had very evidently followed Mayor Walker as his sartorial model.

"Whew! That guy's so damn polite he makes me want to kick him in the seat of his pearl gray pants to see if he'd say, 'Thank you, my dear Mr. McMann! Thank you!'" the detective sergeant growled, when the lawyer had bowed and smiled himself out of his dead client's office. "But I'm glad he came, anyway. Come on in, Miss Lester, and I'll tell you all about it."

Before obeying, Ruth Lester gathered up the four typed sheets of what Birdwell had called a "serial story," folded them into a small square which she tucked away safely in the pocket of the brown velveteen frock she was wearing.

"A man's will is a pretty good index to his character," McMann began didactically, after he and Ruth had seated themselves opposite each other at the dead man's desk.

"And more times than not, when a rich man's been murdered, his will is the police's best bet in looking for a motive. I tried to get hold of Attorney Walters yesterday, of course, but he was out of town— didn't get back till noon today."

"And did you find a motive?" Ruth asked eagerly.

"Not unless we want to believe that Mrs. Borden got impatient," McMann said slowly. "Outside of a few thousands to his lawyer, who, it appears, expected more for keeping Borden out of jail on some of his fake stock schemes, everything goes to the wife and kids—"

"Nothing to Martha Manning's child?" Ruth interrupted.

"Not a red!" McMann answered. "I've just told you that a man's will is a good index to his character. A bastard more or less didn't seem to bother 'Handsome Harry.' At any rate, he makes no provision for the child that Miss Manning claims is his. Maybe he had good cause to question his paternity, but I doubt it. I'd stake my hope of promotion for solving this case on that woman's telling the truth—so far as the kid is concerned, at least."

"I agree with you," Ruth said soberly. "Did Mr. Borden leave a large estate?"

"About a million and a quarter, according to Walters, though the will simply says, 'More than $10,000.' The usual thing, you know," McMann answered. "Of course I asked Walters if Mrs. Borden knew either the extent of her husband's wealth or the disposition made of it in his will and he answered 'no' to both questions. She must have been pretty sure, however, that whatever her husband had would come to her and her children, but since Borden was giving them five hundred a month, I'm afraid we'll have to look elsewhere for a motive that will hold water."

"Mrs. Borden did not kill her husband," Ruth stated quietly.

"You seem pretty sure—oh, all right, Birdwell! What is it?" as his subordinate appeared in the doorway.

"Captain Foster on the wire, sir. Wants to talk with you."

While McMann was arguing and expostulating with his immediate superior, who had evidently just been heckled by *his* superior, Commissioner Weeks, Ruth sat staring at the airshaft window, smiling strangely, her chin resting on her interlocked hands. McMann, glancing at her once or twice for approval of the way he was "standing up" to the police captain, saw to his amazement that she was not even listening!

Something did arouse her out of her smiling abstraction, however. It was the mournful, reproachful call of the black pigeon, which was strutting up and down the broad white ledge outside the airshaft window. With an exclamation of dismay at her own thoughtlessness, the girl jumped up and ran to the outer office, to get the envelope which she had filled with bread crumbs from her own luncheon. But the hungry black pigeon had to wait a minute longer, for Ruth stopped to type one line and tear it, a narrow ribbon, from the sheet of yellow paper. With her message, bread crumbs and a length of black thread, she hurried back into the private office, where McMann was just replacing the receiver, his face flushed with righteous indignation.

"Expect a man to solve a mystery like this in two shakes of a lamb's tail!" he grumbled to the girl, then abandoned his self defense to ask curiously: "What are you doing there?"

"Just feeding the pigeons!" Ruth laughed. "Poor things! I've neglected them shamefully. I hope the next tenant in this suite has a more humanitarian secretary."

"Say! That's a pretty sight!" McMann commented, as he strolled to the airshaft window, where the girl stood, laughing and cooing to the flock of pigeons, which fought greedily for the crumbs she was sprinkling upon the ledge.

"Oh, you greedy thing!" she cried, as the black pigeon boldly settled upon her hand and began to peck at the crumbs it held. "Now you've made me spill half of your dinner!" she added ruefully, as a shower of crumbs fell upon the polished strip of floor between rug and window. "Just for that, Mr. Nemesis, you're going to be punished by being made to work!" And one little hand closed firmly about the gleaming body of the black pigeon.

"What are you going to do now?" McMann asked indulgently, as swift fingers wrapped the narrow ribbon of paper about the tiny red leg of the pigeon, fastening it securely with the thread.

"Watch and see!" Ruth laughed. Then, still holding the message burdened pigeon against her breast, she called in a clear, blithe soprano: "Yoo hoo, Jack!"

Almost instantly the young insurance broker's head and torso were framed in the opposite window.

"Got any crumbs, darling?" Ruth called gaily. "If you have, you may learn something to your advantage," and she released the black pigeon.

"Say! What does all this mean? . . . And I thought you weren't listening!" the detective sputtered. "Look here, Miss Lester! I've treated you almost like one of the force —let you in on everything, but I warn you—if you're tipping off Hayward that he's going to be arrested, so's he can beat it—"

Ruth's lovely face was sparkling with laughter as she answered: "I *wasn't* listening! And please don't scowl at me like that. As Cleo Gilman said, you'd be an awfully handsome man if you cultivated a jolly smile. . . . Oh, look! Jack's caught the black pigeon!"

"I shouldn't think Hayward would ever want to see a pigeon again, after the trick one of them played on him — making those footprints in blood inside and outside this window," McMann reminded her. "If it hadn't been for those pigeon footprints, inside and outside a *closed window*, I doubt if a grand jury would have indicted him—"

But again he was amazed to discover that the girl was not listening to him. She was smiling and nodding, with carefree gayety, to the young man across the airshaft, who, after reading the brief message, gave her a puzzled smile and nod in return, and then tore the ribbon of paper to bits. The pigeons fluttered after them greedily.

"What was that message?" McMann demanded sternly.

"Oh—" Ruth laughed, as she turned away from the window—"Just a novel way of making a date with my young man! Please don't scold, Mr. McMann! I promise you that Jack won't run away—that if, at five o'clock today, you still want to arrest him for the murder of Henry P. Borden, he'll be here and I shan't utter a word of protest!"

"You're pretty damned cocky and sure of yourself," McMann told her, eyeing her with frowning curiosity. "Holding out on me, aren't you?"

"Why, of course not, Mr. McMann!" Ruth disclaimed, with wide eyed innocence. "You know far more than I do—and *all* that I do. But we were talking of Mr. Borden's will. It was rather disappointing, wasn't it? I thought he had more originality than that—"

McMann returned to the desk, sat down and selected a memo from his stack of notes. "I wouldn't say Harry Borden was lacking in originality," he said, with an odd smile. "There's one clause I haven't told you about—the strangest clause ever written into a last will and testament. ...

# CHAPTER TWENTY SIX

RUTH'S attention was wholly diverted now from her own secret schemes and hopes. "The strangest clause ever written into a last will and testament?" she repeated.

"The tabloids will eat this up," McMann grinned. "Well —this is the clause, shorn of the fancy legal trimmings that Walters is so crazy about: In the event of his death by foul play—murder, manslaughter or simple homicide, as the case may be, Henry P. Borden bequeathes the sum of $5000 to the person or persons instrumental in bringing his murderer to justice. . . . Now what do you think of that?"

What Ruth thought was temporarily beyond the power of words to express, but the detective seemed content with her wide eyed amazement.

"No, sir, I never heard of a man so obsessed with the idea that he's going to be bumped off that he took care of the reward in his will," McMann commented. Then, chuckling: "I'm beginning to like that man! I can use five grand. The wife's been deviling me to make a down payment on a house in Floral Park—"

The girl ruthlessly interrupted the detective's happy counting of his chicks before they were hatched. "Did the lawyer say who it was that Mr. Borden feared would murder him?"

"I asked him, of course," McMann assured her, "but Walters says he named no names, just made a great point of getting that clause in exactly right. I asked him if he thought Borden had the Manning woman in mind, but he said he frankly didn't know—that Borden had told him of receiving a number of death threat letters from suckers who'd lost their life savings in his get rich quick schemes, and had even put a number of these letters in his hands, for him to deal with. It seems that Walters restrained him from taking any of the letters to the police, knowing that his client would have simply been sticking his head into the lion's mouth. Now that Borden's dead, Walters can freely admit that his precious client ought to have been in jail years ago."

"By the way," Ruth began casually, "have you found any trace of the old man who came to see Mr. Borden Saturday morning? The poor old thing that muttered he'd get even with Mr. Borden for having ruined him?"

The detective started, and flushed. "So that's what you've been gloating about, is it? Where did *you* pick up his trail?"

"I?" Ruth repeated innocently. "I'm not a detective, Mr. McMann. I just wondered—that's all."

"Well, as a matter of fact, we haven't spent much time on the old bird," McMann confessed. "We had nothing to go on but your meager description, and there's no evidence at all that he came back Saturday afternoon. The elevator operators are sure of that much."

"I just thought I'd ask," Ruth apologized meekly. Then she changed the subject. "I suppose Mr. Walters knew all about Martha Manning and her son—Borden's son?"

"Naturally," McMann agreed. "She'd even called on Walters to get him to use his influence with Borden, but Walters admits he advised his client to fight the case if the woman carried out her threat to sue for support for the child. He did, however, advise Borden to create a trust fund for the boy, but Borden got his back up be cause the woman was hounding him to do it. A stubborn devil—as well as a good many other kinds of devil," McMann added. "But personally, I'm glad he was a vindictive devil as well, for I intend to earn that five thousand."

"By arresting Jack Hayward?" Ruth asked, smiling.

McMann hesitated, looked as if he did not relish the thought of wiping that cheerful smile off a face whose beauty and sweetness had made his grim business a little less unpleasant than usual. "I'm—sorry, Miss Lester, but damned if there's any other course open to me. Police Commissioner Weeks let me hold up the arrest last night, because of his old friendship for your father and his sympathy for you—"

"And *you* pleaded for more time because you knew your case against Jack was more full of holes than a slice of Swiss cheese!" Ruth interrupted vehemently. "And nothing that has developed today has strengthened your case against him! Rather, everything has weakened it!"

"If you mean the Manning woman's story, I don't agree," McMann argued reasonably. "I consider that Martha Manning left us exactly where she found us— even if I did catch her in a lie or two. I think it's a pretty safe bet that she *was* here Friday night, and left those fingerprints. And we have no more evidence that she was here Saturday than that your death threat muttering old man came back. That's right, isn't it?"

"Yes," Ruth agreed.

"Of course, I've got a man detailed to keep an eye on her, but I don't expect anything to come of it."

"And you still don't think Rita did it, that she only robbed the dead body?" Ruth asked, still in that meek, you're a big clever detective and-I'm only a little girl voice.

"A case against Rita would be more full of holes than your piece of Swiss cheese; it would be a sieve," McMann retorted positively. "As far as murder goes, I mean. But as for robbery—she'll do a nice little stretch for that, unless she knocks the jury for an acquittal, with those legs and those black eyes of hers. Which she probably will," he added with gloomy cynicism.

"But of course you'll have done your duty," Ruth sympathized.

"So you see where all this leads us," McMann summed up, almost apologetically. "Mrs. Borden had already got her check. No reason at all for her to come back and shoot her husband, because he'd said a sarcastic word or two to

make her cry. Besides, the elevator boys swear she *didn't*
come back, and I can't see her walking all the way up six
flights of stairs, with cold blooded murder in her heart—
especially since it's pretty evident that she loved her
husband, rotten though he was. Hayward's the only
suspect left, now that the office boy is out of the picture.
And speaking of Benny reminds me of a bad turn the poor
kid did you when he was willing to confess to murder to
help you."

Ruth was startled. "Benny? What do you mean?"

"Just this," the detective began slowly, with dreadful
significance. "I think the kid was telling about as much
truth as lies. What became of your gun and who closed
this airshaft window—"

"I thought you had explained that, satisfactorily to
yourself at least," Ruth interrupted spiritedly, "by
demonstrating that Jack could have closed it from his
own window by using the window pole."

The detective grinned. "It *would* have been a good
trick —and maybe that's how it was done. But let's
suppose that Benny *did* come back Saturday afternoon—
a second time, I mean."

"To murder Mr. Borden?" Ruth asked scornfully.

"Oh, no! For the same reason he came back the first
time—to borrow your gun for target practice. I don't
believe it was gone out of your desk when he came back
the first time, but that Borden bawled him out for
meddling in your desk and sent him packing—just as
both Benny and Minnie have said. But Benny knew
Borden was going to Winter Heaven on the 2:15. Not
knowing Borden had been killed, the kid sneaks back,
and walks up the stairs as he said he did, so that he won't
be seen and questioned, possibly caught with the stolen
gun. He has his key. He comes in, finds the gun gone, and
goes into Borden's office to see if it is there. He finds
Borden dead, and the gun some distance away. No
powder burns on the man's vest, so the kid, used to
firearms as he undoubtedly is, knows that Borden had

not committed suicide. He thinks first of you. I third degreed it out of him yesterday that he had overheard Borden making love to you and your scream. He thinks you did it, and takes the gun to protect you. Then he notices the open window and wonders if it could have been Hayward, who, he knows, has seen and overheard the love making and scream business, too. Furthermore, Micky Moran has admitted that he told Benny, on the kid's first return, about your scene with Hayward at the elevator at one twenty, when Hayward again threatened Borden's life. He closes the window—in case it had been Hayward who did it—Hayward whom you're in love with, and who must therefore be protected, too. With your gun accounted for, and the closing of the window, and with Rita to rob the dead body of the money that was missing, I can't see a flaw in my case against Hayward—and I'm mighty sorry, for your sake."

Ruth brushed aside his sympathy. "And you think you can force Benny to admit to being an accessory after the fact, when he was so anxious to protect me and the man I love that he would confess to murder?"

McMann shrugged. "I've simply laid all my cards on the table. I wanted you to know why it is my duty to arrest John C. Hayward for the murder of Harry Borden."

The girl went very white. There was no mirth, no assumed meekness in her eyes or voice now. She rose, and steadied her trembling body against the desk. "Mr. McMann, you've been so good—so wonderfully kind to me. Won't you please grant me one more favor? Won't you promise not to arrest Jack before five o'clock today? I can't explain now, but if you will let me leave here now, with permission to be gone not more than one hour, I promise you will not be sorry."

The girl's intense earnestness apparently touched the hard bitten detective. "One hour? . . . All right, Miss Lester, but on condition that you do not go to the hospital and do any more vamping on poor Benny."

"I promise. And thank you with all my heart!" Ruth smiled through sudden tears.

"Where you going? Not going to try to take that five thousand away from a poor, hard working detective, are you?" McMann grinned.

"If I do, I'll give you half—for helping me so much!" she laughed, and ran.

It was a quarter past three when Ruth Lester left the Starbridge Building on her unexplained mission, and just four o'clock when she returned, her cheeks rose pink again, her eyes luminous with victory. Just outside the entrance to the building she paused, and took from the pocket of her dress the four tightly folded sheets of what she had ruefully admitted to Detective Birdwell sounded "a lot like fiction." In a blank space on the first page, opposite the numeral 4, she wrote in the answer to the questions which she had gone out to ask. . . .

"And again it is proved—'truth is stranger than fiction,' " she murmured exultingly, as she refolded the typed sheets and returned them to her pocket.

In the lobby of the Starbridge Building she ran plump into just such a bit of drama as every New Yorker lives in the hope of witnessing and so seldom does. A uniformed policeman and a plainclothes detective—one of McMann's innumerable assistants on the Borden case—were struggling with a frenzied young man, a quite magnificent young man of crow black hair, jet eyes, perfect features, olive skin and immeasurably elegant clothes. A young man who was cursing violently in a foreign language.

"What *is* the matter?" Ruth cried, above the hubbub, and the detective, who had just succeeded in linking his wrist with that of the foreigner, volunteered the answer:

"A bird the whole department's been looking for, Miss Lester, and we find him *here! Yes, ma'am!* Walked in not five minutes ago, and I spotted him. When I told him the police want him, he draws a gun on me—says he come to kill his wife, that Dubois dame, for two timing him. with

Borden. . . . Here, you! That's *my* arm you're jerking out of its socket! Come along quiet now, Romero, or I'll bash your pretty patent leather head in!"

Ramon Romero! Rita Dubois' dancing partner at the Golden Slipper and—her husband! Dazed, Ruth Lester followed the trio into the elevator, the crowd having been roughly forced back by the uniformed policeman.

When the elevator doors opened at the seventh floor, Ruth ran ahead to open the door to Borden's suite, for Ramon Romero's frantic efforts to escape were occupying the entire attention of both the policeman and the detective.

In a chair drawn up to the large "library" table in the center of Borden's reception room, the exhausted body of a woman half sat, half lay, her head resting on the table, her arms out flung in a gesture of infinite weariness. And crouching over her, so that the breath of his menacing words stirred the dark, disheveled hair, was Detective Sergeant McMann.

"Sure I'll let you rest, and I'll let you eat and I'll let you have a drink, when you come clean, Rita! You *robbed Borden's dead body!* That's all I'm accusing you of! That's all! Come on now, Rita—get it over with!"

Neither Rita Dubois nor the detective had heard Ruth's almost noiseless opening of the door, but when a moment later, Ramon Romero, dragged to the door by his captors, spat out a foreign oath, the girl's body became electrified, was out of the chair too quickly for human eyes to take in each of her cat like movements.

"Ramon! Oh, my God! Now they've got you!"

The too handsome, swarthy face of the prisoner became convulsed with hatred as his eyes took in the horror stricken face of his wife, but McMann roughly interrupted the torrent of Spanish invectives by ordering the detective to bring in his quarry.

"Where did you find him, Casey?" the detective sergeant asked his subordinate, when the male dancer had been rudely forced down into a chair across the table from his wife.

"In the lobby downstairs," Casey admitted. "Found a gun on him. Here it is. ... And he made no bones of what he'd come for—was layin' for his wife to kill her for two timin' him with Borden."

Ruth gratefully but silently slipped into a chair which the uniformed policeman had drawn to the table for her, and raised compassionate blue eyes to Rita's devastated face. For a moment she thought the dancer was going to faint, but slowly a quivering hand found its customary place on a slim hip, and the supple body regained a pathetic tatter of its old nonchalant insolence.

"Well—" Rita shrugged, and her voice was hard, bitter, weary, with a terrible undercurrent of amusement—"the joke's on little Rita, all right! Laying for me to kill me, were you?—like you killed—" But she bit back the name that had almost slipped out. "You pretty, dancing fool, you! Didn't you know I did it—for *you!*—because you had me so damned ga ga about you—"

"Just a minute, Rita!" McMann clamped a hard hand on the girl's shoulder. "If you're ready to make a confession, it is my duty to place you under arrest, and to warn you that anything you say may be used against you—"

"Oh, dry up!" the dancer retorted wearily. "This is just a little quarrel between husband and wife. Yeah! That pretty boy is my husband all right! Now laugh that off!"

McMann did not obey. "So your husband killed Borden because you were going away with him, and now he wants to finish his job by killing you. That right?"

"Killed Borden?" Rita repeated scornfully, then broke into laughter, which seemed to be born of genuine amusement. "Do you want to know where this dancing sheik of mine was on Saturday afternoon, from one o'clock till four, when Willette "Wilbur and I picked him up? ... Well—and if you don't laugh now it's because your face got froze into that scowl the last hard freeze we had—

Ramon was in Madame Rosenstein's beauty parlor—
'Temple of Esthetic Beauty,' she calls it—shooting the
family bankroll—"

"For three hours?" McMann was heavily sarcastic.

"Sure!" Rita retorted scornfully. "How long do you
think it takes to get a haircut, a shampoo with hot oil
treatment, a facial, a manicure, a pedicure, and an eye
brow plucking? Did you think God make him look like
that?" and she pointed a mocking finger at her husband.

"Check this right now, Birdwell!" McMann flung the
order to the still bored and apparently somnolent
detective seated at Benny Smith's desk.

"Telephone number's Circle 0430," Rita volunteered.
"A little blond homewrecker, name of Nanette, took care
of him. She always does—and how!" she added viciously.
"Oh, you'll find he was there all right, Big Boy," she
turned insolently to McMann again. "And that I
telephoned him a little after half past two. I called from
the lobby of this building to tell him that it was all
right— I'd got the cash for him."

"But you didn't tell him you'd robbed your dead lover's
body to get it, did you?" McMann pounced.

"No! Because I had not!" Rita flashed, her black eyes
blazing. "Say, I'm getting sick of you harping on that line!
If I've told you once I've told you a hundred times that
Harry Borden gave me the other half of the five hundred
dollar bill, of his own free will and accord, and that he
was alive when I left him!"

McMann shrugged, and abandoned that line for a new
one, of more immediate interest. "So the money was for
Romero, was it? What did he need five hundred for? To
pay his beauty parlor bills?"

Before Rita could reply, Birdwell interrupted to say he
had Madame Rosenstein on the wire. The detective
sergeant, after identifying himself, put his questions with
a brutal conciseness and rapidity that must have been a
severe shock to the high priestess of "The Temple of
Esthetic Beauty," but when he hung up there was no

need for him to admit to the room at large that Romero's alibi had been corroborated.

"Now, Rita—no use for me to try to talk to that Spanish jabbering husband of yours—Romero may not have killed Borden, but he'd killed *someone* and needed money for a getaway! Out with it, and save time. You know damned well I'll get the goods on him anyway—"

"Then why should I do your work for you?" Rita retorted insolently.

"I think I can help you, Chief," Detective Casey volunteered. "This is a bird one of them foreign countries— in South America somewhere, the Argentine, I guess it was—told us to keep an eye peeled for. Killed his sweetie down there, for making eyes at another Hot Tamale. We got his picture on file at headquarters. Guess one of the boys from his old home town blew in and piped him at the Golden Slipper and shook him down for blackmail to the tune of half a grand."

As if each of Casey's hard boiled sentences was a bullet which had found its mark in her exhausted body, Rita sagged lower and lower, until she was again in the position in which Ruth, opening the door had found her— half sitting, half lying in her chair, her head on the table, her arms outflung in utter defeat. And across the table, slowly, uncertain of its welcome, came Ramon Romero's beautifully manicured hand. At that familiar touch, Rita raised her head and gazed at her husband with incredulous hope. "You're not mad at me any more, Ramon?" she asked, in such a wistful little girl voice that tears stung Ruth's eyelids. "You wouldn't really have killed Rita, would you, Baby? Honest—there wasn't any other way to get the money but to string Borden along. I didn't ever mean to come across with him—I was going to give him the slip as soon as I got my hands on the cash. Honest to God I was, Baby—"

Across the table Ramon Romero leaned as far as his manacles would permit, and lifted his wife's hands to his lips.

"I go with you now!" he said arrogantly to Detective Casey.

"You're damn right you will!" McMann agreed grimly. "Take this dancing sheik down to headquarters and book him on a charge of violating the Sullivan Act, till we know more about his comic opera past," he added to the detective and the patrolman.

"May I go with him?" Rita begged, springing to her feet as her husband was being led to the door.

"Sure! ... If you'll come across with a confession that you robbed Borden's dead body!" McMann retorted, grinning cruelly. "Maybe they'll give you a cell right next to 'Baby's'—"

"Oh, my *Gawd,* can't you lay off that?" Rita cried with weary scorn, as she wilted into her chair again.

"Please, Mr. McMann," Ruth dared suggest, in the painful silence that fell upon the group remaining after Ramon Romero had been taken away, "it's 'way after four, and the cleaning women are on duty by now. You're going to have Letty Miller in for further questioning, aren't you?"

"Letty Miller?" McMann gave her an harassed, puzzled look.

"Don't you remember?—she's the woman who cleans Jack's offices, and the one who admitted Mr. Borden Friday night with her passkey," Ruth explained meekly.

"Oh, yes!" the detective agreed wearily. "You have some fantastic theory about the scrubwoman's having left Hayward's door unlocked Saturday afternoon, so that any one might have walked in and used his phone and his gun. Won't do any harm to ask her, I suppose. And I might as well check Martha Manning's story about having been here Friday night. If the scrubwoman says she was still working in this corridor and didn't see or hear anything of the Manning woman. . . . Get her for me, won't you, Birdwell? I'll stay out here and answer the phone if it rings."

The detective sergeant had to make good that promise less than a minute after the door had closed upon his departing subordinate. He strode to Benny's desk, lifted the receiver and growled into the mouthpiece: "Hello! McMann speaking. . . . Who? Oh, Carlson! . . . *What? Lost her!* Well, I'll be— What the hell do you think I had you shadowing her for? . . . How's that? . . ." Ruth, listening intently to the one sided conversation, saw a thundercloud settle on the detective sergeant's face. After a long pause, in which Carlson was evidently talking fast to put himself right with his chief, McMann growled disgustedly: "Well, find her! D'you hear? And don't come back till you do!"

He hung up the receiver and relayed the news to Ruth Lester, his voice harsh with disgust and anger: "That was Carlson—the dimwit of a detective I detailed to keep an eye on the Manning woman. And now he calls up to whine a long alibi as to how he 'lost' her. Says he followed her to the door of the ladies' rest room of a department store at a quarter to four, and she gave him the slip somehow, though there's only the one door. He got suspicious when she hadn't come out in twenty minutes, and sent the maid in charge to look for her. Not a trace of the woman, though he's had every female in the rest room paraded before him— Well, Birdwell?" he snapped, as his assistant opened the door.

"The Miller woman will be here in a minute, sir. I found her in—"

"All right!" McMann interrupted impatiently, as he flung himself into a chair opposite Ruth and beside Rita Dubois, at the big table in the center of the outer office. "I've got to think," he muttered, and proceeded to do so, in frowning silence.

Ruth, whose chair faced the open door between the outer office and Borden's private office, so that she had an oblique view of the all important airshaft window beneath which she had discovered Harry Borden's body cold in death and through which McMann obstinately believed that Jack Hayward had shot the promoter, sat silent, too, but with a tiny smile tugging at the corners of her lovely mouth. As the silence continued unbroken, she saw the black pigeon alight upon the sill of the open window, then, made bold by the absence of human beings in the private office and the utter silence of those in the outer room, the bird which Ruth, in a bitter moment had christened "Nemesis," fluttered to the floor.

The girl shivered involuntarily as she saw the black pigeon pecking at bread crumbs spilled upon the very spot where Harry Borden's life blood had left its dark stain. She was glad when the door opened and the slight sound startled the black pigeon into flight, upward and out of the open window. But the next moment her own blood turned to ice in her veins.

For, from just behind Ruth's chair, came a shrill, Banshee wail of sheer terror, rising, rising, breaking at last on a note of supreme horror, as a fainting body fell heavily to the floor. . . .

# CHAPTER TWENTY SEVEN

"GET me some water—quick!" Ruth, first on her feet and first to reach the side of the unconscious scrubwoman, commanded Jack Hayward, who had stepped into Borden's office just as that terrible scream had broken on its ultimate high note of horror.

"What's happened to poor old Letty?" Jack asked, as he sprang to obey.

"I'm afraid she's hurt her head against my chair in falling," Ruth answered. "I'll see if it's cut—"

But to the amazed horror of everyone in the room, the girl belied the tender compassion in her voice by giving a sudden, hard jerk at the dank gray hair that hung in wisps about the ashen pale face of the woman on the floor.

"Ruth!" Jack Hayward cried out angrily.

The girl did not appear to have heard. Her small hand gave another tug at the gray hair, so sharp that the woman's scalp seemed to have been torn off. Ruth cast the thing from her with a gesture of loathing and immediately after it went the cheap, steel rimmed spectacles that had shielded eyes now closed in merciful unconsciousness.

"My God! Martha Manning!"

It was McMann who voiced the identification, his flinty gray eyes wide open at last and staring incredulously at the small, aristocratic head, wrapped tightly with smooth bands of fine, black hair.

"Yes, Martha Manning! Didn't you know?" Ruth answered, but there was no triumph in her voice—only in finite pity. "Give me the water, Jack. . . . Thanks! Her poor head is hurt. . . . There's a great lump swelling . . ."

"But—how did *you* know?" McMann demanded, with angry bewilderment.

Ruth did not answer until her compassionate fingers had dipped into the glass and dabbled cold water upon the death like face now pillowed against her arm. Then, with her free hand, she reached into the pocket of her smart little brown velveteen frock and drew out the tightly folded sheets upon which she had written what Birdwell had called her "serial story" earlier that afternoon.

The detective took them, shook out the folds. The first sentence was enough to mottle his heavy face with the dark red of chagrin.

"Rita! Will you get me some whiskey, please? You know where Mr. Borden kept it," Ruth directed, her interest wholly with the unconscious woman, upon whom the cold water had had no effect.

The dancer, who had been taking in the scene with stupefied bewilderment, ran to obey, but when she returned from Borden's private office the pint flask was at her own lips, and she was drinking deep.

"Gawd! I needed that!" she breathed, as she passed the remainder of the liquor to Ruth Lester. "So Baby face beat you at your own game, did she, Big Boy?"

"It—looks like it," McMann admitted, and began to read aloud from the first of the four sheets of typing that he held in his not quite steady hand:

" 'Martha Manning, in the guise of Letty Miller, a cleaning woman, killed Henry P. Borden. My reasons for this conclusion are:

" '1. The hands of "Letty Miller" and Martha Manning are identical. When Letty Miller was telling Mr. McMann her story, I, Ruth Lester, observed a yellow stain upon the nail and first joint of the index finger of her right hand. When Martha Manning was being interviewed by Mr. McMann, I observed the same stain, and knew that it had been made by nicotine. In all other respects also the hands of the apparently two different women were identical.

" '2. "Letty Miller" wore glasses habitually. Martha Manning was not wearing glasses today nor when she called twice upon Mr. Hayward, and apparently had no need for them when Mr. Hayward gave her insurance literature to read in his presence. Yet across the base of Martha Manning's nose was a small indentation, such as is made by the wearing of spectacles.

" '3. Martha Manning was undoubtedly in this building on Friday evening, when Jake Bailey was here with Mr. Borden, leaving a few minutes after nine through the main entrance. Yet, according to Mrs. Pellow, in charge of the cleaning women, only cleaning women passed through the lobby of the Starbridge Building between nine and nine twenty five Friday night. Therefore, Martha Manning must have been a cleaning woman. Being a cleaning woman, she possessed a passkey, which permitted her free access to all offices, but only Letty Miller, since she cleans Mr. Hayward's offices, could have been familiar with his offices and known of the automatic in his desk. And only a cleaning woman employed on this floor could have entered and left offices on this floor on Saturday, without having been noticed and asked on Monday to give an account of her movements. Repeated questionings of tenants on the floor Saturday afternoon and of elevator operators have failed to give any evidence of visitors in this corridor or in Mr. Hayward's corridor, not already questioned by the police.

" '4. According to the manager of the Acropolis Hotel, and other employes whom I questioned today, Martha Manning, during the last three weeks, has been absent from the hotel on week days, except Saturday, from half past three in the afternoons until half past nine at night. On Saturdays, she has not been in the hotel between a quarter to twelve and half past four. Three weeks ago— the Monday following Christmas Day—"Letty Miller" began her work as a cleaning woman in the Starbridge

Building. Her hours are four to nine each evening, except Saturday, when they are from twelve to four.' "

The detective paused, to shift the sheets in his hand so that the second page of single spaced typing should be uppermost, but Ruth Lester interrupted:

"The rest is just a connected story of the entire case, but please don't read any more now. She's coming to. ... A little more of the whiskey, darling," she added to Jack, who was kneeling beside her.

"I guess I've read enough," McMann admitted heavily. "So *you* win the five thousand, Miss Lester! Well . . . my hat's off to you!"

"I told you I'd give you half," Ruth reminded him. "But, oh, let's not talk of money now. . . . Letty! Letty!" she called softly, her lips almost brushing the deathly pale face against her breast—the thin, lined face that had only needed a complete lack of the brilliant make up that Martha Manning effected to be remarkably well "disguised."

The dark fringed eyelids fluttered, opened wide at last to reveal a pair of great, tragic brown eyes that were content to rest for a moment upon the sweetness and beauty of Ruth Lester's face. Then partial comprehension came, for those tragic eyes became filled with terror, rolled wildly from one face to another in the circle that hemmed her in.

But with comprehension came cunning, for it was not Martha Manning's lovely, throaty contralto that spoke, but the flat, monotonous, timid voice of "Letty Miller":

"I—I'm sorry. I must have fainted. I—I haven't been very well lately. The—black pigeon startled me, fluttering up just as I came into the room. . . . But you—wanted to see me, sir?"

And Martha Manning, who thought she was still "Letty Miller" to Detective Sergeant McMann and all those others looking at her so compassionately, struggled to rise.

Between them, Ruth and Jack Hayward assisted the thin, calico clad figure to a comfortable position in one of the chairs about the big table in the center of the outer office.

"Feeling better? How about a little more of the whiskey?" McMann asked gruffly, but not unkindly, when he had seated himself opposite the erstwhile scrubwoman.

"Letty Miller" shook her head, and lifted one of those betraying hands to her hair. When her weakly trembling fingers encountered the smooth bands of her own hair, in stead of the lank strands of gray which they expected, her eyes went blank for a moment, then widened and widened until they were enormous with terrified comprehension, as their gaze clung to the detective's face.

But not even that hard boiled, third degree artist could long endure the ordeal of meeting those eyes. His own dropped, and with what Ruth Lester knew was real kindness, he answered the question which Martha Manning's terrible eyes were asking by slowly pulling the gray wig from his pocket and laying it on the table before the woman.

"So—you know?" The ashen lips hardly stirred with the whisper.

McMann cleared his throat loudly. Ruth's hand wavered out, was taken in a strong grip by Jack Hayward's. Slowly, portentously, the detective spoke:

"Martha Manning, I arrest you for the murder of Henry P. Borden, and it is my duty to warn you that anything you say may be used against you!"

As those words were being spoken, Martha Manning's thin body straightened slowly, stiffened against the chair back, but before the detective had completed his official warning to his prisoner, her breast rose high on a great breath of what Ruth was oddly sure was relief.

"May I ask—how?" Martha Manning asked then, almost steadily, in the lovely contralto voice which had been described so many times during the investigation.

"Miss Lester—" McMann began, and hesitated. "I thought so." The pale lips almost smiled, but without malice. "She was the only one I feared—because she was fighting for the man she loves. . . . And they say love is blind. ... It may be—sometimes—" and the tragic eyes glanced toward the spot where Harry Borden had fallen and died.

McMann shifted in his chair, either embarrassed or impatient. "If you'd like to make a confession, Miss Manning —though I don't mind telling you the case is pretty complete without it—I'll take you now to the district attorney's office. Otherwise—remand you to jail— preliminary hearing—await action of the grand jury—"

"The district attorney's office?" the lovely voice quivered with dismay, and the great eyes sought Ruth's, appealingly. "I'm willing to make a full confession—oh, not just willing! I *want* to tell—for the peace of my soul, but can't I —make my statement here? Miss Lester is an expert stenographer. I want it to be over quickly, among my— friends." And those tragic eyes flashed a glance of gratitude and affection toward Jack Hayward, who stood be side her, his arm about Ruth Lester's shoulders.

"We—ell, if you won't try to repudiate it later—" McMann conceded.

"I shall not repudiate anything I tell you now, for it will be the whole truth," Martha Manning assured him quietly. "But—if you don't mind, I'd rather—this girl—" and her eyes flickered their first malice at Rita Dubois.

The dancer sprang to her feet. "O. K. with *me*, Miss Manning! But say, don't get any hate on me! *I* didn't want your man! . . . How about it, Big Boy?" and she whirled excitedly toward the detective.

"Miss Dubois had nothing to do with Harry's—death," Miss Manning informed the detective. "He was alive when she came, he gave her the torn half of a bill, and she left him—still alive."

"All right, Rita!" McMann decided, after a frowning silence. "You can rush out to get a lawyer for your husband. He'll need it. Miss Manning's story can't help *him*."

"Thanks a million times, Miss Manning! You're a peach —I don't care what you did!" And Rita paused at the door long enough to waft a fingertip kiss to the murderess, who had turned in her chair and was bravely watching the departure of the last woman who had won the love of "Handsome Harry" Borden.

"Willing to act as stenographer in an official capacity, Miss Lester?" McMann asked Ruth, when the door had closed upon the dancer.

"Yes," Ruth answered, and slipped out of the half circle of her sweetheart's arm to get notebook and pencils.

"Please—in justice to myself, may I go back to the beginning of my—my relationship with Harry Borden?" the contralto voice quivered, when Ruth was ready, with pencil poised.

# CHAPTER TWENTY EIGHT

"I WOULD prefer that you begin your confession with the story of how 'Letty Miller' came into existence, Miss Manning," the detective sergeant decided. "There has been ample evidence to prove your relationship with Harry Borden—your own story this morning, and the evidence volunteered by Frank Ashe, Jake Bailey and Attorney Walters. There can be no doubt that you and Harry Borden were lovers for years, that you have a child born of that union, and that Borden deserted you and refused to continue the support of yourself and that child. I think perhaps your visits to Mr. Hayward's office, ostensibly to inquire about insurance, would be a good starting point."

"Not *ostensibly!*" Martha Manning contradicted. "I really wanted to take out a small policy on my life in favor of my son. I hoped to save enough from my tiny salary, and to earn more in some other part time job, to pay the premiums. The idea came to me when I had followed Harry into the Starbridge Building one afternoon. He did not see me until we were both in the lobby, and he refused to stop and talk with me. When he had rushed into an elevator, I stood in the lobby, gazing blindly at the bulletin board, as if I were looking for the room number of a tenant. After a bit I saw the words 'Insurance Broker' after the name, John C. Hayward, and the office number—742. I did not know Harry's office was visible from Mr. Hayward's window, didn't know it until I was actually standing at that window. I saw Harry at his desk, but he did not see me. Later, a physician in a free clinic told me that I had tuberculosis, and knowing that insurance would be out of the question, I went in person to pass the news to Mr. Hayward, rather than write him a letter. I did want to see Harry again, if only from a distance, and I was so lonely the prospect of talking with so kind a man as Mr. Hayward was pleasant also. But I— had no plans, then."

"Ah! Plans!" McMann commented drily, with a keen glance at Ruth to see if she were getting every word of the confession down in shorthand. "Just when were those plans made, Miss Manning?"

"On Christmas Day, after my humiliating interview with Harry on Christmas Eve," Martha Manning told him, the exquisite, throaty contralto faltering slightly. "I felt that somehow I must be in a position to see him alone— not with his bodyguard, Jake Bailey, present. But to explain how I—managed, I shall have to go back a bit. One evening early in December—"

"Just a minute, Miss Manning!" the detective interrupted. "Until this time—I mean, until the assumption of a disguise—had you ever made threats, verbal or written, upon Harry Borden's life?"

"I had not!" the woman answered emphatically. "Nothing was further from my wish or intention—killing him, I mean. I—loved him."

"And yet—you became 'Letty Miller,' a scrubwoman," McMann reminded her. "But go on, Miss Manning. I believe you said something about one evening early in December."

"Yes. One evening early in December when I had followed Harry to the Starbridge Building, without getting a chance to speak with him, and was waiting for him to came out, a small army of cleaning women poured out of the building. It was just after nine. One of the women— it was Minnie Cassidy, as I learned later— looked so ill that I followed her out into the street. She almost fainted, and I took her home, using the last cent I had for the taxi.

"On Christmas Day, when I was desperately casting about for a way to see Harry alone, I remembered Minnie Cassidy's gratitude, remembered too that she worked on the seventh floor of this building. I went to see her. I told her I needed work very badly, would take anything. She told me that one of the 'cleaning ladies'—her 'partner' on the seventh floor, as Minnie called her—had just quit, and that her place had not been filled.

"It was Minnie who took me to Mrs. Pellow the following Monday, but late Christmas Day I had engaged a room for a week in a horrible old rooming house under the name of Letty Miller, and in the guise of Letty Miller, just in case my address should be investigated. The gray wig and this dress—" she looked down at the faded calico thing she wore— "had been given me as a sort of souvenir of my part in 'Stairs,' a play in which I had made a rather notable success just at the time I met Harry Borden. . . . I played the part of a scrubwoman. Yes, I was an actress—"

"That explains a lot," McMann commented grimly.

Martha Manning ignored the interruption. "No one but Minnie Cassidy knew that the new 'cleaning lady' had seen better days, was younger than she looked. Minnie was a good friend. But don't think she suspected for a moment that I killed Harry Borden," she added quickly as McMann reached for pencil and paper.

"All right," McMann conceded. "I hardly think Tim Cassidy's widow would connive at a murder. But—go on. You laid your plans to kill Borden?"

"No!" Again that flashing denial. "I merely wanted to be near him, to have easy access to his office, so that I could see him alone some night and *make* him listen. I believed he still cared something—for the boy, at least. But Jake Bailey was always waiting when Harry worked at night, and my chance for an interview did not come. Not even Friday night, for it was nine when Jake left, and I had to leave the building, or be sought for and discovered by Mrs. Pellow. But I admitted Harry to his office that night with my passkey and he did not recognize me.

"Friday afternoon I wrote one last urgent appeal to my son's father, and on Saturday morning I telephoned to ask for his decision. He was not in, or would not talk—I could not know which. I called later at half past one, from an office I was cleaning, and Minnie herself answered the phone. I am sure that Minnie had no idea she was talking with 'Letty Miller.' Harry gave her a message for me. I was to call again in fifteen or twenty minutes. I—"

"One moment, please. How did you manage your transformation each day from Martha Manning, switchboard operator of the Acropolis Hotel, to Letty Miller, the scrub woman?" McMann asked.

"It was comparatively easy. Department store rest rooms in the afternoon and any place in the dark—doorways, subway lavatories anywhere. It was merely a matter of putting on or taking off the wig and making up or removing make up, according to the role I was to assume. This afternoon I walked into Gimbel's rest room as Martha Manning, and left it as 'Letty Miller,' without your man, Carlson, suspecting that the two were the same person. This afternoon I changed hats—carrying the extra one in my coat pocket, and turned my coat inside out. It is a reversible tweed, not the garment I wore this morning."

"I see," McMann agreed, obviously chagrined. "Now about the second call to Borden Saturday afternoon—"

"I had just entered Mr. Hayward's office, intending to make my call on his phone and then clean his offices—"

"Wait! You knew all along that Hayward had a gun in the bottom drawer of his desk, I suppose?"

"No. I did not see it until I was 'Letty Miller.' I opened the drawer to thrust in a towel which was hanging out untidily, and saw the gun then. That was early last week —Monday, I believe. But even then I had no idea of ever using it. But I remembered it—later. On Saturday after noon, I entered Mr. Hayward's office at five minutes to two, to telephone Harry as he had requested. I was happy. I thought he meant to listen to me at last. Mr. Hayward came back for his theater tickets, and because the telephone was ringing, I left him alone. I waited in an office across the hall and as soon as Mr. Hayward was gone, I re-entered his office and put in my call. I knew Harry was in, for I had stepped to the window and had seen him sitting at his desk. He answered. I pleaded with him to create a trust fund for the boy, told him that I was ill and might not live long to support Paul myself. He called me all sorts of names—liar, parasite, and—worse. When he finally refused pointblank, I told him a lie—I said I had already put the case in the hands of a lawyer, who would file suit Monday if he refused to settle out of court. He was frightened, finally agreed to see me in his office that afternoon. When he hung up, I stepped to the window and looked at him. His face was black with hatred and anger.

"While I stood there, a girl came in—Rita Dubois. He was apologetic and extremely—affectionate. He gave her, at her request, as I looked on, the torn half of a bill and by her expressions of joy and the kisses she gave him, I knew it was a banknote of very large denomination. I—I nearly went mad then—possibly quite mad."

"Hmm! Insanity defense!" McMann commented grimly. "But—go on."

"I don't think I shall need an insanity defense," Martha Manning retorted, with a strange smile. "When the girl had left, Harry came to the window and stood there, drinking in great breaths of the cold air. I forgot then that I had on the gray wig and this dress and spectacles. I called out to him. I don't know what I was going to say, but—he recognized my voice, cried out, 'My God! Martha!' Then he turned and ran back to his desk and picked up an automatic. I think it was stark fear of me in my 'Letty' disguise, but of course I can't say what was in his mind. I can only tell what he did. I saw him coming back to the window with the automatic, and suddenly I remembered Mr. Hayward's gun. I stooped and jerked open the drawer. When Harry aimed his pistol at me, my own arm was going up, and in my hand was Mr. Hayward's automatic."

"You mean to say," McMann began sarcastically, "that Borden was such a poor shot he couldn't hit a target only eight feet away?"

"His aim was accurate," Martha Manning answered quietly, "but it was deflected by a white pigeon's alighting on his hand just as he pulled the trigger. The bird thought he was offering food—not death. The shot meant for me went wild, but mine, fired before Harry could aim again, did not." The flat breast rose on a great breath—possibility of relief. Then—"I think that's all. I killed him—before he could kill me."

"All!" McMann exploded. "Where are the guns? What about the closed window? The five hundred dollars in smaller bills that Borden had on his dead body?"

Martha Manning's face was gray white with exhaustion, but she answered obediently. "I wrapped Mr. Hayward's gun in a dusting rag and put it in the bottom of my scrub pail. Automatically, I think. But after a long while—or what seemed a long while—I remembered two things: the letter I had written Harry Friday and which must still be in his possession. I wanted it, of course. I did not want my son's mother to ... But I'll go on. I remembered also that I had shot Harry from Mr. Hayward's office, and that he had been kind to me. I did not want the crime traced to him or to his office. It seemed vitally necessary that I close Harry's window, so that no one would suspect that he had been killed across the airshaft.  I took my broom and pail and went to Harry's office, letting myself in with my passkey. I forgot to pull on the rubber gloves I always wore while cleaning, so that Martha Manning's hands should not be conspicuously marked with manual labor. That accounts for the finger prints, I think. But just after I had pushed open the door between the two offices I remembered them, put them on. Then—I went in."

The slight body was shaken with a shudder of horror, but after a moment she continued: "The first thing I forced myself to do was to close the window. I did not notice the pigeon's footprints in blood inside and outside the window. Then—I looked for my letter. It was not in his pockets or in his desk. I don't know where you found it. But in my search for the letter I found the money. I took it for Paul, but also with some vague hope that the police would think Harry had been shot by hold up men. I also took the pistol from his—his hand. I was afraid that if the police found the fired gun they might look everywhere—even outside the window, although I had closed it— At any rate, my instinct to protect Mr. Hayward made me take the gun, wrap it with the other one and hide it in my pail.

"I at first intended to hide both weapons in my coat pockets, and take them out with me that afternoon. But I remembered that Mrs. Pellow has a keen eye for suspicious bulges in coat pockets when she checks us out of the building. I didn't know what to do. I was afraid to keep the guns and afraid to throw them away. I happened to be alone in the supply room just before four o'clock—somehow I forced myself to do my work; it was a relief to be busy—and my eyes, searching desperately for a hiding place for the pistols caught sight of an abandoned, handleless old pail, much less deep than the one I was using. An idea came to me. I tried placing the old pail inside mine and found that the circumference was the same, so that the rims met all around, but that a false bottom was formed—a compartment deep enough to hold the two pistols. I placed them there, still wrapped in the dusting rag, just as Minnie Cassidy and one of the other women came in. They noticed nothing—"

"And where are the guns now?" McMann demanded.

"There!" And Martha Manning pointed to the scrubpail which she had set just inside the door when she had opened it upon her entrance.

"Good God!" McMann ejaculated, when he had separated the pails and stood with the two Colt's automatics in his hands. "And there they were when

'Letty Miller' came lugging that scrub pail into my presence yesterday!"

"Yes. I couldn't think what to do with them," Martha Manning admitted wearily. "And I had to come back as Letty Miller, both to avert the suspicion which would have fallen upon her if she had disappeared, and to keep those pails under my own eye, until I could find some way of disposing of the pistols."

"And you'd have got away with it too, if it hadn't been for Miss Lester," McMann admitted, almost admiringly. "But what I can't understand is why you fainted this afternoon when you were able this morning, as Martha Manning, to sit at Harry Borden's desk with apparent composure."

"It was the black pigeon, taking sudden flight from the very spot where Harry had—had lain," Martha Manning answered, a shudder of horror shaking her thin body. "When I came to close the window and to look for my letter Saturday, a black pigeon that must have flown in through the open window after—after Harry was dead, fluttered up from the body. I didn't realize then that it was—just a pigeon. I thought it was the black soul of Harry Borden going to meet its God."

# THE END

## Murder at Bridge

When an afternoon bridge party attended by some of Hamilton's leading citizens ends with the hostess being murdered in her boudoir, Special Investigator Dundee of the District Attorney's office is called in. But one of the attendees is guilty? There are plenty of suspects: the victim's former lover, her current suitor, the retired judge who is being blackmailed, the victim's maid who had been horribly disfigured accidentally by the murdered woman, or any of the women who's husbands had flirted with the victim. Or was she murdered by an outsider whose motive had nothing to do with the town of Hamilton. Find the answer in . . . **Murder at Bridge**

## One Drop of Blood

When Dr. Koenig, head of Mayfield Sanitarium is murdered, the District Attorney's Special Investigator, "Bonnie" Dundee must go undercover to find the killer. Were any of the inmates of the asylum insane enough to have committed the crime? Or, was it one of the staff, motivated by jealousy? And what was is the secret in the murdered man's past. Find the answer in . . . **One Drop of Blood**

# AVAILABLE FROM RESURRECTED PRESS!

## THE EDWARDIAN DETECTIVES
## LITERARY SLEUTHS OF THE EDWARDIAN ERA

The exploits of the great Victorian Detectives, Poe's C. Auguste Dupin, Gaboriau's Lecoq, and most famously, Arthur Conan Doyle's Sherlock Holmes, are well known. But what of those fictional detectives that came after, those of the Edwardian Age? The period between the death of Queen Victoria and the First World War had been called the Golden Age of the detective short story, but how familiar is the modern reader with the sleuths of this era? And such an extraordinary group they were, including in their numbers an unassuming English priest, a blind man, a master of disguises, a lecturer in medical jurisprudence, a noble woman working for Scotland Yard, and a savant so brilliant he was known as "The Thinking Machine."

To introduce readers to these detectives, Resurrected Press has assembled a collection of stories featuring these and other remarkable sleuths in The Edwardian Detectives.

- The Case of Laker, Absconded by Arthur Morrison
- The Fenchurch Street Mystery by Baroness Orczy
- The Crime of the French Café by Nick Carter
- The Man with Nailed Shoes by R Austin Freeman
- The Blue Cross by G. K. Chesterton
- The Case of the Pocket Diary Found in the Snow by Augusta Groner
- The Ninescore Mystery by Baroness Orczy
- The Riddle of the Ninth Finger by Thomas W. Hanshew
- The Knight's Cross Signal Problem by Ernest Bramah

- The Problem of Cell 13 by Jacques Futrelle
- The Conundrum of the Golf Links by Percy James Brebner
- The Silkworms of Florence by Clifford Ashdown
- The Gateway of the Monster by William Hope Hodgson
- The Affair at the Semiramis Hotel by A. E. W. Mason
- The Affair of the Avalanche Bicycle & Tyre Co., LTD by Arthur Morrison

# RESURRECTED PRESS CLASSIC MYSTERY CATALOGUE

*Journeys into Mystery*
*Travel and Mystery in a More Elegant Time*

*The Edwardian Detectives*
*Literary Sleuths of the Edwardian Era*

*Gems of Mystery*
*Lost Jewels from a More Elegant Age*

**E. C. Bentley**
*Trent's Last Case: The Woman in Black*

**Ernest Bramah**
*Max Carrados Resurrected:*
*The Detective Stories of Max Carrados*

**Agatha Christie**
*The Secret Adversary*
*The Mysterious Affair at Styles*

**Octavus Roy Cohen**
*Midnight*

**Freeman Wills Croft**
*The Ponson Case*
*The Pit Prop Syndicate*

**J. S. Fletcher**
*The Herapath Property*
*The Rayner-Slade Amalgamation*
*The Chestermarke Instinct*
*The Paradise Mystery*
*Dead Men's Money*

*The Middle of Things*
*Ravensdene Court*
*Scarhaven Keep*
*The Orange-Yellow Diamond*
*The Middle Temple Murder*
*The Tallyrand Maxim*
*The Borough Treasurer*
*In the Mayor's Parlour*
*The Saftey Pin*

**R. Austin Freeman**
*The Mystery of 31 New Inn from the Dr. Thorndyke Series*
*John Thorndyke's Cases from the Dr. Thorndyke Series*
*The Red Thumb Mark from The Dr. Thorndyke Series*
*The Eye of Osiris from The Dr. Thorndyke Series*
*A Silent Witness from the Dr. John Thorndyke Series*
*The Cat's Eye from the Dr. John Thorndyke Series*
*Helen Vardon's Confession: A Dr. John Thorndyke Story*
*As a Thief in the Night: A Dr. John Thorndyke Story*
*Mr. Pottermack's Oversight: A Dr. John Thorndyke Story*
*Dr. Thorndyke Intervenes: A Dr. John Thorndyke Story*
*The Singing Bone: The Adventures of Dr. Thorndyke*
*The Stoneware Monkey: A Dr. John Thorndyke Story*
*The Great Portrait Mystery, and Other Stories: A Collection of Dr. John Thorndyke and Other Stories*
*The Penrose Mystery: A Dr. John Thorndyke Story*
*The Uttermost Farthing: A Savant's Vendetta*

**Arthur Griffiths**
*The Passenger From Calais*
*The Rome Express*

**Fergus Hume**
*The Mystery of a Hansom Cab*
*The Green Mummy*
*The Silent House*
*The Secret Passage*

**Edgar Jepson**
*The Loudwater Mystery*

**A. E. W. Mason**
*At the Villa Rose*

**A. A. Milne**
*The Red House Mystery*
**Baroness Emma Orczy**
*The Old Man in the Corner*

**Edgar Allan Poe**
*The Detective Stories of Edgar Allan Poe*

**Arthur J. Rees**
*The Hampstead Mystery*
*The Shrieking Pit*
*The Hand In The Dark*
*The Moon Rock*
*The Mystery of the Downs*

**Mary Roberts Rinehart**
*Sight Unseen and The Confession*

**Dorothy L. Sayers**
*Whose Body?*

**Sir William Magnay**
*The Hunt Ball Mystery*

**Mabel and Paul Thorne**
*The Sheridan Road Mystery*

**Louis Tracy**
*The Strange Case of Mortimer Fenley*
*The Albert Gate Mystery*
*The Bartlett Mystery*
*The Postmaster's Daughter*
*The House of Peril*
*The Sandling Case: What Would You Have Done?*
*Charles Edmonds Walk*
*The Paternoster Ruby*

**John R. Watson**
*The Mystery of the Downs*
*The Hampstead Mystery*

**Edgar Wallace**
*The Daffodil Mystery*
*The Crimson Circle*

**Carolyn Wells**
*Vicky Van*
*The Man Who Fell Through the Earth*
*In the Onyx Lobby*
*Raspberry Jam*
*The Clue*
*The Room with the Tassels*
*The Vanishing of Betty Varian*
*The Mystery Girl*
*The White Alley*
*The Curved Blades*
*Anybody but Anne*
*The Bride of a Moment*
*Faulkner's Folly*
*The Diamond Pin*
*The Gold Bag*
*The Mystery of the Sycamore*
*The Come Backy*

**Raoul Whitfield**
*Death in a Bowl*

***And much more!***
***Visit ResurrectedPress.com***
***for our complete catalogue***

## About Resurrected Press

A division of Intrepid Ink, LLC, Resurrected Press is dedicated to bringing high quality, vintage books back into publication. See our entire catalogue and find out more at www.ResurrectedPress.com.

## About Intrepid Ink, LLC

Intrepid Ink, LLC provides full publishing services to authors of fiction and non-fiction books, eBooks and websites. From editing to formatting, from publishing to marketing, Intrepid Ink gets your creative works into the hands of the people who want to read them. Find out more at www.IntrepidInk.com.